NAPOLEON'S EGYPTIAN GIRL

JOHN W. LIVINGSTON

iUniverse®

NAPOLEON'S EGYPTIAN GIRL

iUniverse books may be ordered through booksellers or by contacting:

iUniverse
1663 Liberty Drive
Bloomington, IN 47403
www.iuniverse.com
1-800-Authors (1-800-288-4677)

Because of the dynamic nature of the Internet, any web addresses or links contained in this book may have changed since publication and may no longer be valid. The views expressed in this work are solely those of the author and do not necessarily reflect the views of the publisher, and the publisher hereby disclaims any responsibility for them.

Any people depicted in stock imagery provided by Thinkstock are models, and such images are being used for illustrative purposes only.
Certain stock imagery © Thinkstock.

ISBN: 978-1-5320-2164-0 (sc)
ISBN: 978-1-5320-2165-7 (hc)
ISBN: 978-1-5320-2166-4 (e)

Library of Congress Control Number: 2017913191

Print information available on the last page.

iUniverse rev. date: 09/06/2017

INTRODUCTION

I FOUND THIS REMARKABLE TREATISE some years ago while doing research in the Ottoman archives in the Citadel in Cairo. It was at the bottom of a dust-covered box containing Mamluk and Ottoman *daftars* (account books) for the years 1808–10. I vividly recall that when the box, one among a jumble of them, was pulled from an ancient wooden cabinet that looked ready to fall apart, a huge black snake slithered out of it and disappeared behind the cabinet and into a crack in the floor. I was fascinated; I couldn't see enough of the long, lovely, shining creature curling so swiftly away. However, the young Egyptian who had escorted me to the Ottoman-Mamluk section of the archives building jumped back in horror and hurriedly left the room. This allowed me to put the treatise in my briefcase and walk out with it, which I had not intended to do. It was only after having read the first few pages of this extraordinary ... what to call it—confession, testimony, love letter to a sacrificed sister—that I decided to keep it, as it had nothing at all to do with Ottoman or Mamluk tax accounts, much less with the economics or administration of the Muhammad Ali government that was ruling Egypt when it was written. If anything, it appeared to relate to the French occupation of Egypt from 1798 to 1801, and not to taxation but to French-Egyptian relations in Cairo. It was a document on how the Egyptians were getting along with their Gallic occupiers, in particular that young, shaggy-haired dwarf of a general, Bonaparte.

What the lengthy treatise was doing there, I have no idea. At first glance it seemed to be a personal narrative of the three-year French occupation of Egypt and its aftermath, when the French were forced out by an Anglo-Ottoman land and naval assault, written by Zaki Muhammad ibn Khalil al-Bakri, the son of Napoleon's foremost Egyptian collaborator,

Shaykh Khalil al-Bakri. As so little had been recorded by the Egyptians who endured the French invasion and occupation, I decided it was better for the sake of scholarship that I take the treatise rather than allow it to remain in a nesting place for venomous snakes and rot away in oblivion.

Having carried it to my apartment off Maydan al-Tahrir—that is, Liberation Square of recent revolutionary fame, and disappointment—I found it to be more a memoir than anything, and as I began reading, I became so intrigued that what I had originally intended to borrow for a while from the Egyptian archives became a pilfered possession, with no one the wiser. I read it and then reread it, profoundly impressed by what appeared to me a sincere portrayal of the events of those critical years, which brought Egyptians, and consequently all Arabic-speaking peoples, into contact with the gifts and curses of Western civilization. So I now present an English translation of it, having covetously possessed this unusual memoir for some fifty years since discovering and stealing it in 1961, during my dissertation research in Cairo as a doctoral student in Princeton University's Department of Oriental Studies, as it was called at the time—back when, if you can believe it, women were not admitted, undergraduates wore suit coats and ties, and our presidential candidates (and our nation in general) were held in high esteem the world over, way back before the 1 percenters and the moral collapse of the country, which seems to me to be becoming more and more like Egypt. As the Ottomans used to say, the fish begins to stink from the head.

Yes, I freely admit it: I am a despondent pessimist regarding the contemporary American scene and the world's future (forget the Middle East, a hopeless basket case since the fall of the Ottoman Empire and the Anglo-French takeover at the end of World War I). I often think I would have been quite content to be born in Egypt during the 1780s, and therefore a mature young man by the time the French sailed into Alexandria bay in the summer of 1798. That birth would have been perfectly acceptable to me, providing that it was into a certain class—say, the child of an Ottoman pasha, a Mamluk bey, or an Egyptian shaykh teaching in Cairo's al-Azhar, the Muslim world's most prestigious Institute of Advanced Religious Studies.

For some few Egyptians, the arrival of the French—the scientists among them, mind you, not so much that swaggering, impish Bonaparte and his blustering, sword-swinging soldiers—was a beacon shining brightly on the promise of a new era, a revival of spirit and intellect clearing the way to science and reason, the birth of a new Islam reinterpreted in the bright sun of the French Enlightenment, where ibn al Haytham and ibn Rushd flowed unobjectionably into René Descartes and Isaac Newton. It was—for a time, and for a precious few Egyptians—a golden dawn that I would have been most happy to be part of. My study of the history of that time has endowed me with the same hope that, for a while, filled the breast of Zaki ibn abu Bakri al-Khalil, the author of this memoir, and that of his tragic sister, Zaynab, so much more. And like both Zaki and Zaynab, I have, as a romantic historian and Arabist, plunged from the peaks of hope for renewal to the depths of despair that nothing changes except for the worse—a truth made all the truer when one civilization prevents another from changing except to serve the interests of the stronger. The French were by far the stronger when kid Bonaparte sailed his troops and scientists to Egypt. They did truly try to do good for Egypt (without, of course, diminishing their power to rule it), and it was the hundreds of first-rate scientists Bonaparte brought with him who most exerted themselves in a sincere effort to do good—those marvelous savants, the last of the true believers of that incredible Enlightenment that had nurtured them in their youth.

And so with that, I present my translation of Zaki's memoir from the Arabic, hoping it will be as entertaining and informative as it is to me—a depiction of those years when the Egyptians had to live under French occupation and get along with the foreigners as best they could. It was the dawn of Europe's colonialist onslaught into the Middle East—a time when hope and despair were like dawn and dusk, and inextricably mingled, in this, the beginning of global interaction.

The Fate of Egyptians under Bonaparte of France:
A Tale of Thwarted Ambition
And Forbidden Romance.

Zaki Muhammad ibn Khalil al-Bakri

1

I BEGIN AT THE BEGINNING. I was a twenty-two-year-old student of religion at al-Azhar when the British came. It was the summer of 1798. Their fleet anchored in Alexandria Bay, and Lord Nelson was rowed ashore, where he was met at the wall of the port by the Mamluk governor of Alexandria. "Have the French been here?" Lord Nelson asked impudently, without even having requested permission to anchor his ship or disembark in an Ottoman port belonging to the lord of lords, ruler of rulers, the great sultan in far-off Istanbul. The rude foreigner hadn't even known enough to bow before an officer of the sultan's empire. I can imagine the stunned look on the governor's face as he stared in contempt at this so-called admiral's strange-looking hat and tight trousers and crude cloak, unadorned by jewels or gold buttons. An admiral? Why, the Mamluk governor was more splendidly dressed in his silk caftan, pantaloons, and crimson turban than this cheeky, pale-faced twit who appeared to have come off the streets. It is reported that when the question was translated to Turkish, the governor regarded the foreigner and the cheap-looking sword sheathed at his side as if he hadn't heard right, and so the question had to be repeated and retranslated.

"The French? Here? In Egypt?" It is said that the proud Mamluk swept back his cape to reveal his gold-and-silver-handled sword and laughed in astonishment at the absurdity of it all. "No, no Frangis have been here. This is Egypt, territory of the sultan of Islam in Istanbul, lord of the world. No Frangis would dare set foot here. And if they did, the Mamluks would crush them under the hooves of their horses and harvest their heads with

1

their swords and roast their infidel hearts on a shish for breakfast! Now take to your flimsy rowboats and begone before we blow you and your miserable pieces of floating wood that you call a fleet from the water!"

"Well, there's a French general named Bonaparte roaming about somewhere in this part of the sea, and we think he's heading here."

The governor scoffed. "So? If this Bonaparte is stupid enough to come, Sultan Salim will send you his head, if you leave an address. And if you don't sail out of here at once, we'll send the sultan your head!"

That was the beginning of it all. The Admiral Lord Nelson sailed away, and the governor of Alexandria reported the strange incident to the Mamluk emirs and beys in Cairo. They laughed. "Let these Franks come!" they boasted. "We will hurl them back into the sea, as our ancestors did the crusaders six centuries ago!"

How proud we were. How arrogant. How little did we suspect what these new infidel crusader Frangis had in store for us. How little we knew of the changes and progress they had made since the Crusades. How little we knew of the world outside our own world of Islam. We had no word for "progress" in the Western sense.

A few days later, Napoleon's fleet arrived. Alexandria, Rosetta, and Damietta fell. The French army was marching on Cairo. The Ottoman governor told us that the French were a cruel, barbarous people who had rejected religion and killed their king and queen—that they would behead all Muslim men; rape and sodomize all girls, women, and children and sell them into slavery; and trample all religion and civilization into the ground. We were horrified. Who were these frightful beasts that imagined they could defeat the soldiers of Islam, that dared invade Egypt, mother of the world, protected by God and sultan?

Stories coming into Cairo went even beyond the Ottomon governor's, beyond anything we could imagine. Villages were reported to have been plundered and burned to the ground, babies roasted alive in the flames and eaten in front of their mothers, the French soldiers laughing and washing down their feast of human flesh with buckets of wine mixed with blood! Some stories had the soldiers drinking their bloody concoction from human skulls, pyramids of which they left in the savage wake of their advancing army.

We trembled. We prayed. We cried. People began fleeing the city, carrying what they could. Some men of religion preached that God had sent the Franks as punishment for our wicked ways and so it was wrong to flee; we had to face our divine punishment. Old women wailed in the streets that it was the end of the world. There were even some highly educated shaykhs who said these things. My father, one of the leading religious figures in Egypt and known even as far away as Istanbul, was himself convinced that the Mamluks would crush the Frangi enemy of Islam, for God would not allow an army of believers to be defeated by an army of unbelievers. God might now and then allow a Christian army to defeat the sultan's army in Europe, but certainly not a Christian army that rejected its Christianity. Everyone my father talked to agreed with him, but that didn't stop many of the religious shaykhs from running in terror for the desert or fleeing up the Nile to Asyut with whatever they could take with them. Even my father ended up fleeing to the desert, saying he would return as soon as God and the Mamluks finished with the infidels. I should have known just from that what soft substance my father was made of.

In their frenzy of fear and consternation, irresponsible Muslims called for the slaughter of all Jews and Christians, and that included all Christian and Jewish Syrians and European merchants residing in the country! Cairo's European community of merchants had already been locked up in the Citadel fortress for security. Mobs of young hoodlums took advantage of the hysteria and roamed the streets, beating people, smashing up shops, and looting the homes and businesses of the wealthy. We were destroying our religion and civilized society ourselves, saving the French the trouble. Looking back on it now, I see we were our own worst enemies, a flock of headless chickens running around in circles, begging God to come save us. We imagined the horrible French as devils in human form, with no real idea who or what they were. Man has no greater enemy than his own ignorance.

We Cairenes waited in dread and fear for the beastly French to come. If we were to be sodomized, skewered, sizzled, slaughtered, severed, and enslaved, we thought, then let it be quick. Mother, however, wanted none of it. She was for fleeing to the desert. When our father, the venerable shaykh, told us the Mamluks would hurl the infidel Frangis into the river, which would flush them down to the sea and take them back to where they had come from, my sister Zaynab (a cheeky girl of eighteen, four years my junior) asked why the Mamluks were waiting until the Frangis got all the way to Cairo before hurling them into the river. Zaynab had trouble knowing her place.

"All in God's plan," my father piously intoned, adding pointedly, "and God we don't question!"

"I'm questioning the Mamluks, not God, Father. Who wants to be raped and butchered?"

"Or even sodomized," I quipped, bravely trying to make light of our terror and save my sassy sister from Father's wrath. Shaykh Khalil al-Bakri tolerated no back talk, but a son had some chance of getting away with a modest dose of it, a daughter none at all, however clever or humorous—and Zaynab was every bit a wit to be reckoned with.

When our fourteen-year-old sister, Noha, asked what it meant to be sodomized, Mother shrieked in horror, rolling her eyes to heaven and begging Father to let us run to the desert. Shaking his turbaned head, the shaykh gave us all a stern look saying that the family would remain and then retreated to his private prayer room to recite the Quran in order to help God's plan along its course.

The days of waiting ground down our nerves. One week became two. Reports of the Frangis' atrocities as they advanced up the Nile grew more gruesome every day. People cracked. More and more of them went running into the desert to die there rather than face the savage, sodomite, blood-drinking Frangi beasts that had been puked up from the sea. People ran through the streets howling to God for mercy, like wild animals bereft of their reason. Others joined the public procession led in prayer by Egypt's chief shaykh and highest religious dignitary, who was just above my father in rank. The Ottoman pasha had given him what everyone believed to be the battle standard of the Prophet Muhammad, and simply the waving of this standard was taken by the pathetic, traumatized people as divine intervention, a triumph delivered by God. They were already celebrating victory and dancing in the streets before the enemy had been seen or a battle fought, while the religious shaykhs paraded through the streets and markets reciting passages from Bukhari's collection of the Prophet Muhammad's traditions.

Even then, long before I was introduced to critical analysis by the French savants who would become my tutors, I was cynical enough to wonder how that would stand up to what we had heard was Bonaparte's fearsome artillery. Most sensible people like me remained in the dark

4

of their homes with the shutters closed and doors locked, praying the Mamluks would be victorious. The sight of the leading Mamluk beys and emirs hauling their valuables from their palaces and packing them on horses, donkeys, and camels to take with them in the event that they had to beat a hasty retreat did not build our confidence.

I had decided to die with honor and dignity. I knew exactly what I would do, and how and when. It was perfectly clear in my mind. I had already sharpened the dagger. The moment I saw the Mamluks retreating for the desert, I would kill my two sisters: first Noha, then Zaynab. At forty, Mother was too old to be raped or sodomized. When I had saved the honor of my sisters, I would then plunge the dagger into the breast of the first Frangi soldier I saw, if not into the heart of that Bonaparte himself, and then drive it into my own heart. Honor and dignity in death would triumph over a life of humiliation and degradation under savage beasts from Frangistan.

The beasts at last arrived. They camped on the other side of the river. The Mamluks prepared for battle—when they were done stowing all their valuables on pack animals.

The morning of the battle I climbed to the top of the tall minaret of Sayyidna Ahmad Mosque some way outside of the city walls, toward the river and across from Giza and the pyramids. It was dawn. The desert was calm and beautiful. The view was perfect. I wanted to know which side was victorious as soon as possible in order to have time to prepare for what I had resolved to do if we were defeated.

The Mamluk beys and emirs and high Ottoman officials with their personal detachments of Turkish slave cavalry had been ferried across the river and were there to meet the enemy at a place called Imbaba, some distance north of the pyramids. Nevertheless, the summer morning being crystal clear, I had a marvelous view from my high perch.

The combatants were a sight to behold. On the one side, the Franks were in identical uniforms and arranged in perfect squares—each side of each square being several men deep, the individual squares themselves forming one great square—and behind the squares were row upon row of artillery in perfectly straight lines. It was a magnificent sight. Seeing it from the height of my minaret, I was reminded of the diagrams in the book of geometry and astronomy written by my grandfather, the country's leading mathematician; it appeared to me that these French had applied the art of geometry to warfare. More remarkable than that, when the fighting began, these squares of men and lines of artillery operated like a machine whose precisely fitted parts worked together in one grand design toward one end. First, the batteries of artillery burst into action, one after the other, row upon row, so that at any given moment there were twenty or thirty shells exploding from their black snouts. And the infantry! What a sight to behold! The front rank would shoot and then kneel to reload, leaving the rank behind a clear field through which to shoot, and the same pattern was followed rank by rank, all the way to the last one in the rear, like a living mechanism. On the ranks went—shooting, kneeling, reloading, rank behind rank—operating so precisely that the soldiers appeared not so much as human than as parts of a machine whose movements were of geometric and trigonometric exactitude.

As though driven by the methodical pounding of artillery, the square formations of the infantry marched menacingly forward, advancing and wheeling, all the parts acting individually and in concert, terrifying in their purposeful movements. It was if this mechanical beast of artillery, infantry, and cavalry had a single mind of its own that drew into it the tens of thousands of individuals—were they truly human beings?—that composed it.

Some several hundred meters away, at the other end of the sandy field of battle, sat our proud Mamluks, ten thousand and more, each in his own mode of dress, grouped in haphazard clusters of cavalry around their leaders, of which there were about fifteen in all. On their colorfully caparisoned mounts, they streaked forward, swords in hand, so proud, each racing the others to make the first kill. The next moment they were falling with their horses and wheeling around in terror, darting this way and that to get out from under the unremitting torrent of exploding shells and zipping musket lead that plowed the desert sands, sowing it with blood and limbs. In spite of the carnage, several Mamluk emirs bravely drew their swords and, with their men behind them, galloped headlong down the corpse-strewn desert, crying, "God is Great!" into the face of the barrage of lead that rushed against them like a wall. Those few who made it across to the enemy side were quickly dispatched by the cavalry, who lopped off heads more expertly than Ottoman cavalry officers knocked polo balls across playing fields. Some of the Mamluks turned back and fled the field of battle.

The artillery having done its work, the Frankish cavalry charged to engage the wings of the Mamluks who were attempting an outflanking maneuver, while over the shallow dunes rolled the French infantry, those geometric squares of red juxtaposed one to the other in a design as fixed as the stars of the constellations and advancing as ineluctably. They were breathtaking to watch. On a signal, the serried ranks fired in unison, one rank firing and then kneeling to reload as the rank behind fired its volley—rank after alternate rank firing, kneeling, loading, rising, firing, kneeling, all in perfect order and harmony. I know I am repeating myself, but I find myself obliged to, so astonishing was this performance of war, something never before seen in Egypt. It was, as I said, like a mechanical device—like one of those complex geometric modular patterns designed to predict a planet's heavenly motion around the Earth. Yes, I said around the Earth, not the sun. Hah! I still can't believe what those Frangis tried to tell us about planetary motion! But more about that later.

As the red squares of infantry advanced behind the wall of fire blowing ceaselessly up the middle from the lines of artillery, the two arching wings of French cavalry came swooping down to keep the scattered remnants of the Mamluk army from escaping. Some Mamluks chose to meet a glorious death against the cavalry closing on them; others swung back to take their chances, fleeing across the field of artillery and musket fire. But most unbelievable of all was the commanding general, who was waving his men here and there in their rout of our proud Mamluks. He looked like a dwarf on a horse.

Perched atop the minaret, I breathlessly gazed down upon the awesome slaughter until the end, which came when the ragtag Ottoman infantry of Janissaries broke ranks and fled, only to be cut down by the bladed wings of the French cavalry, glints of red and silver slicing across the sun-scorched desert, now wetted with men's blood. Mamluks too proud to run or surrender raced their steeds into the hail of fire, while others drove their horses into the river, preferring a watery grave than death at the hands of a Frank. Riderless horses galloped into the desert, leaving behind them the field of dead and dying. And then it was over.

Stunned, I stared down at the harvest of bodies. It was as if the Angel of Death, dressed in red and blue, had swept across the field, felling everyone in sight with its bloody scythe. Some bodies were still writhing in the sand; most were motionless. Then I saw something that amazed me even more than the thinking war machine these devils had brought. After the surviving Mamluks and Ottomans had fled the field, abandoning camp and baggage for dear life, the Franks gathered all the dead and wounded—ours as well as their own. I thought for sure they would desecrate the dead and shoot the living. I didn't want to look on, but I did, and I was dumbfounded to see our wounded being treated by what must have been doctors, and treated no differently than their own wounded. There was no butchery, mutilation, sodomy, or savagery. With the battle ended, these strange Frangis went about methodically cleaning up and arranging things as though the fighting had never been. I didn't know what to make of it. But by the time I climbed down from the minaret, I had for some reason abandoned the plan to kill my two sisters and myself. I was now more interested in observing these strange people from across the sea who had returned after centuries to do battle with us, and this time were the victors. Imagine giving aid to the fallen wounded of your enemy as if they were your own!

News of the defeat reached the city before I did. People were roaming the streets in a daze. Women were beating their breasts, howling to God for deliverance. Mamluks who had survived the battle and made it back to their palaces were busily loading their pack animals for a flight to Upper Egypt or Palestine, if they hadn't already done it before the battle. Wives of beys and emirs who had perished or fled were doing the same, their camel bags stuffed to bursting with gold coins and jewels. Many families that could afford to pack up and leave were also doing so, followed on foot by their slaves and servants. Even poor people went into the desert, barefoot and foodless, blindly following the rich. Along with them went our chief religious leader, Shaykh Umar Makram, abandoning us spiritually and morally, as the Mamluks had abandoned us militarily.

Azbakiyyah, the palm-shaded quarter along the central canal where many of our great emirs had their splendid palaces, was soon a ghost town. The only sign of life was the cavernous wailing of harem women coming from inside the palaces, their Mamluk owners having perished or fled. By dusk, Cairo was a city of the dead. For all the wailing and moaning, and all the mob looting of abandoned homes, it could have been hell.

By nightfall, the wails of bereaved women within the city walls were joined by those of women outside the walls who had fled into the desert and been ravaged by the wild bedouin waiting for them at the edge of the desert. The screams of the bedouin's victims could be heard through the night and all the next day. Men had been robbed and stripped, their throats slit; women had been raped, sometimes by the whole tribe, and left to wander naked through the desert, their children having been taken as slaves along with the younger women. There were stories of women whose fingers were cut off for their rings, hands for their bracelets, feet for their heavy gold anklets. The terrible screams that pierced the night from beyond the walls gave substance to the stories of rape and mutilation, but it was not the French who were the perpetrators.

Come morning, the once-proud harem beauties of our Mamluk leaders—butterflies who had fled in their silks and brocades and with their jewels and gold to escape the savagery of the Franks, only to endure the savagery of the bedu, staggered back through the empty streets to their plundered palaces, weeping to God for their misfortune, holding their hands over their nakedness in dishonor and disgrace.

Several of these pathetic princesses passed naked before our villa at the edge of the lake in Azbakiyya. Nobody dared go out to help them for fear of the Franks who were expected to storm through the streets at any moment. Mother cried in horror and turned back from the latticed window through which we were peering on the top floor of our villa. "If Muslim bedu can do that to women, what will the infidel Franks do to us?"

Father corrected her: the desert tribesmen were not true Muslims.

"But the girls and women they raped and butchered were," said Zaynab.

"God has punished those women for their greed and arrogance."

"God punishes who He wills," I declared in support of our wise father.

"Even the innocent?" Zaynab asked.

"God's terms are not ours, my child," answered Father. "What may appear innocent to you may not be so with God. Come away from that window, girl. God punished those women for their sinfulness, not for you to gawk at."

"Woe to the woman who loses her shame," Mother cried fretfully.

"Look!" Noha's young face was pressed up against the lattice. "Emir Hassan's wife, Hawa! Naked as the day she was born!"

Father hurried to the window. The young woman was barefoot and limping over the rough ground in front of our villa, trying to use her black hair, which fell to her hips, to cover her nakedness. Even from a distance, her feet looked blistered and swollen. We marveled at the sight of the wretched woman. A high-spirited beauty, Hawa was the only wife of a rich Mamluk. She was rumored to have warned him not to take a second wife or bring a slave or concubine into the house if he didn't want her to leave him. He had obeyed, and now, with the defeat, he had left her, fleeing to Gaza or Palestine with his gold. She had run after him, only to be captured by the Arab tribesmen in the desert and raped, sodomized, and shorn of all her wealth.

"It's a wonder they let a beautiful young woman like her go," I remarked.

"They didn't let her go," Zaynab replied. "She probably outwitted those sand-brained lizard-eaters."

("Sand-for-brains lizard-eaters" was how we commonly referred to desert bedu, a variation of what Persians, an arrogant race if there ever was one, called Arabs in general: sand-kicking lizard-eaters. And what did the Persians have to be so arrogant? I was soon to learn that there was a people a hundred times more arrogant than the Persians, and it took me longer to learn that these people did have reason to be arrogant.)

"They only let her go after they did to her what they wanted," Noha said. "Look, poor Hawa can hardly walk."

"It's because of her sore feet," Mother explained.

We were so engrossed watching Madame Hawa hobble naked over the path that we didn't notice that Father had left. Suddenly we heard his voice booming up from the central hall: "Unlock the gate!" Then one of the servants ran out and unbolted the gate, and the next moment Father was, with great dignity, wrapping a Turkish rug over the woman and helping her into the house.

"God is merciful," Mother said sarcastically. She ordered the servant girls to get the fire going in the bath of the women's quarters.

After Hawa had bathed and dressed in one of Mother's robes, she told us her harrowing story while one of our servant girls swathed her bloody feet in the shallow pool in the garden. She described how a tribe of Arab bedu had descended upon her and her escort a half day's journey into the desert. "The men were killed right off, and the women raped and sodomized. When they finished with a woman, they cut her head off. The younger ones they saved for slavery. It was while the stinking beasts were having their pleasure that a detachment of French cavalry chanced upon us and attacked. The filthy lizard-eaters scattered, with the French chasing them deeper into the desert. Another minute and my head would have gone the way of my honor." She broke into tears. "What good is a head when a woman has lost her honor?"

We looked at each other in embarrassed silence while Mother consoled poor, wretched Hawa in her arms.

"The French saved you?" Zaynab asked.

"Would that they had not!"

"They didn't come back to take their pleasure?"

Hawa shook her head and cried harder. "What life is there for a woman who's lost her honor?" Even with imminent destruction threatening our world, we remained faithful to tradition: Hawa veiled her head in Father's and my presence. The fact that we had both just seen her naked didn't matter. The veil was just a gesture of modesty, as it left her face visible.

Zaynab asked, "What kind of men must they be who save a woman from rape and don't come back to rape her themselves?"

"And don't even sodomize her, whatever that is," young Noha added.

"Infidels," Father replied. "Infidels. That's what kind of men they are. And apparently not very manly ones for soldiers."

They had looked manly enough to me the day of the battle, but I held my tongue rather than say anything that might appear to contradict Father. Had I told him that their doctors had treated our wounded Mamluks with the same care they gave their own soldiers, he would have accused me of blasphemy.

"What kind of men are these French?" Zaynab repeated.

"Time will tell, God willing," I replied with a feigned sigh of piety, fingering my prayer beads and turning my eyes to heaven in surrender to divine will.

"God willing," Father said. "There is no power other than His, and we should fear it."

Hawa continued howling most miserably, in fear and disgrace of her lost honor.

We were undecided about whether to resist or open the gates to the enemy. We were undecided because our leading religious al-Azhar shaykh, whose voice would have commanded the most respect and authority after the collapse of our government and the flight of the beys, amirs, and pashas from the city, had also fled, headed for Palestine along with many of our leading notables. Shaykh Umar Makram would have provided a moral force of unity; he would have been listened to and followed, whatever he had decided. He had advocated civil resistance before the defeat, and maybe that's why he fled after the defeat, in fear of not God, but the French. His disappearance had left the civil dignitaries divided, unsure, leaderless, and even as the French were crossing the river and gathering around our walls, the struggle among our pious religious shaykhs to take his place, with my father very much in the struggle, was already in full progress.

Eight leading shaykhs and as many rich merchants assembled in al-Azhar Mosque to decide what we should do. Those who argued that it would be better to resist the enemy and die fighting rather than submit were overcome by the less passionate advocates of, not surrender, but as they cleverly phrased it, "submission stiffened by passive resistance." Father took the lead as spokesman for this policy. Open resistance, he argued, was hopeless and would only gain us a more wrathful enemy, and perhaps even the destruction of the city and its inhabitants. We should open our gates and hope for mercy and moderation while saving our blood for the day the sultan sent an army to Egypt and we could fight with the hope of winning. He argued eloquently:

"Are we to oppose with sticks and stones what the Mamluks couldn't stand against with sword and musket? Are we to bare our breasts to the enemy in mortal defiance of overwhelming force, while the Mamluks, our brave defenders, gallop for Syria or Aswan with their tails between their legs and their saddlebags stuffed with gold and jewels? Is this bravery, or is it stupidity? Is it brave to die for nothing but death and defeat? Is it cowardice to postpone battle until a glimmer of hope shines on the promise of victory? Which is nobler, to die in a suicidal slaughter by an overwhelming enemy, or to gain martyrdom in a triumphant battle? To oppose our enemy today would be a meaningless waste, while tomorrow it would be the shedding of the precious blood of our martyrs in victory. Are we to be dumb, careless, and fanatic, or patient, wise, and victorious? The decision is yours, but let us decide in the light of the wisdom of the Prophet, pray to God and peace upon him, who said, 'Those who act in thought and patience are indeed the rightly guided people of my community.'"

This was followed by a long silence. I couldn't remember having read in any of the six canonical collections of prophetic tradition that the Prophet had said anything like what Father claimed he had said, and I was sure none of the learned scholars could either, but no one challenged him, for he spoke with intimidating authority, and whatever doubt his assumed authority didn't dispel was stilled by most scholars' fear of openly showing ignorance of the Prophet's words. They didn't know my father's cunning in making up prophetic sayings to substantiate an argument. When he was viciously attacked by his academic rival at al-Azhar, Shaykh Sharqawi, who indirectly called him a coward and defeatist, Father replied with restraint and dignity, "Some of us, no doubt, when the infidels rain fire upon our heads, would have the people go on fighting artillery with stones and knives, while they, our great generals in a scholars' turbans, direct the battle from the security of their fortified villas." This drew a laugh from our prosperous merchants, who were generally in favor of submission stiffened by passive resistance, but not too stiff.

It was at last decided that we would open the gates. Father emerged as leader of the so-called peace party, which was labeled "the party of surrender and defeat" by its opponents, while Father called the opposing party, led by Shaykh Sharqawi and Shaykh Sadat, "the party of death and destruction." Shaykhs Sharqawi and Sadat, who previously had been Father's academic rivals, were now his political rivals. Yes, even before the French entered the city, the shaykhs of al-Azhar were becoming political. It was that quick.

After the debate at al-Azhar, I rode home to Azbakiyya on my donkey, musing over the changes that had taken place so suddenly. Shaykh Khalil al-Bakri—a mild, humble man of letters and pious learning, honored shaykh of al-Azhar—had become a political leader. Without our knowing it, the French invasion was already at work, transforming and subverting the traditional institutions that held our society together.

2

HROUGH WE DREADED THE arrival of the French, it was generally hoped that their occupation of our city would not be too long delayed. That's because riffraff from the lower elements of society had been looting the bazaars since the moment it became known that the Mamluks had been defeated and were hightailing it in every direction to save themselves. I hoped we'd never have to see them again—the useless, haughty Turkish slaves who were only out for themselves and had been lording it over the Egyptians; to my mind they were as corrupt and destructive as the hooligans who'd taken over the streets.

By some kind of perverse justice, the first places to be looted were the palaces of those emirs and merchants who had packed up or hidden their gold and raced away to Palestine. By the second day after the defeat, law and order had broken down completely. With each passing hour, the city was given over to more looting, burning, rape, and murder. People locked themselves in their homes and prayed to be spared. A woman whose husband had been beaten and robbed, and his shop plundered and torched, screamed in the street, "Surely the French couldn't be worse than this! God help us, what are the infidels waiting for?"

Boats. The French had brought none, and the Mamluks had burned the ones they didn't use to cross the river back to Cairo after their defeat. It took two days for the French to collect or build enough boats and rafts to float a scouting party across the Nile. Finally, the afternoon of the second day after the battle, the waiting ended. Cairo held its breath at the sound of approaching drums. The looting and arson ceased without the French

14

having to fire a shot. The menacing roll of drums was enough to scare the thugs away.

Led by a small detachment of cavalry, a force of two hundred soldiers surveyed the empty city. They stayed in the middle of the widest streets, their gazes nervously shifting upward and around them at every step and drumroll. In Alexandria, the people had resisted, women included. They had thrown rocks from the rooftops and used knives and clubs to attack small parties of soldiers in cul-de-sacs. We heard they had killed hundreds, including a Frangi general, and seriously wounded the general who was second in command of the army, a man with an unpronounceable name— "Clay Bear" was the best we could make of it. It sounded like another Turk.

But in Cairo there was little resistance. The people locked themselves indoors and peeked through the cracks of shutters to see the terrible enemy. The roll of drums was like the herald of hell, like the Angel of Death marching in to snatch the people where they squatted in the dark of their homes.

Without seeing a single Egyptian, the patrol of two hundred entered Cairo, its streets and shops as still and empty as a graveyard. The patrol traversed the city right to its heart in Azbakiyya, where the ruling Mamluk beys and emirs had their palaces, and not a soul did they see. They must have thought we had died of the plague. A corps of foot soldiers and cavalry passed by our villa. The look of fright and apprehension on their young faces was somehow reassuring.

"They don't look like savage beasts," Zaynab whispered to me. "They don't look like conquerors."

"They look more frightened than us," I said.

"Look how tight their pantaloons are! They hug the skin, right up to their ..." Little Noha giggled without finishing.

"Poor things," Zaynab commiserated. "Maybe they've been cut."

"You mean like the black guards of the pasha's harem?" Noha giggled again, louder. The girl was a bit too precocious, I thought, but innocent enough not to know what sodomy was.

"You wouldn't say that if you'd seen them fight," I said.

Noha wrinkled her nose at me. "Do you need those to fight?"

"You do if you're going to rape and sodomize afterward," Zaynab whispered. Mother told her to hush up.

The detachment of cavalry leading the infantry was passing. A young officer bringing up the rear stopped his horse in front of our villa to wipe his flushed face. "They can't take the heat of our summer," I whispered. "Maybe if it gets warmer they'll just give up and leave, or wither away."

Stories had been told of hundreds and thousands of French soldiers dropping dead from the heat of the desert march from Alexandria. Our sunny climate had done better than our Mamluks.

"This one looks like he's about to fall from his horse." Zaynab's forehead was pressed against the latticework. The officer took a water canister from a belt at the side of his horse and removed his helmet to drink. "Look! How blonde!" she exclaimed.

"Wow!" Noha was even more exuberant. "Look at it! Like silk gold! He's beautiful!"

"Hush!" I ordered.

The soldier looked up and around him, searching the windows and roofs as though he had heard something. Assured there was no danger, he wiped his florid face again, inverted the canister over his head so the meager contents trickled onto it, then ran his hand through his damp hair and over his face. Holding his helmet and loose reins in one hand and the empty canister in the other, he spurred his mount to catch up with the rest of the patrol, which had continued on ahead. We had a mare in heat fenced up in the field behind the villa, and I think the soldier's stallion must have caught an exciting whiff of it, for it suddenly whinnied, reared back on its two hind legs, and bolted forward, throwing the officer backward onto the ground. He landed hard on his back and lay still, his helmet and canister clattering to a stop at his side. The horse bucked and whinnied again and took off for the field. The other soldiers were too far ahead to notice what had happened; they continued on, patrolling behind the relentless drums.

Zaynab grabbed the clay water jug that we kept in front of the lattice for cooling and was down the stairs in a flash.

"Zaynab!" I shouted.

It was as though the devil had leapt into her. By the time I reached the ground floor, she had already unbolted the door and the gate and was kneeling beside the prostrate soldier, swathing his face in the cool water. At that same moment, a dozen horsemen came galloping down on her, swords drawn, shouting in their hysterical language and kicking up a storm of dust, foot soldiers and drummers following behind. They enveloped Zaynab and the fallen officer in a sphere of horses, swords, and bayonets.

Four of them dismounted to seize her. Realizing they thought she had done their comrade harm, and thinking they were going to swing their swords at her, I flung myself against them and was thrown to the ground. A dozen bayonets were aimed at my breast. I screamed at them, trying to make them understand what had happened, but I may as well have been talking to men from another planet. They kept shouting hysterically and jabbing their bayonets at me. Then Mother and Noha, accompanied by half a dozen servants, came shrieking from the house, causing the soldiers to turn their weapons toward them.

Mother, unveiled, knocked sabers and bayonets aside, pushing her way toward Zaynab. The soldiers pulled at her as the servants cried out and shook their fists at them. Both sides were shouting in their own language and threatening each other—one side jabbing and waving their pointed steel, the other shaking their fists—drums beating all the while. Then a resonant voice commanded everyone to stop. Being in Arabic, the command was incomprehensible to the French, but they nonetheless fell silent—stilled, like the rest of us, by the thunder of authority carried in the voice. Everyone turned. Father, standing at the top of the steps dressed in his shaykh's turban and caftan, raised his arms above his bearded head. The soldiers gawked at the imposing figure, who looked like some prophet who had stepped out of their Bible. Even the drums dribbled to a halt.

In classical Arabic, father informed them that he was Shaykh Khalil al-Bakri, head of the Bakri clan and direct descendant of abu Bakr al-Siddiq, the first Caliph of Islam and father-in-law of the Prophet Muhammad, peace be upon him, and any harm that came to his family would be on their heads. Then he lowered his arms and told them to depart in peace. The soldiers continued staring at him without having understood a word.

In the ensuing silence, a groan was heard. The eyes of the fallen cavalier fluttered open. Zaynab was still kneeling at his side. When he saw her big, brown eyes looking down into his own, he blinked, blinked again, and then smiled, and I swear he looked as though he'd awakened to find himself in heaven. Zaynab smiled back down at him. Suddenly self-conscious, she put her hand to the side of her head to draw her veil, but she had no veil and the blood rushed to her naked face. She looked away from the soldier's blue eyes and slowly rose from her knees with the water jug. The soldiers separated to make way for Father, who passed between them and took his daughter's hand to lead her into the house. Before departing, she glanced back at the blue-eyed cavalier who was still staring up at her with a face of angelic astonishment, a look enhanced by a tumble of blond locks. One of the servants had retrieved his horse.

When the troops had helped their comrade to his feet and onto his horse and they had fallen back into formation, the drumming recommenced and the patrol moved slowly on. I had gotten up from the ground and brushed the dust from my robe and was locking the gate when I looked down the narrow road and saw that the cavalry officer had turned back in his saddle, no doubt hoping to catch a last glimpse of his saving angel. In a raised voice, I told him to look in front of him and try to stay on his horse, but the idiot didn't understand.

The French army entered Cairo in force the following day. They paraded through the streets in their indecorously tight red, white, and blue uniforms, marching behind military bands that played instruments never before seen or heard in Cairo. It was an incredible spectacle: the perfectly even lines of infantry looking straight ahead and marching in step (with their muskets resting on their shoulders, of all places!); the officers on horseback in their close-fitting pantaloons and golden epaulets and funny, pointed hats, silver swords rattling at their sides; the rhythmic clack of hooves on the ground in step with the music, as though even the horses knew to keep time with the beating drums; then row upon row of artillery rolling past on polished carriages … it all brought us staring in open-mouthed wonder. All that was missing was our new French sultan, or Caliph Harun al-Rashid on a white charger throwing gold coins to the crowds lining the streets. But the mighty conqueror was not part of the parade that day. When the parade was over, some of the troops marched up to the Citadel while the rest went to Azbakiyya, where the high officers had taken over the Mamluk palaces for their general headquarters and private residences. There was no looting; no one was slaughtered; not a single woman was raped or sodomized. What kind of soldiers were these?

Later that day, a proclamation was posted on street corners and shop fronts—hundreds and hundreds of identical copies distributed over the whole city. They were in Arabic, the characters and words uniformly written and spaced. We stood around looking at the orders, as captivated by their meaning as by the mind-boggling uniformity of the script and the abundance of copies that had been posted. Someone said it must have taken on an army of scribes a month to produce so many copies; but then each scribe would have to have had identical handwriting, in addition to an identical sense of spacing and centering, for each word was uniformly spaced one from the other and the text centered perfectly on each rectangle of paper. There was something here we couldn't understand. We shook our heads and read, and what we read was even more mystifying. It said the French had come to liberate Egypt from the lawless Mamluks who had defiled Islam. The French, the Defenders of Islam and True Muslims, had come to restore God's Religion and the Holy Law of Islam. Accordingly, looting and seizing food without payment were outlawed. Women were to be protected. Any infringement on their rights would be severely punished.

We pondered the inexplicable. The French were Muslims and the Mamluks were not? And what did "rights" mean? Whatever they were, did women have them and not men? Some of the old shaykhs explained it meant the women were to be raped.

The proclamation declared an amnesty. Anyone who had resisted the French was free and would be regarded as a citizen of the Egyptian nation in full possession of legal and national rights. All citizens should continue their daily affairs assured that their peace and security were guaranteed by the French Revolutionary Army of the Republic. The proclamation was signed by Commander in Chief General Napoleon Bonaparte, a true Muslim who had been ordered by God to deliver Egypt from the Mamluks, to free its people from their godless despotism and save Islam. General Bonaparte had come to make men free!

"Free from what?" Father asked as we stood with a group of shaykhs, pondering the meaning of the proclamation and the way it was written, with that curious regularity of lettering and spacing. "What does 'citizen' mean?"

"Obviously they don't know what they're talking about!" a shaykh of rhetoric at al-Azhar declared. "See the errors in grammar! Only hopelessly ignorant people would write like that. And the script! It has no art to it. No beauty!"

Maybe not beauty, I thought to myself, but clarity and regularity—lines as straight, evenly spaced, and precise as the way the French fought and marched. I was too perplexed to begin to make sense of what was happening. And some of the words in Bonaparte's rescript—*citizen, rights, nation, revolution, republic*—were words we couldn't fathom. I felt our conquerors were trying to say something that went beyond our conceptual thinking. I knew the words but not what they were saying. Later, alone in my room, I pored over every word of the proclamation several times and went to the classical lexicons. *Rights.* The closest I could come to it was haqq; plural huquq: truths; deservings.

"What are 'deservings'?" Zaynab asked when I showed her the copy I had annotated.

"To obey."

"Obey?"

"To obey Father, to obey your husband. To be a good Muslim and obey."

"It doesn't mean that here. Look, isn't the word order strange? And the sentences, they don't even rhyme."

"What do you expect from barbarian infidels?"

She took the proclamation from me and reread it slowly, her brow creased in wonder, and when she had finished she murmured as if thinking aloud, "Who are these strange people? Who is this Bonaparte?"

The commander in chief entered Cairo the next day. *Why did he wait a day?* everyone wondered. As I came to know Napoleon, I came to know the reason. He waited so that he would enter on a day charged with religious symbolism, the tenth of Muharram, the Holy Day of Ashura, the Day of Atonement of the ancient Hebrews of Moses, when the Angel of Death passed through Egypt delivering the Hebrews from slavery—the same day of suffering and atonement of the Shi'ite Muslims of Mount Lebanon, South Iraq, and Iran, the day when Hussein, son of Ali, was martyred at Kerbala. The conquering commander entered Cairo on Ashura as a savior, riding a white charger. He entered in a blaze of pomp and glory through Bab al-Nasr, the Portal of Triumph, to liberate us, to set us free—but from what we had no idea. Nothing made sense. Words, proclamations, military parades—we were like a people intoxicated, drugged by things we saw and heard but couldn't understand. Erect on his prancing charger, arm raised to the gawking crowds who had gathered to see him, he cried out in Arabic, "God is great! Allahu akbar, Allahu akbar!" So colorful and awesome was the affair that no one seemed to notice or care how short the great conqueror was or how ridiculous his words. Except Father:

"This emaciated runt of a Bonaparte is a fool," he snorted in contempt.

I never contradicted Father to his face. Yes, Bonaparte was a fool, but one who had crossed the sea and defeated us, something his ancestors of many centuries ago had never been able to do. Though he may have been ridiculous in some ways, he was the leader of a military power the likes of which we had never seen, and it was that power, not the commander, that should have been occupying our thoughts.

The next morning a cohort of cavalry officers dismounted before our villa. With a jangle of sheathed sabers and a thump of boots, they strode to the bolted gate. "Come with me, Son," father said wearily, seeing them there. "It may take two of us to meet the ignorance of all those Franks."

Father opened the gate himself. A civilian dressed in the strange manner of Europe stepped forth from his military escort, handed Father a document, and in perfect classical Arabic introduced himself as J.J. Marcel, savant and orientalist with the French Expeditionary Army to Egypt and chief of the Arabic press. Press? Matba'a? The word was as boggling as the young man's beautiful Arabic, with every verb, noun, adjective, and adverb ending grammatically correct and perfectly enunciated, as if he were formally lecturing to a seminar of leading scholars at our al-Azhar.

At first I thought the troops had mistaken our large villa for one of the Mamluk palaces and had come to search it for weapons and hidden wealth, as they had all the palaces. But then this Marcel fellow explained that Commander in Chief Napoleon Bonaparte requested the honor of the respected scholar Shaykh Khalil al-Bakri's presence at the Citadel that afternoon at four, following the afternoon prayer.

Father stared at him in perplexity. "Four?"

"Four o'clock. The hour of four. The commander in chief will be waiting."

"But the afternoon prayer usually comes after the hour of nine. How does one come after the afternoon prayer and be at the Citadel at the hour of four?"

"Excuse me. We begin counting the afternoon hours of day when the sun has reached its highest altitude. That is the hour twelve, or midday."

Father pawed his beard. "You don't begin counting the hours of day with the sun rising on the eastern horizon, as God intended it should be?"

"No. We don't."

"Strange are your ways, young man."

J.J. Marcel smiled. "Perhaps. But when the sun has reached the meridian, count four parts of the total time it will take for the sun to set. Then when the sun has reached the fourth part, be at the Citadel. Also, my respected shaykh, the sun does not rise. It is the Earth turning on its axis that makes it appear so."

Father stared at him as though struck by lightning, not comprehending a word of it. Earth turning on its axis? What in God's seven heavens was the idiot talking about?

"So the commander in chief will be expecting you at the Citadel at four this afternoon."

Father then brought his little conical sundial from his robe. Having swiveled down the built-in brass adjustable gnomon to the horizontal position and pulled it out to the line marked midsummer, he placed the dial on a flat horizontal stone, with the gnomon in the direction of the sun. The tip of the shadow cast by the gnomon on the line of stereographic projection indicated the day was four hours old. "You see? It's already four o'clock!" exclaimed father in triumph.

J.J. Marcel smiled and looked admiringly at the sundial. "What a beautiful instrument. I collect these medieval pieces for our museum. Would you sell it to me?"

Father proudly handed him his sundial. "My father had this made by Shaykh Jabarti's father, Hassan. He was the leading mathematician and astronomer in Egypt, if not the world."

"But it's only good for Cairo and places at the same latitude as Cairo."

"So? Are we not in Cairo?"

Marcel smiled more widely. I liked his smile. "You're right. We are. But don't go too far north or south with that."

"I don't plan to. There are those who come to Cairo and those who go. Even the Frankish crusaders came and left. One, a King Louis, I believe, was taken prisoner right here in Egypt. Please, take the sundial for your ... what did you call it?"

Father refused to take any money; it was a gift. Marcel in return took a gilded, egg-shaped timepiece from his pocket and presented it to Father. I had seen one of these mechanical devices before. It belonged to a Venetian merchant I knew. Moving dials told the hour and minute of day and night, from one to twelve, on a circular surface. The Venetian had explained that an intricate assembly of springs, balances, sprockets, and gears moved the dials. I had thought it an amazing triumph of mechanical ingenuity.

"Shaykh Bakri, permit me to give this to you as a token of my respect. It's a great honor for me to be speaking to a descendent of the heroic Caliph Abu Bakr and scion of the renowned Bakri clan—a great privilege. All my life I've studied Islamic history and religion, but never did I dream of meeting such a noble person as yourself from this ancient civilization. It's a humbling honor and pleasure." J.J. bowed and straightened in a respectful but servile act of formality we contemptuously assumed to be Persian or Chinese. "You will need it for the new world Egypt will be a part of now." His mission concluded, he gave us a military salute. "Commander Bonaparte sends you his respects and salutes you in the glory of Islam and the Revolutionary Republic. Good day. Until four."

"In the name of God, I will be there at ten, if He so wills."

"Yes, yes, it's his will. You can read it on the invitation General Bonaparte has sent to you."

When Marcel and the honor guard had galloped off, Father spat on the ground in contempt and squinted at the egg as though it had dropped from the devil's anus. "Stupid, arrogant people! How can such savages expect to rule Egypt when they can't tell time?"

He gave me the egg. "Have it melted down for the gold. 'Noble person from this ancient civilization'! What is ancient about it? And what does 'Arabic press' mean? And 'museum'? What in the seventy hells is the 'new world' this idiot is talking about?" As he spoke, Father was opening the sealed document Marcel had given him. It was written in that same, strange script: precisely spaced, uniform letters, words, and lines stretched straight across the page like the strings of a musical instrument.

"What does it say, Father?"

"What of importance can something written as artlessly as this have to say, this ugly piece of Frankish child's play?" he exclaimed disdainfully, waving the paper in his hand while holding it at arm's length away from him, as though an animal had defecated on it. "This is something to be read and done with, to read and tossed in the trash, for all it's worth."

"But it is easy to read, Father."

"So is relieving one's bowels easy for the stomach when it's full of shit."

The document began by declaring Egypt, in the name of God and Napoleon Bonaparte, a free nation under the eternal religion of Islam, God's one true religion. It went on to appoint Father to the new ruling body, the diwan, which would include twelve scholarly shaykhs and henceforth be the supreme legislative and executive council of government. The diwan would draw up a constitution to delimit and define citizens' rights, legislate new laws, regulate taxes, and establish just prices in the marketplace. In addition, the diwan would be the chief authority in proposing, legislating, and executing all new industrial, agricultural, and scientific projects in the country, with the aim of making Egypt a modern national republic with health, wealth, happiness, and freedom for all its citizens, be they landowners, merchants, workers, or peasants. The names of the twelve shaykhs appointed to the diwan were listed at the end: Sharqawi, Sadat, Bakri, Sawi, Musa, Jabarti …

Father took the document from me and read it through again. "Garbage. Nonsense. A diarrhea of meaningless words. Now I know why the Franks use precious paper instead of water to wipe their dirty behinds. Their paper's already covered in shit."

"It sounds … ambitious," I ventured.

"Ambitious? Ambitious? What is ambitious in it? It sounds stupid! Senseless! The ranting of infidels, heathens whose heads are loose in a sea of disjointed words, drowning in an ocean of grammatical mistakes. Ignorant fools. They can't even compose correct Arabic! God save us from such devilish imbeciles!"

He read the document once more. "Constitution, republic, freedom, rights, legislation—what meaning do such words have?" he snapped, shaking his head. "Constitution? Laws? What need do we have of these vague things that evade understanding? We have the Holy Quran. Rights? We have the sacred tradition of the Prophet of God, rest his soul. Laws? We have the Holy Shari'ah, all the law we need, and right from God Himself, through revelation and our holy tradition in Hadith. What are these perverse concepts of the feverish Frankish mind to us? We have all the laws, constitution, rights, and freedom we need, and straight from God, God Himself! Not from the puny mind of mortal man. Not from some stinking infidel of a dwarf Frank who knows nothing of Egypt, nothing of religion!"

"All the more reason you should help him rule by being on the diwan."

"That's exactly the point. He's trying to use us, all the religious scholars. He wants to make it appear that al-Azhar is ruling. That dolt of a runt, with all his blabber about Islam and his being a Muslim—the hypocrite wants us to be his stooges, his props for legitimacy. No, I won't be used.

I won't be used!" Father dropped the document to the floor and went to the window to look out at the fields and palm groves that extended all the way to the lake and Azbakiyya Canal. The Nile was low, and the canal it fed was almost dry. Gazing out at the forest of palms with their clusters of burnt-yellow dates hanging heavily from the upper fronds, like golden beards of old men, he repeated with a slow, studied, quiet determination, "Shaykh Khalil al-Bakri will not be used!"

"Of course not, Father. I didn't intend that. Helping run local affairs in a wise way until the sultan gets the French out of here is not the same as being used."

"Yes, Son. That's right. Helping intelligently is not the same as being used." Father squinted thoughtfully across the palms and fields and canal into the distance. "Perhaps the ignorant French general is the one who will be used."

"Napoleon Bonaparte may not be that ignorant."

"He is a Frank. He wipes himself with paper and can't tell the time of day."

Father turned from the window. His mouth curved into a thin, curious smile as he smoothed his beard downward between thumb and fingers. A thoughtful light twinkled in his eyes. "We will see," he said quietly, looking lost in his own thoughts. "We will see what brains this Bonaparte has, believing the Earth turns on its axis. Maybe I will turn this Bonaparte on his."

I accompanied my father up to the Citadel that afternoon. All the leading shaykhs were there, along with a dozen rich merchants, a clutch of Ottoman officials who hadn't fled, and the patriarch of the Coptic community, who held himself proudly erect, as if it were the Christian Copts who had conquered Egypt. Like Father, the patriarch no doubt had decided to help the ignorant Franks rule Egypt, but instead of displaying the nervous indecision of the Muslim shaykhs, the patriarch acted like he had suddenly become a French commander.

We were ushered into the grand reception hall of the Ottoman pasha's official palace, the pasha being, at the moment, somewhere in Syria and running for Anatolia and Istanbul. "I wonder how our Sultan Selim in Istanbul is taking this Frankish occupation," mused my father in polite conversation with Shaykhs Sadat and Sharqawi, his Azhar rivals for religious and institutional precedence, as we waited for our new French sultan to make his appearance.

"Indeed, I doubt he thinks about it at all, with the emperors of Russia and Austria squeezing in on him from either side," Sharqawi replied.

"He *must* be thinking about it," Father countered. "He must be organizing an army to throw the Franks out." Shaykh Sadat nodded in agreement; Shaykh Shaqawi shrugged and made no reply. He seemed to know a lot more than the other shaykhs about Istanbul and its problems.

Indeed, the sultan would have to do something to regain control of Egypt, but what? The irony of it was that for more than a decade, Sultan Selim III had been using French equipment and officers to remodel the Ottoman army and navy in order to halt the Russians and Austrians, and now a French general had invaded and taken one of the Ottomans' prize possessions. Sultan Selim called his reforming project the New Order. New Order? In trying to make Frenchmen of his army, he'd lost Egypt to them. It was almost funny.

Napoleon Bonaparte made an art of keeping people waiting in suspense. As the minutes passed and the tension mounted (especially for Father, who was finding it increasingly difficult to make small talk with his sharp-witted rivals, Sharqawi and Sadat), the other shaykhs filled the long silences with patient nods, sighs, and sugared smiles, hiding their jealous-thickened disdain for each other as only scholars know how to do. The vicious rivalry between Father and Sharqawi, in particular, was matched only by the murderous suspicion and jealousy that had prevailed among the Mamluk beys and emirs before they went under.

The door opened. A young man dressed in the robe, turban, and caftan of a high al-Azhar shaykh strode importantly to the center of the hall. He was much shorter than the usual Frenchman, though we weren't sure he was one, for in addition to wearing religious attire, he was holding the Quran in his right hand. But when he saluted us in Arabic in the name of God, the Beneficent, the Merciful, and then went on to recite the opening verses of the Quran, we knew. His pronunciation made me cringe. The older generals towering behind him looked at each other in embarrassment.

When I had first seen Bonaparte, he was on his white horse, and though noticeably short, he looked splendid in his uniform and helmet. But standing before us now, he seemed hardly a full-grown man. In fact, in his long caftan and voluminous turban, which drowned his head from above, he looked like an overdressed dandy of a kid. The shaykhs and other Egyptians gawked at him in astonishment. Was this chit of a boy in the ridiculously large turban the commander in chief of the army that had vanquished the Mamluks and conquered Egypt in two weeks? This, our new sultan? Our new Alexander? This twit who looked no older than myself!

Adding to the general astonishment, the diminutive sultan in robes and turban approached the assembled shaykhs, and one by one took their hands and greeted them in Arabic, addressing them by name, all twelve, as though he already knew them. Sawi, Musa, Sadat, Sharqawi, Bakri, Fayyumi ... he had never seen them before, yet knew them each by name! The unbelievable events of the afternoon did not abate. After reviewing the general contents of the proclamation about the governing diwan, this youth, whose mental powers were beginning to dawn on me and make me forget his clownish imitation of a sultan-pasha, declared that the shaykhs and others serving on it would also have control of the national budget. Nobody knew quite what a nation was, much less a budget. (I didn't either at the time.) J.J. Marcel, who was doing the translating, had trouble finding an Arabic word for "budget" and ended up concocting a stew of vaguely familiar terms—*input, output, apportioning, balances, accounting*—that taken together were meant to define a single concept, which was simple enough in mathematical terms (revenues collected equal planned expenditures). But in its application to government and the rapacious officers who, in their arbitrary ways, controlled administrative and financial affairs, the concept remained as mysterious to me as that golden shell Bonaparte had given Father, the magical egg that contained in its yoke the universal gnomon of shadow lengths, solar altitudes, latitudes, and stereographic projections that together were able to indicate the time of day—even at night, when there was no shadow from the sun's rays. I supposed that such things as balance, budgets, and apportioning, and the idea that what was brought in should equal what was spent, made sense and were practicable in Frankistan. But to think that those things could be applied in Egypt was absolute insanity and showed how little the Franks knew about us, our country, and our lordly rulers.

Listening to Bonaparte go on and trying to make sense of Marcel's translation, and assuming that the words somehow made sense and therefore the concepts they expressed worked well enough for the French, I gathered that these people were like magicians, sorcerers who possessed and commanded the jinn rather than the jinn commanding them. Bonaparte looked clownish, but he and his people were cleverer than a thousand devils. And as with devils, I saw how easily people might be attracted to them, though I as yet had no idea where their cleverness lay, other than what I saw in their mathematical precision on the battlefield. I was sure that there were underlying secrets that explained their military prowess, and that those explained their strange ideas about finances and government and law, which I intuited came from the same source. And even back then, during my first meeting with Bonaparte, I yearned to discover that source.

The heady talk of budget finished, Bonaparte went on to say the diwan would share control of the army with the French high command, with whom they would immediately begin planning the financing and strategy for the conquest of Nubia and Syria. The shaykhs would plan finances and military conquests? They looked at Bonaparte in silence and at each other in confusion. Several of the generals exchanged glances as well. Marcel continued translating: "The state formed by the union of Nubia and Syria to Egypt will be governed by Egyptians, Muslims, Coptic Christians, and Jews alike. All religions will be legally equal, with a government office open to all."

Religious equality? Muslims sharing power with Christians, Jews? The shaykhs blinked. What they had heard was absurd. It was as though the universe were coming unhinged. No one uttered a sound. Judging from the expression on their faces, they would have preferred that their women be raped, sodomized, and sold into slavery than their religion reduced to the status of the tolerated minorities. There were always more women to be had. But religious equality? That was the ultimate insult to their manhood and God! Looking back at it now, I have to smile at the expression of mind-melting shock that came to the shaykhs' faces, and mine too, I suppose, as Bonaparte went on and on about religious equality.

He then launched into a diatribe on brotherhood, the rights of man, and liberty, which was just another way of saying that Christians and Jews would henceforth share the same legal and social privileges as Muslims. He let us chew on that for a while before speaking at length on the glory and commercial prosperity that the great nation of Egypt was about to achieve, in conjunction with France, as the center of an empire stretching into Central Africa and Asia as far as India, and including Europe. Together, France and Egypt would rule the choicest parts of the world and monopolize global trade.

We were dazzled. We were incredulous. The merchant notables attending the meeting were salivating. The young general's breadth of imagination and passion was like a whirlwind, remaking the world in his mind's eye, and for a moment he made that world almost real to us—to me—in spite of our negative predispositions. He didn't even look ridiculous to me anymore in his overgrown turban and Thousand-and-One-Nights kaftan and slippers.

And then when he had done remaking the world and the words *greatness of Egypt* were still ringing in our ears, he added almost as an afterthought, "Oh yes, one thing more. Women are included in the general emancipation of Egyptian society from the godless Mamluk tyranny. In the new Egypt, women will be free to enter society unveiled."

A few shaykhs gasped at Marcel's translation: what Bonaparte had uttered went beyond insult. It meant the dissolution of family, society, and civilization. It meant turmoil, chaos, and strife, the end of public peace and harmony among men. Shaykh Sharqawi stepped forth to say something, but Bonaparte raised his hand, saying, "All of this, of course, depends on the decision of the special diwan, and you are its members. I am sure you will all do your duty to yourselves and your nation in following the general will of your people. Now in the name of God, the Beneficent, the Merciful, elect from among yourselves the president of your ruling body and begin your duty. The world awaits the greatness of the Egyptian nation!"

With this, Bonaparte departed. The dumbfounded shaykhs were then instructed on the art of the secret ballot to cast their votes for a leader. I understood what Bonaparte was doing: creating a new office for the fractious shaykhs to fight over, like angry dogs over a bone tossed to them. This youthful, in some ways comical, commander in chief was offering empty prizes to our religious leaders, flattering their vanity—buying them, as Father had said. And there Father was, watching Marcel tally the ballots, wetting his lips in desire, eyes shining at the thought of being the young sultan's wise vizier, Barmak to Harun al-Rashid. And why shouldn't he be? After all, he was the one who had saved Cairo and her people; he had talked the leading shaykhs out of following the hawkish-minded ones who wanted us to fight the French after our departed religious leader, Shaykh Umar Makram, had whipped people into a suicidal frenzy of resistance and then fled to Palestine, abandoning us to our fate.

Father held his breath when Marcel said he was ready to announce the winner.

The vote went to Father's bitter rival, Shaykh Sharqawi. Maybe the shaykhs had voted for him because he had stepped forward to protest Bonaparte's plan to debase the good names of Muslim women by allowing them to be free in society. I stole a glance at Father. He was livid. He looked like he'd received a mortal blow. His eyes stared straight ahead, as though frozen in his skull. He was so reduced that he hadn't the grace to force up a honeyed smile and congratulate his fellow scholar. It was not the first time he had lost to Sharqawi, or to other shaykhs, in the contest for high religious office and honorific titles. I could tell exactly what was going through his head when Marcel shook Sharqawi's hand and draped some silly banner over his shoulder in recognition of his new position. Father's face said it all: the world was against him.

I saw Sharqawi's eldest son, Faysal, standing alone, waiting for his father. Faysal was my age and, like me, a theological student at al-Azhar following in his father's footsteps. In spite of the enmity between our fathers, we were friends and enjoyed discussing history and religion. I could talk with Faysal more than I could with the other students. He had a broad outlook on affairs, and I felt in him a kindred soul. So while Father was doing his best to conceal his disappointment by chatting with some of the other shaykhs who were standing off by themselves, away from Sharqawi and his clique, I went over to Faysal and congratulated him on his father's election. He smiled wanly, saying maybe condolences would be more appropriate, and asked what I thought of this diwan business and Bonaparte's plans. I replied I didn't know what to think; I was overwhelmed, like everybody else.

"It won't happen," he said.

"What won't happen?"

"What he said. About making new laws. Bonaparte's fooling himself thinking he can fool us. He can't change the law of Islam. Religion is fixed. It's eternal."

"You're right, but ..." I held fire. I had to be careful. I didn't want to sound favorable to the French—not that I was or perceived myself to be, not at that early date, in any case—but I had to be careful what I said from now on, even to a kindred soul. Faysal pressed me on:

"But what?"

"Well. In some things, at least, he sounded as though he was trying to do something positive."

"You mean that nonsense about health and industry? We already have that. What more do we need? The man's a clown, but a devil underneath."

"I know. Those are my own words for him." I waited a few seconds, then: "How do you mean, exactly?"

"All that nonsense about wealth and brotherhood, and religious equality. How can one religion be equal to another any more than a peasant is equal to a rich merchant or a religious scholar? And that stupidity about women in society—unveiled!"

I feigned a laugh. "That bit was pretty absurd." There was another pause, and then I ventured to ask, "You really think he's that much of a fool?"

"That much of a devil!"

"You're right. He also needs a good tailor."

Faysal gave a sudden laugh and clapped his hands. "Didn't that shorty look ridiculous thinking he cut the image of a sultan! But his words weren't ridiculous," he added, turning serious. "They were dangerous. I'll bet your sister Zaynab would have danced for joy if she'd heard what our little sultan said!"

It wasn't proper to speak of someone's female relatives, and when I didn't laugh, he took me by the shoulder, as if in apology, and said he'd been joking, and then he added to the joke, saying, "Zaynab should've been born a man."

A twinge of pain in Faysal's eyes belied his smile. His feelings were still raw. The year before, my mother and his had tried to dissolve the hatred between our fathers by having Zaynab and Faysal marry. In terms of family background and social station, it would have been a perfect match, and neither of the two fathers could protest it without showing pettiness. The affair had gone far enough for Zaynab to receive Faysal at home and chat with him unveiled in the presence of the women servants. However, wanting nothing of marriage, Zaynab insisted on conditions Faysal couldn't possibly accept: no second wife, no female slaves or concubines, an enormous payment if he should divorce her, even a clause allowing *her* to divorce *him*, if she should ever wish to. As if that hadn't been humiliating enough, she had half-seriously joked that if Faysal didn't agree to those conditions, she would still marry him, but only if for every additional wife or concubine or slave he took, she could take an additional man. My God! From where did my sister get these evil ideas? That ended the affair. Faysal, Father, Mother, Shaykh Shaqawi—everyone was scandalized, except Zaynab.

Faysal had been so nonplussed by her preposterous remark that he hadn't felt insulted, only boggled, hurt, and disappointed that such a beautiful girl from such a noble family could have a mind so diseased. He pitied her. He took her to be mentally ill.

"We'll see what comes of this stupid diwan," Faysal said to get back to the subject. "It couldn't have any real power." He chuckled. "Maybe it's a trick to keep all the leading shaykhs together in one place every day so they'll be too busy fighting among themselves to organize any resistance against our invaders."

"Right. Since they're so good at talking, they'll talk each other to death in their diwan while our little French sultan rules Egypt as he wants. Maybe that's what he means by representative institutions."

We laughed over that for a moment, and then shook hands and rejoined our respective fathers, who were mounted on their donkeys and waiting impatiently some distance apart from one another.

Side by side, Father and I descended the Citadel road, which was cut from the cliff of the high Muqattam Plateau. We didn't speak. Our donkeys' hooves kicked up the dust with a rhythmic clop that echoed against the cavernous rock gouged out of the steep cliff. I was about to say something, but Father seemed too preoccupied for conversation, and so I continued on in silence, pondering in my mind's eye the theatrical spectacle of Bonaparte in his sultan's garb, the odd juxtaposition of his uncanny knowledge of some things about Egypt and ludicrous ignorance of other things, and his grandiose plans for the country—Egypt joined to France in a world empire of commerce, abetted by a canal linking the Red Sea to the Mediterranean. From there my thoughts drifted to the strange words and ideas I had heard—*nation, freedom,* the *rights* of man, women in society and unveiled—and while lost in the frightening whirl of these unfamiliar things, I heard Father declare out of the blue, "Anyway, who

32

would want to serve on a diwan that lowers Muslims to the status of Jews and Christians! And women free to leave the house, their naked passions unloosed in the streets! Like bitches and she-camels in heat! And why, of all people, Sharqawi?"

3

WHY SHARQAWI? IT WAS a question of bitter memory. Sharqawi's election to the presidency of Napoleon's diwan was eating at Father's heart. It had brought the ghost of humiliation and defeat back from the past to haunt him. Seven years may have dulled the pain in his heart but not the look in his eyes. I had been a boy at the time, but in all those years since, I'd never forgotten the bitterness in Father's eyes.

I should say something here to fill in the historical record regarding the Bakri family. I don't relish the task, for what was painful to Father is painful to me, but it may help explain what later happened between Father and Napoleon, and how poor Zaynab got caught in their web of intrigue. We never escape our past—nor should we. The past is our responsibility, what we must live with and make the best of. We are not victims of our past, for we're the ones who made it. The victims are the innocents we allow to get trapped in it.

Seven years before Napoleon's arrival in Cairo, one of my uncles died— my father's brother. He had been the leading shaykh in the family and in Egypt, and as such held two of the highest religious distinctions in the country. First, he was keeper of the Bakri Prayer Rug. The rug was purported to have been the caliph abu Bakr's and had been handed down generation after generation for twelve centuries, always entrusted to the one who was considered the most excellent of all the elders in mind, body, moral character, piety, and generosity. In Egypt it was a high religious honor to receive the rug, and only members of the Bakri family were entrusted with it. The highest religious honor was to be elected Naqib al-Ashraf, the honorary head of an elite society open to all shaykhs of al-Azhar whose ancestry went back to the family of the Prophet (whose family didn't?). The office of Naqib was awarded by election of the shaykh who was most renowned for character, intellect, learning, piety, and leadership—the same general attributes that went along with being named keeper of the prayer rug. My uncle, an exceptional shaykh, had been elected to receive both honors. Upon his death, Father expected to inherit them both, figuring the elections were no more than formalities. Because of his age, family, social stature, piety, and closeness to his older brother, he was certain that he was the only viable candidate and so the election was a foregone conclusion.

The elders of the Bakri clan pulled the rug out from under him, so to speak, giving it to a lesser shaykh in our large family. As in any extended family, ours had always had a good deal of jealousy and infighting, but this time it got out of control. Some members of the family, a clique of younger brothers, uncles, and cousins to the tenth degree, let it out that Father was too frivolous and unstable to be entrusted with the rug. They dropped hints that he'd drunk alcohol and smoked hashish and taken all sorts of drugs, and had been mixed up in unseemly affairs, even having young boys. No skeleton was too dirty to be trotted out of the family closet to keep Father from getting the rug.

Their strategy worked. Even though most of the rumors were patently false, Father's character was so besmirched inside and out that the family elders, disgusted with the whole affair, settled on an unknown.

Being denied the rug lost Father the higher honor of Naqib al-Ashraf, as there was no way al-Azhar shaykhs could elect someone who had been rejected by his own family. Father was crushed. He cursed and cut himself off from the family. Four years later, when the man who had been given the rug died, the Bakri elders gave it to Father, as though to make amends for the unfair treatment he had received. Father graciously forgave and accepted, expecting that with the rug, he would now be elected Naqib al-Ashraf. But this was not to be. Some still detected the bad smell his character had been given years earlier. Shaykh Sharqawi cast the deciding vote that gave the honor to Umar Makram, the man who ran for Palestine to flee the French devils after having exhorted the poor of Cairo to stand and fight them.

Father wisely countered that irresponsible exhortation, which would have caused untold destruction and death, and now, for his having served the people of Cairo with wise counsel that saved them, even at the risk of his being labeled a defeatist and collaborator, his nemesis, Sharqawi, who had already robbed him of being Naqib, was elected head of the diwan—a dubious honor in my esteem, but it was like fiery acid eating away at Father's innards.

Faysal was right when he said condolences were more appropriate than congratulations. I tried consoling Father by saying the same thing, expressing pity for poor Sharqawi, who would have to bear the onus of acting as a front man for the French. Father agreed, but the coldness of his words and the bitterness in his eyes told me something else. I worried for him. His need for recognition to extinguish the smell of the past had drawn a veil over his eyes.

In the days that followed Father's defeat at the hands of his fellow shaykhs, we all watched in wonder as the French began to exert a strengthening influence on the people. The French were a constant source of wonder, to put it mildly. Everything they did was absolutely horrifying, amazing, or amusing. Some things they did went beyond categorization. For example, one of the first things was to take what they called a census. That is, they counted every person living in Cairo and made a detailed account of everyone's wealth and possessions in every possible form that such things can exist, and in some cases not exist—income, buildings, land, animals, fruit-bearing trees, business, gold, profits from sales that merchants made, and even profits they reckoned to make in future sales, as if our merchants could see into the future like prophets and mystical saints. The devilish French tax agents even counted the eggs our chickens laid, estimated the amount of milk a water buffalo would give in a year, and tallied not just the number of date palms we owned, but the number of dates as well! Then they very carefully recorded everything in their enormous account books, overlooking nothing—not even the unborn camel that still had a month to go in its mother's belly. By the end of their accounting and assessing, they knew how many eggs, chickens, water buffalos, and dates there were in the whole of the country. We couldn't believe it. People said the reason the French soldiers didn't rape and slaughter and burn towns and villages was that they were saving them for the slower death of taxation!

It wasn't long before the French learned that the rich people buried their gold. This got them to digging under the floors of those they suspected of doing so. But to us, the census was especially diabolical. The French claimed that the object was to form an equitable basis for a regularized system of taxation. That sounded suspicious; anything government did was suspicious. Whatever the official description and intent, the underlying design was always a trick to take from the people whatever the other taxes had left them. The Mamluks had simply taken what they wanted when they wanted it from those who had it. That we could understand. When the French claimed that the tax revenue would be devoted to municipal and national development, we thought that sounded like a conspiracy greater than anything the Mamluks or Ottomans ever pulled on us. Muslim rulers always claimed that any new tax they imposed was for Islam and justified by the Quran. With the French, everything was justified in the name of liberty, equality, justice, progress, and brotherhood. We believed one as little as the other.

Imagine our astonishment when, within five days of the first tax collection, men had been hired to clean the streets, collect garbage, and set up lanterns for streetlights and signs to identify the streets in Arabic and French. Not that we needed signs to tell us what street was what, as if we didn't know where we lived. (Streets needed names? There was no end to French absurdity!) But we went along with it; we had no choice. And so the streets were now clean and given names, and—can you believe it?— they even put identifying numbers on some of the houses and buildings. How to explain such queer occupation of their forever-busy hands that were just like their fever-stricken minds—always in search of things to do, no matter how useless or unnecessary. In amazed incomprehension, we watched them buzz busily through the day like excited bees, forever planning and building.

Restaurants were opened. Cabarets, coffeehouses, hospitals, clinics, and some new industries were created, and old ones enlarged and reorganized. New courts of justice were created. It was their system of justice that made it hard for me to hate them. When a high-ranking French general took over Emir Ibrahim Bey's Azbakiyya palace as his personal residence, forcing out Ibrahim's wife, the beautiful and highly respected Sitt Nafisa, she appealed to Bonaparte, who obtained a court order obliging the general to vacate. The court order stated that though Ibrahim Bey was a Mamluk ruler who had fought the French and fled, and therefore must be considered an enemy, the palace was nonetheless his private property, of which his wife was the legal owner in his absence. Rumor had it that young Bonaparte was so incensed at the general that he slapped him—slapped a general who had done nothing but take over the palace of a vanquished ruler. It was hard to believe, but Sitt Nafisa returned to her palace escorted by a ceremonial guard of French officers splendidly attired in red, white, and blue uniforms with gold epaulets, their silver swords unsheathed and held upright. She looked like a queen on parade with her royal bodyguard.

By coincidence, that same day a report reached Cairo about the execution of two French soldiers convicted of raping a peasant girl in Damietta. The soldiers had been executed by firing squad, shot by their own French comrades for raping a peasant girl! When I heard about it, I shook my head in case I was dreaming. Some of the shaykhs grumbled that it was a trick to put us off our guard, to seduce us into accepting them. The shaykhs warned us not to have anything to do with them, to not even speak to them if they happened to know Arabic, as some of their scholars did. Contact with all the French, soldiers and scholars, was to be totally avoided. They were devils, the shaykhs said. But before the end of two weeks into their occupation of Cairo, I had trouble believing it. I mean, do devils shoot devils for rape? Do devils clean the streets? Do devils clown about on donkeys and camels, laughing and having fun on smelly, mangy animals they paid a small fortune to ride on? Idiots do, but not devils.

The younger French soldiers, the ones around my age, were like kids having the time of their lives. Dumb kids though. Who in their right mind would pay so much to ride a donkey or camel? The absolute proof of their mental deficiency was the perverse fun they got out of racing the animals down the street, and each other up the stones of the pyramids in the hot sun. They laughed and chattered and climbed like a tribe of wild monkeys. We derived immense pleasure just watching them. And then some Egyptian kids started doing it to see if it was really fun. It was, in a way. I had the dignity to do it before dawn, when nobody was around. I mean, after all, to be seen imitating the French? Impossible.

It was really strange. Nobody had bothered with the pyramids until the French came and started crawling all over them. No, we were too sophisticated for climbing. We limited our interest to looking for buried treasure. So when I foolishly told Zaynab my intention to climb the Great Pyramid, expecting her to laugh at me, she instead insisted on going with me. I should have known she would go for a crazy idea like that, climbing to the top of a pyramid for no reason but to get to the top, and then climb back down. Well before dawn, she dressed up in one of my caftans and wrapped a turban around her head, and we rode a donkey to Giza. I was surprised by how beautiful she looked as a boy.

We were at the top of the highest pyramid as the sun broke over the horizon. It was quite a sight. I never would have taken Zaynab to do such a thing—it wasn't something a girl did, or a boy or a man, for that matter; it wasn't our tradition—but since the French had come uninvited into our presence, the limits of behavior weren't so clear anymore, at least not for the young Egyptians in Cairo, especially those with some education who came into contact with the French. But that wasn't a whole lot of people.

For example, the day after Sitt Nafisa was royally restored to her palace, she was seen promenading unveiled along the palm-shaded bank of the Azbakiyya canal. Unveiled, like an Egyptian Godiva—I learned about Godiva much later, when I studied in Paris—but our Godiva was carrying a sun umbrella instead of riding a horse. Everyone who saw her stopped in their tracks. Men shuddered in disgust, looking away in horror as though Satan's wife were promenading the canal with an umbrella protecting her from the sun instead of a veil from the animal lusts of men. Girls turned to look in envy through their veils. I didn't know what to make of it. I was aghast. I couldn't take my eyes away. Sitt Nafisa was as beautiful without a veil as she was naked.

The next day I was on my way to al-Azhar Mosque for the Friday prayer when I met Faysal, who greeted me as though his best friend had died. "It's a disgrace," he said, much agitated. "I'm ashamed. It shouldn't happen. It's too much."

"What's too much?"

"You haven't heard?"

"You mean about Sitt Nafisa?"

"Worse. The batch of girls they're offering Bonaparte."

"What?"

"Some of the city notables are offering their daughters. As though he's a sultan or grand vizier."

"In a way he is, I suppose."

"It's filthy. It's not just the Christians and Jews who are in on this filthy thing. Muslims too!"

"Really?"

"You truly haven't heard?"

"No. Not a word. Why?"

He took me by the arm. "Zaki. I shouldn't be the one to tell you. Your sister Zaynab is one of them."

I stared at him, unable to bring words to my throat. Faysal let go of me, diverting his eyes. "There's no honor left in the old men," he said, almost crying. "My father took it as an honor to be elected president of Bonaparte's diwan. An honor! The old men don't know what honor is anymore. They don't know where they are. They've been turned around. Collaboration is honorable! To give your daughter to the infidel conqueror is an honor! Zaki, don't let him do it! Zaynab may be crazy, but she's an honorable Muslim girl. Don't let him debase her!"

We continued together in silence to the al-Azhar gate. I was so overwhelmed by confusion and despair that I gave up prayer and headed back to Azbakiyya. Even God couldn't still the torment in my soul.

With my mind in a turmoil of disbelief and denial, and fearing that Father would do almost anything to replace Shaykh Sharqawi as Bonaparte's chief Egyptian adviser, I hurried back to our villa, where I found Father in the shade of the palm-frond canopy over the open balcony. He liked to spend the late afternoon there, smoking his hubbly-bubbly and gazing out at the dun-colored buildings of the city beyond Azbakiyyah Lake. Hearing the shuffle of my sandals on the stone steps leading up to the balcony, he turned his head to see who was coming. I knew he hated to be disturbed at this hour in the solitude of his balcony, but I could not keep myself from confronting him. He met my confused look with a questioning expression that for a moment discomfited me. Gathering my courage, I respectfully told Father I had heard a rumor in passing about Zaynab being included in a group of girls being presented to Bonaparte. "Of course I didn't believe it for a moment, but I thought you should know about it, Father."

"Do you regard your sister unworthy of Napoleon?" he snapped.

Napoleon. The old man was already on a first-name basis with his new master.

"It's true?" I felt my legs going out from under me.

"What? That your sister will marry the ruler of Egypt?" The forward thrust of his frowning face was commensurate with his aggressive tone. It was his standard defensive posture when his judgment was questioned.

"But … but sir. She can't."

"She can't? Indeed! Why can't she?"

40

"Father. Bonaparte is a Christian."

"I doubt that."

"He's not a Muslim."

"That's only a matter of time."

"You can't believe that propaganda of his, that he will become a Muslim."

"He will if he wants to be sultan of Egypt. He will convert to Islam just as his governor of Rosetta, General Menou, did. Abdullah Menou—what a foolish name."

"He only did it to marry that rich woman. She was already married and divorced. Father, Zaynab is a girl. A virgin."

"Christian Jacques Menou became Muslim Abdullah to marry Zubaydah. So too will Napoleon become Muslim to marry Zaynab. I wonder what name he will take. Nabil? Nabil al-Awn Bun al-Fart?" (I should perhaps mention that Arabic has no letter *P. Bun al-Fart* means "coffee beans in abundance.")

"Please, Father, she can't. I mean … she won't. You know how she is." I had never stood up to Father before. I didn't think I had it in me, but some strange inner force hurled me forth to confront him, the man who had intimidated me all my life, who wielded absolute power over me.

"Can't? Won't? Son, have you fever in the head to claim these strange words for the mind of a girl? Zaynab is my daughter. She will do what she has to do. What she has to do is what she's told to do. I have already told her. What is a girl for, if not to marry obediently? As for Nabil al-Awn Bun al-Fart becoming Muslim, it's only a matter of the right time."

"What does she say?"

"What could she have to say? She said nothing. Oh yes, she did say something, as I recall: 'Hear and obey. Like a good Sheherazade.'"

"That's not like her."

"You're right. But she knows I'm serious, and judging from her lack of reaction, I assume she shares my wisdom in this affair."

"Wisdom?" More whoredom than wisdom. But this I could never say to Father. I walked to the edge of the balcony and leaned my elbows on the balustrade. The sun was a glowing red ball hovering over the pyramids and the western desert. I recalled what J.J. Marcel had said about the sun being stationary and Earth orbiting it. What nonsense! What to believe anymore?

Father was saying, "You know how the French are slaves to their women."

"I've only heard. One hears a lot of things about the French."

"It's well known that Frenchmen are ruled by women. They defer to them in every way. The women rule. They slap their husbands; they forbid them other wives or women while they themselves have as many men as their unruly passions desire. They go about the streets almost naked, doing what they want when they want with whom they want, and spending their husband's money while doing it. They say French women change their style of dress every season, as they change their lovers. And the men don't mind. Zaynab will be very happy. She will get to beat her husband with her shoes, the way French women do." Father sucked deeply on the stem of his pipe, drawing up a gurgling rush of bubbles through the water, and blew out a pale cloud of gray-blue smoke.

"You can't be serious, Father."

"I'm deadly serious. Give him the chance and a Frenchmen will happily spend his life with his face stuffed between a woman's legs. How such tulips defeated the Mamluks is one of the strangest of God's mysteries."

"I mean about Zaynab. That she's agreed to go."

"She has no choice. In any case, why would she choose not to? Zaynab will be the real ruler of Egypt. Better a woman who knows Egypt than a French boy who doesn't. And behind Zaynab …" Father's smile said it all. "I'm doing this for Egypt, mind you. Shajaret al-Durr was Egypt's Mamluk queen for a time. Zaynab will be Egypt's queen for a longer time."

"Father, Shajarat al-Durr was thrown to her death from the Citadel after ruling for eighty days. Think of what you're doing."

He ignored my objection and, with an air of sublime contentment, drew through his pipe another draught of the perfumed tobacco burning away in the tray at the top of the glass vessel. From the whiff I caught, I could tell it was laced with more than ambergis.

Too stunned to protest further, I stood leaning against the balustrade, staring at him in disbelief, my stomach turning in revulsion. Zaynab, my beloved sister, wrapped up and given as a gift to Bonaparte. I wanted to scream. I took a deep breath to control my throbbing nerves and calmly asked, "What makes you think Bonaparte will choose to marry her?"

"How could he resist? All Frenchmen are the same: they only understand force. They worship what they fancy to be the power of women.

Why? Because they want to be dominated. A young wisp like Napoleon Bonaparte wants nothing but to be possessed by a strong woman. His wife plays the whore in Paris, and our great conquering hero whimpers like a dying pup. Wait till Zaynab gets to him."

"Bonaparte is already married!"

"To a woman of mixed blood from some desert island in a sea on the other side of the world, who has slept with every officer left in France. He's going to divorce her—you'll see. Zaynab will be his wife. His only wife. She'll see that it's written in the contract."

"And if he doesn't divorce his present wife?"

"As a Muslim, he will be able to have two. Four if he wants. But it will be the ones in Egypt that count, and Zaynab will be number one. You can bet on that, if you know anything about that sister of yours."

Father's plans had my head spinning. He was so sure of himself. He had it all figured out. Bonaparte would become a Muslim and marry Zaynab, who would be the true ruler of Egypt, another Cleopatra.

I sat down on one of the large cushions lining the walls of the balcony, put my head back, and closed my eyes. Had the French conquest so loosened Father's mind that he mistook fantasy for reality? Absurdity for plausibility? Had his world so crumbled under the shock of Christian rule that he would trade his daughter to outbid Shaykh Sharqawi's preeminence with Napoleon? Sacrifice Zaynab? Everything was wrong in Egypt. Everything was unhinged, hanging in pieces. We had fallen to trading our honor. Next we'd be wearing tight trousers, saying *oui oui* and *non non*, drinking wine, and wiping our asses with dry paper. "They are going to make Frenchmen of us," I said glumly.

Father got up from where he was sitting and settled down next to me with his hand on mine. "No, Zaki. We are going to make Egyptians of them. That is why I'm doing this—for the good of Egypt and our people, for our religion. We have no choice but to work with Napoleon. He conquered us. The sultan of Istanbul is distracted by Austria and Russia. That is the reality of our situation. We do the best with the reality God sends us. Why He sent the French, I don't know; it is all a part of God's wisdom. But I do know that Napoleon is here for a long time."

"How long?"

"For my lifetime. Your lifetime. The lifetime of Zaynab's children. The Greeks ruled us for a thousand years; the Ottomans ruled us for three centuries. Who's to say that Zaynab's and Bonaparte's progeny won't outdo them?"

Father saw how upset I was. He also, I suspect, realized that his scheme was not entirely honorable and felt obliged to defend himself:

"Son, listen. Napoleon will have a successor when he dies, a son. The son will be an Egyptian—my grandson. That is why Zaynab is going to Napoleon."

Father went on speaking, and I have to say that his argument was not without merit. We had suffered a calamity—God was punishing us for our laxity in morals and putting us to the test—and we had to make the best of it by surviving. We couldn't defeat the French in battle, and anyone who said we could was crazy or suicidal. Stones, staves, and knives were no match against artillery and muskets. We could only win over time, by absorbing the French. They were small in number, and no more of them were coming. In a generation there would be no French, only Egyptians. We would survive by drowning them in our blood, by making babies from Egyptian women married to French soldiers and scholars. We had survived Greeks, Romans, Arab tribesmen, crusaders, and Turks. The French would be but another drop in the Egyptian ocean. The union of Zaynab and Bonaparte would be the beginning of our drowning the enemy. General Abdullah Menou and Zubaydah were already leading the way.

"There is no dishonor in this, Zaki. Letting the French marry our women will bring us victory over them. Instead of war, destruction, and hatred, we'll give them peace. Instead of bloodshed, we'll have new blood and babies."

I remained silent. He made it sound so reasonable. But instinctively I felt there was something not right in it, some miscalculation or hidden unknown—many of them, in fact. "You think you can control Bonaparte?"

"Zaynab will control Bonaparte. She's quick, that girl. Quicker than many men I know."

"Maybe God made a mistake when he made her a girl."

"God made no mistake, Zaki. He gave her the beauty of a woman and the mind of a man. Why? To save Egypt. And as God's humble instrument, I am putting the pieces into place, all according to the unfolding of God's divine plan."

I muttered hesitantly, "Isn't knowing God's plan and manipulating Napoleon and Zaynab according to it a pretty tricky business?"

Father slapped me on the shoulder and with a chuckle to soften the arrogance of his words said, "Son, as I put my trust in God, so He puts His trust in me. I sail the ship to the course He sets, and together we ride the waves to destiny. Have confidence. There is nothing tricky in the business of having trust in God and oneself."

This was the first time in my life I had spoken more or less openly with Father regarding an issue we didn't see eye to eye on. That may not sound like an earthshaking event, but in regard to my relationship with Father, it was to me analogous to a woman slapping her husband.

———ɯ——

I went to the courtyard where Zaynab, Noha, Mother, and the two household servant girls were peeling mangos while relaxing on cushions in the shade of an arching trellis of woven palm fronds. I removed my turban and sat between Zaynab and Mother, who said the mangos were the sweetest she'd ever tasted. "They're from the Sudan."

"The Sudan? How did they get here?"

"They were sent to Napoleon by his troops in Nubia. He gave a crate each to all the shaykhs."

"Napoleon," I muttered.

"They say he's going to become a Muslim!" exclaimed Noha excitedly. "And all his soldiers too."

"That should keep the circumcisers busy."

Zaynab and Noha glanced at each other and tittered as Noha dangled a ruddy helix of mango skin between her fingers before letting it drop.

Mother put down her paring knife and handed me a dripping mango, piously intoning, "May God speed the day that the French accept Islam."

"May it be before a Muslim girl agrees to marry one!" I bit spitefully into the mango. Zaynab glanced at me from the corner of her eye with a pleased smile.

"Man proposes; God disposes." Mother, like Father, was a living treasury of pious apothegms.

"I heard that Father has proposed to dispose of a daughter." My words turned Zaynab as red as the skin of the mango she was holding. Mother asked me what I was talking about. "You don't know?" I asked in return.

"What is there to know?"

I turned to Zaynab. "You haven't told her?" She continued peeling her mango in silence. "Father's adding her to the basket of virgin fruit they're offering up to Bonaparte," I said. "He's supposed to choose the one, or ones, he wants. Or take the whole basket."

Mother's hands flew to her breast. "I seek refuge in God! It can't be true. Shaykh Khalil would never do such a thing. It's impossible!"

"No, dear Mother. What was impossible before the French arrived seems to be possible now."

Noha embraced her older sister in joyous surprise. "Oh, Zaynab! I hope it's you he chooses! Napoleon's bride!"

"It's not definite yet," Zaynab said, still blushing as the two servant girls hugged and kissed and congratulated her. Mother started weeping, as was her custom.

"You don't seem so crushed over being given away like a concubine, do you, Sister?"

"Concubine!" Mother's wails grew louder.

"What girl wouldn't want to have a Frenchman?" sang out Noha. "A Frenchman holds his woman's hand in the street and even kisses her on the lips right in front of everybody. Their wives and concubines go unveiled and wear bright, pretty dresses instead of black all the time, and they laugh and talk just like the men, talk back even, and they don't have to walk behind them. I even saw two French women riding donkeys. Can you imagine? They were laughing and joking with each other in the looniest way, and racing their donkeys down the street like drunken Mamluks and having a good old time. I wish I could have understood what they were saying. I'm going to study French and be like a French lady."

"I seek refuge in God!" Mother cried out again. "No daughter of mine's going to pollute her mouth in an infidel tongue!"

"What does Napoleon Bonaparte look like?" Zaynab asked me.

"A bald, toothless dwarf with bulging eyes and a protruding belly and pointed ears like a rabbit."

"Never mind," Noha chirped. "He can be fat as a water buffalo as long as he's rich and lets you do what you want and you can slap him and have fun. Maybe he'll take us to Paris! I'll walk down the street in a dress with my ankles showing and my hair over my shoulders. I'll sit in cafés with a pet monkey and smile at the men, and when they smile back I'll slap them across the face." She sank her teeth into the oozing mango and bit off a chunk, eyes rolling, juice running down her chin. "I'll have fun!"

"No daughter of mine!" screamed Mother.

Disgusted, I returned my turban to my head and stood to leave. Compared to what was happening to our young girls, the Mamluk debacle at Imbabah threatened to be the least of our defeats.

—⁂—

Father initiated the first step of his grand scheme. Zaynab followed complacently, as though she wanted to be given to Bonaparte. She never came out and said she did, but she also didn't say a word against it. Her compliance sickened me. Father sickened me—he was putting her in Bonaparte's bed to leapfrog over Shaykh Sharqawi onto Bonaparte's shoulders. The whole thing sickened me. My scholarly father, pandering to Bonaparte. My beautiful, intelligent, madcap sister—Bonaparte's concubine! I couldn't pray or study for days. Even the Quran offered no solace. And then, after thinking about it, I wondered if Father's plan of absorbing the French through our girls and founding a ruling dynasty might actually work out. From the Pharaohs to the French, Egyptian political history was filled with intrigues a lot stranger than what Father was plotting.

Fourteen girls, purportedly virgins, were offered to our French sultan. There were half as many Muslims as Christians, and two Jewesses. The girls were taken in a group to Bonaparte's residence in Azbakiyya, where he had taken over the Mamluk emir Alfi Bey's magnificent palace.

Before going on, I should say something about the Mamluk palaces that the French took over. Except for Sitt Nafisa's, all the great palaces in Azbakiyya had been occupied by the French. One was made into military headquarters; another was converted to a military hospital; and Qasim Bey's and Hasan Kashif's palaces had been seized along with several others along the canal to house the 165 French scholars who had accompanied the army and would form something called "the Egyptian Institute," which was rumored to conceal a fearsome array of European black magic and satanic devices. The French and other European merchants residing in Cairo, as well as some Syrian and Egyptian Christians, had all flocked to less palatial quarters in Azbakiyya to be near the French, pandering to their new masters.

The French expedition must have come as a godsend for them. In the wake of the expedition had come French cafés, restaurants, and wine houses, all choicely located in the shade of the palm and orange groves along the canal. Azbakiyya, variously called Little Paris, the French Island, or the French Quarter, was a little city in itself, cut off from the rest of Cairo and foreign to Egyptian traditions, manners, and customs in every way, an alien world with all the dark vices and delights of Parisian society, the big difference being that what Egyptians did secretly in the dark, the French did openly in the light of day.

Sick at heart, I watched Zaynab prepare herself for her visit to that iniquitous world of Little Paris. She spent two days making herself beautiful—plucking the hair from her legs with a dried sugar paste, bathing and perfuming herself, washing, brushing, and sculpting her hair, and then applying shades of color to her eyes, lips, and cheeks, thin lines of mascara accentuating her large, oval eyes. She wore an embroidered silk caftan that, when drawn snugly around her waist by a chain-like belt of gold links, clung to her hips and bosom. She left her upper shoulders and neck bare, the way French women dressed, or at least those few we had seen accompanying the army. I told her she looked like a French whore.

"Have you seen many?" she asked.

"Don't be sassy, Sister. And remember what I said: let the French turn your head too much and you might lose it."

"I'm only the obedient daughter. Father commands; I obey."

"The French have turned both your heads." I raised my hand to her as to put her in her place with a slap. She smiled with her face turned up to me. I brought my hand down, lightly caressing her cheek. She took my hand and kissed it and held it.

"It's not Bonaparte," she said. "It's not the French. It's life. I want to live. I want … I don't know what I want. But maybe there's a French window somewhere I can look through to see what it is I want. Even if it's just to see there's nothing there for me."

"What are you talking about? Galloping half naked on a donkey and laughing like an idiot? Sitting in a coffeehouse with men around you? Holding hands in the street? Is that what you want? To be a French girl?"

"No—not just that. Not that at all. Doing something … being … I don't know. Feeling good about things. About myself."

"You've got everything. What more do you want to make you feel good? Men?"

"No. I don't know; it's not just any one thing. It's … it's having some control in my life, I guess."

"You don't know what you want."

"You're right, I don't. I want to find out what I want. Even if I can't get it, I'd like to know what it is."

"As Napoleon's concubine?" I spat the words out.

"I don't know. If that's the only way, then maybe. But I won't find out staying here in the house."

Whore! I wanted to say it, but I didn't; I controlled my anger. The truth was, I was angry and I wasn't sure at what—at how beautiful she'd made herself for Bonaparte, at the French in general, at her spirit in daring to go to them? Perhaps jealousy was better a description than anger for my emotion regarding Zaynab. Truthfully, my stomach burned in anger *and* jealousy—anger at everything, including myself, and jealousy of Zaynab's determination to learn from the French.

Yes, I was jealous of her daring. She had the courage to explore a new world in search of something, she didn't know what, but something she thought she had to seek, even if she never found it. I was jealous of her spirit to go and search for whatever it was to fill the empty corner in her soul. I understood her. She was my sister, my soul mate. I too had an empty corner in my soul. And I loved her. I loved her too much, maybe in a way I shouldn't have. One part of my soul was empty; another, I feared, was twisted by an overwrought love for my sister.

I watched her leave for the French Quarter. Father had arranged for a two-horse French military carriage to take her. When the carriage had gone down the road a ways, I went back to my room, threw myself on the bed, and sobbed.

Zaynab told me the next day what had happened.

The girls were taken to a spacious banquet room in Alfi Bey's palace, where Bonaparte had taken up residence. It was furnished in the uncomfortable manner of French tables and chairs. Instead of relaxing on cushions and low divans with trays of food spread before the guests, the French, as Zaynab described the event to me, ate sitting on chairs with their backs straight up and their stomachs pressed up hard against the table. It was most uncomfortable. They didn't reach into various bowls of food, or use flat bread to scoop up chunks of meat or sauces or to dip into salads; nor did they exchange tasty morsels across the table. Instead, each person had an individual plate filled with food, as though sharing would have been trespassing on private property—whose defense was guaranteed, as it first appeared, by a formidable assortment of silver weapons placed next to the individual plates, such as a knife for cutting and a pronged instrument for jabbing and stabbing, but which were used not for defense but for attacking the food.

After an embarrassing pause at the beginning of the repast, Marcel saw the girls' confusion and astonishment and demonstrated how the instruments should be used. But for all his fluency of explication and clarity of demonstration, the girls could not master the application of these silver weapons to deliver food from plate to mouth, and after several awkward attempts and as many messy mishaps that stained the girls' dresses, the dashing young officers serving them cleared the silver away, allowing the shy young ladies to go at it in customary fashion with their fingers, the officers joining in and having a jolly time of it, all the while drinking wine and encouraging the girls to drink with them, which a few of the more daring ones—Christians or Jews—did.

Dinner was followed by tea and cakes and strained conversation through the translators. It wasn't only the strangeness of French ways that created the strain: the girls had never eaten outside their homes before, and for most of them it was their first time to be unveiled in the presence of men—and the fact that these men were fair-skinned, light-haired, and in some cases blue-eyed, as well as attentive, smiling, and strikingly handsome in their brilliant uniforms, made the experience all the more disconcerting. The girls were in such an emotional boil of desire, shyness, confusion, and fear that they couldn't eat, even with their fingers.

After the banquet they were led to a drawing room where they sat on padded chairs and waited like nervous schoolchildren for Bonaparte to arrive and choose his bride. At last the door swung open and Bonaparte entered in his usual brusque way, as though charging across a field of battle. Zaynab and the other girls stiffened. The commander in chief introduced himself, asked the girls their names, and kissed each one's hand as she told him. He put them at ease with his warmth—his humorous attempts at Arabic proverbs and expressions, and the little jokes he had memorized, in addition to those he had Marcel render from the original French. It was his lightness of blood, as we say in Egypt, his affability and warmth, and his ability to remember the girls' names—Fouziya, Layla, Khadija, Fatima, Hamida, Nadia … all fourteen of them—and address them as though he had known them a long time, that saved the event from becoming a disaster.

He had the girls sit in a semicircle on cushions on the floor, and then, seating himself before them, he asked each girl in turn, like a favorite uncle, what it was she wanted in life. Most of the girls looked at each other and giggled in confusion. Bonaparte had the translator rephrase the question: If it were in their power to remake the world, what place would they give themselves in it? No one spoke up. He asked two or three by name to address the question. They blushed and looked away, understanding him as little as had the al-Azhar shaykhs when asked what laws and political principles they wished to include in Egypt's new constitution.

Zaynab at last broke the embarrassed silence: "If I could remake the world, I would have it so that women enjoyed the same pleasures in paradise as men." Marcel lost his professional detachment as translator and laughed along with the other girls, who clapped in agreement.

Bonaparte seriously considered her reply. "Good. But that's paradise. If Zaynab could remake the world, then why wouldn't she make it as she believes it is in paradise?"

To that she said, "Because everybody lives forever in paradise; the world would get too crowded," which when translated by Marcel brought a smile from Bonaparte, who then asked if Zaynab would have girls and women be equal in her world. No, she replied, men wouldn't look good pregnant and would have a tough time of it giving birth. "So what? Let them anyway!" one of the other girls piped up, and everybody laughed.

Should women be sexually equal to men? asked Bonaparte. Zaynab replied that she had no idea about that, having had no sexual experience, but that from what she had heard, females were more than equal to men when it came to sex. Looking highly amused, Bonaparte then asked her about what the Quran says concerning man's position over woman, and she said the Quran spoke of this world, not the world they were imagining. The commander appeared to like that answer. He then asked her if she thought men and women were equal as it related to things of the mind, and she replied with an emphatic yes.

Bonaparte nodded. Turning from Zaynab, who had broken the tension, he drew some of the other girls out and appeared to have forgotten her. After an hour of this, he abruptly rose, as to a silent signal, invited the girls to study French, history, and natural science at the Institute of Egypt that would soon be opening in Qasim Bey's palace next door, and departed as swiftly as he had arrived, leaving the girls in confusion, for they had expected him to choose from among them the ones he wanted. He hadn't chosen, or so it appeared. As the girls were being escorted out, Marcel motioned Zaynab aside and whispered that General Bonaparte wished her to stay. Zaynab nervously waited behind. When the others had left, Marcel took her by the hand and led her upstairs and to the rear of the grand palace, where the women had had their quarters when Alfi Bey lived there.

"He didn't like the others?" she asked, wondering what she had gotten herself into.

"No, he didn't," Marcel replied. "He thought them fat and too strongly perfumed."

"Oh? What are the girls like in France?"

"All types. Would you accept General Bonaparte's invitation to study at the institute?"

"I don't know; it isn't up to me."

"Why isn't it? The commander in chief invited you."

"To study? Was that why we were invited?"

"Not exactly. Your shaykhs wanted the general to choose a wife—or wives. It would have been impolite to refuse. Instead of choosing a girl to marry him, he chose one to marry knowledge."

"I don't understand."

"That's precisely why you must come to study. I will teach you French. Once you know the language, you will understand everything."

My poor sister was so confused. She'd thought she'd been invited to compete to marry a ruler, and instead she was invited to study in something called an "institute." She told me that she took a sip of wine to clear her head, but she must have been joking, for I doubt she would have dared put wine to her lips—at least not in those early days of our experience with the French.

She asked Marcel if it was true that Bonaparte thought the girls too fat and overly perfumed, which she took as a personal insult—what did fat have to do with anything? Not that Zaynab was fat; on the contrary, an Egyptian man would have considered her painfully inadequate in body mass to heat the bed on a winter night, whereas in France, as I later learned, the saying is that "the closer the bone, the sweeter the meat," which shows how much our tastes differed from those of the French on some fundamental issues.

To her question about Bonaparte's abhorrence of generously applied perfume and fleshy females, Marcel simply and honestly replied, making her blush, "Well, that's Bonaparte. To me you're not fat, and jasmine couldn't smell sweeter. But the general … he has trouble with women. For him they have to be like pure air—odorless, colorless, tasteless, and almost weightless. Then when he marries one, she jumps from bed to bed from one end of Paris to the other the moment he's out campaigning."

"Why didn't he bring his wife with him to Egypt?"

"Josephine didn't want to come."

"She had a choice?"

Marcel smiled. "Of course. It was the commander who had no choice but to accept! A strong-minded French woman like Josephine can bend iron just looking at it. Poor Bonaparte. He rules Egypt, but in Paris, Josephine makes him look like a whimpering pup."

Marcel poured more wine in her glass, and Zaynab put it to her lips, wetting them without sipping the forbidden drink. "Is Josephine beautiful?" she asked.

"Bonaparte must think so," he replied, "but what do soldiers know about beauty or women? They treat women the way they ride a horse or use a bayonet. Jump on, one thrust in and out, and off they fall, like a dead fish, done before it's begun. No wonder Josephine is so unfaithful. Oh, look at what I've done! I'm sorry. I've made you blush."

Zaynab laughed. "You have. The way you talk about love. I've never heard such words. Like a poet drunk on hashish spinning around in classical Arabic. And the way you say them. I have to laugh."

"Laugh away, my girl. I've spent my life studying the language."

"No, please, don't be offended. I didn't mean to laugh at you. The classical words are beautiful, and the way you say them—yes, like a poet. Nobody speaks like that except the shaykhs and imams when giving religious sermons about God and punishment. I'd rather hear about horses and soldiers."

"What's there to hear about soldiers?"

"You're not a soldier?"

"You insult me. Do I look like a soldier?"

"How would I know? All you Franks look the same to me."

"Thank you, but no, I'm not a soldier. I'm an orientalist. J.J. Marcel, professor of oriental languages and literature and chief of the Arabic press in Egypt. A humble savant commissioned to study Egypt and bring it into the modern world."

"What's the modern world?"

"Ah. The modern world. It's a world of marvels. Of science and technology and industry. A world of new things, of machines and mathematics and logic and precision. A world where the perfection of man is religion and natural science its Quran."

"I don't understand a thing you're talking about."

"You will. Come to the institute and learn."

"I'm not a French girl who can bend iron by looking at it and do what I please."

"Your father wouldn't want to disappoint Napoleon."

"My father figured Napoleon had something other than learning in mind for me."

"Ah, but if he's led to think that the way to Napoleon's heart is through his mind, your father won't object. An intelligent man usually doesn't marry a girl with whom he can't converse and share ideas. Although he's a soldier, Napoleon is intelligent. He lives in the modern world, where an intelligent man doesn't choose an ignorant woman."

"Maybe not in your world a man doesn't."

"It's not just my world or your world anymore, Zaynab. It's our world now—one world, yours and mine together. France has come to Egypt in this new world, Zaynab. In eighteen months it will be 1800—new century for a new world."

"It's not 1800; it's 1213."

"It's 1213 for Islam. But Egypt is France now, and France will bring

Egypt into the new world of the nineteenth century. It is our civilizing mission. Come to the new institute and enter the new world!"

"Napoleon will have to ask my father to let me come. Egypt isn't France yet."

—m—

Zaynab's narration of what had happened left my head turning. My sister putting wine to her lips, Josephine jumping from bed to bed, Bonaparte our sultan a whimpering pup, the new world that had come to us, the new institute, a new century dawning, Egypt being France, civilizing mission! And what did this term "modern world" mean? I was in a whirlwind of confusion. I just stared at her as she spoke. No words could express my disorientation.

"Guess what happened then, dear brother." I shook my head at the thought of there being yet more of this madness.

"Talk about how quickly things have changed since the French got here!" she exclaimed. "Imagine! Marcel, who calls himself an orientalist, took my hand and asked me if I was disappointed that Napoleon didn't choose me to be his wife. 'Not as much as my father will be,' I replied, and the next thing he raises my hand and puts it to his lips, so gently I couldn't feel it. Can you imagine such a thing? Just as if I were a French girl. No man except those in the family has ever held my hand, and here was this Frank, kissing it! Well, it was then that I decided to go to this institute they talk so much about."

I was aghast. Kissing my sister's hand! The arrogance! Who did these Frankish upstarts think they were? My breast exploded in boiling resentment at Zaynab's candid account of the sordid affair. We called our beloved Egypt "Mother of the World" and "Creator of Civilization," and these pale-skinned, infidel barbarians from the frozen wastes of the north had come to civilize us? What arrogant presumption! How dare Marcel kiss my sister's hand!

When she had finished speaking, I brought my fists down on the cushions in a fit of impotent rage, and with my steaming blood almost frothing from my mouth, I spat out, "I forbid you to go to that institute! I absolutely forbid it! I don't care what Father says! You're not going!"

"Zaki, be serious," she said lightly, with an amused smile that drove my anger and impotence deeper into me like a poisoned dagger. "If our new sultan commands me to attend the institute, what can I do? Hear and obey," she said meekly, with the cunning smile of Sheherazade.

I wanted to scream. In a rage of frustration, I raised my hand as if to slap her, and when she lifted her head and turned her smiling face to graciously receive the blow she knew would not come, I tore off my turban and threw it on the floor of the salon where we were sitting and, howling like a stricken animal, kicked it so hard that it unfolded in a long band that stretched clear across the room. Laughing in delight, Zaynab got up, retrieved it, rolled and folded it back into shape, and put it on her own head. "I shall be a shaykhah," she said, holding her turbaned head up proudly, eyes twinkling. "A princess of learning to bring Egypt into the modern world! Zaki—do you know it's soon going to be 1800? A new century for a new world! And we're going to be in it!"

4

BEFORE I COULD ASK Zaynab *what* she meant by "it was soon going to be 1800," the thump of hooves in the courtyard came through the open windows, followed by abruptly shouted military commands in French. We hurried to the latticed window.

"It's Napoleon!" she cried out excitedly. "With a military escort!" Our colorfully uniformed sultan was dismounting from his white charger in a sun-reflected glitter of silver sword and gold epaulets. "I wonder why he has come?"

"For you," I replied sullenly.

"Me? He thinks we're fat and smell of too much perfume."

"His tight pantaloons have crushed his instincts."

Father met our little sultan at the gate. Bonaparte embraced him, kissing him on both cheeks, and the two men entered the house arm in arm, boon companions.

"Look at them," I said sarcastically. "Like lovers. Your mission has been a success."

"What do you mean?" she asked.

"Do I have to explain? Father is using you to elevate himself with Napoleon. Toadying up to the foreign invaders! Disgusting!"

"Well, they conquered us, didn't they? So we have to make the best of it."

"You think exactly like our father."

"So?"

"Mind you, sister, the French won't be here forever. Then what?"

"I don't know. But as long as they are here, we may as well live peacefully with them."

"There's a difference between living peacefully and collaborating."

"What's the difference?" she asked.

"The difference is between survival and betrayal. You know what the Ottomans do to people accused of betrayal?"

"Don't be silly. Nobody's betraying Egypt by cooperating with the French. The way you make it sound, anyone would think just learning French would be treachery."

"Some people might think so."

I called for the nearby servant girl to bring tea and a hubbly-bubbly, and we sat comfortably on the cushions with our legs crossed, drinking the sweet mint tea. While I puffed on my pipe and filled the broad room with jasmine-laced smoke, Zaynab played with a little kitten—we had more cats and kittens around the villa than I could count.

"I wonder what Father and our sultan are discussing?" I mused aloud, not expecting an answer.

"There's nothing wrong with cooperating with Napoleon if it keeps the peace and lets life go on," Zaynab said. "I don't mind being used for that. Napoleon's not bad looking, is he?"

"No, and when you kneel, he looks tall for his age," I snapped. "Someone should tell him to get a haircut. And stop referring to him by his first name!"

"What's the difference what name I call him? Here, let me have some of that." She put the kitten on my lap, pulled the stem of the pipe from my mouth, put it in her own, and drew in with gusto, filling the vessel with a storm of bubbles. "I drank wine with Napoleon and Marcel," she said between coughs while blowing out the smoke.

"You have no shame."

"I know. But even if I did, what do I have to be ashamed of?" she asked throwing the pipe down with a frown of distaste and retrieving the kitten.

"Faysal said you should have been born a man."

She was rubbing her nose up against the kitten's. "I'm happy I'm not one. What kind of man do you think I would have made?"

"Father thinks you have a man's mind."

"Do you think I have?"

"I've given up thinking. Nothing makes sense anymore." I returned the pipe to my mouth and, savoring the smoke, listened to the pleasant gurgle of bubbles. "That could be a lethal weapon," I mused, watching the rising bubbles.

"What?"

"A man's mind in a beautiful female body."

"You don't think females have minds equal to men's?"

"Don't be foolish. Of course not."

"Napoleon does. Marcel the orientalist of the printing press does too. And so do I."

"I told you, the French are fools over women. No surprise their women slap them all over the place."

Father entered the room. He had been looking for us. Napoleon had come to invite us to have lunch at his palace and visit the Egyptian Institute that was to open soon. When I told father that I didn't want to go, he replied sharply that I would go, that the French were our guests and we were obliged to treat them with the kindness and generosity of our culture, and that was that.

So now our invaders were now our invited guests!

"By the way," Father added off-handedly, "Monsieur Esteve, Napoleon's director of finance, will be living with us. I'm arranging rooms for him on the top floor. A little favor I granted Napoleon."

Monsieur! Now Father was using French. Monsieur! Molten black bile rose up from my churning stomach like an erupting volcano, scorching my breast. The whole house was becoming a viper's nest of collaboration!

Even though we rode in Bonaparte's closed carriage, Father had Zaynab disguise herself in one of my student robes and caftans with a turban covering her hair. He could give her to Bonaparte but couldn't tolerate her being seen in public. If our morals were corrupted before, and we did things in dark places that we never dared to do openly, what we were now I did not care to say, nor did I have a word for it.

We had never ridden in a carriage before. There were no carriages in Egypt before the French came. Our two rulers, Mamluks and Ottomans, rode horses; lesser Muslims—shaykhs, merchants, landowners, and peasants—rode donkeys, as did Christians and Jews, if they had them. The rest walked. Now the French let everyone ride a horse, even Jews and Christians. But only the French had carriages.

Zaynab and I sat silently across from each other as the carriage traversed the streets to the center of Azbakiyya. I was intrigued by how much she resembled a younger me in her turban and caftan, like a beautiful boy. J.J. Marcel, who was acting as translator and was sitting next to me across from Father, couldn't keep his eyes off her. Bonaparte rode his white charger in front of the carriage, wanting to be seen and admired by the benighted people he had magnanimously liberated. The city seemed to be settling into a way of life under our new rulers, who, I grudgingly admitted, had turned it into a cleaner and more orderly city than it was before. The French soldiers were directing Egyptian workers in sweeping the streets, while other streets were being dampened from a large water tank that Marcel explained was used to keep the dust down.

"What for?" I asked, unwilling to concede any blessing from our occupiers. "When it dries, the dust will only rise again."

"Every day it will be wetted down."

"What a stupid waste of time and water," I remarked, shaking my head.

"Not at all. One of the doctors at the institute claims there's a relationship between the frequency of eye diseases in Egypt and the hot, dry, and dung-laden dust in the air and its fly- infested, filthy streets."

"Eye disease?" I asked. "Is it any less in other parts of the world?"

"Oh yes, much less. I can assure you that!"

Father's eyes narrowed. "If the case is truly as your doctor claims, then it can only be because God wills it to be that way. Sweeping and wetting the streets won't alter God's will."

"No, of course not," Marcel agreed. "God has nothing to do with it. But it will reduce the frequency of eye disease."

The brazen words of implied atheism froze Father's face in an open stare of disbelief. Zaynab glanced at me, almost smiling. I turned and looked at the street to ignore her. What I saw surprised me, but surprise had been my dominant condition ever since the French had arrived. What surprised me now were the large baskets of woven palm fronds that had been set up at the corners with signs instructing the people to keep the city clean and use the baskets for refuse. The arrogance! Telling us to keep our city clean! As if it did any good. Every night the baskets were stolen, and every day the French replaced them, thinking they could train us, as if we were monkeys. The French just couldn't learn. The streets were kept clean by the sweepers they hired; people sold the baskets they stole, and the basket weavers were doing a good business with the French. Our invaders would wear themselves out and go bankrupt trying to change us. And who needed clean streets? They only got dirty again, a simple fact that only the French couldn't seem to grasp.

In Azbakiyya, military officers were promenading arm in arm with their French women, who were proudly erect in dresses that left their arms as bare as their faces, and with their hair piled up on their heads or hanging down over their naked shoulders and half-exposed breasts. Some of the women were dressed in officers' cavalry uniforms—swords, boots, caps, and all. Seeing us gawk at the strange sight, Marcel felt obliged to explain.

"The women are the wives of cavalry officers. They dressed in their husbands' uniforms to smuggle themselves on board the ship in France. You see, the government had forbidden wives and all women from joining the expedition. But you know women, once they make up their minds to do something."

"God forbid I know such women!" exclaimed Father. Zaynab's sandaled foot nudged mine. I refused to meet her eyes, but I could imagine the subtle smile playing across her lips.

A few of the women were riding donkeys; one was riding behind a man with her arms around his waist. It was too much for Father. He fumbled with his prayer beads, mumbling something about half-naked women dressed like men, riding donkeys.

Zaynab, pushing her turban back so it tilted rakishly on her head, allowing a few locks of hair to fall over her forehead, exclaimed in mock horror, "Imagine anyone dressing like a man!"

"You're not dressed like a man," Father scolded. "You're dressed like a student of religion!"

I didn't much like that remark, but of course I kept my mouth shut. Zaynab's mocking smile didn't help my roiling stomach, nor did Marcel's ravenous glances at her. And the insolence of the man, the way he so freely spoke to her! "You look very ... I don't know what the word is in Arabic ... with the times. Stylish, in French. Modern. Fashion."

"With the times? Fashion?" she asked. "What's that?"

"Elegant," he replied. "Some years ago, women's fashion in Paris was oriental. Caftans, turbans, sashes, billowy Turkish pantaloons, Turkish robes, pointed slippers. It was charming."

"What is it now—what you call fashion?"

"For some years now it's been military. Cavalry uniforms and the like. Women and men have been dressing more and more alike since the revolution."

"Oh?" Zaynab's face lit up.

Marcel nodded, saying, "Equality, fraternity, and liberty have taken unexpected forms."

Equality, fraternity, and liberty again! If I'd had the courage, I'd have sent the smug savant sailing out the carriage door onto the dampened road.

In the French Quarter of Azbakiyya, tables had been set up in shaded gardens along the canal, and men and women were sitting together, eating and drinking, and some of them singing as they drank. Zaynab keenly regarded them from our slow-moving carriage. The women were talking as much as the men and looking for all the world like they had something worthy of saying. Their verbal rivalry with the men was amazing enough, but even more amazing was that the men were listening and nodding as if the women actually did have something to say. I glanced at Zaynab. She was watching the couples in complete absorption, and believe me, I could see the curtains of her mind being drawn back to reveal her deepest thoughts, which shone like lights in her wide-open eyes as they feasted on this New World dawning in front of her. She wanted to be one of those unveiled young women in the garden, sitting and talking with a man about serious things.

Among the women were some Egyptian girls, obviously prostitutes from the poorer levels of society. Dressed in the French fashion, they were trying to act French but looked like poor imitations—clumsy, vulgar, overly painted, speaking their smattering of the language too loudly, ill at ease in their unfamiliar, gaudy, badly fitting garb. Zaynab winced. Our eyes met and we exchanged a sad smile. If not understood, the New could be cruel, treacherous, and—even then I intuited it—fatal. I didn't understand this French gift of the New. I feared it; I wished Zaynab did too. It is wise to fear the New. And I soon learned it's even wiser to understand it.

We approached Qasim Bey's palace, which was to be the Institute of Egypt. Napoleon had also designated a second Mamluk palace, the one that had belonged to Hasan Kashif, to house the institute. Both Qasim and Hasan had been killed at the Battle of Imbaba, which was rapidly becoming known as the Battle of the Pyramids, a name Napoleon thought would resound more gloriously to his triumph.

"Other palaces will be added as the institute grows," Marcel explained, and though I was coming to like the fellow, the sound of his voice so puffed up with pride soured my stomach as he went on. "One day it will be a university like our great Sorbonne in Paris."

"We have al-Azhar," Father said. "What need do we have of a university like one in Paris?"

"My dear Shaykh Khalil, with all due respect, al-Azhar only teaches subjects related to religion."

"Only? And what else is there need of to teach?"

Marcel chortled. "You will see." His winking smile to Zaynab added repulsion to my acidic stomach. Gracious as Marcel tried to be, likeable as he almost was, his arrogance kept poking through his fine manners, easy humor, and intelligence. For all his knowledge of Islam and Arabic and his sincere goodwill, he insulted us without having the least inkling of it. His manner was simply the way of a man who was too sure of himself. His sense of superiority was so infuriating to me that as I sat listening to him hold forth in his scholarly Arabic on how the French were going to transform Egypt, I grew sweaty with feverish visions of undoing my turban, wrapping it loop by loop around his neck, and slowly strangling him with it until his eyes bulged and his tongue stuck out.

Then at lunch in Alfi Bey's palace, we had to suffer through two hours of listening to him translating Napoleon's version of this Bright New World that Glorious France—upon which, we were modestly informed, the sun never set—was going to bestow upon Egypt, as if our poor and backward country hadn't sun enough! But did Zaynab suffer listening to the prattle of this pretentious prig? Not in the least! He spoke, and her eyes lit up like full moons illumined by the sun of this new world he gushed on about, as if thinking himself a prophet. This new world that through the progress of laws, science, industry, and medicine our social conditions would be transformed so that Man could attain his moral perfection in a perfectly rationalized civilization and live freely in the guiding light of Humanism and Reason.

What a load of donkey dung! When Father asked where God fit in this perfect civilization of reason and Marcel smartly replied that there was no need for that hypothesis, Father coughed up a chunk of chicken kabob and looked to be choking to death, his face was so red.

God a hypothesis? And one not even needed! Slapping him on the back to get the chicken out, I couldn't help thinking that Father was as deceived in one direction as Marcel was in the other. The coming of the French was robbing me of both faith and reason.

When lunch was at last over, we walked the short way to Qasim Bey's palace, Napoleon having excused himself, saying he was in the midst of his plans to build a canal at Suez that would commercially transform Egypt. My God, the arrogance! Just like that, he said it—with a prissy French gesture of his hand, as if it was just one more little thing among thousands that he had to do in the afternoon. *Oh, excuse me, gentlemen, I'm off to connect the Red Sea to the Mediterranean for our new world of global trade which will enrich Egypt forever; I'll only be a moment.* Who in the hell did these people think they were? Next they'd be talking about sailing our pyramids to Paris for analysis in their great Sorbonne!

The main hall of Qasim Bey's palace had been made into a vast library. Books were everywhere. They were arranged in orderly rows in open cases against the high walls, case upon case, lining the walls with books from floor to ceiling. What struck me, other than entering a fabulous palace and immediately seeing of all things books, was the neat way they were shelved, standing upright on their ends in even rows, shelf over shelf, rather than piled flat on their sides, one on top of the other in high columns, as was our custom. Our way kept them flat and the pages compressed, which preserved them, but the French way allowed one to remove a volume without disturbing any of the others above or beneath it. Whenever during my studies I wanted a particular book, I would find it only after a long search at the very bottom of a twelve-volume column, if I found it at all, and would have to remove all the ones on top to get to it. Their method was so simple and logical I couldn't imagine why we had ever decided to do it the way we did, other than it being a tradition going back to the days of parchment, when the Byzantine Greeks ruled Egypt.

I was also stuck by the silence—a hive of scholars busily working away at their books and instrument-laden tables, with only the rustle of turning pages audible in the cavernous hall. Not one of them was waving arms in intellectual hysteria while boisterously arguing dialectics or variants in the text of a hadith, nor even mumbling prayers. The rooms were funereally silent, as if all the people studying and working in the many rooms had had their tongues cut out—a typical form of Mamluk punishment, by the way.

We were introduced to two other savants, an elderly man with the curious name of Jean Michel Venture de Paradise, head of the institute's orientalist department, and his assistant, a much younger, shy-looking man named Amadeus Jaubert, both of them as fluent in Arabic as Marcel. Venture de Paradise had memorized the Quran, and when Father asked if he had become a Muslim, he smiled in surprise, shrugged, and shook his head. No, he had not. He said it in an off-handed manner, as if religion were a trifling irrelevance.

"But how can a man memorize the Quran and not be a Muslim?" Father asked, utterly boggled.

"Because it is an important piece of oriental literature," replied Venture de Paradise.

Father stared at him, eyes bulging: the word and language of God, the Holy Quran, no more than a piece of oriental literature? I was sure Shaykh Khalil would not make it through the day. It was hard enough for me, and I was steeled to expect anything from these impossible people from Mars.

The three orientalists, Venture, Jaubert, and Marcel, took us through the institute's many rooms and departments, eagerly explaining the organization and purpose of each. I couldn't understand why these French scholars, seemingly all 165 who staffed the institute, were so excited about studying and transforming a place as foreign to their own culture and religion as Egypt. The intensity with which they spoke of their industrial, agricultural, scientific, and medical projects was little different than the fervor that gripped our own al-Azhar scholars when discussing religion. It was only comprehensible when I finally realized that the strange Franks had traded their Christian Trinity for a new one: Science, Industry, and Progress. They talked so much about these things that I think I actually came to have a glimmer of understanding of what they meant.

Zaynab listened to them and nodded as though understanding every word without difficulty, the look on her face as bright and eager as theirs. Father was neither interested nor listening. *So much Frankish nonsense,* his distant look of disapproval said. He frowned every time one of our three orientalists had to conjure an Arabic word in order to explain an unfamiliar machine or scientific concept. Father didn't tolerate innovation in any form, particularly not in language, the tool by which God revealed

Himself and His law in the Quran. But we had no words for many of the things these savants had created or discovered—steam pump, electricity, reagent, chemical affinity, oxygen, hydrogen, nitrogen, batteries, positive and negative charge, electrical resistance, calculus, differential, integral, force of gravitational attraction, acceleration ... New words were necessary. If they didn't exist, they had to be invented. I was gradually beginning to understand this and tried not to look at Father. Zaynab didn't understand a word of it, but she drank it in, intoxicated, beaming, head nodding in affirmation, eyes shining in rapture.

As we went from laboratory to laboratory, the kindly old man Venture de Paradise explained the organization of the institute. It was composed of four main departments: Mathematics, Physics, Political Economy, and Literature and Arts. Each department had twelve savants who would deliver public lectures that were open to all, Egyptians and soldiers alike. Attendance was obligatory for military officers. The lectures would be translated into Arabic for those who hadn't learned French by the time the lecture schedule began. Courses in learning French were soon to begin and would be open to all Egyptians.

Learn French? I could see in Father's reddening visage the shock of coming face-to-face with heresy and denial of faith that the invitation implied. Who on God's earth was going to waste time learning something as useless and irreligious as French? God didn't reveal Himself in French! Unctuous hypocrite that I felt myself fast becoming, I nodded in agreement and felt disturbed, then wretched—not for my hypocrisy but the vituperation of Father's remark: Zaynab had confided in me that she had already started learning the language secretly, but I would sooner have torn my tongue out with my own hand than betray this to Father, for though I had no idea how severely he would punish a daughter for heretical practice, I feared it would be terrible. A shaykh had to set an example, and examples began in the family, particularly with females in the family, making it a curse as much as a blessing to have a shaykh as father. I trembled for Zaynab if she were to be found out.

The institute, it was explained to us, would undertake studies to expand Egyptian agriculture, purify the water, improve sanitation and hygiene, and create an industrial base for the material wealth and prosperity of the country. In addition, the institute would promote technical, historical, literary, and scientific studies for publication in scholarly journals in order

66

to encourage the French in France, along with the Egyptians in Egypt, to build the country. It was news to us that our country hadn't yet been built. As though to prove it hadn't, Venture de Paradise added that the institute had already decided that the Italian entrepreneur Carlo Rossetti, a longtime resident of Cairo, would head a commission with Shaykh Sadat to study the Nile and its delta in order to propose a plan for preserving, utilizing, and expanding its waters for irrigation in the most economic and efficient way. Father winced at the mention of Sadat—another bitter rival, though not as bitter as Shaykh Sharqawi. I expected Father to demand a project of his own, perhaps turning lead to gold—something that measured up to the French madness for what they called progress.

I had to agree with Father on one thing, at least: the French were filled with themselves. The ambitions of these savants knew no bounds. In addition to their legion of mathematicians, physicists, chemists, astronomers, and doctors, they had brought artists and botanists to draw the country's flora and fauna, architects and engineers to study and draw the monuments of the pharaohs and sultans, economists to study I didn't know what. They had brought leading scholars in all fields of learning to accomplish their scientific and industrial projects, scholars whose names I only later realized were already famous all over Europe—Quesnot, Monge, Conte, Dupuis, Berthollet, Costaz, Fourier, Savigny, Saint-Hilaire, Clouet, Vivant-Denon …

The scholars' schemes were as staggering as their names were unpronounceable. The crown jewel of their foolish ambition was the project to cut a canal at the Isthmus of Suez to link the Red Sea and the Mediterranean. When Father heard that Napoleon had already assigned a team of engineers and hydrologists to draw up a plan, he turned to me with a sardonic smile and whispered, "May God drown them in their stupidity as He did Pharaoh!"

Gullible Zaynab was gulping down what the savants planned in open-eyed stupor, as if these French were actually capable of changing the seas and rivers God had made! I swear the savants were as ambitious and arrogant in conquering nature as their Bonaparte was in conquering the world!

But their skills couldn't be denied. In one room, botanists and artists had teamed up to make drawings of animals and plants they had collected throughout Egypt; flowers, herbs, fish, and waterfowl, including some specimens we ourselves had never seen, were rendered in such precision and detail and subtlety of color that they looked about to fly, swim, or grow out of the paper, every feather, fin, leaf, and petal an improvement on nature herself.

In another room, artists were drawing ancient burial tombs, temples, and pyramids with painstaking accuracy. Their precision and fineness of detail seemed beyond human limits. But what on God's earth was there in those old stones to fascinate these Frenchmen, that they would exert themselves to go so far into the desert and up river to collect, study, and draw them so accurately, as though they were as sacred as the Ka'ba in Mecca? The French seemed to worship the ancient past with all its imperfections as much as they worshipped the future with all its promises of perfection. There seemed to be no present, no moment in time's unreeling during which these people could take rest. I was exhausted just looking and listening.

They had also executed drawings of Cairo's great mosques and mausoleums with the same loving intensity for detail and exactitude as they rendered the dead past and living nature. They were a strange breed, these French: they studied the past as assiduously as our shaykhs studied the Quran to enter paradise, and they planned for a future in which earthly existence would be as it is in paradise, the heavenly version of which they couldn't have cared less about! For us Muslims, the past—that is, the time before Muhammad and Islam—was an age of ignorance, yet here were these French savants, studying it as if it were a time of wisdom. My God, what to think of them? They glorified change and called it progress; we glorified God and tradition and called change the path to heresy, the devil's snare.

So how to understand these creatures with their strange gifts that escaped our comprehension? In their drawings, I saw our mosques with a beauty and elegance I had never seen before, though I had laid eyes on them thousands of times. Nothing had escaped their attention: palaces, hovels, sailing boats, animal-driven water pumps turning millstones, dilapidated fortresses, old women, Sufis, mothers nursing babies, shaykhs, beggars, Mamluks. Looking at their drawings was like looking at an instant of Egyptian life, caught and separated from the whole. The fewer than two hundred savants of the institute had accomplished all this in only several months' time. Their plan was to capture, record, draw, and study the whole of Egypt and Egyptian life as it was, from pharaohs to sultans. I was dumbfounded by it, and grudgingly impressed. Zaynab was absolutely transported in body and soul. Father dared not cast eyes on their graven images for fear of sullying the purity of his faith and losing his soul to the devil.

For a long while I hovered between Zaynab's intoxication and father's revulsion. But before our tour was over, I had fallen more toward Zaynab's side, and I remember exactly when and where it happened. It was in the science and mechanical sections of the institute. In a storeroom of sorts, we saw dead but perfectly preserved fish and animals floating in colorless liquid in large glass jars. With a grandfatherly arm around Zaynab, Venture de Paradise explained that these specimens were alien to France and would be shipped to the Sorbonne for further study. The liquid, he said, was formaldehyde, for which no word existed in Arabic. Father shook his head in protest. Of course there was a word for it in Arabic! Father refused to admit that Hermes Trimegistes had left his Egyptian place of birth and was now living happily in France, along with the spirit of Jabir ibn al-Hayyan and all the other great scientists of our gloried past (although at the time no one told us it was the past, and we had not realized it ourselves), which had inspired, as I was to learn, six centuries of European scientists and produced a scientific revolution! No, my pious, tradition-bound father, dyed-in-the-wool Azhar scholar that he was, could never have admitted to lost glory, whatever French wizardry was demonstrated before his eyes.

When one of the biologists showed us a perfectly preserved six-month-old female fetus floating in a jar, Father whispered to me that the curiosity of these Frangis transgressed the bounds of human decency and God's law. I nodded. But I was no longer sure where the bounds were. Where there had been bounds marked by high walls of certainty and buttressed by a thousand years of affirming commentary by ten thousand authorities, there was now the rubble of doubt, confusion, and wonder, the halting questions that undermine certainty. The walls were beginning to crumble. My old world was falling away. I turned to glance at Zaynab. Venture de Paradise was explaining to her the relationship between organic decomposition, oxygen, and the preservative action of formaldehyde. Her walls were far from falling; indeed, from her look of rapture, she appeared much at home in the New World. Her walls in the old world had never been very high or strong. I suspect that she had no walls at all, only the oppressive sense of being imprisoned.

We were next shown something called a "printing press" and given a demonstration of how it worked. Marcel, Jaubert, and Venture de Paradise assembled some tiny lead cubes in parallel grooves on a flat, rectangular plate, smeared them with black ink, placed the plate in the machine, and brought a padded block connected to the machine by a mechanical swivel down on the plate several times as a wheel was turned by a crank, and in seconds we were each given a paper upon which was written in neat, straight lines of uniform Arabic letters, "To Zaynab, Zaki, and the respected Shaykh Khalil al-Bakri, may God bless you all and give you long life in peace and love. From the Orientalists of the Institute of Egypt." It wasn't magic. It wasn't the work of the devil. It was human invention, ingenuity—reason and its mechanical application to the material world, the logic of dialectic theology transposed to matter and the motion of connected parts. The chinks in my crumbling wall deepened. Light was coming through.

The mystery of the sameness of those hundreds of written declarations posted on the shop fronts was at last solved. I stared in awe at the machine and breathed in its intoxicating fumes of ink and oil on engraved metal. Hundreds of identical copies of a written page could be produced in minutes, rendering copyists and their errors of missing words, paragraphs, and pages a thing of the past. Instead of it taking a week to have a book copied, hundreds or thousands of books could be made in days by this unerring machine, with each copy identical to the original! The implications were … revolutionary. I turned to Father with a kind of dumb, awestruck smile.

"It's blasphemous innovation for a machine to write God's name!" he growled at me without anyone else hearing. "Look how plain and ugly the letters are."

"And what's that?" Now Father was looking up at several large paintings on the wall—men dressed in robes and turbans.

Jaubert shyly explained they were portraits of the great men of early Islam. "One's the Prophet Muhammad. The two below are the Caliph abu Bakr, your glorious ancestor, and his successor, Umar. One of our artists painted them."

"I seek refuge in God! Your artist must be an old man indeed to know what men who lived twelve hundred years ago looked like!"

Jaubert regarded him in blank wonderment, not sure whether Father was joking, and then glanced at Zaynab and me with a confused half smile.

From Qasim Bey's palace, we traversed the courtyard and garden terrace to Hasan Kashif's palace. It was a magnificent building, as spacious and airy as any of the famous Mamluk palaces, with high, brightly painted, geometrically carved stalactite ceilings; an indoor fountain of Italian marble; glazed tile floors; fluted columns that towered upwards, supporting the central room's domed ceiling; and a broad marble staircase ascending the palace's three levels. The scent of jasmine wafting in from the gardens through the high, arched windows fused with the strange odor of the machines and chemical apparatus that had replaced the Mamluk furnishings. In the courtyard there was an assortment of large, weird-looking machines. Venture called them steam pumps. Since we had no precise word for "pump," he had to resort to sign language. He explained that the long steel beam at the side was driven by steam—hence the strange name, steam pump. The steam-driven beam turned a giant wheel that could be used to drive other machines to weave fabrics or perform any other kind of labor for manufacturing. It sounded like a kind of mechanical alchemy. Steam? I looked to see if he was serious. How could something as thin and insubstantial as vapors from hot water move a piece of steel too heavy for ten strong Mamluks to lift? When I expressed my doubt, Venture had the boiler filled with water and the furnace in the bowels of the steely beast stoked with wood and ignited. In a while, puffs of steam were issuing with periodic regularity from an exhaust valve (another device for which Venture de Paradise had to create an Arabic term), and soon the giant wheel was rapidly spinning under the smooth, powerful forward and rearward thrusts of the drive shaft, to which it was cleverly pinned. So powerfully was the wheel turning that a hundred horses tied to its spokes couldn't have resisted its pull. Steam. We gazed at the thrusting shaft and spinning wheel as though caught in a sorcerer's spell.

"This is what's going to revolutionize agriculture and industrialize Egypt," Marcel said. "Soon there will be thousands of these machines pumping water into the desert for irrigation and running factories all over the country. Egypt will become fabulously rich exporting its agricultural and industrial products to the world through the canal at Suez we are building."

"I seek refuge in God from such machines!" exclaimed Father.

"But this is exactly what God intended," Marcel assured him. "Machines will do the labor."

"What will men do?" asked Father.

"Perfect their minds and society."

"You have a strange understanding of men," rejoined Father.

The upper floors of the palace had been made into workshops of various sorts. One room was filled with chemical equipment, another with astronomical. In the chemical room, a young savant was filtering a clear liquid. Venture explained that he was testing the purity of the Nile. I asked why. "For cleanliness. Hygiene. To make people healthy," he replied.

I was too intimidated to say that all you had to do was observe the water's clarity to know it was pure, for by now I automatically assumed these sorcerers knew more than I ever would. Not so Father, of course:

"According to tradition, the Prophet said that any water that is running is clean."

Marcel smiled. "Science makes visible what is invisible. It can show what might look clean to be unclean."

If only he hadn't been so damn smug I could have loved the man with all my soul for his wisdom, could have accepted without shame or dishonor this new religion of science and progress. The problem was the way he and these French savants acted. They didn't just expect acceptance of their marvelous inventions; no, they demanded total awestruck, wide-eyed surrender and on our knees in worship of them and their accomplishments. I resented their unconcealed pride, the anticipated amusement that shined in their faces as they waited for our swooning, gushing amazement and cries of delight when they demonstrated their science and machines. And in resenting their pride, their intellectual arrogance, I also resented their inventions, marvelous as they were. This would take time for me to get over. For Zaynab it was already over; the look on her face told me she embraced it all, without question.

We were introduced to Berthollet, a spirited, bright-eyed old gentlemen who was head of the chemistry department and who, as Jaubert told me, was one of the world's leading chemists. Berthollet offered to show us some chemical magic. He first dissolved a chemical in a fuming clear liquid, obviously a potent acid of some sort, and it turned blue. He then mixed the one solution with another and the concoction fumed copiously as it coagulated into a thick, white, jellylike substance. A moment later he impishly turned the fuming vessel over Marcel's head. Zaynab cried out. I was praying the concoction would pour out and dissolve the top of his skull and eat into his brain as a lesson in humility, but it had unfortunately solidified in the vessel. To demonstrate how hard it had become, Berthollet, smirking in self-satisfaction, tapped the surface with a hammer. He then poured another liquid onto it and the petrified substance dissolved into solution again. Zaynab clapped in delight. I followed Father's model of maturity and smiled soberly in restrained amusement. But by then, though filled with resentment and dislike for them and their cleverness, I was a cryptic convert to their science and mechanics, a convert who didn't like what he found impossible to resist, a believing bundle of confusion and contradiction.

Berthollet handed Zaynab a powdery substance and had her deposit it in a glass of clear liquid. Immediately, magically, stalactites of intricately shaped multicolored crystals began to grow from the bottom of the glass, higher and higher, complex and beautiful—but I wouldn't have admitted for the world how magical and beautiful the sight was.

For his next performance, Berthollet mixed chemicals that exploded spontaneously in a burst of light, causing us to jump back, much to his delight. Father gave me a look as if to say, *Well, we must be polite and humor the children.* We were then led up to the roof to peer through a long, barrel-like cylinder Berthollet called a telescope—"multiplying optical lens," it came out in Arabic—but whatever it was, I was too numb to be any more amazed or culturally reduced. They could have told me that they had shot men to the moon through the thing and I would have believed them. Berthollet apologized for the smallness of the telescope, saying the astronomers were going to build a much larger one in an observatory on top of the highest pyramid in Giza. For now, this one would do. He invited me to put my eye to it. I feared if I did I would be sure to lose it but bravely did as I was told was going to get another shock or lose an eye.

In minutes, I learned that the moon was not a smooth, crystalline sphere; that there were more stars than the ancients and our Muslim astronomers had said; that Jupiter had four moons; and that the Earth was not at the center of the universe. The planets went around the sun, not the Earth, and they orbited it in ellipses, not circles, and not in uniform motion but at a velocity inversely proportional to the distance between the planet and the sun. The solar system was but an insignificant drop in the oceanic universe of stars infinities away. In minutes, two thousand years of astronomy were demolished. The theories of Aristotle, Aristarchus, Hipparchus, Ptolemy, al-Farghani, al-Battani, al-Biruni, Nasir al-Din ... all relegated to the dustbin of mistaken constructions. Berthollet said the men who got it right were Copernicus, Kepler, Galileo, Newton. Father couldn't accept it: "But how do you know their theories are true?" By mathematical relationships proving what is observed at all times in all cases, which elevates theory to law. Our universe, Berthollet explained, was run by the eternal rulings of mathematical laws—fixed, unchangeable laws. The mind of God was a mathematical fixity, pure and simple. Morality itself would one day be viewed as a branch of mathematics. Father stared at him, speechless, as if peering into the face of Satan.

Berthollet next amazed me with a demonstration showing the composition of light. Using a dark room, a prism, a candle, and a screen with a tiny hole in the middle, he showed us how light could be broken up into the colors of the rainbow, and then put back together again by passing the elements of broken light through a second prism. White light was composed of a color spectrum, he explained. It could be broken and reassembled. A man named Newton had demonstrated this over a century ago. Shades of our ibn al-Haytham, who had analyzed the rainbow as a complex combination of reflections and refractions of light striking droplets of water—but that was eight centuries ago. How shocking it was to learn, in so brief a period, how far behind we had been left by a people we had always considered our inferiors in every way. I felt there was nothing left of us. First they had taken our balls by crushing the Mamluks in a few hours; now it was our minds, our civilization.

What can I say? Three hours in that institute and my world, its walls, all the years of learning that bolstered our religious beliefs and tradition— all of it was blown away. What I saw there bordered on magic. I would have called it sorcery, like Father, but I was too far gone to dismiss what I saw.

Let me explain. What I saw was not sorcery, but it was frightening. It frightened me because I could see that what the French had put together as something good had the potential to become pure evil. I saw this in one contraption in particular. It was composed of what looked to be a copper sphere. Close by it was a wheel with a handle fixed close to its rim, with wires and a host of other less definable objects attached to it. Berthollet turned the wheel rapidly a number of revolutions, and while still turning it he motioned for me to put my hand to the sphere. I obliged, and no sooner had my finger come close to the surface of the sphere than something like a blue streak leapt out of it with a sharp crack and shot into my fingertip. It raced like fire up my arm and jolted my elbow back, almost jerking my shoulder out of joint. With a scream of terror, I yanked my arm away and jumped back so forcefully I almost fell. The savants were about to expire, they were laughing so hard, struggling to catch their breath. They assured me that what I experienced was no more than a little shock of electricity, nothing serious. Electricity? Berthollet explained it was a force of nature identical to lightning, a discovery made by a famous statesman and inventor named Benjamin Franklin when he flew a kite in a new country across the western ocean. Berthollet said that once they captured this mighty force and put it to work, it would make steam look like child's play.

I couldn't speak. My mind was spinning too rapidly for words. The printing press was understandable, and even simple in comparison to this. The steam pump was comprehensible as well: water in a vessel was heated to make steam, which was then transmitted to a cylinder where it was condensed, causing a rod to move back and forth, turning a wheel. But electricity? Lightning? If these men could actually reproduce lightning or capture it from heaven, what couldn't they do? They had hardly captured steam and they were already moving on to conquer the forces of heaven! The world would be helpless before them. Soon the Franks, along with their new allies led by Benjamin Franklin from over the western ocean, would be sailing armadas of kites across the sky to rain down heaven's thunder and lightning upon us, frying whole cities to cinders in a single zap. With my elbow still tingling from the electric shock, I could see the dark sun of doom rising over the western horizon. The Frankish genius chilled my blood with its evil potential, even as they spoke of progress, the perfectability of man, and health, wealth, and happiness. Filled as they were with their pride and power, I feared how easily they could turn what they'd intended to be beneficial into evil curses that would destroy their enemies as well as themselves. I knew then that we would have to learn from these angelic devils if we were to survive.

Visiting the institute was a hundred times more traumatic than witnessing our military defeat. It gave me a headache. My throbbing mind was lost in the middle of a dark ocean with lightning bolts streaking across the black sky. There was no way out: we had to learn. It would take time for admiration and understanding to displace hostility and suspicion of these people and their inventions, for the disorientation of being lost at sea would not give way easily. It would take time. But at the speed these Franks were going, we had no time.

On the way home from the institute, Father, Zaynab, and I had the carriage to ourselves. I asked Father what he thought of the machines. "Empty cleverness," he replied, glowering at some unveiled girls who were laughing and racing their donkeys down the road. "Suitable playthings for empty-headed men who have abandoned God."

I kept my silence. He had been there, he had seen what I had seen, but he hadn't seen. For him, printing presses, steam engines, telescopes, electricity, the power of lightning captured from the sky were children's playthings, just as the French occupation of our land was an aberration of history soon to be rectified by God's guiding hand, just as that same hand had brought Napoleon to us as a divine punishment.

"Our world is threatened," I told Zaynab when we were back in our villa and walking alone in the garden, discussing the wonders of all we had seen that day. She regarded me curiously and asked why. "We have to learn from these people before it's too late."

She smiled. "Good. We will learn."

"Not you. I forbid you to go back there."

She sighed with impatience. "Come on, Zaki, don't be stupid."

"Don't you be! Napoleon rejected you. You're not going to be his Cleopatra. Father's little scheme fizzled. The case is closed. You stay home where you belong."

She laughed. "Those days are over."

"Over your dead body! No sister of mine is going to cavort with the French and have every tongue wagging. Father's enough of a liability on our honor without you compromising it."

"Zaki. Listen to me."

"No! I won't discuss it."

"Why not?"

"Because there's nothing to discuss. You stay home with Noha and Mother and keep from shame. I'll be the one to go to the institute."

Her smile vanished. With a visage of passive submission, she lowered her head and, putting her hand in sequence to her brow, lips, and heart, uttered in mock humility an oft-used phrase in *One Thousand and One*

Nights, "Sam'a wa ta'a." ("To hear is to obey, oh my master. Your command is my wish.")

"Don't pull that Sheherazad shit with me, Sister! I'm serious! You're not going!"

"Très bien. D'accord."

That proved it. We hadn't a chance in hell against the French.

5

ACH MORNING WE WENT to the institute. To keep tongues from wagging, Zaynab dressed in one of my robes and caftans, with her hair rolled up in a turban, and sat behind me on the donkey. It wasn't long before she talked me into buying her a donkey of her own. Marcel, Jaubert, and Venture de Paradise offered to put a carriage at our disposal, but I refused for two reasons: I didn't want to accept a favor that was really intended for Zaynab; and I didn't want a French carriage showing up every morning at our house. But frankly, as far as the second reason was concerned, I shouldn't have worried. The whole city appeared to be settling into a condition of collaboration with the French. We were getting used to them. Soldiers were seen sauntering unarmed about the streets and marketplaces, laughing and singing and generally treating the people they came into contact with courteously and, to a degree they didn't realize, generously.

Taking advantage of their ignorance, some unscrupulous merchants began charging them four and five times more than they would an Egyptian. Such gross dishonesty in the marketplace was something new, but it was justified in the merchants' minds since the victims were French, rich, and stupid. It soon became a disease of mind to the extent that even Egyptians started falling victim to the merchants' avarice. Father claimed it was a French conspiracy: the soldiers had been ordered to overpay so that Egyptian morals would be corrupted and the country easier to rule. He was not alone in believing this. There were many who blamed the French for everything bad that happened in the country. Whatever they did was bad. There were a lot of people making a lot of money on what the French did, and not just the merchants. Christians, Jews, Muslims, everyone who contracted to supply the French with their needs or entered their service in other ways—laborers, cooks, servants, tailors, purveyors, pimps, prostitutes—made more money than they ever had before. To them, the French were a blessing, a livelihood, a fat cow to be milked.

Change was rapid. Wine houses opened up, and coffeehouses and restaurants and gambling dives, and it wasn't unusual to see Egyptians there—Egyptian girls as well, and Muslims even. At first the sort of girls who frequented these places came from the lower levels of society. Then a few upperclass women began to be seen with the higher-ranking officers. This caused a lot of talk in the beginning. But as the weeks went on and social mingling between French and Egyptians increased, the resentment subsided. Yesterday's abomination became today's norm. What had been collaboration became business as usual. Egypt had gone through so many foreign invasions and occupations over the course of history that you might say we were conditioned to tolerate our occupiers without too much fuss.

There were mixed marriages, eventually so many of them that the shaykhs of al-Azhar felt obliged to issue a *fatwa*—that is, a legal opinion based on their understanding of the Shari'ah, or holy law—that it was not unlawful for a Muslim girl or woman to marry a Frenchman once he declared the Shihada, the profession of faith: "There is no God but God, and Muhammad is His Messenger." With that, they were considered good-enough Muslims, no circumcision necessary, and the shaykhs were paid well for their cooperation, though the guild of circumcisers was a bit huffy about it and had to be paid off.

Those shaykhs serving as members on the ruling diwan were paid very well, to put it mildly. Bonaparte showered them with gifts and tokens of gratitude, and no end of high-sounding titles and offices. Our French sultan unstintingly fed their sense of importance with signs of prestige, dignity, and authority, in addition to feeding their sense of acquisition— some might unkindly call it their greed—with material rewards. Bonaparte appealed to their baser instincts in every way he could imagine: with jewels, gold, high office, honorary robes, and high-quality horses, bestowing titles as noble as the horses to go with them. There were of course shaykhs who resisted Bonaparte's warm embrace, regardless how richly he extended it or dressed it in the trappings of Islamic propriety.

Many of the pious common people declaimed the cavorting and

gambling, the licentiousness and drinking, but there wasn't much they could do about it, and there were more people who reveled in the casinos than were repelled by them. And even among the God-fearing community, there were those who privately conceded that in some ways the new rulers were an improvement over the Mamluks. For example, the streets were now regularly swept clean and dampened down, and there was that daily afternoon ritual called garbage collection, where all debris and waste was supposed to be deposited in designated areas to be taken outside the city and burned by men who earned more than what a hard-working porter earned on a good day. Most people thought this a good thing, but there were always those who complained that it was another French conspiracy, as fewer flies thickening the air was considered detrimental to health and fertility, both human and agricultural.

Streets were illuminated at night, as shops and houses were outfitted with oil lanterns and the street corners with high posts from which hung shielded lamps. People stayed out late now, promenading and playing games and gambling in the illuminated cafés and wine houses, eating and drinking and amusing themselves into the night. The French said the purpose of illumination was to reduce nighttime robberies, and they had a point, but many Egyptians who resented the French claimed it would only help robbers see better at night. When robberies did indeed decline, these same people protested that the tyrannical French were depriving Egyptian robbers of their livelihood. The robbers were said to agree.

Hospitals and clinics offered their services free of charge to everyone, Egyptians as well as French. The military hospital in Azbakiyya where the Europeans all went was also open to Egyptians and also free. Egyptians favored the military hospital despite the rumors that women who went there would be raped and men sodomized and made impotent. The rumor attached to the free dental clinic was that French women went there only to have their pubic areas shaved, and that they paid the dentist by letting him put whatever he wanted in their mouths, as one might expect in a dental clinic. This went along with all those other stories about French women throwing their legs open to everybody and loving to copulate in the street in groups and never washing themselves afterward, or after anything they did. The French were dirty. They never washed, not even their rear ends after defecating. They spit on rugs and furniture, blew their noses on their sleeves, dumped their dead in garbage heaps for the rats to eat. Even some educated people believed the stories, just as they believed that the new irrigation ditches the French were digging would dry up the Nile and Egypt would disappear from the face of the earth—France's final conspiracy against us.

The system of justice instituted by the French was a thing of wonder. When one of their soldiers was killed in broad daylight and the assassin, a young fanatic Muslim Berber sailor from Rabat, was apprehended, rather than chopping off his head right then and there, the French soldiers arrested him for interrogation without even beating him. The assassin confessed proudly to the crime, making himself a hero to the Muslim people. Still not satisfied, the army set up a court that included military officers, savants, even Egyptians—Muslims, Christians, and Jews. Imagine, Jews and Christians adjudicating over Muslims! Talk about going too far. Witnesses were gathered, evidence examined, and testimony taken. We didn't know what to make of it. A soldier had been killed, the murderer had confessed, so why all the fuss? Off with his head! Upon further examination by the court, it turned out the Berber sailor from Rabat had procured women for the soldier and sold him hashish, both of which the soldier refused to pay for. A fight had ensued, the soldier had swung his sword at the Berber's head, and the Berber had run away, only to avenge himself the next day by stabbing the Frenchman from behind. He was found guilty and given his choice between sixty stripes or six years in the stockade. He took the stripes, which were publicly administered, and was then—this was beyond amazing—taken to the military hospital, where his lacerated back was treated! Having been bandaged up and given a free rest with food, he was released to go ply his sleazy trade. Some Egyptians grudgingly admitted there was something to be said for French justice, though we couldn't quite understand it. Others resented the French for having proven a would-be martyr to be nothing but a cowardly pimp and drug dealer—just another one of their conspiracies.

Then there was the episode of the Agha of the Janisarries and the four hundred prostitutes. Napoleon complained to the agha that too many of his soldiers were getting venereal diseases from Egyptian prostitutes and ordered him to have the women cured. The agha's cure was to have four hundred of Cairo's prostitutes drowned in the Nile. Napoleon was so enraged when he learned what the agha had done that he had him publicly beaten and imprisoned. It was generally taken as an example of Napoleon's mercy that he didn't have the Turk beheaded. When a French civilian lawyer called for Napoleon to be charged and brought to court for having inflicted corporal punishment on the agha without formal charges or an investigation or a court hearing, we thought it was a joke. But then charges were brought against Napoleon and the agha was freed from prison and given compensation, with Napoleon having to apologize to him before a military tribunal. I mean, what can you say? The commander in chief of the army apologizing publicly to a fat agha—a corrupt, good-for-nothing slob of an Ottoman? It was an incredible performance. We shook our heads. How could people like this last very long, humiliating their leaders so? We actually felt sorry for poor Napoleon. Our shaykhs who had castigated the French as devils incarnate were stilled to silence. Father had not a word of comment or criticism. All of Islamic legal thinking and political philosophy prescribes that a ruler is under the authority of the law, all Muslims being equal in that respect, even a caliph or sultan. Of course, it never happened in Islamic history that a caliph or sultan was brought before a court and found guilty; assassination was quicker, cleaner, less costly, and less traumatic, and it brought the issue to an irreversible close. And here the shaykhs saw the ideal of Islamic law enacted right before them, by Frenchmen. The spectacle was so humbling that no one dared call it a French conspiracy. (Well, some did, of course. Ironically, it was probably the greatest conspiracy of all in its effect of undermining our confidence in ourselves and our institutions.)

Something else: the French listened to complaints and acted. When Father and the other shaykhs complained that the spread of drinking houses was becoming a scandal because of all the loud men and women they attracted, both French and Egyptian, Napoleon set limits on the number and location of drinking houses. He restricted French soldiers and their Egyptian females to certain areas, mainly Azbakiyya, but that didn't last long. When it was brought to his attention that the equality he had established between Muslims and all other religious communities had resulted in uppity Christians eating and smoking publicly during the month of fasting, and doing a lot of other nasty things to taunt Muslims who, as they saw it, had lorded it over them and humiliated them before the French came, Napoleon ordered that during the daylight hours of Ramadan, non-Muslims could eat only in the privacy of their homes—and that went for all French soldiers and officers as well. He used the occasion to mention that he too was fasting for the holy month, but this was taken as just another example of his deception, the conspiracy of pretending he was a Muslim. But in spite of that, people were impressed by Napoleon and his execution of French law under their judicial system.

According to Father, Napoleon found some of our Syrian and Egyptian Christians to be a pain in the ass. As soon as Napoleon declared what he called the Rights of Man—something else we couldn't comprehend: Men had Duties to God, not Rights distilled from Reason!—and had these so-called rights take the place of traditional customs, the Christians asserted themselves with a vengeance, slaughtering pigs in front of mosques, drinking alcohol in the streets, mocking us with cold goblets of water during Ramadan, galloping their horses down the narrow, quiet streets of Muslim quarters while shouting insults to Islam, haughtily swaggering through the marketplaces in gaudy French clothes, throwing their weight around while speaking a grotesquely garbled mishmash of French and Arabic, and generally acting as though the current occupation had happened just so they could act as arrogantly as they wanted and get back at the Muslims.

They had forgotten that Muslims had suffered as much as they had under the Mamluks and Ottomans. To be fair, Napoleon did try to rein them in, but they refused to be reined in once they'd gotten the bit between their unclean teeth. Equality proved to be a pretty potent wine. It was only a minority of these Christians who behaved so badly, but a loud and aggressive minority they were—mostly people of the lower sort, who, having eagerly sold their services as contractors to the French, had grown rich in no time by overcharging the army even more than the merchants overcharged individual soldiers. They were an embarrassment to the more sober Egyptian Christian families who realized that the whole would suffer for the few, and who regretted the problems equality posed when it was given by a powerful outsider to a weak minority. Also, as God-fearing family people, these Christians were as horrified as the pious Muslim families at their daughters and sons being drawn to what they saw as the French life of heedless licentiousness.

On the other hand, it was mostly Christians and Jews who attended the free school Napoleon opened for Egyptians to study French, located in one of the buildings of the institute that hadn't yet opened its doors to the general public. Zaynab and I were two of the few Muslims there, and Zaynab was the only girl, but passing as a boy in her boots, caftan, and turban. Only one of the shaykhs attended—Hassan al-Attar, a brilliant man who was learned in all the sciences and mathematics but was also considered weird for being too open in his sexual preferences and not keeping them hidden as would have been normal. Venture, Marcel, and Jaubert happily took Zaynab under their collective wing for special lessons in French in the institute's Department of Oriental Studies; they had no choice but to take her bothersome brother and chaperone under their other wing. They made no secret who their true protégé was.

Within a month of intensive study, Zaynab was making her way in the new language. Marcel began giving her little essays to write and was trumpeting her progress through the whole of the institute. The savants gave her the good-natured nickname "Napoleon's Egyptian girl" because every now and then the commander in chief, in one of his fly-by visits, would drop in briefly to see how the shaykh's daughter was progressing, kiss her on the cheek, and assure her she would be ready for the Sorbonne in a few years, or joke that he was going to become a Muslim and marry her. Then off would he fly, his aides-de-camp and generals streaming behind him like ducks following their mother. The few times he noticed me, it was, "Ah, Zaynab's brother! And how is the future shaykh coming in our language? As well as his sister, I trust?" and with a wink to Venture, he would chuckle and pat me on the turban like a dog.

Zaynab's brother! The arrogance! All this attention she was getting made me puke. It was going to her head. Venture, Marcel, and Jaubert were always fawning over her—not to mention some of the other younger savants. It was disgusting. She was already beginning to read books in French, some that Napoleon himself had given her as presents. Her progress came as no surprise to me, but really, a girl outdoing her older brother, an al-Azhar student and future shaykh? Well, by now my self-esteem was so battered I was able to swallow it. She was a precocious girl, and I knew her voracious appetite for learning—something that ran in the family but was normally limited to the males.

Zaynab was anything but normal. Before the French came, she had kept herself from boredom and thoughts of marriage by following my studies—reading and learning what I did, whatever book, whatever subject. Before I went off to study at al-Azhar, Father tutored me at home, and Zaynab had been allowed to sit quietly and listen. Actually she just invited herself, and Father didn't make a fuss about it as long as she kept quiet and didn't pose embarrassing questions. After the lesson, it would be me she bombarded with questions, most of which I couldn't answer. She infuriated me. She asked questions I couldn't answer, and those questions were like arrows shot into my brain; I couldn't shake them off, and her questions became mine. She ruined my education. Everything I had committed to memory would be blown away by the deceptively gentle breath of her questions. One question—How can God know everything and plan everything that will happen in this world and not be responsible for the evil in it?—had vaporized the tortured arguments of three books of theology I had just committed to memory. The origin of evil, divine justice, human responsibility, determination, omniscience, causality, anthropomorphism in the Quran—the simplicity of my beloved sister's questions knocked the logical nexus of all my learning from my novice's mind, leaving the meaningless fragments of my once-integrated theology scattered like windblown pages from a book's unglued binding. What a pain in the ass she was—and now she was outpacing me at the institute. There were limits to what a man could tolerate from a female who didn't know her place. How could I have ever loved her?

I patiently suffered her humiliating progress until one day when I overheard a group of soldiers who were visiting the institute whistle as she passed by, and one of them saying, "There goes the general's Egyptian girl!"

"You mean Cleopatra, the general's whore."

"And the whore of the asses!"

My French was by then good enough to understand what they had said. "Asses" was the soldiers' derogatory term for the civilian savants—a pun on les savants and les anes, anes meaning "asses." They also called the savants "eggheads," while the savants called the soldiers "lead heads" and "sulfur snorters." The soldiers and savants had nothing but contempt for each other. Each side thought the other a stupid waste of money and time, a useless appendage of the expedition. The soldiers generally thought it should have been purely a military venture; the scholars thought it should have been an intellectual one. And now Zaynab was caught up in their nasty rivalry because of her association with the savants and the institute and her imagined relationship with Bonaparte. I shuddered. If the unsavory epithets I had just heard the soldiers bandy about ever leaked from the

French Quarter to the Egyptian community, Zaynab would be considered just that: Bonaparte's Egyptian whore of a Cleopatra. I determined to put an end to it. I had her honor to defend, not to mention my self-esteem, which was being whittled away by her facility with French and overchallenging questions.

6

I APPROACHED FATHER AFTER A lecture he had delivered to his students at al-Azhar, on the categorization and evaluation of individual hadith based on analysis of the chain of transmission, the isnad. The lecture was brilliant. If only the old man would stick to religion and keep his nose out of politics. I had to talk to him about what was being said concerning Zaynab.

"So? What's wrong with her being called Napoleon's Egyptian girl?" he calmly asked as we walked toward the bookstalls of Khan al-Khalili. His response staggered me. I had expected an outburst of rage.

"Her—her reputation!" I sputtered. "Our family honor!"

"A woman attached to a ruler has no need of reputation. The ruler himself is her reputation. Has our young sultan made Zaynab a woman yet?"

The question was another punch that took the wind out of me. "My God, Father! How can you ask that?"

"Well? Has he?"

"Of course not! She's still a virgin."

He frowned. "They say he couldn't give Josephine a baby. Do you think he's—"

"You're not going to restrict her to the house?"

"Maybe it's those tight trousers. Does he show any sexual interest in her?"

"His interest in her is only political."

"Exactly what it's supposed to be. As mine is only religious and historical."

"Why sacrifice Zaynab to an aberration of history? Keep her in the house."

"What a fool I have for a son! It is Zaynab who will undo the aberration and bring history back to where it should be. Napoleon will go. The French aberration will go. They will be sucked into Egypt like into a bottomless swamp and disappear as though they had never been. But Zaynab's and Napoleon's offspring will propagate. They will be Egyptians and not disappear. They will be the legitimate rulers of Egypt—good Muslims from the Bakri stock, descendants of the first caliph of Islam. What greater honor could Zaynab wish?" Father smiled in satisfaction. "That girl has the blood of Ayesha in her."

"She has the blood of Ayesha in her, all right! But she's not a prophet's wife or a caliph's daughter. She can't risk losing her honor. She should be made to stay home with Mother."

"Don't be so narrow-minded. She has her historical destiny to fulfill, as we all do. What does she do with her time?"

"She studies."

"Studies?" Father chuckled. "No wonder Napoleon hasn't married her. She has to put her time to more suitable pursuits for a girl. Make sure that she behaves herself. She must remain pure for our sultan." He scratched his beard and chuckled again. "Studies. That girl has the blood of Ayesha in her veins. It's still in the family. After thirty-six generations."

"That's what she says."

"I'm sure she does. You just make sure she keeps that blood cool—and have her go easy on the studying. Too much of that and she might get intemperate ideas. Ideas are dangerous in the mind of a female; they excite the blood and weaken the mind."

My withering self-esteem aside, what really disturbed me was the possible return of the Ottomans and Mamluks, and the price our family would have to pay for collaborating with the French. Ottoman agents were continually slipping into Cairo, warning us not to have anything to do with the French, warning us that an Ottoman army was on the way, that Sultan Selim's arm was long, that he had ears and eyes everywhere and knew who were traitors and who were faithful Muslims. As it turned out, it was not the sultan's but Lord Nelson's arm that was long.

—m—

The news arrived while Zaynab and I were at the institute, attending an afternoon lecture on the anatomy of the ostrich. Napoleon was there too. The theme was, Is the ostrich made for running or flying? After a long, soporific lecture, the savants divided into two groups and debated the issue for hours without coming to an agreement. It was the only time I didn't regret not understanding French better than Zaynab. Even she was nodding in boredom.

Then, as we were both dropping off, an officer rushed into the lecture hall and whispered something in Napoleon's ear that sent him bolting up as if zapped by a double shot from Berthollet's lightning globes, and he burst out of the hall like a rocket, his aides-de-camp and attending officers frantically charging after him. Relieved to be rid of the sulfur-snorting lead heads, the savants calmly continued their deadening debate on the ostrich.

At the end of it, Jean Michel Venture de Paradise announced that Lord Nelson had delivered the French fleet to the bottom of abu Qir Bay. The entire French fleet! Marcel put on a brave smile that I genuinely believe was as sincere as it was hopeful: "Well, we're in Egypt for good now—those of us who can't swim."

Some other of the savants were less sanguine. They thought of their homes, from which they were now cut off. They were apprehensive that a combined English-Ottoman-Mamluk attack was about to begin. Zaynab and I exchanged worried looks and started for home.

The news had traveled fast. The streets were already empty, the cafés, taverns, and gambling casinos closed. There were no Egyptian girls frolicking with their soldiers. The few to be seen were back in black robes. I was sick with worry. Zaynab didn't speak, a sign that she was more than worried. How would we adjust to a return to the old order?

When we arrived home, Zaynab went straight to her room. I sought out Father to see if he had heard the news. He had. "God may not need Zaynab to set history right after all," he said. He accepted the French disaster as God's will and uttered a pious expression to that effect, but not without my detecting a wistful note of disappointment in his having been deprived of helping God along the tracks of His preordained will. His grand scheme of a Bakri caliphate in Egypt seemed to have come to an abrupt end, as had Bonaparte's to use Egypt as a stepping-stone to India in the creation of an Afro-Eurasian empire under Sultan Napoleon. Both caliphate and sultanate had gone down the drain of historical dreams, the aberration having been rectified by God's uncanny design.

At first, the news of abu Qir was received among the Muslim populace with joy: Islam had defeated the Christian invader; the sultan was about to restore Egypt to legitimate Muslim authority. Upon cooler reflection, however, they realized that Lord Nelson was no more a Muslim than Napoleon. The fleet of one Christian power had defeated the fleet of another Christian power. If the weaker of the two had conquered us with ease, what would the stronger do to us? The new world of Western power dawning upon us made Egypt and the sultan look smaller and smaller. Thoughtful Muslims saw the French defeat at abu Qir as another defeat for Islam, and for Egypt, in that we would be trading a weaker occupying power for a stronger one. There was no reason to celebrate. To the perceptive mind, the sultan's long arm had shriveled to an impotent, atrophied muscle.

"Is this Lord Nelson married?" Father slyly asked me when I finally understood the true nature of the situation. I shrugged my ignorance of the admiral's marital status without getting angry. After all, what was the difference between having an English lord admiral or a French commander in chief for a brother-in-law when an Egyptian caliphate was at stake?

"You want we should start studying English already?" I asked Father.

The old man shook his turbaned head. "These Franks. Is there no end to their power? First France, now English? And what's this about another one of these heathens from over the sea flying kites to steal God's power from the heavens?"

"Poor Egypt," I sighed. "Generations of our children will waste their lives learning languages. On the other hand, if those from over the Atlantic ever come, they at least speak English, as I've heard. That should save us some time."

"They speak English?"

"So I've heard."

"And they're Christians?"

I nodded.

"God is great!" exclaimed Father. "From over the wide ocean, and they speak the same language and have the same religion as the English!"

"All part of God's plan," I said, a bit too flippantly.

"Don't talk nonsense, Son. What could Franks as far away as from over the western ocean have to do with God's plan?"

"I don't know. But a Berber sailor told me they sailed their navy across two seas a few years ago and attacked the lands held by the Dey of Tunis and forced the Muslims to a treaty because of the pirates. The same people that defeated the English."

"By God, is there no end to this Frankish arrogance?"

And with that Father retreated to his private prayer room to read the Quran and pray for the victory of Islam over its Frankish enemies, which were ranked up against it across two continents, a sea, and an ocean.

Fearing that news of their defeat would incite the Egyptians to revolt, the French did what they could to keep it from the people of Cairo. It just went to show how little the French understood our country. One could more easily make the Nile flow backward than keep news of events from spreading. If there is anything faster than sound, light, and electricity, it is the speed of news traveling from village to village in Egypt. Even the Mamluks never thought of controlling the spread of news. That the French thought they could stop it from traveling showed how stupid they were, and if their effort to do so accomplished anything, it was to compromise the favorable impression their sense of justice had made on us.

When Egyptian informers in pay of the French overheard two merchants from Alexandria speaking about the naval battle at abu Qir, Bonaparte, following Mamluk tradition, had the merchants arrested and ordered their tongues cut off. They were well-to-do and respected by the Cairene notables, and so Father went to Napoleon's palace and asked him what could be done to save the merchants their tongues. Sapped of his sultan-like magnanimity by the loss of his fleet, Bonaparte snapped, "I'll indulge you their tongues, if you wish, and take only their heads!"

Father then had Zaynab appeal to him. He tutored her in what to say, but he could have saved his breath, as Zaynab, regarding Napoleon's brutal order not only as a betrayal of principle but also as personal betrayal to her, knew exactly what she would say, and now, given the chance, she said it.

She donned her caftan, pantaloons, boots, and turban, took the copy of Rousseau's *Social Contract* Bonaparte had given her, and rode Father's donkey to military headquarters. Refused admittance on her first try, she persisted and at last was granted entry to see the commander in chief. He was in his private study. She waved away the translator and, without sitting down, placed the book on the desk in front of him and said what she had to say. She told me later what she said, and I doubt her French was fluent enough at the time to convey grammatically and clearly what she told me she said, but apparently it was sufficient for Bonaparte to grasp without trouble.

"I started studying French not because you were strong and won battles," she said, standing upright before the young ruler, "but because of what I saw of your justice and intelligence. And because of the way you included women in your justice. I'm here to find out if I have deceived myself. Those two merchants told the people of Cairo nothing that the people didn't already know. Egyptians love to hear stories. Those merchants were only storytelling. Storytelling is in our culture. That's how we amuse ourselves. It's a passion. Have you not read *One Thousand and One Nights*? If you cut the tongues of the two merchants, even people who like and admire you will turn against you. Until now, I have been able to attend the institute with a clear conscience. If your order is carried out, my position will be compromised; I won't know what to do. I couldn't continue at the institute, and I couldn't return to my old, boring life. So I am appealing to you: for the sake of justice, for the sake of your position in Egypt, for the sake of Rousseau, for my sake, I beg you not to do what you said you would do. That's all I have to say."

Napoleon shrugged, scowled, and said that he could not rescind his order. He would look weak. Egyptians only understood force.

"No, I don't think they do," she said forthrightly. "But they soon will, if they have to."

"What would they think if I changed the order?"

"They would think you wiser than they do now."

"What are the people saying?"

"That you're worse than the worst of the Mamluks. The Mamluks cut out tongues for treachery. Those merchants didn't betray anyone."

"They entered the city when I had forbidden anyone to enter without permission. They betrayed my orders."

"They're just simple merchants."

"Simple merchants who instigate rebellion."

"The people only thought they were listening to stories. They already knew about the fleet." She looked down at the book on his desk. "The general will of Egyptians is to listen to good stories and be left in peace. If you cut out the tongues of storytellers, you cut the Egyptian heart."

Napoleon's eyes fell to the book. He brought it toward him and opened it to the early chapters on general will. "You have learned well at the institute, haven't you?"

"I have learned that we were born free but are everywhere in chains. As a woman, I can't bear mine any longer." Napoleon turned away, as though not wanting to hear, and sat behind his paper-littered desk. Zaynab continued. "You lifted mine from me. And now you're putting them back, heavier than they were before. Spare these merchants and take these chains from me!"

There was a long silence. He leafed through the *Social Contract*. Raising his head to her, he asked, "What would the Mamluks have done to merchants who disobeyed their orders?"

"Fined them. And then fined them again when they'd made more money. And maybe kept on fining them. But to make more money, a merchant needs a tongue to haggle."

Napoleon closed the book. "My compliments. You have argued your case well. But I regret I cannot rescind my order."

Zaynab stared at him coldly. "Why?"

"Those merchants broke the law."

"What law?"

"My law."

She stood facing him a long moment before turning to leave.

"You forgot your book," Bonaparte said.

"I didn't forget," she replied. "I'm leaving it for you to read again."

Zaynab returned home in tears. The next day, however, it was announced that the merchants would pay a fine of a hundred French riyals each and be released. Hours later, a cavalry lieutenant appeared at our gate with the book Zaynab had left behind. A note was enclosed between the pages:

> Please accept my gift of the book once again. It is our
> General Will you return to the Institute.
>
> Napoleon Bonaparte

Father hurriedly collected money from the other shaykhs and notables and then paid from his own pocket twenty that was still lacking of the two hundred riyals. I hoped that if the day came when we were back under Ottoman rule, and the accounts of collaboration were tallied up and served for payment, it would be remembered what Father and Zaynab had done to preserve the tongues of those two merchants.

The French lost much of the prestige they had won since their arrival. The humiliating loss of their fleet was bad enough, but to make matters worse, they levied new taxes to make up for their material loss. The naval defeat at abu Qir shook French confidence. Napoleon now insisted that all Egyptians wear the French Revolutionary Rosette, a symbolic decoration made of three cloth circles, each with a different diameter so that one circle fitted inside the other, like a three-layered red, white, and blue flower. He thought wearing this silly thing would assure our loyalty to him, as if loyalty could be assured by three circular scraps of different-colored cloth, when all it did was further alienate people who might otherwise have been satisfied to leave bad enough alone. While the new taxes heightened resentment against the French, having to wear the rosette raised contempt and pushed otherwise moderate people into open resistance. When, during a ceremonial meeting of the special diwan, Bonaparte pinned these tricolored rosettes on the robes of each of the member shaykhs, Shaykh Sharqawi plucked the thing from his robe as though it were a cockroach or a scorpion and threw it on the ground, stunning the assemblage of Egyptian and French dignitaries. Bonaparte glared at him and ordered him to pick it up. When Shaykh Sharqawi refused, Marcel, who was translating, explained to the shaykh that the commander in chief only wanted the shaykhs to wear it as a token of his friendship. He was honoring them and increasing their authority by bestowing upon them the insignia, which would raise them in the esteem of the people and the military.

"If our esteem would be raised among the French," Shaykh Sharqawi replied with quiet dignity, "then it would be lowered before God and our Muslim brethren."

The pupils of Napoleon's eyes burned like points of black fire. He stormed out of the meeting, leaving one of his generals to retrieve the rosette from the floor. From that moment on, the French considered Shaykh Sharqawi an enemy, which automatically made him a hero to Egyptians. In such a whimsical way, because of three scraps of colored cloth, did we gain a leader against foreign occupation.

People generally wore the rosettes in public, as there was a stiff fine for being caught without one, and this forced obligation to wear something we understood as important only to the French not only catalyzed our hostility, but also gave us something to stomp on in anger at home, while enriching the Egyptian tailors who spent day and night stitching up the silly things and selling them to the French at a bloated price.

Common Egyptians developed poisonous feelings against the French and against other Egyptians who were seen or thought to be associating with them. Shaykh Sadat was accosted by a group of people upon being seen coming from Napoleon's residence. They asked him what his business was there and roughed him up. If Sharqawi was their newfound hero, Sadat was their goat. The political algebra of the day would put Father in the same boat as Sadat. Attitudes were so sharp that Zaynab and I were scared to continue our studies at the institute.

To divert people's attention and defuse the mounting tension, the French staged extravaganzas of cannon fire, music, military parades, and fireworks that canopied the night sky in multicolored constellations of flowers and showers of shooting stars—rockets streaking upward, exploding and filling the sky with fiery butterflies of different colors, as if God himself were throwing down the stars from heaven. We had never seen anything like it. But it didn't keep Cairo from exploding in fiery revolt. The French had descended upon us in July; revolt broke out in October.

It was the taxation that did it. We thought the Mamluks knew something about taxing people, but they were amateurs compared to the French. First, Napoleon levied a 2 percent tax on property. This was unheard of. We thought Napoleon had lost his mind. Not satisfied with this, he demanded that everyone who owned a house, a store, a building, land, or property of any kind prove ownership by producing a deed. Who in Egypt had deeds? Most property had been held by families for generations, centuries. Everybody knew who owned what. But not the French. If a family couldn't produce a deed, a punishing tax was levied, and then a heavy fine for not having a deed, and finally a stiff fee for a deed to be drawn up. Those who couldn't afford to have that done had part of their property confiscated. Those who did happen to have a deed were charged a fee to have it certified and stamped, in some cases the fee was so crippling that the owner had to give up a good part if not all of his property to pay it.

There were other taxes and fines and fees, all equally cunning and arbitrary. Napoleon and his financial advisers must have been up day and night dreaming of ways to squeeze money from the people. We were charged for not keeping the walks and streets in front of our shops and homes perfectly clean. Garbage was one fine, animal dung another, a dead cat another, and so on. A week of this and Cairo must have been the cleanest city in the world. It was bitterly joked that the next tax would be based on the length of a man's penis, leaving the French tax-exempt. I never thought I'd see the day when people cried to have the Mamluks back!

When rumors were buzzing like flies in summer that a combined Ottoman-Mamluk army was two days from Cairo, the shaykhs and notables met in small groups, secretly because the nervous French had forbidden congregations of more than ten adult males (another hated innovation). Each group discussed what should be done when the attack came and appointed a leader to represent it. Then the leaders of each group gathered as an executive command council and discussed the various proposals. The decisive meeting was at our house. In case the French had us under surveillance, Father told Napoleon that he was hosting a special dinner for the diwan in order to discuss the new taxes. Napoleon was welcome to attend if he wanted. As Father expected, he declined.

It was a lively meeting. Zaynab and I watched through a wooden screen along the upper-floor railing overlooking the central hall downstairs. Our house, something between a modest palace and a palatial villa, had been built a century earlier by a wealthy Ottoman pasha who had been appointed governor of Egypt. (That was back before the Mamluks took control of things and began building their own marvelous palaces as almost-independent rulers.) The pasha had the villa modelled on the sultan's imperial palace, which included a concealed alcove whose tightly constructed latticework allowed the sultan to peer down and hear what was being said by whom in the large room below, where government ministers met to discuss state affairs. Zaynab and I loved hiding in this alcove and listening in on Father's discussions with the other shaykhs. Listening in now, we saw clearly that the council was unequally divided between two factions. The majority wanted to begin immediately organizing the populace so that they would be ready to attack the French the moment the Ottomans commenced their siege. Shaykh Sharqawi led this faction, supported by Shaykh Sadat, who must have been frightened after being roughed up and who now, with things looking not so favorable for the French, wanted to get back on the side of the "citizens." The other faction, led by Father, advocated doing nothing to incite the people until the Ottoman attack had begun and had shown itself to have a reasonable chance of success. His was not a popular stand. I was beginning to learn that sensible ones were usually not.

I turned to whisper something to Zaynab and saw how full of worry she was. Her new life was dissolving in planned violence right before her eyes. "Don't worry," I said, feeling miserable for her. "Even if the French are forced out, they can't take with them what you've learned." She smiled, but the tears in her eyes spoke for the turmoil in her heart.

"How do we really know an army is on the way?" Father was asking. "We've been hearing rumors of an Ottoman army coming since the first day the French arrived. The Ottomans and our brave Mamluks have done nothing but send agents armed with quick tongues and promises. The only action taken against the French has been by another Christian power. We have no reason to believe the sultan has sent an army. If an army is coming, it is probably an English army. Should we have our people revolt against the French to make it easy for the English to take their place as our masters? As for a Mamluk army, you saw how they sat around doing nothing but counting their gold until the French were upon them, and then when they at last acted, it was to pack up their valuables in readiness to run, as though they knew they would be defeated. They rode faster in retreat and into the desert than they had ever run against an enemy. If we pin our hopes on them, God have mercy on us and those we incite to attack the French." He paused, surveyed his audience, and held up his arms to still the mixed murmurs of acquiescence and opposition before continuing.

"Now, supposing there is an Ottoman army coming, but only a small one to reinforce the Mamluks in the desert, and we do attack—can we take responsibility for what the French would do to us and to the people we have incited? How can we in good conscience order the people to take up arms when we have no idea of our chances of success? If we knew for a fact that the sultan was sending at least thirty thousand troops, I would say revolt. Without this knowledge, we would be irresponsibly asking people to sacrifice their lives, and how many thousands would be killed? In the absence of a full-scale Ottoman army, the French would turn their artillery on us in an all-out slaughter. Our city would be turned to rubble and dust and swept away in a river of blood."

Father went on to remind the shaykhs that they would be asking a defenseless people to face artillery, infantry, and cavalry. No mercy would be shown. Bonaparte had convinced himself that the shaykhs were his friends; his vengeance for being proven wrong would be most bloody and cruel. He was young, and the young were extreme in vengeance. "Wisdom tells us to be cautious and do nothing until we see a reasonable chance of victory."

A respectful silence followed Father's argument, which was delivered eloquently in the high Arabic of the Quran. Some of the pro-revolt shaykhs then argued that to do nothing was weak and defeatist. When these hotheads had had their say, Shaykh Sharqawi took a moderating position, saying that he agreed with Father and that the revolt shouldn't begin until the sultan's army had already launched its attack. But for the revolt to have a chance of success, the people needed to organize and prepare. "We should begin that now," he concluded.

Father countered by asking what would happen if the French were to discover the people's preparations to revolt before this hypothetical Ottoman army arrived. He declared that preparations should wait until the army arrived, and that the revolt should not begin until the third day of fighting, in order to see which way the battle was going. The army could retreat if it went badly, but a city can't retreat. "I do not place my full confidence in the Ottomans' skills in warfare," Father bravely said, daring to imply that a Christian army could fight better than a Muslim one. "Look at what the Austrians and Russians are doing to them."

This brought more grumbles: the idea that Muslim soldiers could value their own skins more than martyrdom and paradise, or be defeated in their struggle against infidels, was downright irreligious. As though the fleeing Mamluks hadn't been Muslims! Ignoring the grumbles of protest, Father battled on, arguing that the sultan and the Mamluks were responsible for defending us against the French. They lost Egypt, and it was their duty to restore it to Islamic rule. The duty of the shaykhs was to protect the people and preserve the customs, traditions, and laws of Islam. It was not for them to take up sticks and knives against artillery and muskets and bring even more affliction upon the people than what they already were forced to bear. "We preserve Islam in society during its time of troubles. It is not for us to defend the borders or take on the responsibility of soldiers and pashas who have failed in theirs."

The shaykhs argued the issue for hours, and at last Shaykh Sadat voiced the majority consensus, saying they should trust in God and begin that very day to prepare the people to revolt. God would decide. God was good. God was great. God would favor the Muslims. God, God, and more God. Had the French been there to hear this, they would have pissed in their tight britches from laughing so hard. God favored the rational, the strong, the organized, the efficient, the side with the best and most weapons. I was inclined to laugh myself, and I would have if Zaynab had not given me a look of such wretched despair that it tore my heart. She feared that her beloved institute was about to be destroyed.

The day after it was decided to organize a revolt, the wooden triumphal arch the French had constructed in Azbakiyya in celebration of their revolution collapsed. The common people took it as a sign from God that French power was about to be thrown down. What brought the arch down was simply an overflow of water from the Nile running too rapidly through the irrigation ditches and loosening the soil. The fallen arch was clearly caused by a logical sequence of natural events, beginning with the Nile in flood, which also destroyed the crops of many devout Muslim farmers, but that part of it was ignored. To the common people of Cairo, it was an unquestionable sign from God that we were about to destroy the French. The shaykhs who supported a revolt—and who as educated Muslims were entrusted to protect the gullible people from believing in omens and other occult nonsense—betrayed their trust and their duty by encouraging the people in their belief that the fallen arch was God revealing His will to them. It wasn't intentional deception. The shaykhs were so desperate to be rid of the Christian French that, as fervent Muslims, they were prepared to believe anything that might encourage the people. Father deplored the way the shaykhs were resorting to omens. For all his faults, there was much integrity and wisdom in the man.

The French didn't take the fallen triumphal arch as an omen. They simply rebuilt it stronger than it was before and planted a "tree of liberty" under it, the tree being mounted on a high wooden pillar that jutted up from the earth like a long prong. The people referred to it as *al-khazuq*, which loosely translated means a long wooden stake with a pointed end. Ottomans used it to impale enemies of the state. By expertly inserting the sharpened tip into the anus and avoiding vital organs as the stake was driven into the body, executioners could keep the victim alive for days as a terrifying lesson of what happened to those who defied authority. The jabbing motion of an extended middle finger, which we called the khazuq, was a common gesture expressing anger at whom the finger was pointed, and calling the French Tree of Liberty al-khazuq was considered a clever insult, but except for a handful of savants, our mocking humor was completely lost on our French guests. They never knew and never learned what we were laughing at or what we were angry at, and this was like a wall that made life for everyone more miserable than it needed to be. The savants were open to learning about us, and a number of them learned, but precious few in the military community. I could understand why the savants called the soldiers lead heads and sulfur snorters. Bonaparte gave the appearance of being eager to learn, but in reality, he arrived convinced that he knew everything already, and that, in spite of how mentally quick he was, closed his mind to what made us a people, our character.

As for us, except for a few shaykh Attars and Zaynabs, our minds were closed, locked, and sealed when it came to learning about the French or about anything that wasn't in books of religion or already long known and written generations ago.

Planning for the revolt went ahead. Each shaykh, Father included, was responsible for organizing the people in the quarter of the city where he lived. A communication system was established using imams from the hundreds of mosques scattered throughout the city. The imams spread the word of insurrection to their congregations, and they also collected and hid in their mosques and cemeteries all the things that could possibly be used as weapons against the French, even sticks. When the fighting began, they were to shout down orders from the tops of their minarets, directing attack groups to and from this or that street or alley where the French were coming or going. Local commanders were appointed to each quarter. These were mostly young religious scholars like myself, and the sons of leaders of Sufi mystical orders. I was appointed command of a section of Azbakiyya, the one closest to French military headquarters and the institute.

At home, when Zaynab accused me of conspiring to destroy her institute and her life, I defended myself with more passion than I really felt. "I'm fighting the French," I protested, "not destroying your life!" I didn't tell her I had done nothing to collect and hide weapons and had no intention to.

"Yes! My life!" she cried.

"Sister, I hate to disillusion you, but the French didn't conquer us to give you a new life! You don't mean a damn thing to them. They're using you. Open your eyes!"

"I'm the one using them!"

"Sure, like Father was going to use Napoleon. Come on, don't be naive. They're foreign invaders. We have to fight them."

"No you don't! If they go, the institute goes. If that goes, what's left for us?"

"That's not all there is in the world."

"Stop fooling yourself, Zaki. That institute means as much to you as it does to me. Who is it who said we have to learn from the French if we want to be as strong as them? Shaykh Attar said it. You said it. If the institute goes, where are we going to learn? You're going out to kill the very people who are teaching you. You're a traitor! Killing your own teachers. Marcel, Jaubert, Jean Michel, Conte, Berthollet!"

"I'll only kill soldiers!" I exclaimed boldly, as if I were capable of killing anything larger than a cockroach.

"Traitor!"

"Bitch!"

I had to push my way past her to get out of the house and start organizing.

7

THE PLAN WAS TO launch a surprise attack on the third day of the Ottoman siege, and strike hard. Our strategy was to divert French artillery and musket fire from the Ottomans to us, making it easier for the Ottomans to penetrate the city walls. Taking the brunt of the pounding would be the price we paid for liberation. "Liberation for what?" Zaynab had scoffed. "To be ruled by Ottomans and Mamluks again?"

As it turned out, Father was right. We paid the price without liberation coming with it, whatever liberation was supposed to mean. The grand Ottoman army rumored to be at the city wall was a mere token force meant to unnerve the French, and with the first volley of French artillery, the motley gang posing to be an army scattered into the desert faster than the wind. That should have ended it, but tensions by then were so high that at the first sound of artillery, the revolt broke loose—three days before schedule. So much for all our meticulous planning. The misfire was sparked by a street urchin who threw a stone at a soldier who was chasing another urchin who had thrown a stone at a soldier who had been chasing another urchin who had snatched the purse of an officer's wife. The soldier was then stabbed by yet another youth who had been waiting nervously for the revolt to begin. This led to other assaults against isolated soldiers and Frenchmen, who within minutes were being attacked throughout the city. In spite of the tensions that had risen daily since the sinking of the fleet, soldiers were still circulating freely in the streets, unarmed and unafraid, as if they were at home among friends, making them easy targets, even though their assailants had only knives, axes, and clubs.

The first attack was led by the blind leader of the beggars' union, whose stronghold was just outside the gates of al-Azhar Mosque. Armed with the crudest weapons, the blind leader and his beggars took the French by surprise and slaughtered a hundred or more of them in minutes. The beggars' brigade was not to be outdone by other assault units. During the first hour, more than three hundred soldiers fell in various parts of the city. One of Napoleon's favorite generals, Dupuy, was surprised along with a small number of troops, forced into a cul-de-sac, and killed along with practically all his men.

I didn't know what to do when the fighting broke out. With no Ottoman attack, I hoped the fighting would die down and so I stayed home, and I would have remained there had the men of my group not come to get me. I sought advice from Father, but he had locked himself up in his prayer room in one of his unpredictable mood changes and wouldn't see me. When it came to talking and planning and envisioning great schemes, he was a pillar of intelligence and confidence. But when the action started and swung out of control, he turned into a frightened snail and contracted into the shell of his prayer room with his nose stuck in the Quran.

Zaynab pleaded with me not to leave home. I would have gladly obliged, but my men were clamoring for action, and so in a false show of contempt for a girl's advice, I turned my back to her and, like a good leader, blindly followed my men.

Armed with some staves, axes, knives, and farm tools, we advanced on military headquarters only to find that it was already under attack by several other groups. Thinking the revolt won and this merely the last battle, my men broke out in a joyous cry of "God is great!" and joined the attack. I followed behind at not quite a safe distance, but safe enough. Several of my men dashed into a palace that had been vacated by the residing general and emerged carrying armloads of booty. I ordered them to stop it and press on with the attack or I'd report them to the Executive Command Council. They ignored my order and ran on. I gave up, entered the abandoned palace, and climbed up to the safety of the roof, the better to direct my men in battle.

The attack groups—really a motley collection of mobs—had surrounded the French compound in Azbakiyya, killing soldiers as well as Copts, Syrians, European merchants, and anyone who had collaborated with the enemy and many who had not. Their homes were torched, their stores looted, and their women and children raped, sodomized, and murdered. From the roof of the palace, I watched men hacked to death while defending their homes. Women, young girls, boys, and adolescents were dragged out, had their clothes torn from them, and were viciously assaulted from front and rear. Some came screaming out of their burning homes only to be hacked down or raped. Even the homes and families of respected Muslims fell victim to the mobs, as though the demons of hell had taken possession of the city. The beggars' brigade leading the way, the revolt soon turned into a savage war of the poor and wretched taking vengeance on the rich. Those families who had been wealthy before the occupation were treated no differently than those who had grown rich serving and cheating the French.

It took only hours for the French to regain their balance. The revenge they exacted was every bit as terrible as the vision given me by Father's description of it when he had tried to talk the shaykhs out of revolting. It was a contest between stones and clubs on the one hand and muskets and heavy artillery on the other. Once the French had thrown back the attack groups from Azbakiyya and created a line of movement through the city, they hauled their artillery up the road they had cut to the Citadel and the heights of the Muqattam Plateau. By midafternoon, a firestorm from hell was raining down on the populace below. Al-Azhar was the main target, for Napoleon knew the shaykhs were the only ones with the brains, courage, and organizational network to plan and launch such a coordinated and large-scale assault. Now they would pay, and pay dearly. Again, as my father had foreseen, Bonaparte saw the shaykhs' action as nothing less than the basest treachery.

Buildings were destroyed, whole quarters leveled—nothing like it had been seen since the razing of Baghdad by the Mongols five and a half centuries earlier. As the cannons belched their murderous fire down on us from the commanding heights of the Citadel, the soldiers emptied their muskets on us from the city walls. Thousands upon thousands perished— for every Frenchman, a hundred of us. Those who weren't shot from above or slaughtered in the streets by the cavalry's storm of flashing swords were buried beneath the rubble of buildings that had collapsed under the hail of artillery that continued on through the day and into the night, when at last the artillery mercifully fell silent, only to resume even more murderously at daybreak, for the French had by then tripled their firepower from the Citadel and the plateau.

For three days, death and destruction rained down on us. No place was safe from the artillery. From one end of the city to the other, with every bursting shell, with every collapsing building, with every cry of pain, the lesson was driven home: defy the French and Egyptian blood would flow deep as the Nile.

At the end of the first day of bombardment, Bonaparte sent a message to the shaykhs of the diwan ordering them to come to him. None of them dared. They were too afraid—afraid of the young general, and even more afraid of looking like traitors to the revolt that had turned into a looting party by poor, lawless mobs. So the shaykhs stayed in their homes or in al-Azhar Mosque, praying to God for protection from the savagery that had been let loose from both sides, the French and the mob, with the civil populace between them.

On the second day of bombardment, Father saddled his mule and braved the murderous streets. Alone, he climbed the road up to the Citadel while the artillery pounded down from above and the mob raged below. When he had come within view of the guardhouse, the sentries leveled their muskets at him, ordering him to halt. Shaykh Khalil ignored their cries and, remembering to pin his tricolored rosette to his robe over his heart, as though to give the sentries an easy target, continued on. Thinking him perhaps gone mad from the bombardment, the sentries stared at the approaching turbaned graybeard on a mule, and were then even more dumbfounded by his demand to be taken to General Napoleon Bonaparte.

Bonaparte, surrounded by his grim-faced generals, furiously rounded on Father. Why had it taken the diwan so long to respond to his appeal for peace? Was it the shaykhs' intention to sit on their asses and watch the city be destroyed? Why were they doing this to their city and their people? Had they no conscience? Were they nothing but bloody butchers? The slaughter had to stop! And what was wrong with Shaykh Sadat and Shaykh Sharqawi that they didn't come? Trembling at the aggressive reception, Father thought the French interpreter had mistranslated, for nothing he heard made sense to him. He replied that he hadn't been informed of any peace appeal, and that he had come on his own, not on behalf of the diwan. He begged that the bombardment be stopped.

"I beg *you* to stop it!" returned Napoleon.

"Excuse me?"

"I beg you to stop it!"

Father was sure something was wrong with the translator's Arabic. He repeated, "On my own authority, I accept any condition you demand, but please stop the bombardment."

"You certainly waited long enough! You could have put a stop to it before it began! Why didn't you? It's criminal what you shaykhs are doing! Criminal! Barbaric!" In red-faced fury, Bonaparte brought his fist down on the map-covered table behind which he and his generals were standing. The rattle of wineglasses could be heard above the booming artillery. "Are you happy to see your city destroyed?" Gesturing his innocence, Father put his hand over his heart and in abject appeal stared at Napoleon with teary eyes. "Is that what you and your colleagues want?" Napoleon thundered. "To see the city leveled to dust?"

Father shook his head. "I accept any conditions for the ending of the bombardment."

"You should all be executed! Every last bloody one of you! I appeal to you so this terrible bombardment can be stopped, and you ignore my appeal! You allow your own city to suffer fire and destruction and death while I send appeal after appeal for peace and wait for you to respond, and you fail to come. Only now does one of you come! Where are the rest?"

"I have come on my own because I can't tolerate what's happening."

"Nor can I! Listen to the artillery! Look at what you've made us do! Your cruelty sickens me!"

"On my own authority. I accept all and any conditions."

"Don't listen to him!" one of the generals retorted. "He's trying to trick us! They don't want peace. They want to kill us and drive us out. Let them destroy their city if that's what they want. It's what they deserve for killing General Dupuy."

The other generals nodded, gruffly voicing their agreement. "Execute them all!" shouted another general. Sabers rattled.

Father wiped the sweat from his brow. "We want peace. We accept all conditions."

"Don't believe him, General. It's one of their sneaky gypo deceptions. Turn and they'll stab you in the back, filthy gypos! They place no value on human life."

Father pleaded with Bonaparte to tell him what he had to do for the bombardment to end. He promised on his honor to do whatever he was told, if only it would stop. "On my honor!"

"Honor?" cried out General Kleber, second-in-command to Bonaparte. "They killed General Dupuy. It's our honor to let them continue destroying themselves. Bloodthirsty savages. I wouldn't trust them."

Bonaparte replied that the conditions were the same as those he had communicated to that traitor, Shaykh Sadat. "The rioters must surrender their arms and return to their homes, and the leaders of the revolt must be delivered to us. By leaders I mean those who planned and incited this treachery."

"How can I deliver the leaders when I don't know them?"

"You see, General? They want the bombardment to go on!"

Bonaparte raised a hand to silence his generals. "You know who the leaders are, Shaykh Khalil. We both know them. Sharqawi is at their head. You don't have to deliver them. Just tell me who conspired with Sharqawi. Sadat? Ghazzawi? Sawi? The names only."

"I can't do that."

"You can't? Then listen to the artillery that your irresponsibility has let loose! You hear it? Every blast is the death cry of one, two, perhaps three of your countrymen. Count them! Count and tell me how many innocent people you can let die before facing your responsibility and ending their slaughter."

The booming artillery pounding against his ears, Father looked hopelessly from Bonaparte's angry, penetrating eyes to the icy faces of his generals. Then, shrugging and holding his hands clasped in front of him, he looked down at the floor and said quietly, "I can only take responsibility for ending the rioting. If you then need someone to execute as a leader, I am as good as anyone."

"Listen to the old charlatan! He thinks he's a Christ!" one of the generals snorted. "Offering himself for sacrifice!"

"The arrogance!"

Napoleon raised his hand. His generals hushed up. The roar of the artillery punctured the ensuing silence. Napoleon was staring at Father. "No. Not you, Shaykh Khalil—you won't be executed. It's the others. I gave those shaykhs power to run their country. They were nothing under the Mamluks, and I gave them power, and they betrayed me. I who liberated Egypt, who want only to bring your country into the modern world." He shook his head in disgust. "You complain of taxes. But what taxes? A few percent! Less than you paid to the Mamluks and got nothing but strife and tyranny. And what are we doing? I will tell you. Your agriculture is being expanded, new crops are being planted, new industries are being founded, your drinking water is purified, your streets are clean, there is law and order, a daily Egyptian journal is to be printed, a canal will be cut at Suez connecting the Mediterranean and Red Seas to increase your international commerce. When I take India from England, Egypt will be at the crossroads of world trade. Egypt will be the jewel of the East. Her sun will never set. Immense wealth will be yours. Already your merchants are growing fat on us—and they want to pay nothing in taxes when they stand to make fortunes! I expected at least you savants, you the men of religion of your country, I expected you to understand. But instead of seizing the hand of glory and destiny, you revolt! Small-minded people! I offer you a world, and you throw a dagger! Sharqawi! Sadat! They will pay for their small minds!" His hand came down on the handle of his sword with a rattle that made Father jump. Several of his generals rattled their swords along with him. "Is not all that I am giving to your country worth the names of a few worthless traitors?"

Father stood silently with his head down and his hands folded before him. Napoleon gave him a long, penetrating look, then smiled in understanding. "No, of course it isn't. With men such as us there is honor. You are a good man, Shaykh Khalil. Come. I have something to say to you in private."

Accompanied by the interpreter, Napoleon led Father to the privacy of his office and sat down next to him. "You are a brave man to have come here on your own like this," he said, glancing at the rosette pinned over Father's heart. "A loyal man. I won't forget it. The destiny of Egypt and the Franco-Egyptian Empire of Africa, Asia, and Europe depend on our cooperation—yours and mine. But you must understand the delicacy of my position, as I understand yours. My generals want to destroy Cairo for the murder of General Dupuy. He was much loved. For that reason, the bombardment can only be halted when the rioting stops and I am able to appease their fury by giving them a few heads. Between you and me, whether they're the heads of the real leaders is not important. They must at least appear to have been the leaders. I know who the leaders are, as you do—and I also know you were against the revolt. I have my sources of information. But I can't execute the true leaders. If I had any of the high shaykhs executed, I'd have an implacable populace on my hands. My purpose for coming to your country would be lost. So until I have a few names, any names, you and the leading shaykhs are responsible for the bombardment. It is up to you. Your city and the lives of your people are in your hands. Do you understand?"

"God willing, we will do everything in our power to stop the rebels."

"And the names?"

"The names are known to God. If He wills, you will know them."

"And if He wills, the bombardment will stop. I think we understand each other. Go in peace, Shaykh Khalil. It is fortunate we see things in the same light. Much good will come of it, you will see. I have great plans for Egypt. Together we will bring a new dawn to this ancient land. Asia awaits a master. Like an open oyster with its pearl exposed for the taking, it lies before an awakened Egypt in alliance with France. Together we will have oyster and pearl, and Egypt will be great again! For that, Egypt needs you, Shaykh Khalil!"

I can imagine how quickly Father's head must have been spinning. Before taking his leave, he asked, "So the bombardment will definitely stop? We are of one mind on that?"

"Shaykh Khalil, you and I, and God, have been of one mind from the beginning. Would that you had come to me earlier, this meaningless bloodshed could have been avoided altogether. From now on, we must work together. Closely. Destiny demands it."

Napoleon stood and offered Father his hand. Father took it. Because of Father's height over his own diminutive stature, Napoleon stretched his arms up to embrace him, kissed his cheeks, and holding him by the shoulders intoned majestically, "Glory awaits Egypt, Shaykh Khalil. The moment is yours. Don't let it slip through your hands. Seize it!"

The bombardment had halted by the time Father's donkey had descended the road from the Citadel. You can bet Napoleon's words were still ringing in the old man's ears.

The revolt fizzled to an end when the ragtag mob's ammunition was depleted and enough of them had been slain. The French army then cleaned up the remnants, attacking their strongholds by surprise during the darkest hours of night. By the morning of the fourth day, the last of the rebels had been dispatched. The head of the blind leader of the beggars' brigade was paraded through the streets on a pike in traditional Ottoman fashion, and then left on display in the middle of the city for three days for the people to see and the flies to feed on.

Commander-in-Chief Bonaparte issued a general amnesty assuring the populace security of life and property and urging them to resume their normal daily lives. Everyone breathed a sigh of relief, though rumors were predicting an orgy of beheadings and firing squads. I suspect they were spread by Bonaparte's agents in order to make him appear all the more magnanimous and merciful when they proved to be false.

But his generals had to be appeased. The bombardment had been death and destruction at a distance—mechanical, impersonal. The generals needed something closer, more intimate, a private revenge they could smell and feel and walk their horses over, blood running through their hands. It couldn't be something trivial—but it couldn't be a massacre either. Napoleon wouldn't allow it. So he let the army enter al-Azhar Mosque and College, the symbol of Egyptian prestige and pride, the treasure of our spiritual heritage. It cut deep into the Muslim soul.

They rode their horses into the mosque, smashed the book cabinets in the library, and tore up the books, urinating and defecating on them, and then they tore pages from the Quran and from precious illuminated manuscripts and used them to wipe themselves. They wrecked, polluted, defiled, and desecrated everything sacred that the bombardment had spared. As an added touch of French finesse, they smeared their feces over the Quranic verses inscribed in glazed tiles on the walls. For a long time, I hated the French.

I should add, though, that J.J. Marcel, orientalist and director of the Arabic printing press, and Zaynab's ardent mentor, literally risked his life at al-Azhar to save many valuable manuscripts, among them a precious six-century-old Quran, even as the place was being trashed and smashed and desecrated by his fellow countrymen in their frenzied rage of revenge.

When vengeance had been taken and life had returned more or less to what had come to be considered normal, Napoleon had nine leading shaykhs arrested, Sharqawi and Sadat at their head. That Shaykh Khalil wasn't among the arrested was like the kiss of Judas. Father made it even worse by prevailing upon Napoleon to have the arrested shaykhs transferred from the Citadel prison to our house, thinking they would be safe with us. Napoleon was only too glad to give his good friend Shaykh Khalil custody of the prisoners. When I found out about it I was aghast, and I communicated my feelings to Father as politely as I could, as an obedient and respectful son.

"Father, are you sure of the wisdom of this? Making our house into a French prison for Egyptian prisoners?"

"They will be safe here with us."

"Yes, but what about us? What happens when the French leave? Do we go to France with them?"

"They will never leave. Though we may hate them, they are here to stay. The revolt proved that."

"What if one day the sultan sends a real army?"

Father scoffed at the suggestion. We revolted, and where were the Ottomans and Mamliks? We revolted and failed because they failed to show up as promised. From now on, he said, we had to think and act for ourselves; we had to give up any ideas about getting help from the Ottomans and live as best we could with our present rulers.

Zaynab agreed. "Better we live in peace and learn what we can from them before we destroy what we have left. Look what happened to the institute."

Yes, the institute. How could I forget? During the first hours of the revolt, a mob had broken into one of the palaces housing the institute and had smashed and torn up everything in sight: astronomical equipment, mechanical calculators, chemical apparatus, books. The damage would have been much worse if the savants had not taken up arms and fought off the attackers. Zaynab was more depressed by the damage done to the institute than by what the soldiers had done to our al-Azhar. I shared her feelings about the damage done to her precious institute, but I took it as another symptom of our family's blindness that her feelings weren't balanced by the wounds inflicted on our own Egyptian Islamic institute.

We had gone down the road of no return. Our villa had been turned into a French prison for nine elderly shaykhs; the French chief of finance, Monsieur Esteve, was our permanent houseguest; Father was bosom buddies with Bonaparte; and my liberated sister worshipped the stones of a French institute more than she did al-Azhar, more even than the holy stone of the Ka'aba in Mecca.

Maybe Father and Zaynab were right: maybe I was too cowardly; I wasn't sure. I wasn't sure of much anymore. But of one thing I was sure—I felt it in my bones—and that was that something terrible would happen to our family because we had cozied up to the French. My fears were heightened the next day when, at the al-Azhar Mosque for prayers, I overheard some shaykhs, among them my friend Faysal, Shaykh Sharqawi's son, asking themselves if Shaykh Khalil was protecting the incarcerated shaykhs in his home or working for the French as a prison guard.

After prayers, Faysal spoke to me and we commiserated about the filthy things the French had done to our al-Azhar, and before we parted he warned me to be careful—people were talking, the Bakri family was being accused of serving the French too eagerly. I thanked him for the warning, told him I could understand the reason for the gossip about us, and explained Father's altruistic reasons for keeping the imprisoned shaykhs in our house. Faysal said that he believed me, but what he believed was inconsequential; it was what others believed that could be troublesome. Before leaving, he gave me a friendly hug and repeated, "Be careful."

8

AFTER THE NINE SHAYKHS had been incarcerated in our house long enough for the people of Cairo to be well aware that Shaykh Khalil had agreed to be prison keeper for the French, Napoleon ordered them transferred back to the Citadel. They were taken in the middle of the night. It was always in the deepest part of night that the French did such things. Father tried his best to keep the troops from taking them, but Napoleon convinced him that they were only being taken for questioning. Shaykhs Sharqawi, Sadat, and Sawi were released a few days later. The less important remaining six were secretly executed, their bodies flung over an isolated cliff of the Muqattam Plateau and not discovered until many days had passed. On each of those days, Father banged on the doors of the Citadel, demanding that the six shaykhs be released to his custody, and each day he was told they were still being interrogated and would soon be released, and all the while the six bodies were rotting in a ravine at the bottom of Muqattam. At last, with rumors rife, Napoleon admitted to Father that the shaykhs had been executed without his orders. The responsible officer would be court-martialed.

Father was able to retrieve their bodies and give them a proper funeral, but that didn't help deflect public suspicion that he was somehow involved in their murders. That should have been more than lesson enough for Father to stay clear of Bonaparte. But no, Father had a religious mission. He would not be deterred or cautioned. To this day I truly believe that the old man believed in what he was doing, and I also truly believe he had grand visions of himself in the duplicitous game of beat the devil that he was playing with Bonaparte. The visions so filled his eyes that they blinded him to the dangers of the game.

Not too long after the corpses of the shaykhs were found, Bonaparte appointed Father president of the special diwan, and he accepted. Bonaparte then had the diwan appoint Father rector of al-Azhar. Father accepted. Bonaparte had him elevated to Naqib al-Ashraf, the highest religious honor in Egypt. Father accepted. Every day it was another office, another honorary title, another ceremonial gift: a thoroughbred stallion, a saddle decorated with silver and semiprecious stones, a cloak of rare fur decorated with precious stones, a banquet in his honor. Father gave Bonaparte rich gifts in return. They were inseparable.

When the Prophet's birthday rolled around, Napoleon gave Father several hundred gold riyals to pay for the celebration. Most people thought it improper to celebrate it while under French occupation, much less to take money from the Christian enemy for the pious occasion. Father argued that since the French took the money from the people in taxes to begin with, it was properly Muslim money, and that if we waited until the French disappeared from Egypt, we might never celebrate the Prophet's birthday or any religious holiday.

So celebrated it was, and in a style grander than anything that had been seen under the Mamluks or Ottomans, and perhaps the Abbasids, Fatimids, and Ayyubids, for that matter. Cairo was illuminated over three days of festivities: there were fireworks, rockets, parades, and military marching bands playing their strange French music, sometimes on rafts in the middle of the Muski Canal or Azbakiyya Lake. The concluding event was a sumptuous ceremonial banquet at our house attended by Napoleon, his top generals, and the creme de la creme of the savants: Venture de Paradise, Marcel, Jaubert, Berthollet, Fourier, Savigny, Monge, Saint-Hilaire, Vivant-Denon, Quesnot, Lefevre, Costaz—and answering to them on the Egyptian side of the crème de la crème, forty leading shaykhs and notables of Cairo: Sharqawi, Sadat, Musa, Sawi, and the rest, including a few Copts and Jews and European merchants, and of course the Italian merchant Carlos Rosetti, who seemed to have lived in Egypt since before the pyramids were built. Also attending was an anonymous Dane, a Dutchman, and even a crazy English explorer, Bruce something or other, who claimed he was searching for the source of the Nile; he had been residing in Cairo when the French invaded and had stayed for the adventure. It was Cairo's first truly international event since Julius Caesar sailed the Nile with Cleopatra.

As for food, there were French dishes as well as Egyptian, twenty tables of them. The French guests sat on chairs at tables set with cutlery and bottles of wine, cognac, and champagne. The Egyptians sat on cushions and ate with their hands from trays. The savants, hostile as ever to the lead-headed sulfur snorters, joined the shaykhs on cushions and ate "oriental." Disguised as a student in caftan and turban, Zaynab sat cozily on cushions like a pet kitten, surrounded by her fawning orientalist trinity of Marcel, Jaubert, and Jean Michel Venture de Paradise, all proudly smiling at their prodigy, or so it seemed to me—I was as envious as ever. Napoleon and Father sat at a table at the head of the banquet. Father had by then learned to use a knife and fork.

The whole affair was sickening. So accustomed or benumbed had we become to French ways that the shaykhs seemed not to notice or care about the many bottles of alcohol that surrounded the trays of food. Napoleon recited a poem in Arabic that he had memorized eulogizing the Prophet, and I swear the shaykhs applauded more loudly than the Europeans. The two groups toasted each other, the French raising their glasses of wine, the shaykhs their glasses of rosewater, though a few of the old boys were drinking from opaque cups to conceal the wine and cognac they couldn't resist. It was a sight to behold. A few weeks earlier we had been killing the French, and now here we were, feasting and drinking with them in celebration of the Prophet's birthday. How we had caved in to them! There was something soft and gooey about Egyptians and their quickness to surrender, like those melting chocolate-cream cakes that the French had introduced us to, soft and gooey to the core.

Our house thereafter was an unofficial center of French-Egyptian administrative interaction—that is, a kind of business bureau for everything imaginable: petitioners wanting Father to intercede with the French on their behalf for one reason or another, or needing a contract to supply the French with some service or other, or seeking exemption from paying taxes on anything from obtaining a liquor license to selling a piece of property. There wasn't a moment that our house wasn't besieged by a dozen people or more beseeching Father for some favor or service. Our once-peaceful home was turned into a government halfway house that made it seem like

Egyptians could get nothing done of an official nature without resorting to the intermediary efforts of Shaykh Khalil. The place got so hectic at times that our uninvited houseguest, Director of Finance Monsieur Esteve, threatened to leave us. I swear, is it possible that there is any people on God's earth more haughty than the French?

With the revolt crushed, the institute was repaired, refurbished, and reopened. More and more locals visited it. The general populace came to accept the French more and more, grudgingly at first, then open-armed. After pondering the matter, I concluded that the failed revolt had convinced the people, as it had Father, that the French were a permanent fixture in Egypt and we'd best accept our fate and get on with life, stuck as we were with them, for better or worse. If we could make the effort for the better, then maybe the French would too, and life would be tolerable. Maybe some of our Egyptian generosity and good-natured humor would rub onto them and they wouldn't be so damned arrogant. Of course, there were those Egyptians who never accepted the French at all, just as there were those who threw themselves into their arms like she-camels in heat.

Our females generally chose to play the latter. A good number of girls and women had gone French before the revolt; but after it, when the dust had settled and it was deemed safe, they rushed to the French like the Nile to the sea. Upper-class women learned French and started dressing French. Marriages between them and French officers, which had been something of an event before, now had become almost commonplace, although even before the revolt there were enough mixed marriages that the shaykhs had been obliged to issue a legal opinion allowing them as long as the men went through some quick and easy religious conversion. It was no more than a perfunctory ritual for the shaykhs to save face by preserving a social semblance of religious propriety, and, as I previously mentioned, it didn't even require circumcision, much to the disappointment of the professional cutters. What had been considered shameful before became, if not exactly fashionable, acceptable. Some fathers acquiesced in their daughters' marrying Frenchmen. Some, because of the abundant money the French seemed to have, actually encouraged it. Most fathers whose daughters married Frenchmen had no say in it; if a father denied permission, the girl just did it anyway and her family couldn't do a thing because she was now protected. Families either passively accepted what they could not prevent or they pretended to, because by openly opposing it, they would in the end be humiliated by either the daughter or her French protectors. The French even gave women the right to divorce and inherit equally with men. One woman was now legally equal to one man; in court, her testimony carried the same weight as a man's. Our balls were being squeezed off turn by turn—first one, then another and another. What kind of mad, upside-down society did these people live in back in France?

Needless to say, Zaynab didn't see it that way. For example, Sitt Hawa—the woman Father covered in a rug when she came limping by our house naked after having been raped by a tribe of wild bedouin and later repudiated by her husband, a Mamluk bey who had fled—well, Sitt Hawa married Niqula Qabtan, some Levantine in French service, and Zaynab rejoiced as if it were a blessed event.

"What to rejoice?" I asked her, wounded, emasculated, confused. "What can a Frenchman give a woman that a Muslim can't give more and better?"

"Respect" she exclaimed peremptorily, her old persnickety sister superior self again now that we were back at the institute busily at work translating—under Venture de Paradis's direction—a copy of Montesquieu's *Esprit des Loi*.

"Who could respect women more than we do?" I defended, searching the French-Arabic lexicon for the meaning of a French word that apparently had no Arabic equivalent.

"To protect is not to respect."

"These savants at the institute have spoiled you rotten!"

"Yes, I suppose they have."

"They've filled your head with a lot of nonsense. They're seducing you through empty flattery."

"I'll just have to suffer through it, I guess."

"Bitch!"

"What's wrong with you?"

"You're starting to think so much like a Frenchwoman, why don't you dress like one?"

"I'm happy the way I dress. What am I doing that's French other than studying their language?"

"Water takes the shape of the vessel."

"What's that supposed to mean?"

"If you fill your head with their language, you'll fill their clothes with your body, whether you know it or not."

She laughed. "You sound stranger than Father."

"And you act like Father—sucking up to the French."

"Then maybe I will wear a French dress one day. For now I'm happy with the way my body fills my clothes, thank you."

"Watch that you don't dishonor yourself."

"Tell me, brother, how do men dishonor themselves? Maybe if you had a Frenchwoman, you'd learn something."

"Just watch it, bitch! The French aren't going to be here forever!"

Back at home, I slammed the door and nursed my wounds in the solitude of my room, reading verses of the Quran, which I'd opened randomly to (wouldn't you know it) the sura called The Women, in which God reveals the law making females half a man in matters of litigation, testimony, and inheritance. Unable to shake my fit of temper, and muttering, "How could the French make into one what God made to be half?" I slammed the Holy Book shut and took up my prayer beads, rubbing them furiously between my fingers while repeating one of the ninety-nine names of God with each bead, and ended by flinging the string of beads across the room before I had reached even thirty. They hit the wall and spilled across the floor from their broken string, as scattered as the pieces of my broken soul. *The damn bitch!* I couldn't control my jealousy of her. The clarity of vision and optimism with which she accepted our changing conditions under the French were torture to me. Her revelry in what she called liberty was my misery. Adding salt to the wound, as if the wound weren't deep enough, she had gone through four chapters of Montesquieu to my one and a half! Arrogant, French in-the-making bitch!

And what the hell was the big deal with this thing called "respect" she kept hitting me with?

Every indication pointed to the French being here until Judgment Day. Everyday Cairo became more and more Paris on the Nile. The French instituted a long series of public festivals, one after the other, in celebration of one occasion or another. The anniversary of the revolution, the Christian

New Year, the Muslim New Year, Bastille Day, the rise of the Nile, the beheading of Louis XVI, the flight of the Prophet from Mecca to Medina—even something as frivolous as the sun entering a new sign of the zodiac was celebrated by the French, and celebrated with a zeal that could only be described as religious. It was enough to make one suspect that the revolutionary French had substituted sun and nature worship for their traditional Christianity, just as they had substituted the traditional names of the months for names reflecting nature's changes during the year: Brumaire, Thermidore, Fructidore, and so forth. Each festival was celebrated with fireworks and huge bonfires, music, dancing, parades, and feasting and drinking and singing through the night. Shops and markets were kept open until dawn in the brightly illuminated streets, while in the canals and river, white-sailed falukas filled with tipsy girls and soldiers left in their wake the laughter and singing of joyous youth, and the whiff of burning hashish that was carried to shore by the autumn breeze off the desert.

One of these celebrations was unforgettable. Printed posters tacked up all over the city boldly announced that on the occasion of the sun entering Virgo, French engineers would perform a feat never before seen in the land of Egypt or anywhere in the world: four men would ascend high into the air and sail over the countryside, to descend far away. People couldn't talk about anything else. Men flying! Father said if God had intended men to fly, He would have given them wings. Zaynab, always ready with a smart remark, snapped back, "Then how is it they sail over water and don't have duck's feet? And why do ostriches have wings?"

Some shaykhs said it was just a French conspiracy to debunk the story of Muhammad's midnight journey to Jerusalem on the back of the angelic horse, Buraq. Then the shaykhs started debating the issue in terms of high scholastic theology based on Aristotelian theories of time, motion, gravity, natural place, and the structure of matter. One scholar claimed it was indeed possible for men to fly, according to the high Islamic theology of time being atomistic, which annihilated cause and effect and natural law, preserving God's power of making miracles that went against all that Greek stuff. The scholar who was arguing this claimed that the French savants must have been able to calculate with their astronomical equipment and mathematics when a moment of nontime would occur, and it would be then, between two atoms of time, that the men would fly up to the sky.

When it got around town that a shaykh of al-Azhar had proven that men could fly, the odds became sixty to one that men could fly, and even some of the shayhks started laying bets.

The day of the promised spectacle at last arrived. People's excitement was at fever pitch. A high wooden structure had been erected in the middle of Azbakiyya and anchored firmly to the ground; apparently the men were going to leap up to heaven from the top of it. Father and several dozen other shaykhs sat solemnly with a few dozen notables on a platform reserved for them. Another platform was reserved for the European community. Bonaparte and his officers had their reserved area, and the savants theirs. The rest of us just stood or sat on the ground, as close to the ropes as we could get.

By noon the place was packed. Balconies and rooftops were so crammed with excited people struggling to get a good view of the show that a number of them fell to their deaths in a kind of prelude to the spectacle of flying men, though the expectation was to see them flying up, not down. When the excitement of the crowd was at its peak, a wagon was rolled out, and from it was taken a huge bundle of material that was hoisted by pulleys to the top of the wooden structure and unfolded, like a mountainous umbrella. The immense field of cloth had been stitched together in three broad horizontal bands—the uppermost red, the middle blue, the lower white, reminding me of a squashed rosette. The engineers attached a basketlike carriage to ropes at the lower hem of the cloth, and then ignited several naptha canisters and, using bellows, pumped the hot air produced by the burning naptha into the innards of the cloth that was suspended from the top of the structure. The hot air that was pumped inside rose to the top, and the sagging rosette quivered to life, its overlapping folds filling and puffing up, as if the breath of life were indeed being blown into the inanimate beast. People screamed. The beastly thing slowly billowed out like a painted octopus, its loose folds expanding little by little until, after an hour of bellowing, it took on a spherical shape (really more like a bulbous teardrop) and strained upward from the ropes that tied it to the basket, which was anchored to the ground. The puffed-up beast looked about to tear itself apart or break loose from its moorings to attack us. Mother fainted.

Some of the burning naptha canisters were extinguished so that only enough hot air was pumped in to maintain a steady level of buoyancy. Then, when all was ready, a military band struck up with a roll of drums, and four men dressed in shiny uniforms of red, white, and blue, with bonnets and boots to match, popped out of a horse-drawn carriage, pranced to the basket in a kind of lively, hand-waving skip that was between a dance and a march, and then, after saluting Napoleon, who had taken his place in front of his generals on the platform, the four gaily colored wingless birds nimbly hopped into the basket. Band playing, drums rolling, cymbals crashing, the ropes were untied and the balloon lifted slowly from the ground. The crowd gasped. A few women screamed. Mother opened her eyes to look and, hands clutching her breast, fainted again, this time most convincingly. The four men waved, and as the balloon slowly lifted them up, they tossed flowers down upon the gaping spectators. At a certain height, one of them threw a few sacks of sand from the basket and they floated high into the blue. Hushed murmurs of "God is great" rose from the astonished crowd. Zaynab clapped enthusiastically. Noha jumped up and down in sheer joy. Men were indeed flying!

Caught by the desert wind, the pear-shaped octopus was carried toward the river, up and away—a red, white, and blue bubble soaring through the cloudless sky—and soon the basket beneath it was just a speck. Mother, revived, was gawking in terror at the rapidly diminishing bubble. "Will they really go up to heaven?" she asked.

"They will once they reach Jerusalem and catch the flying horse," quipped Zaynab, whose blasphemy flabbergasted me.

When the bubble was almost out of sight, Father joined us for the journey home. "What's so wonderful about filling a sheet with hot air?" he asked.

"I'll tell you, Father. It will not be long before these Europeans are dropping grenades and bombs on our cities from the sky while we're still waving swords at them," I replied, staggered by his blindness to the possibilities of what we had just witnessed. That he couldn't foresee the next generation of European soldiers dropping bombs on us, or zapping us from above with Berthollet's bolts of electricity, or swarms of kites and balloons raining death and destruction, frying us and our cities to a crisp as we bravely fought on with kitchen knives and sharpened sticks, that Father couldn't see this coming cataclysm crushed any faith I had in him as a leader, and any hope I had in our future.

Napoleon did everything to divert our attention from the politics of foreign rule. One spectacle followed another. No sooner had the flying men in a balloon come and gone than we were treated to a festival in celebration of the new moon. Then came Napoleon's ultimate weapon in making Cairo Paris on the Nile. It was called Tivoli.

Patterned after the Tivoli Gardens of Paris, Tivoli Cairo became the principal center of entertainment and fraternization between the French and Egyptians. Built in an area of Azbakiyya by the canal where most of the French and other Europeans now lived, along with a community of Egyptian Jews and Christians who were growing rich serving the French, Tivoli encompassed a vast area of verdant gardens, palm-shaded parks and promenades, and a carefully manicured green zone, at the center of which stood a complex of substantially built edifices of brick and mortar that housed entertainments of every sort: clowns, jugglers, singers, dancers, musicians, magicians, wrestlers, snake charmers, game rooms for billiards and cards, gambling and dancing halls, reading rooms, restaurants, cafés, taverns. The centerpiece of the great Tivoli entertainment complex was the Grand Hall, where men and women could dine and dance to music. Seeing French men and women dancing in each other's arms had come as a shock. At first we thought they were having sex through their clothes. But once over the shock, we observed how different their dancing was from ours. First, with us, men and women didn't dance together. When our girls or women danced, they danced alone, almost naked, and it was erotic, the dancer's motions a virtual simulation of sex—not at all the way the French danced, even though men and women danced close together. It was strange to us and hard to understand. They touched each other and held each other as they moved smoothly with the music, and though sex may have been on their minds and a culmination of the evening, they looked to be enjoying the moment and the music, with sex the furthest thing from their thoughts. I couldn't for the life of me figure out these people and their customs.

Tivoli also had outside areas for eating, drinking, and relaxing. For more frivolous moods, there were carousels, swings, seesaws, all kinds of simple amusements we had never seen before. There were also animal rides: donkey, mule, horse, camel—it still dumbfounded us that people would pay money to ride an animal with no other purpose than to ride it in a big circle. Where they got on was where they got off, no matter how big the circle. They didn't go anywhere. The French were a mystery that defied unraveling.

Around the buildings and play areas there were outside pavilions where people gathered at scheduled hours to hear music. The French military band performed every day, and soldiers in brilliant uniforms marched up and down the parade grounds executing a remarkable series of turns, retreats, and charges, and doing all sorts of queer antics with their rifles. The surviving Mamluks who had run for their lives from the French and returned in rags, and were now reduced to begging in the streets for food from the French, had the audacity to laugh in scorn at the way the soldiers marched.

These poor, ragged Mamluks joined the great number of the city's beggars that congregated around the vast grounds of Tivoli. It got so congested with them that the French rounded them all up, put the sick and deformed ones in hospitals, and gave the healthy ones the choice of either working as street cleaners and garbage collectors or being forced into the desert. Posters reading "Clean It or Leave It" in big letters in French and Arabic were put up all over the city in a campaign to keep it clean and at the same time free of the beggars, hustlers, and tricksters that buzzed around the French Quarter and Tivoli like bees around flowers and flies around excrement.

When Tivoli opened, it was at first frequented only by the military and their female companions. But it wasn't long before a number of our Christians and Jews joined the French, aping them imperfectly as always, which earned them contempt from the French and hostility from the Muslims. After the Christians and Jews came the Muslims, who like the Christians and Jews made a mockery of themselves showing off their few phrases of atrociously pronounced French and smoking French cigarettes. Tivoli rang with excitement. Zaynab and I were among the early wave of respectable Muslims to have an experimental look at it. I told her I highly disapproved of the place, and went there every evening I could.

Tivoli became the nexus of social life, where East and West met in relaxation and recreation. It was where many Franco-Egyptian business ventures were conceived, many friendly and romantic liaisons born, and many hearts broken. Nightly, the music poured out onto the canal, melded with the laughter and the singing; the angry accusations of arguing lovers;

the raucous revelry of clowns, buffoons, and bursting balloons, of gamblers, hustlers, card sharks, and clacking billiard balls, of hawkers and tricksters out to cheat a coin from some French sucker. Village girls in cheap, cotton French-style dresses hung on to the arms of their corporals. Upper-class women and girls—that is, women left behind by the Mamluks; daughters of merchants, professionals, scribes, and administrative officials; daughters of landowners and shaykhs—they went for the officers in brilliant uniforms. It was amusing to see how the corresponding classes of these two societies found each other.

Tivoli at night turned into a garden of love, as though it had been lifted right out of our *Thousand and One Nights*. Couples hid in the darkness of the palms, away from the colored lanterns that lit up the place in festive gaiety. Moans of lovers by the edge of the lake sometimes broke through the music, reaching the dance hall, where former wives of Mamluks draped in silk caftans danced in the arms of major generals, and French women dressed in true revolutionary fashion, as hussars in caps, boots, and swords, held themselves as proudly as their officer consorts. Tivoli was beautiful, ugly, vulgar, exciting. I hated it. I couldn't stay away from it.

Zaynab would go dressed in the caftan and turban of an al-Azhar student, but no longer to disguise herself. Her tight sash and the rakish way she tilted her turban back, with teasing locks of hair falling from under it, made her sex obvious. In fact, her mode of dress was a statement no less stark than that of the French women in their military uniforms.

Many romances were born in Tivoli. One evening while attending a banquet, we were invited into the Grand Hall of the casino and were sitting at a table with Marcel, Jaubert, and Jean-Michel, when a boisterous party of young officers swaggered in and seated themselves around a table next to ours. They ordered a bottle of cognac and were eyeing the Egyptian girls who had come there hoping to meet an officer, when one of the men turned in his chair and began boldly staring at Zaynab. I gave him a look as though to tell him to look somewhere else before I broke his neck, but his blue eyes were so riveted to her that he didn't notice me. The three savants were also disturbed by the young officer's liberal gaze at their prize protégé. I was about to say something, but then I saw that there was no affront in the man's eyes, only an intense, searching, innocent look, as though he were trying to comprehend an ecstatic vision, like a Sufi beholding the angelic epiphanies. Then I vaguely recalled having seen those awe-filled blue eyes somewhere, and I tried to place the occasion. I turned to ask Zaynab how we knew him and saw her staring back at him with an intensity no less than his. It took a moment for my question to register. "The day of the occupation," she explained.

"Right! The one you saved!"

"Saved?" Marcel was frowning, perturbed.

"He fainted from the heat and fell from his horse," she explained, making Venture de Paradise chuckle and say how typical, a cavalry officer falling from his horse without the decency of having been shot.

"Give him time," Jaubert said. "He'll get himself shot."

"No doubt," Venture agreed. "Look how starry-eyed the boy is. What did you do to him, my girl?"

Zaynab blushed, then blushed deeper when the young officer started over. He bowed to us and asked Venture to ask her if she was the girl who had brought him water that day. Ask her yourself, Venture returned. Confused, the young officer addressed her in French, and when Zaynab rejoined in his language, with what I took to be pretty good pronunciation, that she was indeed the girl, his eyes widened in astonishment, and it was a moment before he regained himself and thanked her for saving his life.

Marcel was measuring the officer up and down. "Tell us, Lieutenant, how was it you fell from your horse?"

"I am a captain. Captain Raymond Bertrand Belmond." He bowed slightly.

"Next time smear glue on your saddle. No, better not. You might fall out of your captain's britches." The young captain stiffened. Marcel then asked, "Were you one of those brave cavalrymen who had their horses shit all over al-Azhar Mosque?"

Belmond's blue eyes remained icily on Marcel. "No. I was defending you and the rest of the asses in your institute." He turned to Zaynab. "Please accept my gratitude. I will never forget that moment. Your face and goodness are locked in my heart and mind forever."

"That's good," Marcel interrupted testily. "Both mind and heart. If you lose them in one place, you'll have them in the other. But be careful not to break your mind the next time you fall on your ass from your horse or donkey or whatever it is you mount."

Captain Belmond ignored him. "My Egyptian Joan of Arc, who saved the life of a simple soldier of France, I thank you." He bowed again, kissed

Zaynab's hand, and rejoined his fellow officers. Zaynab was blushing so deeply, and no doubt her heart pounding so hard, she didn't say a word more.

"Well!" exclaimed Venture breaking our silence. "Egyptian Joan of Arc! Didn't I tell you? The boy's a hopeless romantic."

"A dumb sulfur snorter!" snapped Jaubert.

Zaynab was biting her lip. "Why were you so hard with him?"

"How else do you treat a fool?" replied Marcel.

"Who is Joan of Arc?" she asked.

Just then the music stopped. The soldiers present snapped to attention. Napoleon and his generals entered in a clattering glitter of uniforms and swords. One of the generals, hardly older than a boy and impossibly handsome, was hanging on to Napoleon's arm like a lover. Zaynab and I exchanged looks. The orchestra struck up their national anthem, another ridiculous innovation: a song that was supposed to represent a country. Whoever heard of such imbecility? When the robust singing came to an end and Napoleon and his officers took seats at a table reserved for them, Napoleon put his arm around his little boy general and kissed him on the cheek.

"Now I see why Napoleon didn't choose an Egyptian girl," I remarked. "Does the army enroll boys for the enjoyment of their generals?"

"She's neither boy nor officer," replied Jaubert. "She's Madame Pauline Foure. Our real commander in chief."

Madame Foure removed her hussar's bonnet to release a field of golden hair that, with a shake of her head, tumbled to her shoulders in long, undulating waves, like flax in the summer sun, turning her into a woman of extraordinary beauty.

"He met her here at Tivoli," Jaubert explained, and then told us the story, which added to the *Thousand and One Nights* aura of the place.

Madame Pauline Foure was an officer's wife who had smuggled herself aboard a military transport ship dressed as a soldier. She and her husband had been married only days before the fleet departed Toulon, and not wanting to be apart, they decided to make the invasion of Egypt their honeymoon. The young beauty captivated the commander in chief the moment he saw her and she set her big blue eyes on him.

"What about her husband?" Zaynab's attention kept drifting from Madame Pauline Foure to Captain Raymond Bertrand Belmond. My precocious sister had shed the protective cover of a veil before having mastered control of her eyes.

"He was conveniently sent on a secret mission to Malta," Jaubert continued. "From Malta he was to be sent to Italy, and from Italy to France. The plan was to keep him going from place to place for a few years. But the British fleet captured his ship a day out of Alexandria, and instead of taking him prisoner, they sent him back to Egypt. They must have known what was going on through their spies here and wanted to embarrass Bonaparte."

"Did they?"

"Hardly. By the time Lieutenant Foure arrived back in Egypt, Pauline was set up in a palace adjoining Bonaparte's. He tried to keep the lieutenant in Alexandria, but the young man suspected something and came on his own to Cairo and saw what was what. When Pauline refused to leave her palace, the lieutenant was granted a military divorce. The divorce isn't legal in France, but that doesn't matter here."

"The lieutenant is still here?"

"No. His request for transfer was granted. He's back in France, trying to legalize the military divorce."

"Divorce is hard to get for a man whose wife sleeps with another man?" I asked.

"It's a matter of proof."

"Proof?"

"It isn't easy to get a divorce in Europe, for the man or the woman."

"At least we're more advanced than Europe when it comes to that," I quipped.

"Not when it's the woman who wants the divorce, dear brother." Zaynab's eyes returned to Pauline. "She's the most beautiful woman I've ever seen."

"There's talk of Napoleon divorcing Josephine to marry her," Jaubert said. "He wants a son, and Josephine doesn't seem able to give babies."

Zaynab smiled in sarcasm. "It couldn't be his fault, could it?" From Pauline, she glanced back at Captain Belmond, whose eyes, I covertly observed, never left her.

"Does Napoleon's Egyptian girl impugn the conquering hero's virility?" Marcel's question had a grating edge to it. His thin, nervous laugh cracked and sputtered to an end, freezing on the lips of his taut mouth. The pupils of his eyes were cold, dark crystals burning into her. I wondered, Was it Napoleon or Captain Belmond who had aroused his jealousy?

"What does impugn mean?" she asked.

"Perhaps," he snapped in answer, "you should concentrate more on your French and not gawk like a simpleton at gaudy uniforms." Zaynab regarded him in astonishment. Venture and Jaubert looked away.

Marcel's exposure of emotion dismayed me. I hadn't known that the French were capable of such feelings, that beneath their cool, mannered exterior, Frenchmen could feel the same jealous anger as Egyptian men when it came to women. I could have hugged Marcel for it. "Now you know why we keep our females veiled," I said.

Napoleon looked over and saw Zaynab and his savants. When he came to greet them, he called Zaynab "Zenobia, Queen of the East" and kissed her on the cheeks. It was a while before he noticed me: "Ah yes, Zaynab's brother!" he exclaimed with false enthusiasm. He searched my face in quest of a name to go with it. "Zayd! No—Yazid!"

"Zaki."

"Of course, Zaki! I could never forget." He patted me on the turban as if I were some kind of a pet and invited Zaynab to his table to meet Madame Foure. "It would be good for you to have a young Frenchwoman as a companion, no?" Zaynab nodded in agreement. Napoleon took her by the arm and, beckoning the rest of us to follow, led her to his table. Everyone at every table in the casino watched them go, arm in arm.

Marcel said that he hoped Zaynab would be amused by those military peacocks.

"Don't be hard," Venture told him calmly. "She's a young girl."

"Liberation is strong wine when it comes all at once," Jaubert said.

"For females it shouldn't come at all," I rejoined.

"You're right!" Marcel agreed. "The veil and the harem."

"Now, now." Venture put a fatherly arm around Marcel's shoulder. "She's still finding herself."

"I wish her luck finding herself with them!" Marcel got to his feet.

"Shall we join them?" I asked.

"And go brain-dead with boredom talking about tactics?" Marcel said he was going back to the institute; he had work to do. "You'd better look after your sister."

Venture and Jaubert left with him.

As I was heading for Napoleon's table, Captain Belmond rushed over and seized my arm, asking excitedly, "Who is that girl?"

"You don't know?"

"No! Tell me! How does General Bonaparte know her?"

"Why, she's his Egyptian girl, that's who she is—Zenobia, his queen of the East."

He stared at me, stunned, as though his saving angel's wings had been clipped. I pulled my arm from his grasp and left him standing there, proud of my halting French and feeling as haughty as a Frenchman.

Napoleon introduced Zaynab to Madame Foure and his generals. The golden-haired Frenchwoman regarded the younger woman in turban and caftan as though she didn't appreciate the competition, but soon they were chattering away in French like old friends, with Julius Caesar beaming at his two Cleopatras. I stood unnoticed at the end of the long table. One of the generals, thinking me a waiter, called me "boy" and ordered me to fetch four bottles of champagne. It didn't matter. My ego was by now so bruised, scarred, and scabbed over in wounds it had grown a hide of leather.

Zaynab and Pauline Foure were chirping away like birds of a feather who'd found each other after years on a desert island. Different feathers from different worlds, but under them two young women discovering each other—one a virgin in scholar's turban and caftan, the other an adulteress in hussar's uniform and boots, both pretending to be men in a man's world but knowing they were desirable women made all the more desirable by the audacity of their pretense.

Madame Pauline. I had never known eyes could be as deep blue or hair as soft and golden as Madame Pauline's—or breasts as white and wonderfully plump. Pressed together as they were in the specially tailored low-cut bodice of her hussar's uniform, they appeared to be pushing each other out of their crowded confines to get a breath of fresh air. The disgusting sight of them stole my breath away and sent fire raging up and down from my loins, loosening my knees in lust. When at last I was able to tear my eyes from those poor breasts trying to free themselves, I took a deep breath and recited verses from the Quran until the attack of hot blood had subsided somewhat.

I was too far down the table to hear what the two Cleopatras were saying, but I saw Pauline's eyes search across the hall in a long arc as Zaynab was whispering in her ear. When her eyes stopped, I discovered that the object of their search was none other than Captain Raymond Bertrand Belmond, who was getting ready to leave by himself. Pauline jotted something on a card that she gave to Napoleon, who read what was on it, smiled, and then handed it to his aide-de-camp and brother-in-law, Eugene Beauharnaise, who in turn handed it to one of his aides, who gave it to a junior officer. The officer, after making a few inquiries of other officers, headed across the hall, intercepting Captain Belmond as he was on his way out.

Zaynab removed her turban, shook loose her long, dark hair, as she had seen Pauline do earlier, and smiled to receive her captain, who, gazing into her eyes as he prepared to sit next to her, looked like he was about to fall off his horse again. My eyes went from the virgin to the adulteress. Even from the opposite end of the long table, the blueness of her eyes drew mine into them. Her golden hair danced when she gave a jaunty toss of her head at some joke of Napoleon's, and as she laughed, her white breasts swelled upward, struggling to burst free. I poured myself a glass of forbidden wine to drench the rekindled flames, but it stoked the rage all the fiercer, so I refilled the glass. What difference did it make? Maybe father was right: the French had come and were here forever. If not, we'd all go down together, one big happy family.

9

NAPOLEON GAVE A BANQUET in Father's honor. It was originally to be in celebration of the vernal equinox, but when a cargo of champagne and cognac slipped through the British naval blockade and was unloaded in Alexandria and shipped up the Nile to Cairo, Bonaparte declared the celebration to be in honor of Franco-Egyptian unity, the spirit of which was embodied by Shaykh Khalil al-Bakri. For three nights the illuminated streets were filled with wobbly-kneed soldiers and the skies with showers of fireworks. We had grown used to that, but something new was added to this particular festivity.

On a high platform, French engineers raised an immense square frame made up of a latticework of crisscrossed planks. Lanterns were attached to the planks in such configurations that, when lit, they simulated actual objects. The people were delighted. One configuration looked like a giant camel. Then the men on the scaffolding rearranged the lanterns and it became a horse. Then it was the three great pyramids of Giza, a mosque, the Holy Ka'aba. It was amazing how precisely the juxtaposed lanterns resembled what they were supposed to, as though an artist had painted the object in colored light across the dark sky. One of the more complex configurations was that of a French soldier with his arm around a bearded man in robe and turban, while above the figures was written in Arabic GOD'S WILL MADE MANIFEST. This was followed by some verses from the Quran, and then several famous sayings of the Prophet, one of them being SEEK KNOWLEDGE THOUGH IT BE IN CHINA, and then the lanterns for CHINA were rearranged to read FRANCE. The final configuration was that of a bearded and turbaned figure in a robe. In case no one guessed, SHAYKH KHALIL AL-BAKRI was illuminated in Arabic beneath the figure. Above the figure was the word GOD. Beneath GOD shone the words EGYPT AND FRANCE, and beneath them were the words UNITY, STRENGTH, BROTHERHOOD.

The crowds were in open-mouthed awe, and then all the more so when the figures on the screen moved, simulating action, in black and white and then in color. Artillery thundered, military bands drummed and trumpeted, strutting soldiers in their brilliant uniforms twirled their rifles, rockets were hurled in fiery constellations, lighting up the sky, and the people gazed up at the splendid lantern-lit spectacles of many colors on the wooden screen. The literates of the crowd read the words for those who couldn't read, and without doubt, both literate and illiterate got the message, though either it meant nothing to them or they shrugged it off as just so much more cleverly executed French frivolity.

I appreciated the mechanics and methods of Napoleon's political genius, which in France may have been effective but in Egypt went for naught but amusing theater. When it came to holding a people down, Bonaparte's bombs and zaps of artificial lightning from flying balloons would be a far better bet than his illuminated messages wrapped in theatrical amusements, and in regard to the military modalities of destruction by fire and exploding metal, we didn't have a chance.

After the light and sound show came the banquet. Father sat next to Napoleon. At the banquet's conclusion, with fireworks gloriously canopying the sky, Napoleon draped an honorary cloak over Father's shoulders, embraced him and kissed him on both cheeks, and announced he was to be president of the special diwan and Naqib al-Ashraf for life. Father presented Napoleon with a silver-and-gold-covered Quran and returned the kisses. A few disgruntled shaykhs murmured that Shaykh al-Bakri didn't deserve the religious honor and that Napoleon had no authority to confer it, but most of the people were either too intoxicated by the martial music and spectacular amusements to care, or were actually convinced that Napoleon had done the right thing for the shaykh, who had been unfairly passed over before the arrival of the Franks.

Revolted by it all, I retreated to the promenade the French had built along the canal bank. In the light of the exploding rockets, I saw Zaynab among the strollers, between Pauline Foure and Captain Belmond. I caught up with them and angrily asked Zaynab what she thought she was doing, and without waiting for an answer I clenched my fists and turned to Belmond. "Don't you know it's a dishonor for my sister to be seen in public with a man?"

But before I could thrash him and pound him into the ground, Pauline grabbed my hand and pulled me to her side. "Behave yourself," she chided.

She kept hold of my hand as she led me down to the end of the cornice, where we hired a faluka to sail up the canal to the river. My insides were a molten inferno. We sat close together, and she was grasping my arm as I had seen French women do with their lovers, but I didn't know what to do, trembling as I was with sexual energy, but without the experience or knowledge of how to release or share it with Madame Foure, with whom I had fallen desperately in love. So we sailed up and down the river for an hour, watching the sky explode in fireworks, like my innards, and then returned to the canal and the cornice, where we docked and disembarked from the faluka.

"Come to my palace tomorrow," she said with a squeeze of my hand as we parted. "Nappy will be busy at military headquarters, planning his invasion of Syria." She said it slowly and distinctly so that I would understand, assuming correctly that my French was in need of all the help it could get. Then she kissed me good-bye on the cheek, the soft warmth of her lips and intoxicating perfume of her body melting my joints in desire.

That's how it began with Pauline and me.

I became a frequent visitor at Pauline's palace, as did Zaynab and Captain Belmond, and it was there that I came to understand Zaynab's infatuation with the man. His fine looks and dashing youth, his ardor and manners, and his rare mix of boyish innocence, sensitivity, and masculinity—not to mention his cavalry uniform and smell of horse and leather—all alchemically combined to endow in him a magnetic charm that, in comparison, left scholarly Marcel and Jaubert as gray, frayed, and nondescript as their academicians' cloaks. Belmond made me wonder if it was possible that Frenchmen in general, even soldiers, were at least a bit likeable once you got them to shed all that superior haughtiness they so adeptly dressed themselves in every morning.

One defect of his that stuck in my craw was his undisguised deference to Zaynab. It sickened me. It reflected my own enslavement to Pauline. I didn't make an issue of Zaynab meeting Belmond at Pauline's; it wouldn't have done any good if I had. And not being blind to the fact that the only reason Pauline bothered with me was so that I would not object to Zaynab's being with Belmond, I had every reason not to object. So powerful was my passion for Pauline that I agreed to pander on behalf of Zaynab. Out of a sense of duty to protect my sister, however, I tried halfheartedly to disenchant her of this soldier to whom she seemed so intensely drawn. As we were riding our donkeys to the institute the next day, I turned to her and asked what it was about Belmond that infatuated her.

"Infatuates me?" she returned, half smiling, half frowning.

"What do you like about him?"

"He makes me feel like a woman."

"Woman? Are you a woman now?"

"I'm still a virgin, if you have to know, but I know what it is to be a woman."

"And he makes you feel like one."

She fell silent for a long moment as she considered my question. All around us on the busy street, people were going about their daily affairs. My donkey brayed as a beggar ran in front of it.

"Yes," she replied at last. "He makes me *happy* to be a woman. Even proud to be one."

"Marcel doesn't do that?"

"How can I explain? With Belmond there's ... there's something. Passion, I suppose."

"Passion only enslaves you to your lowest instincts."

"It can give me strength."

"Strength for what?"

"For me to be proud as a woman. For the first time in my life, my passion can go into something meaningful. Life has meaning."

"My god, how the French have fuzzed up your mind."

"No, Zaki, they've cleared it. Tell me, where can a woman's passion be expressed in a proud way with us? Look at them. Like Mother. Whatever passion we have left by the time we become women is wasted in cunning

134

intrigues to keep their husbands interested in them and keep their position in the house. I don't want to waste myself having to do that. Belmond respects me. He's not jealous of my time at the institute. He's proud of the interest the savants show in me. You see? The more I'm valued, the more he values me, and the more I value myself—and him. The French call that a harmonious relationship. They say it is the door to love."

"Love? What's that?" We had reached the institute and were dismounting.

"Being happy. Raymond makes me happy to be a woman. It's as simple as that—or for me it is. Doesn't Pauline make you feel like a man?"

"I suppose." In truth, Pauline made me feel like a whimpering dog in heat, begging and sniffing for a smell of her body, but how could I tell my sister that? I was nothing but a plaything for Pauline, and accepting that, I accepted Belmond visiting my sister. And the young officer was not at all arrogant once I got to know him. In fact, he turned out to be quite likeable, an honest and sincere fellow who had a sense of honor not unlike mine, and so I had no qualms about his visiting Zaynab at Pauline's, as long as I was there too, and you'd better believe that I was there as often and as long as Pauline permitted.

The autumn days passed pleasantly. The sun's mild heat felt warm and comforting, and while we Egyptians enjoyed it, the pasty-faced French took to worshipping it as if seized by the spirit of ancient Egypt and the sun god Ra, and they did something we had never seen or even imagined: they stripped off half their clothing and lay in the sun. Yes, they would just lie there on their stomachs or backs, eyes closed and periodically turning themselves like skinned lambs roasting on a spit! At first we suspected it was a form or religious worship instituted by the French Revolution's rejection of Christianity, but it turned out to be no more than the French belief that the sun's rays were health inducing and that a tanned body looked good. Weird but true. Well, thank God, we already had our healthy tans and were spared having to imitate the French in that respect, but yes, on the French, it was true—their tans did exceedingly improve their otherwise sickly, bloodless, death-like whiteness. They began to look, in fact, healthy, and with that transformation, life appeared brighter, even happy—even with the continuing change of things, change being something Egyptians normally feared and shunned.

My head spun with the pace of events changing our lives. While

Zaynab and I were spending our time between the institute and Pauline's palace, where we met our respective infatuations, Napoleon and Father were busy spending a good deal of time together, exchanging visits and planning, among God knows what other things, the new Franco-Egyptian global commercial empire. At least once and sometimes twice a week, Napoleon would come to our villa to confer with Father, who was now the most important Egyptian in the country, having attained what he wanted: to be Napoleon's adviser, the grand vizier ordering the affairs of state for a sultan cut off from the conquered people by race, religion, language, and culture. Shaykh Khalil, scion of the Bakri clan, fox of foxes, had mastered the lion to become the "Egyptian Machiavelli," as Venture de Paradise had put it.

There was a mystery between Father and Napoleon. Napoleon periodically gave Father gifts, some wrapped up and secretly delivered. Among the gifts Napoleon openly gave him were young Turkish, Georgian, and Circassian slave boys, whose numbers grew to become Shaykh Khalil's own private Mamluk harem. In all, Bonaparte gave father twenty-five of them, each one a handsome, strapping lad between fourteen and twenty years old. A barracks had to be built for them next to the villa. They were a nuisance, a headache—scrapping all the time, a rowdy bunch of boys from the central Asian plains and highlands. When I asked Father why he needed all those boisterous and troublesome kids around, he merely shrugged and said they were given to him by Napoleon.

"But what for? What can you do with them?"

"They can help around the place."

"Help? They don't help. They only eat, drink, and fight. They're a waste of money."

"They're presents from Napoleon."

"What for? You're not a Mamluk emir. You don't need a bodyguard or a private army. Why did he give them to you?"

"We don't question the sultan's will. Excuse me—it's time to pray."

"It's not time yet."

"I'm doing supererogatory prayers."

And with that he withdrew into his private prayer room, which was now kept locked. He had never performed supererogatory prayers before. He had never locked his prayer room before.

"There's a mystery in our house." I was breakfasting on the upper balcony facing the gardens and the lake with Mother, Zaynab, and Noha. Several of Father's boy Mamluks were brawling down below in the garden, raising a hell of a noise. "Those accursed Mamluks!" I snapped. "I'd like to burn their barracks with them in it!"

"Thank God they're gone most of the time," Mother said.

"Not enough of the time," added Zaynab.

Noha asked, "What's wrong with them that you don't like them?"

"What's good about them?" I asked back. "What are they doing here?"

"I wonder where they go?" mused Mother, standing to look over the balcony. "They leave every morning, return to eat lunch, and then go out again. They always leave one by one, never together. Sometimes they stay out until late at night."

"How do you know?" I asked. "Are you spying on them?"

"I hear them. They're so loud they wake me up."

Their raucous roughhousing sounded like it had reached a howling climax. I threw an orange over the balcony in the direction of the barracks, hoping it would hit one of them on the head, the one place they wouldn't feel it. "Drunken louts!"

"Not all of them," Noha defended. "Rustam doesn't drink or stay out."

"Rustam?" My eyes narrowed on Noha. "Who's Rustam?"

Mother returned from the balustrade. "Rustam Raza. He's the head of them. Shaykh Khalil has promised Noha to him."

"To a Mamluk!" I screamed.

Mother sighed. "Worse. He's secretly a Christian. But who cares these days?"

I looked at Noha in disbelief. But why in disbelief? With all that had happened since the coming of the French a mere six months ago, incredulity should have been the least of my reactions to anything that involved our family. Zaynab expressed an attitude more attuned to our actual condition: she laughed.

"Father wants me to marry Napoleon and Noha to marry a Mamluk. He's scheming something, the old fox."

"With Noha and some slave Mamluk from the hills? How does that figure?" I asked.

"I don't know … maybe Bonaparte is planning a French-Mamluk army with Father's daughters leading it like two Joans of Arc."

"Who's this Joan?" Mother asked indignantly.

"The peasant girl who led the French army and saved France from the English. She had the dauphin crowned King of France in the cathedral of Rouen."

Mother squinted at Zaynab in suspicion. "I seek refuge in God from your lies! No decent girl would do such a thing, not even a French one!"

"She wasn't decent, Mother, she was a virgin." Noha clapped her hands at Zaynab's smart remark, and the two girls burst into laughter.

Mother's hands went protectively to her bosom: "God save us from Zaynab's tongue!"

Marcel and Jaubert had told us the story of Joan, but we didn't believe a word of it—an illiterate peasant girl leading armies and defeating the English to save France! I mean who could believe such nonsense? It was wilder than anything in *One Thousand and One Nights*, but just to be sure, we checked it out in the encyclopedia at the institute. After reading the history of Joan, we were ready to believe anything of the French.

I asked Noha what she thought of Rustam Raza. "He's kind of cute," she replied, wrinkling her nose. "He's from Georgia, by the Caspian. Real light skin, you know, dreamy green eyes, long reddish hair tied in a bun at the back like a Mamluk prince, and he's got the sexiest accent when he speaks Arabic. Oh lord, I get all prickly when I hear him. He speaks French too. He's très Français in his views."

I stared dumbfounded at my fifteen-year-old sister. Zaynab laughed. Mother begged God to pardon her wicked daughters. Even little Noha was coming undone. The Bakri family's surrender was now complete.

Zaynab and I were about to leave for the institute when a soldier who looked younger than me arrived leading a donkey-drawn cart. He was right on schedule. The soldier removed one of several boxes from the cart and carried it to the entrance, where one of Father's boy Mamluks was waiting with a box just like it. The Mamluk received the newly arrived box in return for the one that had arrived a week earlier. We watched the exchange from the balcony.

"It's been a month this has been going on," Zaynab said. "What do you think?"

I replied that I thought it was part of the mystery.

"I wonder what's in the boxes," she said.

"Father says they're things from Napoleon he has to see before his meetings with him, confidential things—papers, documents, reports, things of that nature. When I pressed him for details, he said they were engineering plans for chemical and fertilizer factories, spinning mills, agricultural projects, the canal at Suez. He even threw in something about future student missions to Paris and then winked, as though I might soon be going to Paris to study. He was trying to put me off."

"French engineering plans in Arabic?" she asked incredulously.

"That's what I thought. Father doesn't read French, and what the hell does he know about engineering?" We looked at each other a moment in mutual search of some explanation.

"It's puzzling," I said. "Those boxes started arriving about the same time Bonaparte started giving Father the young Mamluks. There's a connection."

"Well, let's find out what's in the boxes!" she exclaimed. "That should solve the puzzle."

Zaynab and I left the balcony and caught up with the soldier a short ways along the dirt road that led to and skirted Azbakiyya Lake. He seemed to be in a hurry and didn't stop for us.

"What's in the boxes?" I asked in my French, panting after the run.

"What boxes?"

"The boxes in your cart."

"Oh, those boxes. I have no idea." He was smirking in amusement at someone in a robe and turban speaking more or less understandable French.

We had come to where the road turned into the one circling the lake, which at this time of late autumn was filled with migrating ducks and geese. Fields bordering the lake spread out all around us. Except for a few peasants tending vegetable and flower gardens, we were alone. I thought of grabbing a box and running, but the rifle slung over the soldier's shoulder quickly convinced me to forget it. His pace quickened. He tapped his switch across the donkey's rear to speed it up.

"Your general sends boxes every week to my father, and you don't know what's in them?"

"How would I know, and why would you want to know?"

When I offered him a French riyal to let me have a peek in one of the boxes, he turned surly and, motioning as though to take the rifle from his shoulder, ordered us to get lost. It was obvious we weren't going to find out anything from him, and so we let him go.

Zaynab said, "Well, at least we know that what's in those boxes is meant to be secret!"

We rested at the edge of the lake, watching the birds frolicking in the water and wondering how to find out what was in those boxes and how these mysterious deliveries related to the mystery of Father's growing Mamluk contingent. What was going on?

10

EARLY THE NEXT MORNING, I stopped the young chief of Father's boy Mamluks as he was leaving the grounds of our villa. He looked like a Persian prince, flamboyantly attired in high military boots of soft leather, a blue silk blouse with pearl buttons, a crimson sash, and a gold-embroidered tunic, and with the end of his magnificent white turban hanging down his back like a fashion statement, as the French would say. Of all the heads that the French presence had turned, it was the proud but rootless slave youths whose heads were turned the most, as made obvious by their ostentatious dress and outrageous hairstyles, cosmetics, and jewelry.

"The rebellious narcissism of youth," Venture de Paradise called it. The French had a word and a category for everything.

"Rustam! Hey you, Raza! I want to talk to you."

He turned at the high gate he had just come out of. "Master Zaki?" He was a nice-looking young man—broad-shouldered, with long locks of russet hair falling over his forehead from under his turban, a faint tint of mascara highlighting his green eyes, the subtle aroma of French perfume, and a gold ring in his ear distinguishing him as Georgian.

"Where are you going, Rustam?"

"To the city."

"Where in the city?"

"Where?" He shrugged, paused. "Al-Azhar."

"Al-Azhar? Aren't you a Christian?" We walked together up the road from Azbakiyya and the lake toward Khan al-Khalili and al-Azhar.

"I was when I was in Georgia. I became Muslim when I became a slave of the Ottoman governor Tashkopru Pasha."

"Do you pray?"

"Sometimes."

"What are you going to al-Azhar for?"

"The tranquility."

"I hear you're engaged to my sister, Noha. Is that right?"

"Not officially. Your father promised her to me, but we're not officially engaged."

He seemed anxious to be rid of me, but I kept pace. It was a long walk from our villa to al-Azhar; normally I would have ridden my donkey. When I asked him why he was walking instead of riding his horse, he said he liked the exercise. Remarking that he seemed to be bursting with good health and as strong as Sultan Baybars, a Mamluk hero of old, I reached inside my robe, brought out a leather pouch, and handed it to him.

"What is it?" he asked, loosening the leather string at the top and extracting the mahogany-colored ball of Lebanese hash.

"Let's go down to the Muski canal and have a quick smoke. We should get to know each other if you're going to be my brother-in-law."

He looked at me in indecision; then at the shiny, resinous ball of hashish; and finally behind us, back down the empty road toward the villa. "Where's your father?"

"Locked up in his private prayer room, where he usually is these days. Reading secret documents in French, which he doesn't know." I threw my arm over Rustam's shoulder. "Don't worry about the old man. Come on. It's Mount Lebanon's best. From Baalbak."

He looked down at the hashish in his hand, put it back in the pouch, and smiled. "Why not?"

We sat in the reeds along the bank of the canal and smoked. I pretended to inhale deeply and started acting giddy after a couple of pipes. We intermittently laughed while watching the tiny river flow past in its lazy current, carrying on its surface the season's colorful birds looking for their breakfast as they dipped their heads in and out of the water. We talked about Napoleon, Pauline, the delights of Tivoli, the French way of life, and the ridiculous animosity between the soldiers and the savants, and by the middle of the third pipe we were howling in laughter like drunken brothers over the Egyptian reaction to the French flying men in the balloon, and then we grew serious discussing the quality of French arms and horses—subjects that Mamluk Rustam knew a lot about. He admitted to loving horses more than women. Following yet another pipe, he grew dreamy-eyed, then turned sad and started talking about his tragic life.

When he was twelve, he and his mother were traveling through the Caspian highlands to visit a sick relative in another village, and a gang of Turkish slave traders seized, raped, and enslaved them. His mother was sold as a servant to a wealthy merchant in Istanbul, while Rustam was taken to Belgrade and sold to a high Ottoman official who was later appointed governor of Egypt, where Rustam was then sold to a leading Mamluk emir who was killed battling the French, upon which Rustam was taken by Bonaparte as his personal Mamluk.

"That's really funny," I said. "Our self-proclaimed liberator takes a slave."

"What's wrong with that?"

"Nothing. Liberation is in the eyes of the conqueror. And then what happened to you?"

"And then he gave me to your father."

"Why?" Rustam remained silent. "Didn't Bonaparte like you?"

"Of course he likes me! We slept in the same room together. He promised to take me to Paris."

"Then why would he give you to my father?" Rustam shrugged and looked out across the canal. I prepared another pipe. "What are all those Mamluks doing for my father?"

"I'm sorry, Master Zaki. I must go."

"You know, don't you?"

"I must go."

"To pray at al-Azhar?" There was a long silence. "What's your real job, Rustam?"

"I am your father's slave."

"Slave my ass! You've got mascara around your eyes, you reek of French perfume, you've a gold ring in your ear and one on every finger, and you're dolled up in purple and gold silk, and expensive leather britches and boots. Slave! I'll bet you go to one of those French coiffeurs in Azbakiyyah to have your hair styled."

Rustam rose to his feet. "Thank you for the hashish, Master Zaki. I like you. I do. You are a good person. But I have to go."

"What's the business, Rustam? Tell me, or I swear to God I'll break your neck and throw you across the canal! I have a right to know!"

"I am sorry, Master Zaki. *Right* is a meaningless word to a slave. I have one master I serve, and only one. That's the way it is. I hope we will remain friends." He offered his hand to help me up. I took it.

"Okay, Rustam, we're friends. Here." I gave him what was left of the hashish. "But answer me one question. Only one. Who is your real master, Napoleon or Shaykh Khalil?"

"I find no difference between them when it comes to serving. One is the other. They are like soul is to spirit, like mind is to thought. I must hurry now, Master Zaki. A thousand apologies and ten thousand thanks." He pressed my hand, put his hand to his heart, bowed, and ran up the sandy track. I remained awhile in the reeds, thinking and watching the kite hawks turn, circle, and dive over the canal in search of fish they never seemed to catch. I had a bad feeling.

Pauline had convinced herself that if Zaynab married Belmond, Napoleon would marry her. Why else would she open her palace to Belmond and Zaynab, or praise him to her as she did? Pauline wanted Napoleon legally, and she would do anything and use anybody to that end. That Napoleon already had Josephine in France was irrelevant. Egypt was another world; he could drum up a military divorce for himself, as he had earlier for her. They would have a double wedding: Napoleon and Pauline, Belmond and Zaynab.

And where was humble religious student Zaki al-Bakri in all this as he listened to Pauline go on about Bonaparte and her plans in her splendid salon, with its white marble floor and French sofas and open balconies overlooking the lake and its palm groves, with every word he heard scraping away his, as the French called it, *amour propre*? Every time Pauline mentioned Bonaparte, my face twitched in jealousy as another flake was chipped from my dwindling self-esteem. Thinking my father had influence over Bonaparte, she even urged me to mention her to him, telling me that she loved Egypt and its people, and that as Napoleon's wife she could help unite them with the French. It was torture, a humiliation that I endured only in order to remain in her presence, a payment in self-abasement that I gladly made just to have her take my arm or run her hand playfully over my cheek and through my hair. I paid for the pleasure with pieces of my soul. Forget self-respect—that had gone long ago. As the payments continued, the currency was debased.

You have to understand: to me, in those early days, all European women were whores, and here I was, a young man from the highest class of Egyptian society, allowing my amour propre to be pounded and pulverized by a French courtesan, a simple seamstress's daughter from some peasant village! I wallowed in self-loathing and disgust. I waited like a hound dog in heat for Pauline to brush against me or to bend down so I could glimpse the rest of her half-naked breasts. I was a disgrace to my turban. But I couldn't help myself; I was enslaved by the burning passion her beauty and laughing voice stoked in me. Like a beast in human form about to explode in animal heat, I sat those evenings in her salon, pretending to be my sister's chaperone, forcing a calm smile as Pauline spoke of the great plans she had for herself and Napoleon and Egypt—plans that outdid even Napoleon's and my father's! I sat there listening in the opulent ambience of her salon, looking cool as the soft winter breeze that wafted through the open balcony from over the lake, while my loins melted in lust and my guts burned in resentment, humiliation, and jealousy.

When she wasn't singing about Napoleon, it was Belmond's song she chirped. Once when Belmond wasn't there and we were idly gossiping in her salon, I suggested (with jealousy fuming beneath my tranquil exterior) that a scholar might make a more suitable husband than a soldier.

Pauline laughed. "A scholar?" she scoffed, her voice rising with derision. "What could be more boring or sexless? Musty books, myopia, and bad breath … No my darling, a cavalry officer is what a real woman should have. Action, excitement, passion, satisfaction. They crush you in their arms. They know how to please and satisfy a woman to exhaustion. That's from their experience with their horses."

"Oh? Their horses?"

"It's true. They canter, they trot, they gallop, they charge. They know to bring their mounts forward and backward and to the side. They know when to jump, when to go fast, when to plunge fully into the breach. And when the action is over and the fortress taken, they know to walk their mounts to cool them slowly from the sweat of battle, to brush them down and soothingly massage their weary limbs."

My god! What torture! I was consumed in flames by her description as I imagined myself riding her, and was thankful for the loose robe that gave ample concealment to my growing condition. "Very descriptive," I coolly remarked, innards and loins on fire.

Zaynab, smiling in utter enjoyment of Pauline's description, mischievously asked her friend if she thought a woman was really like a horse to a man.

"Only in bed under certain positions and a full moon," replied Pauline without a moment's pause. "Women ride too, you know. Some men are too intimidated for that. But then, they're not whole men."

"What is a whole man?" I ventured to ask, feeling totally emasculated in spite of the painful tumescence hidden under my scholar's robe.

"A man who knows women so well he is one himself and has the self-confidence to embrace it."

Zaynab clapped at that. I smiled in dour tolerance, yearning at once for Pauline and for the calm days before the French came. I was a mental and physical mess.

"It's true, my dear Zaki. With a cavalry officer, you feel there's a man in the saddle who knows how to ride and be ridden. They know horses as well as they know women, and love them both as they love themselves. But a scholar? You're lucky if their legs reach the stirrups. As soon as they mount, they slip off, finished before they've begun."

The bitch! I hated her as much as I loved her! "Belmond has trouble staying in the saddle," I remarked with amazing aplomb.

"It was the heat," Zaynab defended.

"But I would think that when things are hot would be precisely the time you'd do best to stay on. What fun is a cold mount?"

Zaynab shrugged at my flippancy.

Pauline said, "A good soldier knows to warm his horse before he rides."

"Is Napoleon a good horseman?" I asked.

"We're talking about Captain Belmond," she replied stiffly, momentarily flustered.

"Apparently he's had some trouble satisfying Josephine, and I hear she's very beautiful." I wanted to stick the knife in and turn it.

"Josephine? The slut! Napoleon needs a more spirited filly. One that knows something about fidelity."

"Can a girl tell if she's truly in love with a man without first making love with him?" Zaynab's question brought a smile to Pauline's face. "Of course she can tell."

"How?"

"Her breasts swell. She's wet all over. That's God's way of letting us know. Why do you ask? You can't possibly still be a virgin?"

Zaynab nodded hesitantly, as though ashamed of it.

"Well," Pauline consoled her, "don't let it bother you. We all start out that way. Virginity in a young lady might even be charming. In fact, it can be an advantage if you know how to use it properly."

"I always thought virginity was something a girl lost the moment she put it to use." I think I overdid my effort to sound cool and witty.

"Don't be naive, Zaki. A smart girl can have her cake and eat it too. Mind you, Zaynab, I don't mean to sound prudish, but don't let Captain Belmond pluck the rosebud until a date is set for the marriage and the engagement made public. A man should be made to feel he's worked hard for what he's going to receive. The more one puts into something, the less inclined one is to pull out of it."

"I haven't thought about marriage."

"It's time you should. As Napoleon's wife, I would be in a position to help your captain's career—just as you could help mine with Napoleon through your father. There's no Egyptian whose opinion Napoleon respects more than his."

"Two foxes trying to outsmart each other," I interposed, and then I gave the knife another turn. "Speaking of Napoleon, if what is said about his being unable to impregnate Josephine is true, his manhood hardly matches your description of his riding ability."

"I told you, he chose the wrong filly."

"He's not too short in the spur?"

"Zaki!" Zaynab flashed me an admonishing look and said in Arabic not to be disgusting.

"As a matter of fact ..." Pauline bit her lip, as though debating whether to continue. "As a matter of fact, if you wish to know ... well, I'll tell you, but in all confidentiality: we've been working pretty hard at making a baby the last few months. And we still are."

"Oh? It's hard work, is it?" I remarked as superciliously and poignantly as I could.

"As hard as Nappy can get it. He blames me for it. Do you know what he told General Dumas? He said that silly little fool, meaning me, doesn't know how to make a baby! Me! But it's not my fault! I do what nature meant me to do, and I've been told by people who should know that I do it pretty well."

"I'm sure you do, but you don't shoot an empty musket in a dry well and expect to catch a fish."

"What does that mean?" asked Zaynab, scrunching up her pretty face.

"My well's not dry, I'll have you know!" Pauline cried out. "If anything's dry, it's his musket! And now he's going to Suez because of that stupid canal he wants to build, and as soon as he returns he's leading a campaign to Syria, and how are we going to get a fish in the well with him gone all those months?"

Having calmed herself, Pauline called for her Coptic femme de chambre and in Arabic asked her to serve tea and cakes. "The problem is," she resumed, "Nappy's mind is taken up by too many things. Impossible things. That ridiculous canal—all the wealth and power it's supposed to bring Egypt and France, when everyone knows that as soon as the two seas are connected, all the water from the Red Sea will rush in and flood Egypt and half of France! What good is an empire under water?"

"But Pauline," Zaynab explained, "as much water will flow from the Red Sea into the Mediterranean as flows from the Mediterranean into the Red Sea."

"I hope so," Pauline said, looking in distress out the balcony toward the lake. "Maybe it will flood India and drown all those horrible Englishmen who took it from us, and make one less country Nappy thinks he has to conquer. What good is conquering a damn swamp? Let the English drown in it!"

The tea and cakes arrived. Pauline poured and served us these tiny little multicolored, multilayered cakes that I found disgustingly delicious. It had taken me a long while to admit that the French knew the first thing about food and how to cook it.

"The problem is," she was saying as she served the cakes, "half of what Nappy wants is mad, and the other half is impossible. I tell him to forget his crazy dreams and come to bed, but no, he has a canal to build and a world to conquer—Syria, Persia, India. Asia! Europe is too small for him; he needs more spacious worlds to conquer. And then he blames me for not being able to make a baby! I can already feel his resentment because I'm not pregnant." She faltered, brought her hands to her eyes, and burst into tears. When Zaynab put her arms around Pauline to console her, she broke down entirely, heaving and sobbing in Zaynab's arms.

Tormented by her tears for Nappy and by her drivel about the baby he couldn't give her, I wanted to wrap my hands around her beautiful white neck and choke the life from her. Instead, I knelt down next to her to join Zaynab in comforting the poor, suffering woman who had stolen my heart while torturing me with her fantasies about her beloved Nappy and his sexual shortcomings. When I put my arms around Pauline, Zaynab misinterpreted it and warned me in our language not to take advantage of a woman in distress. After asking for a translation from Zaynab, Pauline said through her tears that she never allowed a man to take advantage of her unless she wanted him to. "And Zaki would never take advantage, would you, Zaki?"

"Never. I'm a scholar, not a soldier."

"Ha!" scoffed Zaynab. "You're a man!"

"And a beautiful and gentle one." Pauline reached out for my hand and drew me next to her on the sofa. "And a friend," she added, smiling through her grief. "A friend is a thousand times more precious to a woman than a lover."

"And a thousand times more precious than that is being both," I declared boldly.

"Impossible, my dear Zaki. No man can be lover and friend. It's either one or the other. And marriage, I fear, ends both love and friendship."

"Then why are you so eager to marry Napoleon?" Zaynab asked.

"For love, my dear Zuzu. A love as mad and passionate and destructive as his own love for himself as a man of destiny. And to give him the legitimate heir he desires. For that I can sacrifice myself to history. And if you knew what sacrifices I have made, what desperate measures I have taken to make a baby—even compromised my religion!"

"Oh?"

"Yes. And all for him."

"How's that?" I asked.

"How's that? Come, I'll show you."

She led us from her salon up the marble staircase to her bedroom and flung back a satin curtain covering a corner of the room. Standing in a hemispherical niche built into the wall was a squat granite statue about three feet high, with a gigantic penis half as long as the figure was tall. The granite penis was pointed at the bed. "It's an ancient Egyptian fertility deity that one of the savants found digging around the Sphinx. Since nothing else worked, not even the herbs and secret potions that the Sufi woman gave me, I tried this. It's my last hope."

My inveterate Muslim abhorrence of idols struggling against my urge to ingest the secret power of this exaggerated emblem of masculinity, I stroked it, running my fingers over the upward-curving length of polished stone, wondering if it was true: the bigger, the more pleasure for women.

"Stop! You'll ruin the magic by touching it!" She pushed my hand away as though it had been up her dress, and then kissed the monster's bulbous tip in ablution of its being defiled by an infidel hand. I asked if she didn't think she'd hurt herself on the stone. "Don't be silly, it's not used for that! It's a talisman. I'm getting a female one for Nappy, in case it's him and not me."

Zaynab was blushing, gaping open-eyed at the statue. "How can a stone get you pregnant?"

"The Sufi woman said it has magic powers."

Pauline's femme de chambre entered to announce the arrival of Captain Belmond. We descended to the salon and Belmond was standing in the middle of it, his uniformed presence, enhanced by his tanned face, bright-blue eyes, and sun-bleached golden locks, seeming to radiate a halo around him—or was it Zaynab's eyes that lit the salon? He bowed, shook my hand, and kissed Pauline's hand and then Zaynab's cheeks. He apologized for being late: Napoleon had called an emergency meeting of all cavalry officers assigned to the Syrian expedition. "We are leaving within the week."

The news crushed Pauline. She broke into tears so torrential that Zaynab took her to an adjoining room, leaving Belmond and me alone in embarrassed silence. His face was flushed, his eyes unusually blue. The tension between us was greater than I had previously sensed it to be. After a minute of silence, Belmond took an audibly deep breath and came out with it: he wanted to marry Zaynab.

"Oh?" The monosyllabic grunt was about all I was able to muster these days of revolutionary change that had emptied me of all expression of surprise and shock. But in truth, his words came like a horse's kick in the stomach. "Oh?"

"With your father's permission, I want us to marry when I return from the Syrian campaign." He took another deep breath and smiled his clean, boyish smile of innocent candor. "Whew! Am I relieved to get that out!"

"Zaynab accepted?"

"I haven't asked her, but I love her and I know in my heart she feels the same way."

"Your heart does not deceive you. She loves herself more than you can imagine!"

"I didn't mean it that way."

"It doesn't matter how you meant it. Father will never accept. He still thinks of Zaynab as Napoleon's Egyptian girl."

"Would *you* accept?"

"Me?"

"I believe you're dearer to her than her father."

"What do I have to do with it? You run the country. You have the power. You French are able to do what you want. What do you want from me?"

"Your blessing."

"It's not worth anything."

"It is to her." He paused and then added, "It is to me also, Zaki. I know you don't think highly of me—a soldier, a sulfur-snorting lead head. But I like you. Zaynab loves you. I respect that, and I respect you. What's important to her is important to me. You, her studies, her family and traditions—"

"You don't mind being a woman's slave, do you?"

Belmond's brow arched in surprise. "I don't think of it that way. *Partner* is the right word. Helper. Mate."

"I call it slave."

"To allow a woman to follow her will and share it? Is that to be her slave?"

"To surrender your will to her is."

"I haven't surrendered my will, no. One has to ..." He halted in confusion. "What I mean to say is, I wouldn't hold her back. She has her own character to develop."

"A woman belongs at home, not running around developing character." It surprised me how much like Father I sounded when anger blew words from the top of my head.

"And if she belongs at home, then home is the factory of character, and woman is director general. Strong women, strong mothers. Strong mothers, strong children. Strong children, strong nation."

"What rot! Pauline is up there sniveling her heart out because your heroic general can't get it up to give her a baby, and you're talking about I don't know what—strong nation? We don't even have a word for it. I'll tell you what, Belmond. If we'd had your artillery, we would have blown you French fuckers down the Nile to the sea in a hailstorm of steel and fire!"

"But you didn't have. You had Mamluks. Slaves. You were slaves to slaves. Haven't you learned from your defeat? You call me a slave to your sister, and still you don't know that a civilization that locks up its women is doomed to be slaves to those that do not. Zaynab is too strong for you people. Too strong for weak men who disgrace themselves by defeating their own women when they can't defeat an enemy of men."

My arm stiffened. I rose to my full height, neck craned, and looked up into Belmond's eyes, some elevation above my own, waiting for the right moment to smash my fist into his mouth to shut him up and then break his back over my knee. But before the right moment came, he said something that momentarily stilled my volcanic emotions, which had been about to erupt in violence. What he said about Egyptians was a French version of something I had been mulling over in my troubled mind:

"You may be brave individually, but as a people you don't cut it, Zaki. You're afraid of strong women. You've condemned them to serve you, and in doing so you've lost the best of yourselves. Europe surges forward in revolution, while you wallow in tradition wrapped in a god and a thousand-year-old holy book that has become empty of meaning. You condemn yourselves and take down with you the strong women you have, and deprive the others from growing strong. Better for you that women were your rulers. You memorize verses of an ancient book until your mind is numb and your eyes are blind to the world around you, and put your boots to the necks of women you fear for their strength! You deserve to be defeated, ruled, and humiliated!"

There were some things he said that I would have liked to discuss, but my emotions had taken hold of me, and so, casting self-restraint and reason to the wind, I took his words as an insult to me, to all Egyptian men, and to my religion, and shouted up at him with wild eyes as he stood towering above me, "Infidel pig eater! You have no religion! You'll never have my blessing to marry Zaynab!"

"Zaynab's too strong to be held back by a blessing. And I don't like pork, if that's what you mean by religion."

"That won't save you!"

"From what?"

"From this!" In blind rage I reared back and threw out my fist, grazing his chin. He regained his balance, grabbed me, knocking off my turban, and threw me to the floor. Gaining my knees, I sprang forward quick as a striking cobra and wrapped my arms around his legs, bringing him to the floor, where we grappled and rolled and wrestled for some minutes until my strength began to give out and he pinned me down. With one last effort, I reached out, grabbed the end of my fallen turban, and struggled to wrap it around his face, finally winding a loop of it around his neck. As I tightened it, I felt his grip on my shoulders slacken, and a wheezing gurgle came from his throat. My god, I was choking him to death! In horror, I started untwisting the band of cloth, and we lay there, panting and gasping in exhaustion, with Belmond on top of me.

"I'm sorry, Belmond," I gasped, trying to catch my breath. "Please forgive me. I didn't mean to hurt you. You're a guest to our country, even though we didn't invite you." I put my arms around him, begging his forgiveness and then kissing his cheek. He hugged me back, saying it was okay, it was his fault. We lay there for a minute in exhausted embrace, and then I asked him to get off of me, as he was crushing me, but before he could move, a stern voice in commanding French broke through the room: "What's going on here?"

We looked up. Napoleon was standing in the doorway. We remained frozen in position for a long moment, like the copulating princes in *One Thousand and One Nights* who'd been turned to stone by the evil sorceress. Belmond at last broke the spell. He climbed to his feet, and flushing in shame as though caught sodomizing a nanny goat by the Almighty Himself, snapped smartly to attention and saluted. When he opened his mouth to explain, no sound came out, so frozen was he in humiliation.

"Captain Belmond? What do you have to say for yourself?"

"He struck me, General. I was defending myself."

"Not very well, I would say." Napoleon looked more amused than angry, though a soldier, particularly an officer, brawling with an Egyptian, particularly the son of a shaykh, was an offense that normally would have called for a court martial and severe punishment. He turned his attention to me.

"Zubayr, what did Captain Belmond do for you to strike him?"

"Zaki," I replied, climbing to my feet. "My name is Zaki, sir."

"Of course. Zaki. I wouldn't forget that. What caused you to wrestle each other?"

Belmond, still standing at attention, rigid as an obelisk, shot me a look of pleading despair. A vein on the side of his head was throbbing as though he were already facing the firing squad. I remained silent. Napoleon repeated his question.

"He said things—nasty things I didn't like to hear."

"So you hit him instead of showing him where he was wrong for saying what he did?"

"Well, that was part of the problem, sir. I don't know if he was all that much wrong."

"But you didn't like hearing what he said?"

"No. Not from him. It—it was not his place to say what he did. Not the way he did."

"It was more the way he said it than what he said?"

"Both. But he said it and it's over."

"Do you want me to have him placed before a court martial and shot?"

"It's not that serious, sir."

"But it is. He's one of my officers."

"Yes, but he also may be my brother-in-law. Zaynab will be punishment enough for him."

11

A BANQUET WAS GIVEN IN celebration of the Syrian campaign that was about to head out. It just happened to fall on the eve of the new moon, supposedly an auspicious time for starting new ventures. Napoleon didn't openly espouse astrology, nor did Father, but I have a strong suspicion that Father, with his smattering of astronomical knowledge, had conned the commander in chief into believing that he was as wise in interpreting the stars for him as he was wise in advising him on ruling Egypt, and had assured him that his campaign would be successful if launched at the new moon. Well, if the campaign's success had anything to do with my father's knowledge of astrological principles applied to astronomical exactitude of observation and computation, then little wonder the campaign was a total calamity—and even that is to understate what happened.

The banquet Napoleon gave to celebrate the launching of his Syrian venture would have led one to think that Alexander himself had returned to march off in conquest of Asia. Cairo's tailors were busy for weeks sewing gowns for Egyptian girls and women who had been invited by their French friends, lovers, and husbands. Those tailors—Armenian, Coptic, Syrian, Muslim, most of them working from French patterns they had been given—showed surprising skill in their productions and even originality in producing creations of their own, patterned along the simple but elegant lines of Persian and Turkish caftans and blouses and the local djellaba. Zaynab sketched a caftan-like gown of her own design, with a modestly daring slit up the side and the slightest hint of exposed cleavage, and Pauline prevailed upon Napoleon to have Francois Bernoyer, his personal tailor and the chief tailor for the Army of the Orient, do the sewing. Pauline liked the result so much that she gave up her hussar's uniform and had Bernoyer make one for her as well. Zaynab's was of white satin and Pauline's of scarlet velvet, with matching turbans. The respective colors of their gowns, it struck me, appropriately matched the divergent states of their sexual experience.

As was customary for such French occasions in Egypt, the festivities lasted three days. There were the rockets and incendiary displays, the bands and military parades, and all the rest of it, in addition to another highly publicized flight of men in a hot air balloon, an exhibition ending in total disaster the balloon deflating and the men plummeting into the lake with the balloon over them, almost causing them to drown. The episode cast Napoleon into a deep gloom, as he saw it as an omen that cancelled out Father's auspicious horoscope of the new moon.

A banquet in Father's honor was given on the second day of celebration. It brought together shaykhs, officers, and savants, and culminated in a candlelit evening procession from Napoleon's palace to our villa. Napoleon was dressed in Islamic garb, and like a dutiful son led by his father, he held Shaykh Khalil al-Bakri's hand as they solemnly led the procession between rows of illuminated trees, the military band following behind playing a subdued triumphal march.

I couldn't believe my eyes. The whole sight so totally appalled me that, cringing in disgust and embarrassment, I searched for a tree to hide behind, but they were all lit up with candles and colored lanterns. Had the people so lost their minds that they could fall for this phony theater of political absurdity? Could it be that all these people—French and Egyptian, soldiers, shaykhs, and savants—simply went along with it because they were stuck with each other and there was nothing else to do?

Rustam Raza attended Father and Bonaparte, his two masters who were one, as he said. As the feasting progressed, I noticed that Rustam became a bit unsteady on his feet. Napoleon's brother-in-law Eugene Beauharnaise, Josephine's brother, was giving him glass after glass of champagne, thinking it a big joke to get the young Mamluk drunk. I counted six glasses he had downed, and there were many others I failed to count, judging from his rubbery legs. Eugene threw his arm around Rustam and clinked glasses with him and merrily sang out, "La bonne de France!" That's what they called the champagne they were drinking.

Rustam Raza and the whole affair was an abhorrent sight. Father frowned in displeasure, though he himself was nipping something from his opaque glass, and from his ruddy face I could tell it wasn't water or fruit juice. By the end of the banquet, poor Rustam was hardly able to put one foot in front of the other without stumbling.

When the party had ended and everyone had gone home and the lanterns had been extinguished in the courtyard, I heard a commotion through my bedroom window. I went to the balcony and saw Father holding Rustam's arm and giving him a rough shaking, admonishing him for drinking too much, the way a father would a son. Another dagger of jealous anger pierced my heart as I watched from the darkness of my bedroom balcony. Father could give Zaynab to Napoleon, could suffer me to drink and do as I wanted, but young Rustam was too dear to his heart to be left to drink with the French officers. Tears of rejection moistened my eyes as I watched the tender love scene of Father scolding son Rustam.

But then the scene turned ugly. Rustam jerked his arm free and passionately hissed loud enough for me to hear, "I'm finished with that business! Finished! I can't take it anymore!" Father lunged after him, and Rustam backed away, repeating in heated words that he was finished. "I can't do it anymore! It's too dirty! Find another boy!"

Then Rustam turned and ran. Father cried out his name and followed him, his arms stretched out in appeal, but after several paces he stopped and stood staring into the night in the direction that his beloved boy had disappeared. A moment later, Father's arms dropped to hang dejectedly at his sides, and he returned on heavy feet to the villa, a defeated, pathetic figure.

I returned to bed but was unable to sleep. I lay there staring into the darkness, feeling alone and empty in a world that was sickly, corrupt, and degenerate. The changes that had come so rapidly I could bear no more. But of course I had no choice but to bear them, and I would. That was my life now—an uplifting part of which was hearing myself say that I couldn't bear it anymore.

On the third and last day of the celebration came the final banquet, and females were invited to this one. Pauline and Zaynab were stunning. Pauline must have taught Zaynab to dance, for she danced with Belmond, and it pained me how beautiful they looked together, how harmoniously they turned in those shameless dances that allowed man and woman to touch and press their bodies together. Pauline added embarrassment to my pain by hustling me off to a private room where she tried to teach me how to dance. "Napoleon doesn't know how either," she complained. "Another of his hang-ups as conqueror. Imagine, a man who doesn't like to dance! No wonder he can't make a baby!"

Pained, angry, intoxicated by desire, I clumsily fell over my feet as she led me. Then I stopped, and taking advantage of being alone with her at last, I grabbed her around the waist and brought her forcefully to me, crushing her breasts against my chest. "I'll make a baby in you if that's what you want!" I whispered passionately between clenched teeth.

"Zaki!"

I pressed my mouth against hers. She resisted. I persisted. She at last accepted her fate. Her tongue slid into my mouth and searched for mine. I responded in kind. Our arms tightened around each other as our tongues curled and pushed in and out of each other's mouths like starved eels in an eating frenzy. Taking this tongue-in-mouth copulation as the French way of inviting the real thing, I held her breasts. "Zaki!" she was panting. With my other hand I reached through the slit in her caftan, fingers finding their way between her legs, to her silky underwear.

"Oh god, Zaki! No! Please! Not here! No, don't! Hold me!" She pushed her groin against mine. Her fingers dug into my back, her long nails piercing my robe, cutting into my skin like tiny daggers. During the hysterical frenzy of simulated copulation, my turban fell over my eyes. "Oh god," she panted, taking her mouth from mine. "Stop!" My fingers found their way inside her moist flower. "No, please!" Her lips returned to mine. Her tongue hungrily inserted itself deep into my mouth. The pulsations of her pelvis against mine grew fiercer. I held her tighter. My desire was exploding; I lost control. A minute later, while squeezing her in one arm and pushing in rhythm with her, and two fingers of my other hand inside her, I groaned as my seed burst forth. She felt me throbbing against her and gripped me harder, moving to my fingers inside of her, moaning, "Oh! Oh! Oh!" as though sharing in my explosive release.

We clung to each other, panting like wild animals. Then, when it was over and our blood had calmed, she led me outside to a fountain in a corner of a garden, pulled up my robe, and washed me. "Are all Egyptians as hot-blooded as you?"

"I don't know." I felt ashamed, embarrassed. "I'm sorry."

"Don't be. I wish he were like that."

"Don't talk about him. It hurts me."

"I'm sorry. I meant to compliment you. Are you jealous?"

"Yes."

She took my hand. We sat on the edge of the fountain, hand in hand, waiting for my robe to dry while listening to the music and looking up at the stars over the desert.

"We should go back in," she said after several minutes. "Nappy will be looking for me."

"I'm going home."

"What's wrong?"

"Nothing."

"You look sad."

"Make sure Zaynab gets back all right."

"I will." She kissed me on the lips and returned to her banquet and Napoleon, leaving me alone, miserable, rejected. Napoleon had Pauline, Belmond had Zaynab, Father had Rustam, Rustam had Noha, who would have to share him with Father, and I had no one. I had just made love to Pauline through our clothes, and instead of being happy I was miserable, alone, and rejected, oh so horribly down, in a world turned upside down and black.

I walked slowly home along the edge of the canal, the fading music behind me a sad echo of my emptiness. Sighing heavily, I trudged along the bank toward Lake Azbakiyya, yearning for something to fill my aching, hollowed-out insides. Nothing was right: Father was lost; Zaynab was lost; Pauline would go. I looked up at the stars. The French had opened a new world of great possibilities and expectations without having provided the means to attain them. I felt condemned to a life of desire, frustration, envy, and futility, of endless searching to fill the void. Only the stars hadn't changed since the coming of the French.

As I was staring forlornly at the sky, the night was rent by a terrible fracas: Father's Mamluks were brawling in their barracks. They sounded like they were tearing the place down—I could hear things being hurled and bodies thrown against bodies in a wild cacophony of Turkish, Georgian, and Cherkes dialects, as though they were shouting their Mamluk war cries and charging into battle. As I reached the villa, the barracks door swung open with a splintering bang. In fear of violence, I ducked behind a cluster of palms. A second later, a gang of young Mamluks came bounding out, kicking, punching, pushing. They had surrounded one of their own and were pummeling him with fists and feet. I wanted to run out and help the poor fellow, but I was afraid they'd do the same to me. To justify my cowardliness, I told myself he was only a Mamluk slave getting what he deserved.

The guy was swinging his fists wildly in a futile effort to defend himself, but his wobbly legs finally buckled beneath the vicious blows raining down on him from every side. Hunched on his knees with his arms over his head, he took the pounding for a long while. His assailants kept punching and kicking him until he fell forward and lay prostrate before them. For a while they stood around, kicking him and laughing, and then at last they laid off the poor guy and returned to their barracks.

When the barracks door had slammed shut behind them, I crept over to him. It was Rustam. His fine silk garments were a torn, bloody mess. The earring had been ripped from his lobe. He was unconscious. I fetched a pitcher of water from the fountain in the courtyard and washed the blood from his face. His eyes opened. He moaned and sat up, holding his head and squinting at me.

"Are you all right?" I asked him.

He held his open hands to his battered face. "I'm fine."

"You don't look it. What happened that you lost your popularity with the boys?" I helped him to the fountain and finished cleaning him up. His eyes were almost closed with swelling. His cut lips and cheeks were puffed up like balloons. His whole head looked like a bloated, rotting melon.

"You don't know?" he asked, the words sounding punch drunk as they staggered over his bruised and swollen lips. I shook my head. "Your father didn't tell you?"

"We don't speak a whole lot these days. Even if we did, he wouldn't tell me. Why'd they beat you?"

"I wouldn't give them cognac."

"Cognac? Why would they expect you to give them cognac?" He winced in pain without answering. After a long minute passed, I asked him what he and all those Mamluks were doing for my father. "Why did Napoleon give them to him?" He turned his face away from me. "What's wrong, Rustam, you can't confide in a friend who saved your life?"

160

He sighed with a muffled groan, either from physical pain or some mental suffering. It was a long time before he spoke. "You really don't know?" he asked.

"How would I know if I know, if you don't tell me what I may or may not know? No, I don't know! What's to know?"

"You've seen it come in often enough."

"Seen what?"

"The cognac. Once a week. Every Friday after prayer."

I pondered. Then it struck me like a bolt from Berthollet's globes. "You mean the box?"

"The box."

"Cognac?"

"Cognac, wine, champagne, opium. Six bottles, two of each, and a pouch of Anatolia's richest poppy juice, one delivery a week."

"What does Father do with it?"

"What do you usually do with it?"

"Father?"

"The pious shaykh himself."

"All that? A box every week?"

"Not by himself—I stole some. Some he gave away to the shaykhs. Did you think he was reading the Quran all those nights in his prayer room?"

"I can't believe it!" The French had been here how long, and I could still say something as dumb as "I can't believe it." I could believe anything.

"Sorry, Zaki. I never would have told you if he hadn't done me bad."

"How did he do you bad?"

"He broke his promise. Your sister Noha—he's giving her to someone else now."

"Who?"

"That new Mamluk kid Napoleon gave him. Circassian son of a bitch! He talks Turkish worse than an Armenian."

"Is that because of the night before?"

He looked at me through the narrow slits of his swollen eyes and cheeks. "What do you mean?"

"I saw you from the balcony. It's something sexual isn't it? Go on, tell me—nothing can shock me anymore."

"Are you serious?"

161

"Of course. By now I believe anything is possible. Were you his little boy love?"

He laughed, winced, brought his hand to his jaw. "I have to get to the French hospital. I think they broke my jaw."

"What was going on between you and my father?"

"Not what you think. Though if he'd had the chance …" He broke off. "Forget it, Zaki. I'm angry because he gave my Noha to that new guy and made him chief."

"Then what was that you were shouting about? You said that you were finished with the business, that he should get another boy. What business? Why did he need another boy?"

"Forget it."

"I will as soon as you tell me, and you're going to tell me or I'll rip your jaw from what's left of your face."

Rustam patted me on the shoulder. "You don't want to hear it, Zaki."

"Why are you still protecting my father?"

"It's you I'm protecting."

"Thanks. What was it? Selling cognac to the shaykhs?"

Rustam laughed. "Selling cognac." He slapped his thigh, then grimaced in pain. "Selling cognac in al-Azhar Mosque. That's great! Oh god, I ache all over." The pain didn't keep him from laughing.

"Hashish?"

He nodded, threw his arm around my shoulder, and tried to smile. His face had swollen into a ball that sucked up and devoured all his features—nose, eyes, cheeks—leaving his smile and bloated lips looking like a gaping wound.

"So that's it. Hashish."

"That's it. Who would have guessed?"

"Then why were you so happy to take the little bit I had, if you were dealing big in drugs? Come on, Rustam, tell me what the business was or I'll crush your head between my hands like an overripe watermelon!" I stood with my fist poised about a centimeter from his fractured jaw. He pushed my fist away and sighed heavily.

"Don't ask, Zaki. You'd never be able to live with yourself."

"I'm beyond being shocked or disillusioned. Tell me the business."

"I don't want you to suffer like me."

"The business! What was it?"

"Espionage."

"What?"

"Your father's running Napoleon's intelligence agency."

"What intelligence agency?"

"The one your father and I set up for Bonaparte. What do you think those twenty-five Mamluks are for? For him to fuck? They're agents. They gather information from all over Cairo. I was their chief. I stationed them. They reported to me, and I reported to your father. I gave him the information I got from the boys, and he analyzed it and wrote up a weekly intelligence and surveillance report he gave to Napoleon. The next day a few Egyptians would disappear forever. Troublemakers vanished in the night to go for a swim in the Nile. It still goes on, but I'm out of it. You father's new boy runs the agents now."

Revulsion rose up like acid from the pit of my stomach and scorched my throat. I felt the vomit rising, hot and stinging. I sat down before it came or I fainted, my head spinning. I reached into the fountain pool and splashed cold water on my face, and then I looked up at the starry sky and breathed in deeply. The stars were the only things that hadn't changed in what used to be my comfortable little world. God how I yearned for the good old rotten days of Mamluks and Ottomans.

"How many Egyptians do you think were executed because of those reports?" I asked.

"Too many. I couldn't take it. I was always afraid Noha would find out, or some Egyptians. I couldn't sleep. I was afraid if I did, I'd wake up one morning without my head."

"That's why Napoleon gave you to my father? To spy?"

"It didn't sound so bad when I agreed to it. It was to maintain law and order and keep the peace. Your father and Napoleon made it sound like it was the moral thing to do for everyone's good, for the security of society and the nation. Viva la patrie!" He spat the words.

"So you quit, and Father gave Noha to your replacement."

"I couldn't live with myself. I like the French, but I couldn't spy for them anymore. That's why those Mamluks turned on me—for quitting. They don't know how it is to feel you have the blood of innocent people on your hands. They don't care; they're not from here. They're slave kids from across the desert and over the mountains. They don't even speak Arabic. But your father does. Your father knows about the innocent blood of Egyptians. That's why he drinks so much—he can't face it. He keeps saying it's to keep the peace, and that too many innocent people will die if the plotters aren't caught before they destroy the peace. He needs to drink a lot to keep himself believing it. That's why I drink too. I like the French, but since they came I don't know what's what anymore. I only know I can't spy for them. Not anymore." Rustam tried to get to his feet but gave it up. I asked him where he was going. To the French, he replied. He had nowhere else to go.

"There are plenty of Egyptian households that would love to have you. You're a Mamluk. You speak French. You're in with Napoleon."

"I'm not safe among Egyptians. When the French leave, everything will be known. They'll kill me. I've got to stay with the French, and leave with them."

"What makes you think they're going to leave?"

"Napoleon's already thinking about it. He thinks more about returning to France than conquering Syria. He wants power and glory and he'll have it, believe me. Also, there's that business with Josephine playing the whore in Paris. He wants to be done with her once and for all. He'll be leaving for France when he's done with Syria, you'll see. And when he goes, the French will fall apart here. Napoleon is their heart and soul. Without him, the French are lost; they'll go to pieces. They'll be out of here within a year. And watch out when they go. Anyone who's served them—off with their heads."

"Then we'll be a headless people. Who hasn't served the French one way or another?"

"I'm telling you, Zaki. Watch out."

"How do you know all these things?"

"I overhear Napoleon talking to his generals and brother-in-law. They forget I know French, or maybe they don't care. Like I'm a dumb oriental. They can be arrogant sometimes."

"Sometimes?"

"It's just their way. Learn to be arrogant like them and you won't notice it."

He managed to get to his feet and stood unsteadily, holding out his hand. I took it.

"Remember what I said, Zaki. Everything seems calm now, but don't believe it. If you worked the job I had, you'd know. One thing I learned running a spy network: things are always happening beneath the surface. The deeper you go, the more that's happening. The ground beneath us is trembling in rage, every street and quarter of Cairo, but you can't see it. Everything looks fine, but it's not. Good luck, Zaki. Maybe see you in Paris one day." A moment later and he had vanished into the night.

12

THE NEXT DAY I gathered my courage and confronted Father in his private study with the awful truth I had learned. He didn't see it the way I did. He put down his pen, stood up from his writing table, and said that the Prophet himself had made peace with his pagan enemies for the sake of sparing bloodshed, even at the expense of incurring the doubt and anger of some of his people who failed to understand his wise leniency. If Muhammad could make peace with the pagan polytheist idol worshipers of Mecca, why couldn't he make peace with Christian monotheists? Because the Ottomans would see it as collaboration, not peacemaking, I told him. Forget the Ottomans, he said.

"No. They'll return one day and you'll be seen as a paid agent. You have to stop, Father. Please."

"Stop and let the people be swept into another bloodbath by troublemakers? Not on my life!" Face flushed in passion, he slapped the flat of his hand on the writing table, sending the bottle of ink jumping up in its bulbous compartment hollowed into the desk. "Let Bonaparte leave! I have a responsibility to myself, to the people, and to God! You saw what happened the first time the people rose up. I can't let that happen again."

"Why compromise yourself? If they want to revolt, let them revolt. You don't have to be their sacrifice."

"They don't want to revolt. They don't know what they want. They want only to be fed and led. They have to be told what they want and sternly guided to it. You know as well as I do that the people are mindless sheep who think with their stomachs and sex organs. Well, I am their shepherd. That's my duty as a shaykh."

He returned to his writing table and took up his pen. Discussion over.

Father's quest for power and prestige had made him either hopelessly foolish or recklessly courageous. Maybe on some super-sighted, metapolitical level of vision, he was right. There were times he seemed an innocent fool, a Jeremiah, an old man who actually believed he was called by the voice of God to sacrifice himself to the enemy for the noble cause of peace. But then when I thought of all the religious titles and offices and honors that Father had so coveted and Napoleon had heaped upon him ... I didn't know what to think of the old man.

—◊◊◊—

Napoleon departed for Syria with fifteen thousand of his best troops and a corps of savants and engineers, which included, among many others, Malus, Savigny, J. J. Marcel, Amadeus Jaubert, and Jean Michel Venture de Paradise as interpreter in chief. Their mission: take Syria; advance to Mesopotamia; stabilize the Fertile Crescent under French control as a base for the conquest of Anatolia, Iran, and Afghanistan; and then—ultimate prize of the grandiose campaign—seize India, bastion of British imperial power. England would then fall easily.

In the cool days of early March, our French Alexander rode grandly out of the city walls with his small army to conquer half a continent, as though he were going on a weekend picnic or a field trip to collect specimens with his savants. The bands played, the tricolors waved, officers and soldiers kissed their women farewell, flowers were gallantly thrown upon them in the breeze, and the expedition marched proudly off. The festive air belied the grim task of war, death, and conquest ahead of them. What did the French know of the blazing Sinai desert, Gaza, Palestine, or the bloody Butcher of Jaffa, Ahmad al-Jazzar Pasha, ruler of Palestine? They thought that because it was spring, the march would be cool; there would be morning showers and springtime flowers and cloudy skies blocking the sun, a pleasant jaunt along the seashore. When I told Belmond not to fall off his horse and get stung by a scorpion, he smiled his blue-eyed smile of disarming innocence that ill-matched his uniform and sword. When he tilted back his plumed, silvery helmet to embrace Zaynab, a tangle of blond locks tumbled boyishly across his brow. He kissed her full on the lips. She later told me that was her first kiss on the lips by a man. She hardly looked that virginal, dressed as she was like an emir ready to march off with the troops: high, black riding boots; purple Turkish pantaloons that were exaggeratedly voluminous at the knees and narrow at the bottom, tucked into her boots; blue silk blouse with a double row of closely spaced buttons braided in silver thread down the length of the front; crimson sash drawn snugly around her waist; and a turban the color of her pantaloons, with raven hair falling from under it to her shoulders. Looking at her, I could understand the wisdom of our traditions concerning the withdrawal of females such as Zaynab from public view. Allow them out of the house, and they made themselves so ravishingly desirable that men were damned to an erotic suffering of hell on earth, tantalized by seminaked temptresses they could see but not touch.

Pauline was equally breathtaking. Watching her dab her eyes and wave good-bye to Napoleon as he pranced off on his white charger like the conquering hero, looking every inch the man he wasn't, I had an outrageous urge of raw lust to yank her cavalry britches down to her boots and rape her from behind right there on the spot.

By the time the rear guard had marched through Bab al-Nasr (The Gate of Victory" -- some irony there), the French engineers had finally gotten another of their red, white, and blue hot air balloons off the launching station. It rose, hovered a moment, and then, collapsing in a sudden rush of air that sounded like the flatulent release of a belly full of long-digested beans, descended like a shroud onto the hooting onlookers and piles of horseshit left in the wake of the departing cavalry. The next day, six Egyptians were arrested for sabotaging the balloon. I was too sickened by it all to ask Father if it was his agents who had fingered the six.

We received news of the campaign through the grapevine, and the news we got differed as night from day compared to the official dispatches that Bonaparte sent to military headquarters in Cairo. At first, progress went as planned. The army advanced unopposed along the Red Sea, taking al-Arish and Khan Yunis as it traversed Sinai, and then turned up the coastal strip of Gaza and southern Palestine. Ramlah fell, and Jaffa and Haifa. According to the reports that Napoleon sent back to Cairo almost daily, the people of the "liberated" towns greeted the French with joy and flowers. With each new city that opened its gates to the liberators, Ottoman flags and war trophies were sent back to show the Egyptians how powerful Napoleon and his army were. Every week a new batch of war-tattered Ottoman banners arrived to be paraded and flown upside down over the Citadel and al-Azhar Mosque in a humiliating display of Ottoman weakness or a proud display of French strength.

The French completely misunderstood the psychological reaction this caused among most people. They thought we would humbly accept French power as a divine decree; in fact, we were humiliated by it. Our humiliation bred not acceptance, but seething resentment.

The French thought they had cut us loose from our Ottoman sultan, had destroyed our Islamic sense of his symbolic power of political legitimacy. They didn't realize that in humiliating the Ottomans, they were humiliating us. They acted as though a French victory were an Egyptian victory and presumed we accepted it as such. Had they understood anything about us, had they kept their conquests quiet and not proudly paraded their war trophies and banners around with such boisterous hullabaloo, we would have been more impressed than humiliated. The savants were right: military people were hopeless idiots in all things but killing and destruction.

In all fairness, the French could be excused on grounds of ignorance. But not our Egyptian and Syrian Christians. As defenseless minorities, they should have known better than to join in open rejoicing at each French triumph as though it were their own. When news of the fall of Gaza and Ramlah arrived, they took to wearing swords as though they had just been made French officers. They ate pork and drank wine in public, rode their horses in an aggressive manner, and with stinging insults pushed Muslims out of their way. Like unruly children sticking out their tongues, they publicly flaunted their excesses. I pitied them if a day of reckoning ever came, as Rustam Raza said it would. I pitied Egypt. I pitied everyone, except for our Jews. They acted as they always did, going quietly and humbly about their business, avoiding the slightest display of petulant revenge or showy excess because the French were running the country. I admired them for that.

It appeared that Napoleon was going to march all the way to Istanbul. Taking his growing power as an established and irreversible fact, more and more upper-class women led the rest of their sex in going French as more and more Cairenes learned French, dressed French, and frequented Tivoli and the French cafés and restaurants that were multiplying and making a little Paris of our city. Distilleries were opened to meet the growing consumption of spirits; and tanneries, textile factories, boot shops, tailors, and perfumeries to meet the growing demand for boots, jackets, dresses, and women's undergarments. Soldiers, sure they would never see France again and with no regard for the future, spent their money freely on these things to satisfy the insatiable, whimsical desires of their Egyptian girlfriends and wives.

As Napoleon was driving into Syria and Cairo was being transformed into Paris on the Nile, news from the grapevine began arriving—interesting vignettes brought by merchants plying their trade along the ancient caravan routes between Egypt and Syria. We learned, for example, that the notables and religious shaykhs of the towns and cities taken by Napoleon had, in most threatening terms, forbidden the people to have contact with the French in any way, shape, or form. Legal fatwas and religious opinions supposedly based on the Holy Law of the Shariah were issued toward this purpose. Claiming to know the divine will no less than Napoleon and my father, the ulema of Palestine warned the people that God would hate and punish any Muslim who even looked at a Frenchman or came within earshot of one. The faithful were not to read their lying publications, not talk to them, not sell to them or buy from them ... nothing, absolutely nothing. "Not even a button or cup of water," as it was stated in a copy of one of the fatwas I chanced to see later. Anyone who associated with the French in any way would be dealt with accordingly on earth by the religious authorities and in the hereafter by God, to whom the culprit would be speedily delivered. Women in particular were warned—rather, threatened—not to succumb to the seductive allure of the French and their evil ways. This, while our shaykhs in Egypt were issuing fatwas legalizing marriage to the French! As I said, there was something soft and gooey in the chocolate-cream center of the Egyptian people that made them too happy-go-lucky, lackadaisical, forgiving, accepting. Palestinians and Syrians were different. Iraqis were from another planet.

The shaykhs in Palestine had heard what happened to Muslim women in Egypt and did everything possible to prevent it from happening there. To those northern Arabs, it appeared as if Egyptian men opened their arms to the French, and the women their legs. Only some did. The truth of the matter, though, is that Egyptians are given to live and let live. We are a warm-blooded, easygoing lot compared to that motley tangle of fanged vipers up north: Christians, Palestinians, Lebanese, Syrians, the brutish bunch of them bogged down in fanaticism, hostility, and murderous greed. So I ask myself, even if those miserable northerners had opened themselves to the invaders, why in God's name would the French ever have wanted to associate themselves with such unsavory riffraff?

According to the stories we got from merchants and travelers from Syria, the march was going badly for the French. The army had advanced to Akka (or Saint John d'Acre, as the French called it), the city with the famous crusader fortress on the sea, and never got beyond it. They were halted by its ruler, Ahmad Jazzar Pasha, the Bosnian Butcher, who had at one time been a Mamluk emir. Napoleon was unable to take the city; the dirt and stone walls of the fortress had withstood French artillery. There was another even more powerful defensive structure opposing Napoleon: a British naval squadron in the command of a Sir Sidney Smith, who was serving under the grand lord admiral of the British fleet, Nelson. With the British greedily elbowing their way into the Islamic world, Sir Sidney supplied the Bosnian Butcher with artillery, muskets, ammunition, and food, and maybe some training in the art of modern warfare. And so while Napoleon pounded the city walls and fortress with his artillery, Ahmad the Butcher pounded Napoleon with English artillery, with Sir Sidney joining in the fray from the sea. Unable to skirt Acre and advance farther north for fear of being cut off from the rear, Napoleon threw everything he had against what he would later, in exile, contemptuously call "that heap of sand that changed the history of the world." (He would forget to mention Sir Sidney and the British squadron.) Like a deadly sea serpent, Sir Sidney's ships sailed back and forth along the shore, keeping just out of range of Bonaparte's artillery, and with telescopic eyes fixed on the wounded prey writhing on the beach, Smith would swoop in, pummel Napoleon with a broadside, and then cut out again before the French gunners could effectively hit back.

Yet it was an enemy worse than Sidney Smith and the Bosnian Butcher that destroyed the French. Soldiers dropped like flies, half their numbers being carried away within weeks by a plague so virulent and excruciatingly painful that men were said to have welcomed a blast in the head from an English ship rather than suffer the horrible agony of the disease. Stricken men were driven crazy with thirst, but drinking water caused them such pain that they went crazy anyway. The religious leaders in Acre declared the plague a blessing from God, even though it put ten times more Muslims than French in the grave. But, as Father said, God acts in strange ways that must not be questioned.

Then came rumors of a French retreat. Stories that Napoleon had ordered his doctors to inject poison into the dying and wounded to expedite the withdrawal flew to Egypt on the lightning-fast wings of merchants and migrating bedouin tribes. Since food, water, and medical supplies were running low, wasting what was left of these precious things on those who would probably die anyway seemed totally unreasonable. But basking in the spring comfort of well-watered Cairo, we didn't see it as all that reasonable, Bonaparte reduced to poisoning his own troops.

Between nature's heat and God's divinely sent plague, joined by Sir Sidney Smith and the Butcher of Bosnia, the French sultan's great plans of world domination had crumbled like a sand castle in the waves rippling up the Palestinian shore. The Muslims of Syria, Palestine, and Egypt rejoiced: God had helped his favorite people win victory over the Christians. They also didn't mention Sir Sidney's squadron or Lord Nelson's fleet. God worked in strange ways, most of them carefully selected from a long list by men of religion.

The rumors blew in from Palestine, one after the other: Napoleon's army was in full retreat, with thousands perishing of thirst and disease in the burning desert. Swarms of marauding bedouin tribes swept in for the kill, snapping like hungry jackals at the heels of the beleaguered army, devouring the stragglers and drenching the parched desert with their blood. A rear guard of two hundred soldiers were captured by bedouin, castrated on the spot, and taken to Tunis to be sold as white slave eunuchs. Another company of soldiers, captured in the desert by those horrid barefoot, lizard-eating Arab tribesmen, were sodomized before and after being decapitated, their heads and corpses left to rot; some captives were merely sodomized and left to die of thirst in the desert's baking sun. With every story of defeat, death, plague, sodomy, castration, and decapitation, Zaynab shuddered and closed her eyes in silent prayer for Belmond.

At last the survivors started to arrive. They were a pitiable sight. Napoleon had the nerve to parade the miserable remnants of his once-proud army through the Gate of Victory with a band playing, as if celebrating a grand triumph. Crowds of women, both French and Egyptian, awaited them outside the city walls in dread fear that their loved ones wouldn't be among the ragged wretches limping in. Almost half those who had left failed to return. Captain Raymond Bertrand Belmond was one.

Most had been carried off by the plague; Belmond was carried off by tribesmen outside the walls of Acre. As I later learned from a Tunisian merchant, poor Belmond might have become a blond, blue-eyed eunuch serving the dey of Tunis and his royal harem. The account Napoleon gave Zaynab of Belmond's death was heroic but utterly fictitious: her beloved was singlehandedly fighting off a storm of tribesmen when he was overpowered and killed after having felled a dozen or more of the enemy. He died a hero's death, Napoleon assured her, handing her what he claimed to be Belmond's sword.

"What good is the sword of a dead hero!" she cried out and flung the sword clear across Pauline's salon, cracking a wall-length mirror. "Give me a live coward! Keep your empty heroism!" Napoleon turned on his heels and left Pauline's salon. It was the only time I saw him intimidated to the point of speechless retreat.

Zaynab stayed with Pauline, crying for days without sleep. Fearing she might die of grief, Pauline tried to get her to drink a potion of opium, hashish, and wine so she might sleep for a while and forget her loss.

Zaynab refused: "If I didn't run from the love he gave me when he was alive, why should I run from the pain his death gives me now?"

Pauline insisted: "You haven't slept in days, Zuzu. Please. It will help you get over this terrible thing."

"I don't want to get over it."

"You must. Here, drink it. When you wake up, you'll feel like a new woman."

"I *am* a new woman." Zaynab angrily pushed the vial away, causing its contents to spill over Pauline's hand. "And she will suffer the loss of him to death as she loved the joy of him in life."

I never realized how brilliant my sister was. She was now able to express in French the suffering we reserved for poetry in Arabic. I also discovered another dimension of her strength. When she and Pauline were waiting by the Gate of Victory to greet their returning soldiers and Belmond wasn't there, Pauline had embraced her to comfort her from the blow. Zaynab had freed herself and walked away, without word or sign of her grief. Other Egyptian women were wailing and shrieking, tearing their clothes, pulling out their hair, slapping themselves in the face, and throwing dirt over their heads.

Marcel told me a different story concerning Belmond's fate. According to him, Belmond met his end at the edge of a stream, but not singlehandedly holding off a band of bedouin tribesmen, as there were no tribesmen within a hundred meters of the stream at the time. The truth was, Belmond's horse was shot in the head and fell sidelong into the water, pinning him under it. He was either drowned or taken prisoner by a tribe of bedouin who charged the stream right after he and horse toppled into it. If taken prisoner, he was either sodomized and decapitated, or sodomized and castrated and sold into slavery as a white eunuch, in which condition he might be found in Tunis, Algiers, or Marakesh. Marcel told the story with a trace of glee, which caused me to suspect that he might have embellished it here and there. But I believe that what he told me was essentially correct, and what the Tunisian merchant told me much later led me to believe that Belmond was a slave and had lost a leg. I could imagine him struggling under his horse, his arm jutting above the water's surface, waving frantically for help, which was on its way in the form of a hundred shrieking, lust-ridden, lizard-eating sodomites of the desert. Poor Belmond. He had stayed on his horse the one time he should have fallen clear.

Napoleon's Syrian debacle decimated the ranks of the institute. Fatherly Venture de Paradise was gone, along with a dozen or more scientists and engineers. No longer did the shocked shriek of some unsuspecting Azhar shaykh, followed by the mischievous chuckle of Berthollet holding his brass balls and wires, produce the amusement and jovial warmth of earlier days. Something of the spirit had been lost; I could see it in Marcel and Jaubert and the other savants. I felt the loss within me as well. I had, in a way, loved old Venture. He was a good teacher. When I would recite by rote for him whole pages of a French book, he would shout at me, "Think! Don't memorize! That is not learning. Socrates, Plato, Aristotle, ibn Sina, ibn Rushd, Tusi, Descrates, they knew what real learning was. To think is to be godlike. They knew. So be a god, Zaki. Clear your mind of memorized garbage from the past and think!" His words came hard on my ears. We worshipped the past, we memorized the old texts the way we did the Quran, and he was telling me it was garbage.

I passed my time at the institute reading French political philosophy and pondering the critical condition of my civilization.

Assuming that the French were finished after their defeat at Acre, an Ottoman army invaded by sea at abu Qir, where Nelson had undone the French fleet the year before. Napoleon rushed out with fifteen thousand troops and threw the Ottomans back into the sea. Then, feeling he could return home a conquering hero, he left Egypt like a thief in the night. Secretly.

He didn't tell us or his generals that he was returning to France in order to take over the government and become a dictator; he said he was going to reinforce the fleet and would be gone only a month or two, and when he returned he would convert to Islam and build the greatest mosque the world had ever seen. He didn't fool us about becoming a Muslim, but he did about being away only a month or two. Even Pauline didn't realize he had abandoned his army and left Egypt for good.

When we learned that he was in France and had become its ruler, we were dumbfounded. Pauline collapsed on the spot in a limp heap, looking as if the news had dissolved every bone in her beautiful body. The army and savants felt they had been abandoned. Their leader had acted irresponsibly by departing for France without orders from Paris, leaving them behind to die in an alien land. Egyptians who had cursed Napoleon and called him the devil became downcast in deep worry over what would happen to them now that he was gone, and over who would replace the Sultan al-Kabir ("the Great Sultan"), as we called him, and only half in jest, for we knew that in some way he was, although short in stature, a giant among men. How cruel and unjust would his successor be? How much would he raise taxes, and what new ones would he invent? Bonaparte could laugh and joke, the people now started to say; he was light-blooded, and as often as he ruled unjustly, he ruled justly. He'd had his faults, but ...

And on the people went, praising Napoleon as I had never in my life heard a ruler of Egypt praised. They even ascribed virtues to him that he had never had, which told me how deeply distressed people were over his departure. If Egyptians were that worried, it was beyond me what the French were feeling, if Pauline's crumbling in a dead faint to the floor was in any way emblematic of it.

Father locked himself in his prayer room for days. When he emerged, he looked as stricken as Pauline. "How could he have done this to me?" Father's dream of siring a ruling dynasty from the loins of the great general and his daughter had vanished. It was a cruel joke but not undeserved. Zaynab, Napoleon's Egyptian girl, was coldly comforted by his disappearance. She detested the man, thinking him a grim reaper stalking the vineyards of the young. He selfishly consumed the lives of young men to batten his power and glory. To her he was a curse, but for completely different reasons than Muslims cursed him. They cursed him for being a Christian invader from the West. Zaynab cursed him for being a man who hurt women by leading men to their deaths as tribute to his personal glory. He had killed her Belmond, and he had wounded Pauline so deeply that Zaynab (Zuzu, as Pauline dearly called her) thought the wound might be mortal, owing to her too-frequent allusions to death being preferable to life and her questions to Zaynab about Egypt's poisonous flowers and vipers and other killer snakes.

As Pauline had comforted Zaynab over her loss of Belmond, Zaynab now comforted Pauline over her brutal abandonment by the great conqueror who was supposed to marry her. When Zaynab wasn't at the institute, she stayed with Pauline and even slept in her bed, which eventually led me to suspect—and then believe, after an embarrassing unannounced visit to Pauline's chamber—that their comforting each other had reached a point beyond which neither my tongue can speak nor my pen move. Well, if it saved Pauline and gave them pleasure, then all the better, but in truth, I would have given my life if I could have traded places with my sister for a night. And I had high hopes that I might, once Pauline got over Bonaparte and realized that as a man, I was far more suitable for giving her pleasure than Zuzu. But that part comes later.

General Kleber was our new ruler. He was no Napoleon. He didn't laugh or joke or, thank God, spout empty professions of Islamic faith or play the clown in robe and turban while mincing around with the Quran balanced on his head. General Kleber was more interested in getting his troops safely out of Egypt and back to France than in nurturing Napoleon's whimsical marriage of two peoples to sire a Franco-Egyptian commercial empire. He seemed to neither like nor dislike Egypt and Egyptians; at least he was honest. He was outraged at Napoleon's abandonment of his troops. He called it treachery—flying the coop without orders to stage a coup d'etat back home, while thirty thousand surviving French soldiers languished in a hostile land. Kleber, who truly cared for his troops, called for Bonaparte's court martial and execution. Rumor had it that Kleber was secretly negotiating an evacuation treaty with the Ottomans and the English. He wanted to go back to France and run his sword through Bonaparte's egotistical breast. He wanted to take his men back home, and they wanted to go. The Egyptian venture had become a debacle, one disaster after the next: the fleet sent to the bottom of abu Qir Bay; the revolt of the previous October; the disastrous Syrian campaign; the plague; and now the commander in chief abandoning his post and his men, leaving them to survive the best they could or slowly die off, one by one, until there would be nothing left of them but their graffiti inside the pyramids as a reminder that there had once been a French colony in Egypt with dreams as big as the world.

Pauline told me that the rumors of negotiations were true, but talks had broken down. The English government demanded total surrender, but Kleber said his army would be allowed to leave in possession of their weapons and with their heads held high or they would die defending their honor. It looked like it was going to be the latter.

Another Ottoman army invaded, and Kleber led his troops into the desert to meet it. While the French were routing the main force, a smaller one advanced on Cairo and claimed that the French had been defeated. The stratagem worked: the city exploded in revolt for the second time. Again it was the rabble and wretched with nothing to lose that started it.

Zaynab and I were with Pauline at the institute when we heard shouting and then musket fire. From the sound of it, Azbakiyyah was surrounded by insurrectionists. We went to the roof to see what was happening. The few hundred soldiers who had been left to defend the city were withdrawing to military headquarters in central Azbakiyyah. The Ottoman troops entered Cairo unresisted, but they were few compared to the thousands of riffraff storming through the streets, looting and burning. Columns of smoke were rising up from every quarter of the city. The French Quarter of Azbakiyyah was surrounded by howling mobs risen up from the bowels of squalor. Soon the warehouses and affluent homes of the consular and merchant quarter were in flames. The Coptic and Jewish communities were attacked, and then the homes of well-to-do Muslims. The mobs made no religious distinction in its frenzy of looting, burning, rape, mutilation, and murder.

Men fleeing the burning buildings were clubbed and hacked to death; girls and women were raped and then their throats slit. A man and woman in western clothes leapt from a second-floor window by the canal without injuring themselves and were running toward military headquarters when a gang of club-wielding youths in rags saw them and took off after them with blood-curdling shrieks. The woman stumbled in the field; the man turned back, grabbed her by the arm, and was pulling her after him when one of the youths caught up with them and struck the woman down with a blow to the back. Her European companion fended off the youth, who was wildly swinging his club, but within seconds the man was surrounded, struck down, and beaten. One of the youths drew a long blade from under his galabiyya and swung it across the man's neck. Two more whacks and his neck was severed, his head rolling onto the dirt. Then they threw the screaming woman down on the ground, tore off her clothes, and raped her in turns. One man who had finished raping her took the bloody, dirt-covered head, drove it upright onto the pointed end of a pike, and held it aloft, crying, "God is great!" over and over again while his companions continued in turn raping the screaming woman—wretched young men and boys, the downtrodden getting their own back on the rich.

The French soldiers up at the Citadel poured musket and artillery fire down on the popular quarters of the city, but there was nothing the French could do to halt the attack on Azbakiyyah for fear of hitting their own people.

From the tops of minarets, muezzins were calling the people out into the streets to kill the French with whatever weapons or tools they could find. The cry was carried from minaret to minaret, quarter to quarter. Soon the canals were clogged with corpses. A hail of fire from the few hundred troops guarding military headquarters cut down the front ranks of the mobs that were pouring out of the streets and heading for the canal bank and Azbakiyya. The attackers kept charging against the relentless fire, the bodies of their fallen comrades mounting around them. Still they continued forward, and by the time they reached the outer perimeter of military headquarters, their numbers were so few that they turned in retreat, running and stumbling over the dead and dying. Seeing what was happening, the Ottoman officers directed their troops against the looters, ironically making the French and Ottomans allies for the moment.

Having given up on overtaking military headquarters, the mob turned to the buildings of the institute. Zaynab took my arm. Her eyes bespoke the fear and confusion that possessed us both. We were Egyptians in a French institute being attacked by Egyptians—illiterate dregs, but Egyptians nonetheless. Where did we belong in all this madness? Our world was slipping away. The raging chorus of "God is great!" from the poverty-stricken boys about to die played to the crack of muskets laying them low, as their death cries and corpses joined those of their victims.

Jaubert handed me a musket. "Go with Zaynab and Pauline to the commander in chief's palace," he said. "You'll be safer there. Two soldiers will accompany you."

"No. I'll stay here with you."

Jaubert shrugged, the way the French do. "As you wish." Marcel glanced at me and also shrugged: "Comme vous voulez." He and the other savants were holding their muskets as if they'd never held one before. The dozen soldiers assigned to protect the building were already firing at the approaching rabble. From the roof, I watched Zaynab, Pauline, and their escort run the short distance across the courtyard and garden to Alfi Bey's palace. They were concealed from sight of the attacking mobs by a garden wall and hedged path that Napoleon had built to connect his palace to the ones housing the institute. When he installed Pauline in the palace across from his, he had the walls and hedges extended between those two palaces as well so they could visit each other unobserved.

When I was sure they had made it across safely, I turned from the balustrade at the edge of the roof. One of the soldiers was glancing at me in cold suspicion: what was an Egyptian in a turban armed with a musket doing with them? I took the hint, leaned the musket against the balustrade, and went downstairs. Soldiers and savants were nailing planks over the doors and windows and barricading them with chairs and tables. Several other savants were hurriedly packing away their research papers, books, and scientific equipment to keep them out of harm's way—regarding them, it seemed to me, with more care and importance than they did their own lives. I returned to the roof, not knowing where to go or what to do.

Artillery fire from the Citadel was raining down on the rebel-held quarters, which meant practically the whole of the city except our little island inside Azbakiyyah. The rebels—or liberators—had either seized or fabricated several pieces of artillery and were firing on military headquarters. Encouraged by that bombardment, feeble as it was, another mob of rebels braved the musket fire coming from the institute and charged the outer guard posts, running over their dead into the exploding shells of their own artillery. They reached the outer defenses and streamed into the courtyard, where they were cut down like stalks of sugarcane.

From the roof I could see another horde of rabble swarming toward Alfi Bey's palace, the commander in chief's residence. They made it to the outer gates and were left hanging on its spikes, riddled by the steady fire coming from behind the protective walls. Their bodies piled up at the gate and formed a mound for other rebels to climb over and leap into the courtyard. Primitively armed with hatchets, knives, and sabers taken from fallen troops, they ran for the palace, howling their war cry, "God is great!" I thought of Zaynab and Pauline inside and closed my eyes.

13

THE INSTITUTE WAS ABOUT to succumb. A motley horde of screaming rebels was pounding staves and clubs against the doors and boarded-up windows. I crouched in a corner beneath the crenelated parapet and waited for the end. The musket that Jaubert had given me, expecting without a second thought that I would use it against my fellow Muslims in defense of the French, our occupiers, was leaning against the parapet where I had left it. A soldier next to me dropped his musket and slumped down against the wall with a line of blood trickling down his forehead, his glassy eyes staring at me as though accusing me of something.

Just then artillery fire started pouring in from outside the city walls onto the rebel-held quarters. Two more soldiers came up to the roof to fire down on the attackers. One of them said that the artillery bombardment was coming from General Kleber, who must have just arrived and was pounding the city into submission. The soldier hoped he pounded it to the ground. "That won't do us any good," replied the other soldier, a sentry a year or so younger than me who was stationed at the institute and whom I had gotten to know and found to be friendly and likeable. "What do you think, Zaki? Do we have chance?" he asked me with a brave smile, but before I could speak, he twirled around with a sharp cry, dropped his musket, brought his hands to his neck, and fell to the ground. For a minute he lay there gasping for air, making a gurgling sound as blood flowed from his throat. Then he fell silent and stopped writhing. Staring at him as his last seconds of life wheezed away, I was sure I saw in the young soldier's face my own end that was near at hand.

I looked over the parapet toward Alfi Bey's palace. The mob had broken through. People who had taken refuge inside were running out in an attempt to escape. A wounded soldier was seized, and as his head was being cut from his neck, his screams echoed across the field. A woman was pursued and thrown down by half a dozen men and her European clothes torn off. Ignoring the risk of being shot, the men held her down to take turns raping her. I aimed my musket at the one lifting his robe to be first, missed, and ran down from the roof to meet my end.

Soldiers and savants were firing point-blank through the splintering boards of the windows. Then the doors gave way and the muskets couldn't be loaded fast enough to keep the attackers from clambering over their mounting heaps of dead and wounded to come plunging through. The soldiers emptied their muskets and then drove their bayonets into them. Jaubert swung a sword across the neck of a young boy who had broken in. The boy's head fell limply forward from his neck like a broken stalk as he was momentarily paralyzed with his arms flung out and then fell back onto the floor next to the corpses of several other youths. I backed against a wall and waited for death.

The French were at last overwhelmed. The soldiers were the first to be dispatched because of their uniforms. They fought to the end. It was a matter of professional pride. As soldiers and officers, they knew it would be useless to expect mercy. They were right. A few of the savants threw down their swords and empty muskets in surrender only to be cut down by the young men and boys in rags crying out the greatness of God. Jaubert took a vicious sword strike to the shoulder; the blade cut deep, almost severing his arm. He cried out and went down. Marcel and four or five other savants were still left. A Maghrabi sailor crashed through the door with a musket. He aimed it at Marcel and thumbed back the flintlock. I wanted to cry out in appeal to the Maghrabi's sense of Islamic justice to let the men surrender, but my tongue had frozen to my palate. Marcel's eyes found mine and widened in recognition of my presence. His mouth opened as if to say something, and at the same instant an explosion jerked his head back. I closed my eyes. When I opened them, another Maghrabi was hacking Marcel's head off.

A young beggar leapt in front of me. The tip of his bloody sword pressed into my stomach. He was smiling when I closed my eyes to meet death.

"Hold off! He's not one of them. Have respect for his turban." An older man pushed the sword away from my stomach.

"He's with them!" the beggar shouted. "He dies!"

"No!" I shook my head. "I was a hostage. I'm a student at al-Azhar!"

"He lies! Let the steel strike his neck!"

"I swear it! By God! They arrested me as a hostage!"

"Leave him," the older man ordered. "He's a man of religion."

"Man of religion! What religion?"

"Islam! The one true religion of God!" I cried out.

"What's your name?" he asked me.

"Bakri. I'm the son of Shaykh Khalil al-Bakri."

"Bakri?" The beggar spit on me and drew back his sword to swing it at me.

The older man stayed his arm. "Leave him! He's only the son."

"He's one of them!"

"I swear to God I'm not!" I put my hand over my heart. I couldn't keep it from trembling. "I was brought here by force and held hostage!"

"Leave him, we have enough heads. We don't need a turbaned one. Here, try this on the end of your sword." The older man drove the dripping base of a head onto the end of the beggar's weapon. It was Marcel's. He was still staring at me. I turned my head away like the sniveling coward I was.

Heads and sex organs were being hacked off the dead Frenchmen. Those unfortunates who hadn't yet died of their wounds were stripped and sodomized, then mutilated. The uncircumcised sex organs would bring a handsome reward from the Ottoman pasha. The heads were mounted on pikes and swords and paraded outside, away from military headquarters and its two hundred soldiers who hadn't stopped firing away.

In the courtyard, Jaubert was being sodomized by two beggars. Blood was still running from his shoulder; I couldn't tell if he was dead or alive. The brute finished with him and rolled him over for mutilation. As one of them stood over him with an ax aimed at his neck and the other drew out a knife to sever the organ, there was a volley of fire from an adjacent building that had been retaken by a body of soldiers advancing from headquarters. The shots felled several rebels and scattered the rest, including the two who had been about to dismember Jaubert.

I unwound my turban and crawled to him. While I was attending to him, wrapping the long band tightly around the deep gash in his shoulder, shots from French military headquarters whistled past. The cloth turned red, but Jaubert's bleeding stopped. Having done what I could, I sprang back to the protection of the building. Three or four shots rang out behind me. After having stood by in mute cowardice and watched Marcel being brutally killed, I had risked my life to save Jaubert, who was probably dead or minutes from being so. I prayed that helping Jaubert somehow made up for my cowardice and that I could live with myself for the little time I had left. Just being able to live with myself would be enough. I knew I would never have peace. How could I know peace when I didn't know which side I was on? Did I have a side anymore? It was a blessing that death's cloak was already descending upon me.

Laden with booty, the rebel mob was dancing in wild triumph through the streets, chanting God's greatness and glory. High over their heads, bobbing up and down in tempo with them, the heads of their victims looked like sacred totems borne aloft in celebration of some fiendish cult. To blend in, I threw up my arms and chanted along with them. As we approached Alfi Bey's palace, I braced myself for a worse horror. Slowing my pace, I let the chanting mob leave me behind, and when they were far enough ahead, I turned to make sure no one was looking and then made a mad dash across the dirt road and into the field fronting Alfi Bey's palace.

The blood on the tile floor stuck to my sandals. I stepped over the mutilated corpses, turning the severed heads of the females. Had Zaynab's and Pauline's youth and beauty saved them for a life of slavery? Would a quick and brutal death after being raped multiple times be preferable to life as a harem slave? Having searched the palace and inspected all the heads, I followed the hedged-in path to Pauline's villa and ascended the stairs to her bedchamber. At the entrance, the heads of her two Coptic chambermaids had been placed between their naked, spread legs. Blood was everywhere.

But not in Pauline's empty bedchamber. The fertility statue with the long, erect penis had been smashed, like everything else that was breakable. Bits of porcelain, crystal, and marble crunched under my feet. I was relieved to find no other bodies. I sat on the edge of Pauline's bed, looking around at the destruction, searching for traces of blood. The satin curtain that had hidden the fertility statue in its niche at the head of the room had been torn from its rod and lay across the floor like a burial shroud. On the other side of it, lying at the back of the niche, I saw one of Pauline's or Zaynab's slippers—only one. I picked it up, looking for blood.

There was none. Its mate was nowhere to be found. Wondering how one slipper had ended up behind the curtain in the niche, I picked up a length of the enormous penis that hadn't been properly smashed and, rubbing its bulbous head, pondered the mystery of the single slipper.

I turned to the niche and squatted. I had once told Pauline that these great Mamluk palaces were always built with a secret passage so the emir could escape in case a rival Mamluk or an assassin sent by the Ottoman pasha or the sultan in Istanbul came to finish him off in one of their perennial power struggles. Each palace had its own unique secret passage, and the story was that the architect who designed a palace was killed when it was finished to prevent him from telling anyone where the passage was. The problem with that story, Pauline had remarked, was that no architect would have been willing to build a Mamluk palace after knowing the fate of the first architect to build one. Probably because it was such a good story, I hadn't bothered to think about it and discover that flaw on my own.

Pauline had smiled and told me that Nappy had discovered her secret passage one night when she was playing hide-and-seek with him in the palace, adding mysteriously that her secret passage was now guarded by something larger and more lasting than any man. I hadn't known what she meant. I thought at the time that maybe she was alluding to some bizarre sex play she had with Nappy, and that her secret passage was an allusion to her vagina. But of course! I understood it now, in a flash: she had meant the fertility statue!

I kissed the bloated knob of the penis and tossed it onto the bed and then got on my knees to search the niche. There were no architectural hands or jutting stones that were levers in disguise. I pushed against the marble slabs that formed the arch of the niche, and then the stones at the back and sides of it. Nothing budged. I kept pushing here and there on every distinct section of marble and granite until, in frustration, I pushed hard against the backside of the niche. I felt it give. I pushed harder. There was a slight movement, a hairline separation along the joint between the side of the niche and the wall. I got on my back and pushed my feet against the side. The concave formation swiveled on a vertical axis with a grinding creak of stone on stone.

I crawled into the dark opening. Handgrips on the backside of the moveable wall allowed it to be opened from inside the passage. I closed it and crawled on in the dark. A short ways inside, I found by feeling my way that the passage became larger, allowing me to stand. I advanced forward.

How cleverly those architects had constructed the passage. The trigonometry of construction was remarkable: the slope of descent from the second floor of the palace to the ground was set at an angle that made passage in the dark as easy as it was safe. As the exit of the tunnel was designed to be a good distance beyond the outer walls of the palace, the descent was gentle, which prevented broken necks and ankles in case of a stumble or fall. Physically safe as the descent in total darkness was from a structural point of view, there was a worry more disturbing than tripping and falling, and as I progressed through the darkness, I kept repeating to myself aloud that the earthy smell of the dark and dank air would be most inhospitable to poisonous snakes, spiders, and scorpions.

The passageway leveled off, then started to narrow and diminish in height, forcing me back to crawling on my hands and knees. Slits of light appeared ahead. I could make out a hewn, cube-shaped stone set at the end of the tunnel. Above the stone, light filtered through a circular patchwork of what turned out to be a woven cover of palm fronds and weeds. I climbed onto the stone and pushed the cover away. The light hurt my eyes. When they adjusted, I saw the surface of the sandy ground and the tall palms, and beyond them the line of reeds. The canal was just ahead. I pulled myself out of the tunnel and crawled to the lush, damp growth of reeds along the bank. Across the canal, the quarters where the poorer classes lived were on fire. Hundreds of columns of black smoke were rising up and spreading to form one dark cloud over the whole city. Bulaq, the Nile port of Cairo and the section where all the warehouses were located along the riverbank, was hidden in a dome of smoke and fire.

Concealed in the reeds, I watched the shouting mobs go about their work of destruction, as if the city had to be burned to the ground and plundered before the task of driving out the French could begin. There was a symmetry to the destruction: while the wild mobs were doing their share, General Kleber and his artillery were busily at work doing theirs from outside the city walls, as if the city had to be destroyed before it could be saved from the looting gangs.

I searched the forest of reeds and tall grass and found Zaynab and Pauline hidden in a thick clump of growth between the palm grove and the canal. They were lying in each other's arms, holding on for dear life and crying in terror, as much from the thundering artillery as from the wild, high-pitched shouts coming from both sides of the canal and fusing in a hysterical Franco-Egyptian chorus that called for the slaughter of all French, all Muslims, all Christians, all Jews—one insane call for the slaughter of all. This, I feared, was to be our future. France had brought us the West's version of civilization.

I joined Zaynab and Pauline, and after we had all hugged and cried, we lay concealed in the high grass and reeds at the edge of the water, holding hands and listening to the thunder of war and the crazed cries for slaughter. When the sun was close to the horizon, we entered the secret passage and returned to Pauline's palace, where we remained hidden until the violence at last abated.

Fighting raged in the city for eleven days. Day after day, the muezzins in their minarets cried out to the people to fight on, saying it was their religious duty—fight on and God's promise would be fulfilled, the armies of Islam pounding at the city walls would deliver them from the evils of the French. The problem with that was it was the French who were pounding at our walls and bombarding the city; the army of Islam had long been routed and sent packing back to Syria and Istanbul by General Kleber. At the peak of the violence, fifty thousand Cairenes were in the streets, armed with everything from stones to muskets, as well as twelve artillery pieces—eight they had seized from the French, four they had primitively fabricated based on the French model, an accomplishment that stands as our first wobbly step into the world of modern technology.

The French battled the rebels house to house and street to street, hurling down their superior firepower from the Citadel and the fortified towers along the city walls, which they soon recaptured. As the killing and burning progressed, the social order was turned on its head. At first the mob attacked Christian homes and establishments. Upstanding Muslims and their imams said it was in revenge for the way the Christians had lorded it over the Muslims when the French were in command and so it was God's will: the Christians deserved exactly what they were getting. When the Christians' property had been plundered and the mobs turned on the Muslims and the rich in general, the rabble then went from being the agents of God's will to agents of Satan, rebels against the true religion. Who knew what that was anymore?

The revolt became a bloodbath overthrowing all order and structure: the poor and lawless took from the rich and lawful, the weak became the strong, the ignorant overpowered the intelligent, the lowest lorded it over the highest, the scum and dregs of society rose to the top. When the poor had taken from the rich and were now rich themselves, those who were even poorer rose up to plunder the newly rich. There was no end to it. Day and night, one took from the other in an endless cycle of burning and looting.

After days and nights of unceasing bombardment from within and without, buildings started collapsing on people, mud brick hovels crumbling along with marble and granite palaces. Whole sections of the city were laid waste under the incessant rain of fire and iron. People lived in the streets for fear of being buried in the rubble of their homes. At night they huddled together in the open air, seeking refuge beside the mountains of debris, praying that the shells hurtling down wouldn't find them. Animals and people starved in the streets, their moans fusing with those of the wounded dying beneath the rubble. The stench of the dead was unbearable, as the historians say, but people seemed to bear it, at least those who survived. There were no hospitals where the wounded could be taken, as the mob had pillaged them too. In any case, so many people were dying from wounds and lost limbs that hospitals would have made little difference.

Women maddened by the ceaseless thunder of cannons and the crying of their starving children ran screaming in the streets, tearing at their hair and breasts, slapping their faces in terror as if the hellish cataclysm were in some way their fault—which it was, if one believed our imams and other pious Muslims who declared the torment was God's will to punish the sinful people.

Starvation took as many lives as the cannons and slaughtering mobs; a pouch full of coins might buy a handful of rice, cup of milk, or mouthful of honey, but most people were eating dogs, rats, cats, cockroaches, lizards, worms, snakes—anything that ran, hopped, crawled, crept, or slithered. People no longer cared who won the battle as long as it came to an end. Most people didn't know who was fighting whom or who the enemy was, for in the madness of bloodletting, plundering, looting, and vengeance in the name of religion, the French were all but forgotten.

As in any cataclysm, there were heroic acts of bravery and selflessness. A few rich shaykhs and merchants gave large sums of money and food they had stored in their homes to the poor and suffering. Others who had nothing to give risked their lives crawling through a hail of musket and shell fire to drag the wounded to safety. Many people were killed trying to save another person's life. There were cases of Muslim families risking their lives by giving refuge to French people.

At last the bombardment halted. The artillery in the hands of the rebels had already fallen silent for lack of powder. The leaders of the rebel mob, mostly the sons of low-level shaykhs and young men from the lower levels of the religious class, were captured and executed. Leaderless, the revolt broke apart and was destroyed piecemeal in short order. The end came so quickly and unexpectedly that people claimed it a miracle, a sign of God's pleasure.

God works in mysterious ways. What brought a quick end to at least the fiercest part of the fighting was a bit of treachery that was breathtaking even for people used to Mamluk ways. The emir Murad Bey, seeing which way the contest was going, abandoned both the Ottomans and the rebels and signed a treaty with the French, in return for which he was made governor of Upper Egypt, in service of the French. To show his and his army's sincerity, Murad Bey supplied General Kleber with a list of what he claimed were the names of the revolt's leaders. And they called Father a lackey! If God's will prevails, there is something seriously wrong with the human concept of justice, goodness, and fairness—a theological issue that has caused much debate among our scholastic theologians ever since our first rationalist religious thinkers discussed it a thousand years ago, and which still hasn't been settled.

Father and several other leading shaykhs had gone up to the Citadel to make peace with the French, hoping to end the bombardment and establish law and order before the rootless mob devastated the whole of society. A couple of those shaykhs happened to be on Murad Bey's list and were imprisoned. Sadat and Sharqawi were at the top of the list as leading conspirators. The angry generals wanted to execute them on the spot, but Kleber agreed only to slap a stiff fine on them: the French still needed the shaykhs as intermediaries, just as they had when Napoleon ruled.

An agreement was drawn up between the French generals and the shaykhs who had been chosen to represent the people. In return for general amnesty, the people would pay a sizeable indemnity to the French for the material loss they had suffered. The lives of the imprisoned shaykhs would be spared, and the French would put an end to the mobs and the looting. When the shaykhs came down from the Citadel and were making their way through the barricades of one of the rebel-held quarters where the looting was still continuing, they were fired upon by the mob and had to flee. In another quarter, they were accosted by a mob of youths and citizens who cursed them and called them lackeys and traitors, no better than Frenchmen. Father defended the shaykhs. He said it was Murad Bey and the Mamluks, not the shaykhs, who were the lackeys and traitors. "We have brought you peace," he declared (a little too pompously, I thought, considering the circumstances). "Is dealing with the French for the security of the city, is that, in your eyes, being French? Is saving you from the fires of the devil by taming the devil, is that being in league with the devil? By the Almighty God who with but a breath scatters sun and stars to dust and crumbles mountains to butterflies, if the French are devils, I saved you from the devil and his evil. Does facing evil to save others from evil make one evil?"

A voice from the rear shouted, "Yes!" Everybody turned. It was a blind religious teacher. His turban and frayed robe showed him to be at the lowest level of the profession, an ignorant villager whose instruction consisted of Quranic memorization. The peasant boys who were his students were barely able to read at the end of their schooling, though they had memorized the Quran, its words and skewed meaning carved deeply into their young minds, inscriptions on a block of stone forever ready to be recited, if not read and understood. The man's eyes stared glossily ahead of him like petrified jelly, like the eyes in those heads being carried aloft on the ends of pikes. Though sightless, he had put fire into the brains of his pupils, and they would blindly follow his fiery words, blind leading the blind to destruction.

"To associate with a Frangi is to be a Frangi!" cried the shaykh-teacher, his dead eyes locked in hollow sockets, spittle spraying from his mouth and hanging from his unwashed beard. "To rub against evil is to be evil!" He nudged a small boy at his side and the boy hurled a rock that flew by Father's head. Several people around the preacher started chanting, "To

190

rub against evil is to be evil!" The chant was taken up by the crowd. "No to peace, yes to holy war! Death to the French and those who serve them!"

The shaykhs had to run for it. The mob was in control and wanted nothing to spoil their free-for-all plundering spree. To emphasize their point, they looted and burned down one of the houses Father owned in a part of the city they now controlled. They also burned down Shaykh Mahdi's house. Mahdi, the secretary-general of the special diwan, had earlier given Marcel a collection of his stories to translate and have published in Paris. People knew about this, and both Mahdi and Father might have come to worse ends had not some cool-headed and responsible Egyptians come to their aid. From then on, the shaykhs left it to the French army to snuff out the remaining fires of revolt in their own way. The brutal contest between well-armed, organized violence and poorly armed, disorganized violence was quickly decided.

The revolt was a turning point. It discouraged one side as much as the other in their respective aspirations. It made Egyptians realize they could not drive the French out by force, and the French that they could not make Frenchmen out of Egyptians. Napoleon had been the driving force behind the Franco-Egyptian marriage, and with him having absconded to France, the French he left behind wondered what in the world they were doing in Egypt, so far from home and with no way to get back. Their gold and silver were gone, their numbers had been cut in half, and the remaining half was rapidly dwindling. A year had passed since Napoleon fled, and he had sent no reinforcements or material assistance from France. He had led his countrymen here, he had become Sultan al-Kabir and then had abandoned them for his greater glory as dictator of France and promptly forgotten them. Egypt had been for him but an adventure, a stepping-stone to more power. The second revolt brought a brutal close to Bonaparte's Egyptian adventure. The men he abandoned wanted to go home. General Kleber set his policy to that end.

Having decided to withdraw from Egypt, Kleber was not so concerned about Franco-Egyptian harmony. Taxes became oppressive. If a man couldn't pay his share, his property was confiscated. If that didn't cover it, the burden of the remainder fell to his neighbor. "Collective communal responsibility," it was called. Anyone suspected of anti-French activity was executed on the spot and his home blown up. The home of anyone who left the city trying to escape the oppression would also be blown up; fleeing was now a subversive activity. The demolition of family homes was a form of punishment we had never before experienced.

After the revolt, the French relied heavily on our Christians, particularly the Syrian Christians, for support. The French created a Coptic brigade of five thousand troops to police the Muslims. They marched around in French uniforms, pushing us out of their way and shouting, "The rule of Islam is finished! We rule over you now!" That wasn't wise for a small religious minority dependent on foreign rulers who were only too eager to abandon Egypt and their Egyptian supporters. One generalization you can never go wrong with: people are stupid.

Zaynab and I returned home from Pauline's palace and resumed studying at the institute once it had been speedily repaired. It wasn't the same. Napoleon's departure and the revolt had cut the heart out of it. Berthollet and Monge had absconded with Napoleon; Venture de Paradise and Marcel were dead; and many of the savants, though carrying on with their work, were only waiting until it was time to pack up and go home. Zaynab hoped that day would never come. "Without a fleet, how can they go home?" she asked when we were back at the institute library, finishing up our translation to Arabic of Montesquieu's *Esprit des Lois*.

I shrugged at her question the way the French do when they don't know something (and often when they do). "Their numbers get less and less. They have no purpose here. If they don't leave, they'll die out in a few years."

"They can keep marrying into the population and have children. They don't need to go home."

"Kleber wants them to go home."

"Too bad for Kleber. The savants like it here."

"Do they?"

"Most of them do. Some of them. Amadeus does."

Amadeus Jaubert lived, minus an arm, and if it hadn't been for me, he'd have also been minus a man's dearest organ—or at least that's what I liked to think. With Marcel and Venture de Paradise and Berthollet and Napoleon gone, Jaubert assumed a protective role over Zaynab that was more akin to Venture's fatherly feelings than Marcel's romantic inclinations. I didn't mind. I was grateful to him for having survived. It let me believe I had saved his life, which relieved my sense of cowardice and loss for having helplessly stood by as Marcel was killed. I never told Jaubert or anyone else that I had saved him. It meant more to me as a secret of my own.

With his one arm, Amadeus resumed his task of cataloging the Arabic and Turkish manuscripts that the French were planning to take to Paris, but how they were ever going to get there, nobody knew. Zaynab and I helped him do the cataloging, contributing to the French looting of our literary heritage, but since it looked like the French had become prisoners in Egypt and would die there, we didn't see it that way. Especially Zaynab. She refused to accept that the French would ever leave. She resisted believing it even after Pauline slipped away on a Dutch frigate, expecting Napoleon to greet her with open arms and marry her when she got to Paris. Before she left, I went to her palace in a fit of lust.

"I'll not play Napoleon for a cuckold like that bitch, Josephine!" she declared, unwinding my turban before we jumped into her bed. "That's not my way. So I had better get my fill while I can. But don't get the wrong idea, Zaki—my heart still belongs to Nappy."

"It's not your heart I'm after."

"Just don't get me pregnant."

"I thought that's what you wanted."

"Only from the ruler of France."

After we slaked our lust the first time, she clung to me, hot and sweaty, her reddish-blond hair covering my arm. "Nappy may be short on some things," she sighed after a long silence, "but a woman has to sacrifice something if she's married to the ruler of the civilized world."

The next day Pauline was gone. Zaynab was heartbroken again. She had lost Belmond, then Marcel, and now Pauline. Some of the most brilliant lights of the institute were gone. Pauline's departure left her desperate. If Pauline could leave, then why not the savants, one by one, emptying the institute of its soul, of all its promise and magic?

I shouldn't have pitied Zaynab as I did. Pity so utterly concentrates us on our own weaknesses that we tend to underestimate the strength of those we pity, as though the suffering we read in others, when reflected back onto us, is magnified by our own exaggerated sensitivities, in the fashion of one of those French reading glasses that can focus sunlight to burn through wood. Now that I look back on it, I see that Zaynab showed more strength than I did, bereaved as she was at having lost her loving officer, her mentor-scholars, and her dear, sisterly friend and companion, Pauline.

I remember when we returned to the institute following the end of the revolt and found Jaubert there, mulling over some manuscript in the translation room between the library and the rooms of the printing press. Zaynab embraced him and cried, and he put his one arm around her and she kissed him as though she were kissing all of them—Belmond, Venture, Marcel, Pauline, Berthollet ... They clung together, holding each other as though reaffirming their lives. Holding his hand and mine, she gazed at the papers strewn over the floor, and at the large globe of the world that had been cleaved in two during the fighting. Using strips of bloodstained cloth, she bound the two halves and set the broken sphere on its stand. *Our world wrapped in bloody bandages,* I thought, watching her cradle the misshapen globe in her arms to keep it together in its stand, *our fractured world that she couldn't bear seeing split.* But split it was—as split as she was. As for me, I didn't know where I was or where I stood, so how could I feel split? I felt splintered.

Gradually Cairo returned to life. The taverns and cafés reopened, Tivoli was rebuilt, men and women mingled in public in more numbers than they had before. Many Egyptian families had become impoverished: a daughter with a French soldier meant survival. On the surface, Cairo was once again Paris on the Nile. But beneath the wrappings of conviviality, the wounds festered. The anti-Muslim slogans of the Coptic brigade in their French uniforms were daily infusions of venom that curdled our despair into cold hatred. To compound our humiliation, a Copt was appointed head of the French tax-collecting crew. Dressed up in a fancy French officer's uniform, he was escorted by a corps of wreckers armed with axes, picks, and sledge hammers to level the homes of those who didn't or couldn't pay their taxes. Many families saw their homes and possessions smashed before their eyes; larger homes were blown up. The owners were prohibited from removing any of their furniture or possessions. The result was that in their effort to rebuild the city, the French ended up destroying more and more of it.

The Copt who headed the wrecking crew was named Shukrallah—"Thanks-To-God." Thanks-To-God and his wreckers were zealous in their work and enjoyed it; they loved finding people who couldn't pay their taxes. They looted the homes before destroying them and were paid a commission on each house they leveled. They grew rich on destruction. Some merchants who could well afford their taxes let their businesses be wrecked rather than pay taxes to the Copt, Thanks-To-God, who was made all the richer by their bravery. A few responsible leaders of the Coptic community warned Shukrallah and the Coptic brigade that what they were doing was wrong and might go against innocent people one day. They laughed. They didn't know a sword has two edges. Just because it was cutting on one edge today didn't mean it couldn't be turned to the other edge tomorrow.

While Thanks-To-God and his demolition crew were growing rich making families homeless, the French built a theater called the Comedy. All the plays were in French; none were translated into Arabic. The theater was built with money that had been squeezed from the Egyptians—from those who paid taxes as well as those who suffered homelessness—and the French had the nerve to call it the Comedy. Zaynab's French was by now good enough that she could have easily understood the plays—mine was too, to an extent—but neither of us went. We saw nothing to laugh about, and no comedy could change that.

14

N O SOONER DID THE second revolt end in late spring than a plague broke out in early summer. Nature was intervening in its season of rebirth to finish off what the winter of revolt had spared. By the first week in June, people were dropping like flies. The plague was more democratic than the revolt; it carried off everyone: weak, strong, rich, poor, French, Egyptian, Christian, Muslim, Jew. No family, no community was spared. Not even French artillery could defend against it.

We had a time-honored way of dealing with plague: we ignored it. If it infected a family member or friend, we accepted it as God's inscrutable will and held communal prayers for the victim's recovery, and then held the funeral, all according to tradition and the bottomless capacity of Egyptians to accept suffering and go on with life, smiling and making jokes in the cruelest of conditions. The French would have none of this hallowed tradition. Thinking the plague to be preventable, and even curable when it struck, they made no jokes and gave no room for humor, as though they regarded sickness and death as either an aberration of nature or a flaw to be corrected by science and medicine. Their physicians presumed to have a cure for everything. Our shaykhs and Egyptian doctors ridiculed their description of the cure, which was publicly posted in Arabic and claimed to do what only God could do. They called it "fumigation and quarantine." We laughed aloud when the French community stripped down their bedding, washed it in boiling water, and then swept and scrubbed their living quarters and furnishings. Our laughter turned hysterical when quarantine regulations ordered that no one enter or leave a house inhabited by a victim of the disease, which included us pious Muslims. The shaykhs of the diwan refused to endorse the quarantine and urged people not to adhere to the rules, which they considered too ungodly, an abomination of all that was sacred, as evil as Satan's breath. The French had ordered that no one was to visit the sick; that the dead were to be buried quickly and without ceremony in a communal pit outside the city; and that the house of a deceased person must be sealed off immediately, as if it were possessed by the devil French physicians presumed to usurp the power of God, the almighty who decided who should live and who should die of plague.

Egyptians hid their dead to keep them from the men in white gloves and masks who collected the bodies every morning and dumped them in their pits like garbage. Egyptians hid their sick from the unholy French doctors and held secret funerals in accordance to sacred tradition, which required the deceased be buried before the third day after death. We couldn't figure out how it was that the plague swept up Egyptian households and their visitors so swiftly, one after the other, like an insatiable, starving beast, while in the French Quarter, where the scrubbing and ungodly quarantine regulations were strictly enforced, there were comparatively few deaths. People wondered at the discrepancy. Was God saving the French for a worse fate? We couldn't imagine anything worse than death by plague, but no one doubted that God would be able to whip up something pretty nasty when the time came.

Called by the French to account for the huge difference between French and Egyptian deaths, our wise shaykhs and doctors patiently explained to them that it was simply due to Fate, in other words, God's will, as was everything in the universe, which the French took to be an inadequate explanation seriously lacking in science. Some shaykhs went so far as to claim that the French deaths, even though many times fewer than the Egyptians', proved irrefutably that burning bedding, scrubbing, quarantine, and immediately burying the dead were satanic superstitions designed by the French to seduce Muslims from their faith. No one questioned the logic—not openly, anyway. Well, no one except Zaynab. Father had to tell her to shut up, that she had lost her faith, she was no Muslim, and when she agreed that it was true, she had indeed lost it, he looked nearly apoplectic and hurried to his prayer room as if running from a daughter who had sprung from some devil's loins. I kept my doubts to myself. Really, I didn't know what I believed or didn't anymore, so how could I have doubts?

The plague was in fact a blessing in disguise, at least for those who believed that anything that forced the French to leave was a blessing. Our purveyors of God's inscrutable design were on target there, if God's will in sending the plague was to punish the French for their cruel and evil quarantine rules. The French could not afford to lose their troops to plague the way we could afford to, Egyptians being many and doing what they could to reproduce themselves, like there was nothing else to occupy them day and night and twice over but the sweaty effort to procreate.

My prognosis of an inevitable French departure was borne out sooner than I expected. While Zaynab and I were at the institute, helping Jaubert catalog Turkish and Arabic manuscripts, he said he'd let us in on a secret. After we vowed on our honor never to repeat a word of it, he told us that Kleber wanted the French out within a month and had already secretly submitted the draft of an evacuation treaty to the sultan in Istanbul. Her face ashen, Zaynab rose from her chair and without a word left the leather-bound medical treatises stacked high on the table in front of her and went to one of the room's fractured windows.

"You'll have to come with us," Jaubert said to her.

Zaynab kept looking out the window. "Leave Egypt?"

"Of course. You have no choice. It won't be safe for you here when we're gone." Jaubert was speaking to both of us, but it was obviously Zaynab he was worried about.

"I can't leave Egypt."

"You'll have to," Jaubert persisted. "I'll take care of you."

She looked at me. I looked down at the astronomy manuscript I was cataloging for shipment to Paris. Jaubert asked her if she had any idea what her people would do to her without French protection.

She shrugged in the French manner and returned to her cataloging. "I can't leave Egypt."

Jaubert looked at me in appeal. I shrugged in the French manner, having no idea what message the gesture was meant to convey.

It was during the height of the plague that it happened, just as General Kleber was coming to terms with Sultan Salim for an honorable withdrawal from Egypt (with Zaynab biting her nails in deep anxiety over what would happen if the French were actually to leave): General Kleber was assassinated. Negotiations for an evacuation ended. Kleber's successor, General Menou, declared that the French would be in Egypt forever. Egypt was France. Egyptians and French would form one people. This was General Jacques Menou who had become a Muslim, taken the name Abdullah, and married a divorced Egyptian woman, Zubaydah, who came from a wealthy merchant family in Damietta and had just given birth to a son, Sulayman. Zaynab was elated at the sudden turn in events. She even prayed in thanks to God for her new lease on life, the hypocrite. She didn't believe, she never prayed, but she did now, zealously, for the institute and its savants, who would be staying.

Father was beside himself. It was not Zaynab, but Zubaydah who would produce Egypt's new line of sultans, beginning with Sulayman the not-so -magnificent, son of the not-so-Napoleonic Abdullah Menou. For Father, the prospect of a French departure was bad enough, but that Zubaydah and not Zaynab would be the uncrowned queen of Egypt, and that a merchant from Damietta and not Shaykh Khalil al-Bakri would be the scion of the new Franco-Pharaonic dynasty ruling Egypt—it was too big a blow for the old man to take standing. He took to his bed with his beads and Quran.

He was devastated. In fact, he had been since the day Bonaparte abandoned Egypt. The news of Nappy flying the coop had crushed him. It was days before he had been able even to consider that Napoleon's departure might be true and not a vile rumor spread by his enemies, by which time he had gone livid, eyes staring vacantly into space, lost in a twilight where denial and acceptance fused to become indistinguishable, leaving him sleepwalking, the walking dead. He had been deceived, betrayed, sacrificed. He had prayed and recited the Quran day and night that Bonaparte wasn't lying in the letter he'd left promising to return soon and become Muslim and build the world's largest mosque. The second revolt had ended any hope Father had of that. I suspected he was hoping General Kleber would take Zaynab as a second wife, the way Marc Antony had taken Cleopatra after Julius left her. Who knows what was in the old schemer's head, but something must have been, judging from the way he reacted to Kleber's assassination and then General Menou's ascent to commander in chief. Was he hoping that rotund, middle-aged Menou, who looked like one of our portly bawwabs, would divorce Zubaydah and take Zaynab? Or take her as a second wife? The odds of Zaynab accepting were as slim as Menou was fat and undistinguished.

News of Kleber's assassination threw people into a fit of despair and fear, for they were sure that the army would destroy the city over again in vengeance for the assassination of their popular general who had been about to take the French back home. Taking upon himself another mission of mercy, mixed generously with self-interest, Father mounted the horse Bonaparte had given him and went up to military headquarters and begged Jacques Abdullah Menou not to destroy the city.

"We have no intention of destroying the city, Shaykh Khalil. General Kleber's death was the result of one man's work, apparently."

Father was surprised that Menou could manage himself in Arabic, and even more surprised and delighted to hear that the city would be spared. "Apparently?" he asked.

"So far we know only that he's a Syrian from Aleppo."

"A Syrian! Thank God! Wouldn't you know it would be a dirty Syrian!" Father kissed Abdullah's hand, repeatedly thanking God that it was a Syrian and not an Egyptian. "What a relief! Thank God for dirty Syrians!"

Abdullah cautioned Father not to presume the dirty Syrian's guilt, saying that he would be adjudicated by a court after being tried.

Father thought that he had misheard or that Menou's Arabic had fallen short. "Court?" he asked. "A court is needed to find the murderer guilty?"

"That's the normal procedure."

Father couldn't believe his ears: everyone knew who did it. General Kleber's military guard saw him. They themselves stabbed him in the arm. The culprit cried out that he had done it. "Death to the French!" he had shouted.

"You can't be serious, my dear Abdullah."

"Yes, I am perfectly serious. Everyone's testimony will be recorded and presented in court as soon as the accused has recovered from his wound and is released from the hospital."

"Hospital? The dirty Syrian assassin is in the hospital?"

"My dear Shaykh Khalil, where else do you treat a wounded man?"

Father had to sit down. Struggling to come to terms with French military justice, he took out a handkerchief and wiped his face. It was hot. He felt woozy. Abdullah's wife, Zubaydah, entered the office with turkish coffee and glasses of ice water. She was dressed in a French gown that was open at the shoulders, and her hair was done up in the French style, piled high on her head and surmounted by a jeweled tiara. Her every finger sported a ring of gold or diamonds. Probably every one of her toes as well, Father suspected; he later described to me in detail Zubaydah's display of ostentatious vulgarity.

"The ice comes from Mount Lebanon," she explained proudly.

Father forgave for the moment her arrogant implication that he had never seen ice before, as the cold water pleasantly filled his mouth and ran down his gullet to slake his thirst. "So, there will be a court trial for a miserable, dirt-caked wretch of a Syrian beggar who openly plunged a dagger into your commander in chief's heart?"

"The case is strong against him. Shaykh Khalil, let me confess, I was under the impression that you had come to plead for the life of the accused."

"I seek refuge in God! Why would I care about a crazed, louse-ridden Syrian from Aleppo? It is our city I came to appeal for. Bonaparte bombarded us and it was worse than seventy hells."

"That was Bonaparte. Under me, there will be no bombardment or punishment of any kind inflicted on the people. They are innocent. Justice must prevail. How could we blame a whole city for an act of terror presumably committed by one man?"

Presumably? Father sipped his turkish coffee. Something was seriously wrong with the logical connections of the Frankish brain. Their ideas on justice were as inscrutable as God's will. Perplexed as he was, he nonetheless rejoiced at the wonderful news that our city would not be bombarded.

Inscrutable as the French were and as perplexed as Father was, one thing was clear: our new French Muslim sultan, Jacques Abdullah Menou, was obviously a decent man, a worthy successor to Napoleon—even better than him, as he was much older and more than a little stupid looking; a pudgy, balding man more appropriate in the garb of a bawwab, butcher, cook, or bath keeper than in a general's uniform; a soft, squishy kind of fish, unlike the aristocratic Kleber or the stormy, eagle-like Napoleon. Abdullah Menou, Father told me later when recounting his visit, would need guidance to rule Egypt, as had Bonaparte. He would need the wise counsel of a learned and experienced shaykh far more than had Napoleon.

Yes, the old schemer was at it again. The French had a term for it: *déjà vu.*

Emboldened by his first encounter with our new ruler, Father visited him again the next day. This time he dragged Zaynab and me along with him to the Citadel, probably thinking that his good friend Abdullah might offer her a marriage proposal and me a high post on some government diwan.

"My daughter Zaynab," Father began, introducing us to our new ruler. "She speaks French, I am told," he added, as Menou gave her a long, appreciative look.

"Indeed she does," Menou replied, taking her hand and kissing it. "Fluently. I have heard from my wife, Zubaydah, all about you, Zaynab. She thinks highly of you. You must visit us when your work at the institute permits it. Our house is yours."

I was surprised that Zaynab could still blush like an Egyptian girl.

Menou's invitation gave Father his opening: "You wouldn't mind if Zaynab called on your wife?"

"She would be most welcome."

"Thank you. Already twenty or twenty-one, my daughter, but still a tender girl. You would think she was sixteen. And still a virgin, mind you. You don't find many of those around these days."

Now she was really blushing, a deep crimson-purple. She turned her head toward me with a grimace of mortification.

"Please, we would be honored to receive her. And you as well, Shaykh Khalil, and you too, Zakariah. I am forming a new diwan, and I will need your help. I don't have to tell you that your cooperation has been invaluable in the past. Our First Consul Napoleon Bonaparte mentions you often in his correspondence. In fact, in his last letter he instructed us to give your wife the revenues of ten villages in Buhayrah Province in appreciation of your services. And to that I will add ten more Mamluks to add to your household slaves. We were caught off guard with the last revolt—and now this terrible assassination. We don't want a repeat performance. We must work together to build Egypt's future and nurture wise leadership that has the confidence of the people."

"Indeed we must!" Father agreed spiritedly, eyes brightening.

On our downward way back home from the Citadel, Father was humming happily, and I saw that his gait had more of a bounce to it. I thought it may have been because we were now going down instead of up the plateau, but when he said that history was back on track and that God's ways were becoming clearer to him, I realized the bounce was in celebration of his having saved history from going the wrong way.

—◆—

The dog days of late summer slowed the pace of life in Cairo. The French, still unaccustomed to the heat after almost two years, melted in the sultry sun that hung over the city fifteen hours a day, refusing to set. When at last it did set, the heat released from the buildings rendered night little better than day. The evening breeze, which drifted off the desert like a panting hound dog, only added the sand's heat to that stored in the bricks and stones, sending people flocking to the river's edge for relief from the suffocating night air. In desperation, the French sequestered all sailing craft between Helwan and Mahallat al-Kubra, hoping to escape the heat of night by retreating to the middle of the river with their Egyptian women. All night long, the river was clogged with rocking boats that broadcast into the warm, still air the uncontrolled sighs of rapturous lovers. In such amorous ways did the River Nile morph into the Seine.

The city too continued apace in its metamorphosis. It became not uncommon to see our women wearing "summer clothing," another disgusting French import. Arms and legs tantalizingly naked up to the elbows and ankles, half-exposed bosoms, a broad-brimmed hat and parasol to protect her ladyship from the burning sun, but nothing to protect her naked face and body from the burning eyes of tortured men!

I supposed Zaynab's affection for Amadeus Jaubert grew out of her love for Belmond—the love of an intelligent but emotionally immature girl for a handsome face and a tall, strong body in a uniform. I had told her as much before Belmond marched off to Palestine. "You may be right, Brother, I don't know, but tell me, what chance do we have to mature?" she had asked in defense of my analysis of her emotions.

Belmond had awakened something in her that neither the consolation of tradition (she had gone back to her robe and head veil for the traditional forty days of mourning in memory of him) nor the intellectual challenge of the institute could replace once the dashing Belmond had been plucked from her life. Marcel had been there for support, a man of flesh and blood, a scholar and pillar of understanding who spoke Arabic like a prophet and whose protective love was a poultice drawing away the pain of her wound, and drawing her to him—the older, wiser man. Now it was Amadeus Jaubert who was the protector: almost twice Zaynab's age, missing an arm, and even less dashing than Marcel had been, but someone to lean on, a grown man who made no effort to hide his slavish devotion, who professed himself to be her servant.

It made me sick. He called her Zu Zu; she served him coffee and tea, and filled and lit his pipe, knowing exactly how much sugar, how much tobacco. He would be about to ask for an ashtray and it would already be there.

But he was the real slave. They would be translating a passage from Arabic to French together and no sooner would he reach for the Arabic-French lexicon in search of a word than she would ask him the word he was looking for and, being told, would give him the French equivalent right off, as though she'd turned herself into his lexicon, and he would look at her in admiration, like the orientalist fool he was, all goo-goo-eyed in love with this Egyptian genius, this young beauty who, judging from the way he gawked at her, was to him some heavenly incarnation, a genie from Aladdin's magic lamp, a pharaonic princess resuscitated from the pyramid's tomb to reveal the mysteries of the ancients that the French were all nutty about. I often regretted having saved the idiot's life.

Zaynab and Amadeus knew each other so well that it seemed one of them could anticipate the other's desire or need without anything being said. They collaborated in silence; language seemed hardly necessary. They spoke with their eyes, shooting messages across the space between them like those bolts of artificial lightning that used to leap across Berthollet's spheres. It was as though they shared one mind.

Zu Zu's caring behavior toward him amazed me. Having gained freedom, she now surrendered to the customs she had so fiercely resisted when cloistered in the women's quarters of tradition. I hadn't thought it was in her to serve a man. I suppose it took losing Belmond to bring out this humility in her. It had something to do with realizing our vulnerability and the tenuousness of things we hold dear in this world: only after we have lost our great loves and suffered do we truly, humbly appreciate those who love us, and return love for love, in appreciation of that precious thing so easily lost.

When we were alone in the manuscripts room, I asked her point-blank if she had gone all the way with Jaubert, and she replied, "Not as far as you went with Pauline."

"You don't love him that way?"

"It's not that. I'm afraid."

"What's there for a woman to be afraid of now?"

"I don't know. Of our traditions." She rose from her chair, put a bound manuscript in its place on the shelf and started cataloging a new one. "It was easier to break away from traditions with my mind than it is with my body."

I was silent. It pleased me to know that she was still a virgin; we hadn't surrendered everything to the French.

Having read several pages of the new treatise she was cataloging, she looked up: "Zaki. What do epicycles do?"

Happy to know something she didn't, I explained with great affectation that an epicycle was a small circle whose center was on the circumference of a larger circle, and if you imagined a planet such as Mars or Venus to be fixed on the circumference of the smaller circle, and you set both circles to rotate on their respective centers in the same angular direction so they completed one revolution in the same amount of time, then the trajectory of the planet, as viewed from the center of the large circle, where Earth was situated, would account for the retrograde motion you see at certain times of the year as the planets orbit the Earth.

She gave me a snooty smile. "Much obliged, Brother, but haven't you heard? The sun is at the center."

"It wasn't back when your treatise on astronomy was written."

"Who was it? Copern— No, Galileo!"

"Wrong, Zu Zu. Al-Biruni."

She shook her head at me in disgust and returned to her epicycles. A minute later, she said, her face over her open manuscript as if talking to it, "I wish I could do it. Raymond Belmond died without tasting the pleasure he wanted so terribly to have with me. I'm not proud of my chastity. It's only fear that holds me to it—not virtue or religion. It's stupid letting a living lover suffer for a dead tradition."

When I told her it wasn't stupid; it was wisdom, she said, "It's not wisdom, Zaki. It's fear of being possessed, enslaved by passion. To a man. They say women are weaker when they've had sex. My mind tells me to go ahead, but I can't."

"I know. You're afraid of being hurt."

"The way Pauline hurt you?" She took me by the hands.

I removed my hands. "Forget it—it's not important. What I meant was, you'd have been all the more hurt if you and Belmond had … you know … and he disappeared."

"I'm not sure. I regret not having given myself to Raymond. But what was it that kept me from it? There was nothing to fear. He didn't want to possess me. Was it family honor? There wasn't much left of that to be saved. The only dishonorable thing now is to get caught cheating on your taxes."

I laughed. "Welcome to what our French friends call the modern world."

"Welcome to the new century! In a few months it'll be the year eighteen hundred in Europe. Do you know they make vows for the new century? I vow to cast off my childish fears."

"Don't cast them too far, dear sister. Our friends may not last a century here." I wasn't kidding. The Ottomans in Syria kept making feints, as if preparing to march an army through the Sinai desert to retake Egypt, so we never knew when the real thing would come, while a fleet of British ships sailed like giant hunting sharks along our coast, just out of reach of French artillery, as everyone in Alexandria could see, knowing full well that when those French guns were turned against the invading army of Ottomans, the British ships would come sweeping in to unload their troops for the kill. I tried to push thoughts of that inevitable reality out of my mind, and most of the time I was able to, thanks to the institute and the near-daily spectacles of our occupiers. One of the grandest of them was the trial of Kleber's assassin.

Sulayman, the Syrian assassin from Aleppo, was found guilty of murdering General Kleber and sentenced to death. The trial was full of surprises. Apparently Sulayman's father had been in serious debt and risked losing his business, and Ottoman officials in Syria had promised the young man that if he assassinated the French leader, his father's debts would be paid and the business saved. If he accomplished his mission and was caught, a martyr's death and the sensual pleasures of paradise, with its crowd of lusty young virgins, would be eternally his. It came out in court that he'd almost had a nervous breakdown deciding what to do. He didn't want to die, but the Ottomans kept pressing him, and in the end he felt he had no choice but to accept the offer, more for his family's sake than for the virgins that awaited him. Some Egyptians said that the French had rigged the trial in order to deprive us of a hero, that their justice was a façade. In any case, young Sulayman from Aleppo was scheduled for public execution on New Year's Day, and people were encouraged to come see the gala celebration. It came in two acts.

First, his hand, the one that had held the dagger, was thrust into glowing coals and held there until it was cooked off. People fainted at the sight, but not once did Sulayman cry out. I had to look away. Zaynab and Jaubert returned to the institute before the end of the act. We don't generally care much for Syrians, but the bravery Sulayman showed in killing Kleber and withstanding torture won our hearts, despite his having committed murder for no greater reason than to get his father out of debt. I think I would have gone for the virgins, which were in my opinion the best part of the whole deal, but unfortunately I had by then lost my belief in such things.

Having roasted Sulayman's hand off, the French executioners heated a long, thin steel rod that was tapered to a point. When the rod was hot, Sulayman was stripped and then harnessed into a leather seat rigged to a hoist. The seat had a hole in the middle of it so that the glowing rod could enter his anus unobstructed as he was slowly lowered onto it after having been hoisted up. The audience gasped. The sizzle of his cooking organs was audible. His executioners skillfully guided him down so the shaft didn't pierce any vital organ and end the show too quickly. It took a half hour before the tip of the shaft at last broke through the skin of his shoulder. For two hours he hung on to life, suspended on the hoist for all to see, like a human kabab on a skewer. Then, mercifully, he expired. His body was left there as a warning.

The multitude of spectators seemed pleased with the show. But I, gutless coward that I was, walked back to the institute feeling sick. Zaynab and Jaubert weren't in the library or the manuscripts room, or anywhere on the first floor. I went up to Jaubert's apartment on the second floor and tapped on the door. When there was no answer, I opened the door to look in. Strange sounds were coming from one of the rooms. I approached and put my ear to the door. My heart jumped; Pauline had moaned the same way. I listened awhile, wondering what to do, and finally I left, closing the door quietly behind me. Two years earlier I would have had to kill my sister to save our family's honor. Now I rejoiced in her liberation. That's how far gone I was under French influence, although I still fought and denied it.

While I was happy for Zaynab, I wished the man she loved had both his arms. When properly employed, arms are so useful in enhancing and fulfilling a female's pleasure, as Pauline had taught me in the brief time we had together. I hoped that Jaubert made up for his lack of an extremity by being gifted with another, and from the smile on Zaynab's face, the light in her eyes, and especially her calm manner when we worked together cataloging—her sharp tongue now softened and free of its cutting witticisms—I concluded that he had.

Summer gave out to autumn and autumn to our balmy winter, and for months, almost half a year, life went on pleasantly enough for me to hold at bay those chilling thoughts that it was all doomed to come to an end, a brutal end.

On New Year's Day—1801 of the Christian era, 1215 of the Islamic era—Zaynab and Jaubert had a more or less secret marriage: more with respect to the Egyptian community, less with the French. Held in the oriental library of the institute, it was attended by a dozen or so savants; Zubaydah Sultana and Sultan Abdullah Menou; and Generals Desaix, Bellier, and Dumas, whose son Alexander, named after our city Alexandria or maybe Alexander the Great, was destined to become a great writer of adventure stories when I was with him in Paris. Portly, mustachioed, common-looking Sultan Jacques Abdullah Menou, smiling like a jolly gatekeeper, hosted a little banquet at his palace during which his wife, Zubaydah Sultana, swore everyone to secrecy about the marriage and toasted the newlyweds. I think I got a little drunk with all the toasts to their health, happiness, and many future children, one of which was already on the way. Zaynab told me that without a blush when I bluntly asked her why in the world she wanted to complicate her life with the burden of marriage when she was already enjoying the pleasures that decent girls went without until forced into matrimony. I wasn't surprised when she told me the reason: she was three months pregnant. Nothing could surprise me anymore.

"How long do you expect to keep all this secret from Father?"

She shrugged. "Until the time is right."

I patted her stomach. "Father will go crazy. He wanted a grandson from Napoleon, not from a grungy, one-armed scholar."

"He'll have no choice. Sultan Abdullah Menou gave his blessings. He's agreed to be the child's godfather. God and sultan: what shaykh dares go against that combination?"

"Poor Father. He'll be crushed."

"He'll be all right when he sees the baby. If it's a girl and marries Zubaydah's son, Sulayman, he'll have won at least half his gamble."

Father had already won half his battle: he had become Sultan Abdullah's unofficial grand vizier. He was convinced that Zaynab, who had taken up semipermanent quarters in the royal palace as a lady-in-waiting rather than a courtesan, would soon become Abdullah's second but favorite wife, Ayesha to Abdullah Menou's Muhammad.

15

THE FRENCH PUT ON a terrific revolutionary celebration in comemorization of the execution of their king. Everybody loved it. They made an effigy of him by stuffing straw and rags into some ridiculous knickers; long, silken socks; and dainty, high-heeled, pointed shoes. A realistic head was made from a melon that had a face painted on it; it was rouged and powdered and then crowned with a wig of curling locks that fell to the shoulders. I swear, if French kings resembled anything like that tulip, no wonder they killed off the dynasty.

A great crowd gathered for the execution. The roll of drums grew louder as the king was brought onto the platform and made to kneel with his head on the block, and then the reenactment came to a blood-chilling crescendo as the heavy blade was released at the top of the tower and came slamming down with a whizzing, metallic screech. The melon head had been stuffed with a sausage casing filled under pressure with fresh animal blood. The bloated casing was coiled inside the head and extended down through the neck of the effigy, so that when the blade struck, blood and guts shot out in a mighty jet, as if from a fountain, spraying the spectators closest to the platform. The French gasped, and then they clapped and sang their national song as though they had witnessed the original event, which indeed it could have been for how real it looked and felt. The sight sent a chill of horror through my body. The head had rolled away, still spurting blood from the severed casing. A torrent of blood was also spouting out of the neck from the other half of the casing, which due to the sudden release in pressure was whipping wildly side to side out of the bloody stem of the neck, like a snake in torment.

Zaynab had gripped my arm the moment the drums began rolling and the realistic-looking king was escorted to the platform. Her grip had tightened with the release of the blade, and now the expulsion of blood from the head and neck so affected her that she held me in terror and cried. Jaubert and I tried comforting her.

"It's only pretend," I said.

She looked at me in appeal, with fear-filled eyes. "It looked so real to me."

The invasion began the next day.

Reports continued to arrive of an approaching Ottoman army from Palestine into Sinai. Then the story was that the English navy had taken Rosetta and was besieging Alexandria and Damietta. A battalion of marines was already advancing by land up the Nile. People we knew and trusted who had arrived from Alexandria assured us that it was true, they had seen it: the English had at last invaded. The sudden arrival of Zubaydah's brother from Rosetta, tired and haggard from forced travel, confirmed that the English had taken the port city.

Ottoman agents who'd slipped into the city did their best to stir something up, but the people jeered them. Some of the agents were even beaten, stripped, and marched out of town. One obnoxious agent, bearing a proclamation signed by the sultan claiming that God had sent the plague to punish Egyptians for their failure to rebel against the French, was thrown howling and screaming into a deep pit full of rotting corpses reeking with plague. "If it's true, as the sultan says, that the plague is God's punishment on Egyptians, then you should be safe down there, since you're not an Egyptian!" someone in the crowd cried down at him as he sank into a stinking, stomach-turning, fly-infested stew of flesh.

When the French closed the city gates and forbade anyone to come or go, we knew the Ottomans and English were close. Soldiers manned the walls, looking out into the desert with their spyglasses. The muzzles of the cannons were turned from the city to the outside. The Ottomans were coming by desert from Suez. The English, who like ducks were never far from water, were sailing up and marching alongside the Nile. The distant thunder of artillery in the desert froze our blood; the dreaded thud reminded us of the destruction we had twice suffered. Abdullah Menou issued orders warning the populace to remain calm. The directive was made into a joke. Whenever someone broke out in a fit of nerves, he would be ordered in the name of Abdullah to calm down: "This is your last warning! Be calm or be shot!" As a concession to the people for their neutrality, the French relaxed the quarantine regulations. And to ensure that the populace remained neutral, the leading shaykhs were arrested and held hostage in the Citadel. The French could have saved themselves the trouble. We were so neutralized we could barely move.

Unfortunately, Sultan Menou esteemed Father so highly that he wasn't arrested—the French kiss of death that sealed Father's fate. What made it worse was that Father once again offered himself as a hostage for the release of Sadat, Sharqawi, and the other shaykhs. Menou thought Father's gesture so noble that he presented the old man with a ceremonial caftan and had an honor guard escort him back home. Menou might just as well have had him shot right then and there and saved him from the disgrace awaiting collaborators. In desperation, Father cloistered himself in his prayer room and waited.

As the sounds of war grew closer, people fled into the desert only to be finished off by the bedouin tribes. It was July 1798 all over again—déjà vu, as the French called it. They had a word for everything; we had a joke.

Menou led an army to beat back the English who were attacking Alexandria, but only managed to get himself cut off from Cairo and besieged in Alexandria. The two main cities were now isolated from each other. One of the generals under Menou who was fatally wounded in the action, enraged at the commander in chief's incompetence, told him he wasn't fit to cut onions in the greasiest soup kitchen in Paris! The Coptic brigade dissolved into thin air. Thanks-To-God Shukrallah burned his French uniform and went into hiding in the caves of Mount Muqattam. The low-life Syrian Christians took refuge up in the Citadel, then slithered like scared lizards back into the scum from where they had come, back before the French came and used them as they had used the Copts.

Menou managed to make it back to Cairo, barely, and in desperation urged Father to harangue the people to fight for God and religion by assisting the French in their holy war against the enemies of Islam. Menou was an even worse politician than he was a general. Father refused. His neck was already on the chopping block; Menou wanted him to pull the lever of the guillotine with his own hand. "Now is your chance to do something in return for all we have done for you," Menou persisted. "Do not be ungrateful, Shaykh Khalil."

"Who would listen to me?" Father replied, resenting Menou's bullying attitude. "Besides, would cooperating with the enemy of the sultan's army be fighting for God and religion?"

Menou stammered some reply. General Bellier—a tall, thin, insolent man with aristocratic pretensions and a nervous twitch—struck Father across the face with the back of his gloved hand. "Impertinent gypo!"

Menou was aghast. He apologized for his short-tempered general, but Father turned and left without listening. Three years of service to the French in the interest of peace had ended with a slap in the face and an insult to his Egyptian heritage. And that was the least of it. On his way home, a gang of rabble-rousers who had seen him enter and leave military headquarters stopped his horse and shouted insults at him, calling him an agent of the French, a drunkard and collaborator.

"He gave his daughter to the French!" one of them shouted.

"He's not a Muslim—he's one of them!"

"Pimp!"

"His own daughter!"

"Filthier than a Frenchman!"

They pulled him from his horse, knocked his turban off, and threw him to the ground.

"Kill him!"

The commotion drew a crowd of more responsible and respectable Muslims from their homes and shops. They pulled Father from the mob and protected him until they had dispersed the ruffians, and then restored his turban and escorted him home, patting him on the back in sympathy and saying these were terrible times that a respected shaykh could be insulted and thrown to the ground and threatened by riffraff from the streets.

As Father was brushing himself off and preparing to mount his horse, he overheard someone say, "But it's true—the horse was given to the shaykh by Bonaparte, and in return he gave his daughter to him and then she went with all the French!" Not wanting to hear any more, Father nudged his horse to go.

The old man never left the house after that. He was sure the mob would have killed him had he not been rescued, but even his rescuers looked upon him as a collaborator.

Facing the defeat they had anticipated ever since being abandoned by Bonaparte, the French generals started accusing each other of incompetence and insubordination, culminating with Menou publicly stripping Bellier and Dumas of their rank. The French were falling apart. The beautiful machine of clockwork precision I had seen destroy the Mamluks at Imbaba three years earlier had come undone. Their days were numbered. The pretense was over. The pain of defeat written across their faces made it plain that they knew it better than we did.

The savants were packing up their books and equipment. The shelves of the library were almost empty. The institute was vanishing in crates before our eyes. When I told Zaynab she would have to leave Egypt, she retorted angrily that she didn't want to leave, that she wanted everything to remain the same as it had been. "Nothing is the same anymore. You've got to leave. You're seven months pregnant."

"So?" She picked up a quill and resumed her cataloging. A moment later she threw the quill across the room and put her hands to her face. "No! I won't leave!"

Jaubert arrived, breathless: the treaty of evacuation had been signed; the French would be out within sixty days. "You'll have to leave with us, Zaki."

"Leave? My home is here."

"Your home is where you can live. The people will be out for vengeance." He looked at Zaynab. "Especially against the women. You should hear the stories the brother of Menou's wife tells about what the people of Rosetta did to their women."

"The Ottomans promised no one would be harmed for cooperating with the French," I said, knowing full well the worth of such a promise.

"Zaki, don't be foolish. The Ottomans will promise anything to help us leave with a clean conscience, and Menou will agree to anything that makes it look like we are leaving with honor. Promises, agreements, guarantees—they don't mean a thing, even in peacetime. Why do you think the Coptic patriarch has taken refuge in the Citadel?"

I left them and walked along the corniche promenade to Elephant Lake, to be alone. Soldiers directing their gangs of Egyptian forced labor were destroying mosques and sections of the city around Azbakiyyah to build barricades and fortifications in case "perfidious Albion," as the French called the English, launched a surprise attack. Around Elephant Lake, once the most beautiful nature preserve in Cairo, with gardens, pools, fountains, orange groves, and palms, everything was being devastated in the name of national defense. The birds and gazelles that abounded in the little forest around the lake didn't know where to go, and neither did I.

I spit and kicked the ground with my sandaled foot. The French had come to build, and they ended up tearing down even what had been here before them. They had come preaching liberty, fraternity, and equality, and they were leaving like pharaohs—enslaving us to carry out their destruction, using the Copts against us, calling us gypos. They had come to civilize us, and they were leaving us a wasteland. I had learned their language, read their books, drunk from the wisdom of their great thinkers, and they'd left my soul a hollow shell. They'd failed me. They'd failed themselves. And now they were retreating like criminals, in defeat and disgrace, shabbier even than Bonaparte's shameful departure in secret at night. At least the troops he betrayed were making no secret of their departure. I had secretly thought them gods, but they were only flawed men, as duplicitous in living up to their professed ideals as Rousseau was in writing his *Social Contract* while consigning his five children to orphanages. How do you measure such craven people capable of such wonders, such iniquities, such monstrous failures as this one they had brought to Egypt—promising such glory, but leaving such wreckage? I stood and shook my fist at the lake and cried out in rage and despair, "God damn you, Napoleon! Traitor! Destroyer! Hypocrite! May you never sire a child!"

Zubaydah's brother who had fled Rosetta told us that the people of the city had dragged the women who'd fraternized with the French out into the streets, stripped them naked, and beheaded them. Zubaydah implored Zaynab to leave with her. "Even the daughter of a shaykh might not be safe. And what about your husband?"

"Many Frenchmen are staying," Zaynab replied, confused.

"Some soldiers serving the Ottomans as mercenaries, perhaps. But no savants are staying."

In tears, Zaynab asked Zubaydah how she could think of leaving her home, Egypt, Mother of the World.

Zubaydah sighed. Her voice trembled. "Because I fear what would happen to me here. Believe me, it's not easy. No one loves Egypt more than I do. But my brother has seen the future. Think of your baby. How can you not leave?"

Sobbing, Zaynab shook her head, saying no, she couldn't leave; it was impossible. She would remain right where she was, in the institute with Jaubert.

It was impossible talking to her. She was sure Jaubert would remain.

People who felt their lives threatened went up to the Citadel to live. Zubaydah and her brother went there; Copts, Syrians, Turks, and Greeks who had served the French as police chiefs went there; informers, executioners, procurers, and the like, joined by the many Egyptian girls who had married or lived with soldiers—all of them went there.

Niqula Qapitan, some Levantine Christian who'd been the chief of Murad Bey's navy and arsenal in Giza, also went up there with his wife, Hawa, who had been, and still was, the wife of one of Murad Bey's Mamluks, Hassan Kashif. Almost three years earlier, when Murad Bey fled to Upper Egypt after the Battle of Imbaba, Hassan Kashif had gone with him, leaving his wife behind, just as Murad Bey had left behind the beautiful and elegant Sitt Nafisah. Niqula Qapitan remained and took up service in the French military, and then took up with Hawa, Hassan Kashif's abandoned wife. Assuming that her husband would never return and that the French would never leave, Hawa—or Eve, as the French called her—claimed her husband had been killed, and married Niqula. As it turned out, Hassan Kashif secretly returned to Cairo and got word to his wife in the Citadel that he wanted her back. It didn't matter what she had done while he was away—he loved her, he forgave her, he only wanted her back. If she agreed to return to him, he would send up two donkeys and a driver to bring her and her things down the midnight after next. She agreed.

The French searched for her after her disappearance, threatening to blow up homes or even whole quarters if she was found in any of them. They searched for days. They finally found her. Her head was on a pike planted in the ground in front of the house where she and her husband used to live, not far from Azbakiyyah. The rest of her body was beneath it, naked as the day she hobbled by our house, more than a thousand days but also an eternity ago. I tricked Zaynab into accompanying me to the institute and instead took her to see Hawa's head before the French removed it. The long, black hair fell halfway down the pike, the bloodless face veiled in buzzing flies. An old crone in passing stopped to spit on it. "Whore!"

Zaynab decided to leave with Jaubert.

It was up to me to break the news to Father. I found him where I expected I would, in his prayer room with his nose in the Quran. "Tell Zaynab to come home!" he ordered before I had a chance to speak. "She's not to associate with that whore Zubaydah or the French anymore. And she's not to go to that devil's den of an institute ever again!"

"Zaynab's leaving, Father."

He slammed the Quran shut. "What do you mean, leaving? She's to come home. Her French adventure is over. Finished. Thank God they're going."

"She's going with them."

He looked at me as though he hadn't understood. "Who's them? She's marrying Shaykh Musawi, that's the 'them' she's going with!"

"Musawi! He's sixty years old!"

"All the better for her. His wives are all old—thirty, forty. She'll be well taken care of."

"She won't marry that dried-up old fart!"

"He's a shaykh. Have respect for his beard and turban. Zaynab will marry whom I want! I'll not tolerate any of her ... her tergiversations."

"She won't do it, Father. You know how she is."

"It's not for her to decide one way or the other. Have her come home. My family is through with those French hypocrites. Their day is over in Egypt. Zaynab will follow tradition and marry Shaykh Musawi."

"What if she says no?"

"What if the Nile stops flowing?"

"She is not a river. She is a person with her own mind."

"What does that have to do with anything? Her mind is to obey me, fear God, and follow tradition."

"She may not see it that way, Father. She's been with the French for three years now. She has her own ideas about things."

"Don't worry. What the French have corrupted, piety can cure. Bring her. She'll learn soon enough to have shame."

16

THE ENGLISH HAD CONTINUED to advance on Cairo in violation of the treaty of evacuation. The French engaged them, and the skirmishes that followed led to Cairo's third bombardment in as many years, with the English army reaching Giza and the pyramids. The Ottoman army, reinforced with a Mamluk contingent under Ibrahim Bey, was camped at Imbaba. Yusuf Pasha, the grand vizier leading the Ottoman army, finally managed to effect a cease-fire between the French and English, but it was never quite kept; there were always skirmishes and sporadic exchanges of artillery. Yusuf Pasha did his best to keep the peace between the Europeans. He promised the French safe conduct and four hundred camels for the soldiers and savants to carry their loot, and he made the English promise to remain a certain distance away in the desert and out of sight of the French as they sailed and marched to the coast, where English ships awaited to take them back to France. He also forced his English allies to let the French keep their arms. It was a simple matter of honor that the Ottomans had no trouble understanding, but that seemed to totally escape the English mentality. How the English got the reputation of being honorable, I will never understand. I have now lived in France for more than two decades, and I can tell you authoritatively that the English are the most dishonorable of any people on the globe.

Now that the French were leaving, we began to see a lot of good in them. Some of the troops and officers had tears in their eyes, as much for leaving Egypt, which had been their home for three years, as for the humiliation of having to be carried back home on English ships. They said it would have been better to die fighting than to leave this way. But they would at least march out carrying their arms—and, I should add, carrying a great many of our monuments. Jaubert, who wasn't even a soldier, raged until frothing at the perfidy of Albion: "If I see as much as a hair of an Englishman, I'll blow his fucking head off!" I was sufficiently sensitive to his humiliation not to ask how he would manage that with only one arm.

The French didn't want to see, smell, or hear the English. They didn't even want to know they existed. When Menou assembled the shaykhs for a final address (still stinging from his slap in the face, Father didn't attend), he spoke for an hour about the truce and imminent evacuation without once mentioning the English. He spoke of the misguided policy of the Ottoman sultan, who really loved France, and of the love and the richness of common experience that bound Egypt and France together, and similar nonsense. Napoleon, he said, had brought to Egypt independence, freedom, science, newspapers, and democratic institutions; Kleber had brought a measure of economic equality; and he, Menou, had brought religious dignity and harmony. The French would leave, but their friendship would remain and grow stronger as the seeds of liberty, equality, knowledge, and industry planted by the French took root and grew ever more powerful.

It was a beautiful farewell address, maybe even sincerely meant, for Menou's eyes were moist at the end of it and I noticed that even a few of the shaykhs were affected. You'd have thought that the French were leaving because they had chosen to out of the goodness of their hearts and their love for Egypt, and that it was breaking our hearts to see them go. You could also have thought from the speech that the English either didn't exist or were a rain cloud of doom that had yet to come or had passed. I felt sad for Menou. He was a plain man—overweight, with a round, beefy face; utterly nondescript; and apparently not much of an officer—but he had married an Egyptian beauty from a wealthy family, converted to Islam, and risen to commander in chief, ruler of Egypt, and he seemed to genuinely like Egyptians and relish his life among them. He had everything that such a simple, undistinguished person could ever hope for in life, and now he was forced to give it all up and return to France, where he would be socially recast among his countrymen commensurate with his mediocrity.

It baffled us how the French and English could hate each other so much and yet look and act the same—different languages, yes, but the same sickly, gloomy, pallid-faced, frosty-eyed, humorless tribe of Christians from the Nordic ice flats, hairs of the same beard. But there was no doubt of their mutual hatred. Their mere proximity was enough to set the sparks of artillery flying, like those lightning-charged globes of Berthollet's when brought close together.

For days, English shells had been peppering the French Quarter in Azbakiyyah, and the French had been firing back at the English camped in Giza by the pyramids, as if that's all they knew to do to relieve the boredom of waiting—blow each other's brains out. While we Egyptians passed the time praying or playing chess and backgammon, they exchanged musket and artillery fire.

I felt sorry for the French. No one had invited them to Egypt, and they were getting what they deserved, but I pitied them—poor men led by leaders with false dreams, left to perish or get out as best they could. And they were perishing in the most miserable manner: ravaged by plague, felled by a sniper's bullet, poisoned by their Egyptian cooks, their throats slit from behind while locked in a prostitute's embrace, hung from trees, mutilated in atrocious ways.

Passing the gutted ruins of Tivoli, I came to a crowd of Egyptians standing around another French soldier hanging by his neck from a tree. At first I thought they had killed him, but then I saw pinned to his uniform an official notice from the French army declaring that he had been executed for stealing money from an Egyptian citizen and then murdering him when the Egyptian resisted. A man clucked and shook his head. "A soldier who steals is given the same punishment as Sulayman, who killed Kleber, their sultan? They should have just cut his hand off."

I kicked my donkey in the ribs and continued on to the institute, where I tethered it to the post at the front entrance and entered. It appeared to be empty. No one was in the library or any of the laboratories. Crates were piled up everywhere. The shutters were closed against the sun, casting the rooms in a somber gloom of abandonment. All that remained were several bottles on Berthollet's shelf, chemical wonders whose magical power the old sorcerer had conjured to thrill and terrorize Egyptians. I smiled wistfully and returned to the main salon.

I was about to go upstairs when a soldier, hatless and disheveled, suddenly appeared at the top of the staircase and started down two steps at a time, hitching up his belt. Seeing me, he stopped in surprise. A grimace of fear twisted his face, which was cut up and bloody on both sides. His hand went nervously to his head, as though to straighten or take off his cap. Discovering it wasn't there, he half-turned to retreat up the stairs, then turned back to face me standing at the bottom. Lip curling in a snarl, teeth bared like those of a vicious dog about to attack, he drew a long dagger from the scabbard in his belt as he came down the stairs toward me.

"Dirty fucking gypo!" The hate in his eyes froze my blood more than the dagger did. The hairs on my neck and arms stiffened in cold fear. "Life for a life." He coiled back and leapt down the remaining stairs with the dagger aimed at my chest. I turned and ran, with a cry for help. Knowing I wouldn't have time to open the main entrance door and get out before his dagger was deep in my back, I dashed down the corridor toward the laboratories in the hope of flying out an open window or door. Finding no way to escape from Monge's or Berthollet's former workrooms without forcing open a shutter, I squatted behind two crates stacked one on the other and held my breath.

The maniac was panting at the entrance. I heard his boots quietly step in and stop. The panting was getting closer. I removed my sandals and flung them across the room. He didn't move. We remained like this for I don't know how many minutes. The boots approached again, took two steps, then stopped. The panting had ceased; it sounded like he was climbing on top of a crate. I thought of running out and up the stairs where I could jump off one of Jaubert's balconies, but I was so paralyzed by fear that I couldn't make my legs move to run for the adjoining room.

My heart was about to explode in the silent terror closing around me. I wanted to get up and run, but my legs were now shaking so badly I feared they'd buckle at the knees. Suddenly a flying shadow swooped over me, followed by the pounding of boots on the crate next to where I was hiding. I sprang up and started for the entrance, but before I could make it, he jumped from the crate and blocked my way. I stopped. He brandished the dagger with a maniacal cackle and grinned. "Life for a life, gypo boy!"

I turned and made another run for it around the crates, with the maniac three steps behind me, howling like a bloodthirsty hound from hell. Dodging around the crates, looking for something with which to defend myself, I made it to Berthollet's old laboratory with the maniac only two arm lengths behind, expecting the steely blade to slash into my back and lay open the core of my spinal column like a filleted fish. As I was circling the scattered crates, trying to get an angle on him to streak by into the corridor, he pushed the crates aside one by one, blocking all escape routes and closing in on me. I felt the wall at my back.

Berthollet's bottles were over my right shoulder. I grabbed one from the shelf and threw it at his head. It sailed past him and smashed against a crate across the room in a shower of glass and steamy vapor. His fiendish laugh was like that of a jackal thirsting for blood to drink and flesh to eat. I grabbed another bottle and cocked my arm back as if to fling it at him, but I feinted the throw, trying to catch him off balance and get a good shot at his head. I kept feinting and cocking my arm back as he advanced cautiously, his head and the dagger waving side to side like cobras.

"You fucking people killed my mate! Life for a life, gypo."

"I didn't kill him," I cried out in French.

"Let's say you did so I feel better when I cut your eyes and balls out."

The embossed letters on the bottle pressed into my fingers under the force of my grip. I jumped forward with my arm reared back as if to send the bottle into his face, causing him to back off a step. In the second's advantage, I glanced at the letters on the bottle: aqua regia. I knew what this was from Monge and Berthollet.

The maniac was advancing again, rocking his feet and jabbing the dagger out in front of him. I went to open the bottle but the glass stopper was sealed to the narrow neck with a thick coating of wax, so I smashed the neck against the marble slab of Monge's workbench. The maniac thought I meant to use the jagged edge as a weapon and left his face unguarded. I swung my arm out and quickly jerked it back so the aqua regia went flying into his face. I did this several times in rapid succession, all the while moving along the wall to keep away from his dagger, which was slashing the air in front of me. I let him have dose after dose. He paused to wipe his sleeve across his face and grinned. I couldn't understand it: the fumes were burning my eyes and nose, but the maniac seemed unaffected, maybe because his skin was so thick and coarse and partially protected by his bushy beard. As he advanced on me, I saw the acid fizzing hideously in the blood of his cut face, but he kept coming as if he didn't feel a thing. When he lunged for me, holding his dagger out to the side in order to swipe it across my throat, I let him have the rest of it, right in the eyes, and then I threw the empty bottle at his head and backed away as it bounced off. He hadn't ducked fast enough.

As his head came back up, a terrible howl came from him, and with one hand covering his eyes and the other swishing the blade blindly in front of him, he staggered after me as though he'd been shot in the head. He flailed his arm, jabbing the air in a wild frenzy. His howl turned to a staccato shriek of agony; a stricken, blinded animal, he knocked up against a crate and stumbled to his knees, still stabbing the air and rubbing his eyes. I left him groveling and screaming and climbed the stairs to the upper story, his shrieks fading behind me, sucked up by the heavy granite stones of the former palace.

I called out Zaynab's name and opened the door to the apartment. The fragments of a shattered vase cut into my bare feet. She was lying on the bedroom floor, naked. I cried out. Blood was oozing from between her spread legs into a small pool. Another pool had collected beside her head.

I covered her in the torn gown that was on the floor, gathering it tightly between her legs to prevent more loss of blood, and then I separated the strands of matted hair at the side of her head, exposing a shallow cut over a swollen mound. I put my ear to her bruised lips, felt the warm but faint breath, then hurriedly fetched a basin of water, towels, soap, and antiseptic. After cleaning and bandaging her head and face, I knelt with my hand on her huge belly and felt the thump of life inside her.

While I was cleaning the blood from between her legs, a warm stream of watery blood broke forth onto my hand. I cried out in horror, thinking her insides were pouring out, and cupped my hand between her legs to hold back the flow. Then her stomach began contracting and expanding in spasms. Acting on instinct, I spread her legs, kneeled between them, and raised one onto each of my shoulders. The flow thinned to a trickle; the spasms grew more violent. I leaned forward with her legs slung over my shoulders and pressed my hand gently over her stomach in time with the increasing contractions. The spasms stopped, then began again. Sweat was running down my face and dripping off my nose.

At last something appeared inside the parted lips between her legs. I slipped my fingers in and carefully worked them over the top of what felt like an incredibly tiny head. Several heaving contractions pushed the thing far enough out for my hand to get around it. It was like a small melon covered in warm dew. Working in time with the contractions, I tugged the tiny head out little by little, until the rest of the baby emerged in a bloody stream. I held it in my hands, not knowing if it was dead or alive, nor knowing what to do if it turned out to be alive. It coughed out some liquid as I was holding it by the feet to drain, and then bellowed out its little lungs with a cry that made my heart leap in such fright that I almost dropped it. I turned it right side up and held it flat in my palms. It was a perfect little girl.

Crying and shaking from nerves, I bit through the umbilical cord, tied it with a strip of cloth I tore from Zaynab's ripped undergarments, and then washed the little thing and wrapped it in a blanket. It stopped howling when I tucked it in the crook of its mother's arm and guided the tiny mouth and hands to Zaynab's breast. It was not an easy maneuver. Only after I had gotten Zaynab onto her side and her arm at the right angle was I able to place the newborn so that she could instinctively go to work. Watching her suck away, I was so swept away by this instinct of nature and tiny new life that to me was miraculous that I broke into a fit of sobbing. It shocked me to discover that I had the depth of emotion and love as to be so affected by this simple act of a baby at its mother's breast, sucking away as ferociously as one of those steam pumps the French used to drain the swamps.

Zaynab remained unconscious. I washed and dried her, cleaned up the mess, and kissed her cheek. I was on my way out of the room when I stopped, turned back, and kissed the little girl who was still hungrily sucking at her mother's plump breast.

A military cap was on the bed. I took it with me and went downstairs. The soldier was groping his way down the corridor toward the bright, sunlit hall, one hand over his face, the other feeling along the wall for guidance. His shrieks had subsided to whimpering moans. Hearing me approach, he called out for help. I told him to save his breath; it was the dirty gypo come to cut his tiny French cock off. He backed up against the wall and, with his arm extended in front of him like an insect's probing tentacle, lashed out with the dagger. Avoiding the blade, I kicked him in the groin. He collapsed onto his hands and knees with a groan and curled up against the wall like a dying spider. I wrenched the dagger from him and pulled his head up by the hair. His face was a scorched mess of raw flesh, his skin acid-eaten, his eye sockets bloody blotches of cooked mucous. With a length of rope I found in one of the workshops, I bound his feet together, then his hands behind him, and cut away his trousers to carve off his genitals. To keep him from screaming, I jammed my fist in his mouth and drew out his tongue. It was like a slippery fish. I brought the blade across it and kept slicing until I had it. Proud as a Mamluk, I threw it across the room, stuffed a rag in his mouth, and went to work applying the blade to the wretch's genitals, which joined his tongue across the room. Then, like an enlightened Frenchman, I sought out a doctor to tend to the blinded scoundrel.

Jaubert was with the other savants receiving instructions for the evacuation at military headquarters at the Citadel. I waited for him to come out and told him Zaynab had just given birth to a girl. He looked at me blankly as if not comprehending. I repeated what I had said, showing him the dried blood on my hands and robe, and we went running for the institute.

I should have known by all the fuss the French made about soldiers killing peasants and raping girls that they would not take lightly the mutilation and murder of one of their soldiers, even though he had raped my sister. The soldier died of his wounds in the hospital, saving the expense of a military trial and execution, for which I should have been rewarded, not threatened with prosecution. Because the case involved Zaynab, the wife of an honored savant, General Menou ordered that the investigation be dropped.

Amadeus Jaubert had seen the mutilated wretch writhing and blubbering in his blood in the corridor when we had arrived at the institute, before the soldier was taken to the military hospital. "You did that?" Jaubert asked incredulously, looking down at the rough-looking brute, then at me. I drew myself up to my full height, puffed out my chest, straightened my turban, and then nodded in my casual, off-handed way. From then on, Jaubert showed me a respect that verged on fright, which was an odd experience for someone as gentle as myself.

It made me sick the way Amadeus—supposedly a grown man and great savant—clucked and cooed over the baby. To think I had risked my life saving such a wimp. Even Zaynab wondered at his excessive hugging and kissing and bouncing of the baby. It wasn't manly. He would rock the baby in his single arm and sing some ridiculous, nonsensical rhyme while rubbing his big nose into the poor little thing's face. I could have sworn I saw what looked to be a slight grimace of irritation on the baby's face, though still less than two weeks old. Stranger yet, behind the smiles at Jaubert's silly antics, I could see faintly in the baby's mouth and eyes an Egyptian visage of pained tolerance at his French effeminacy. When he asked me if I wanted to hold the baby and proffered the child cradled in the crook of his arm, I backed away. "Of course not! What do you think I am?"

"You delivered her."

"There was no one else around."

Zaynab laughed. She was propped up in bed, looking pale but well. She had gained consciousness without remembering much of what happened the day she was assaulted, and under the care of the French doctors, she'd speedily recovered. She asked me if I had told Father and Mother that she was leaving.

"I did. Mother cried, of course. Father said you can't leave—you are to come back home."

"Back home? Tell him that in chess the pawns don't move backward."

Jaubert laughed without having an inkling of what she meant. He whispered in the baby's ear, in his awful and childish baby talk, what Mama Zu Zu had said, rocking the poor little thing to and fro in his one arm, which I am sure was pure torture for her, judging from the look she gave me to come save her.

"Father doesn't know anything that's happened," I told Zaynab. "No one knows."

"No, I suppose they wouldn't. It's two different worlds, here and there, isn't it? How's sister Noha?"

"She acts happy as a bird in summer since she married that Mamluk of Father's."

"I have to see them before I leave. I may never have another chance."

"Don't. Father might not let you leave."

"How could he? It's all arranged. I'm a married woman."

"He doesn't know. He thinks he's still the master."

"I'll visit when I'm feeling stronger."

"Why bother? I'll bring Mother and Noha here before you leave."

"Why not Father too?"

"It would only upset him. He's got enough trouble with the French leaving."

"Why? He's a shaykh. They won't do anything to the shaykhs. It's only the women they'll punish. Like Hawa … Eve." She crossed her arms and shuddered. "Poor woman. I still see her head stuck up on that post."

"Now, now, Zu Zu, my little flower, don't think of that." Jaubert kissed the baby and placed her in her mother's arms. "Think of her. She's our future." Zu Zu smiled down at her daughter and made baby noises worse than Jaubert's. The child wasn't amused.

"Have you thought of a name yet?" I asked.

"No. We want something that's French and Egyptian, like her. Nadia is all we've come up with so far."

"How about Junaynah—Little Paradise?" I suggested.

"Little Paradise?" Jaubert asked sourly.

"In honor of Venture."

"Ah, Venture de Paradise! Of course!" Jaubert exchanged looks with Zaynab. "Junaynah," he repeated thoughtfully. Zu Zu repeated it after him.

"You can call her Ju Ju in Paris," I quipped—a bit too sarcastically I suppose, though I was serious about the name Junaynah. The memory of my great teacher, Venture, burned bright within me. I hadn't forgotten any of the principles he'd taught me: Think, improvise, create! Analyze, don't memorize! Understand! Between motion and stability, take motion, for motion is life, while stability is death. Life is mind, imagination, and action. Write or speak no word in excess! Science and nature, like good composition and eloquence, demand clarity, simplicity—nothing in excess! How I loved Venture de Paradise. I still do.

"Junaynah," mused Jaubert, sniffing the name as he would a glass of wine or cognac, first critically wrinkling his long nose at it, then letting it roll over his lips and tongue, delicately tasting and swallowing, repeating the silly parody that went as French style. "Junaynah."

Yes, I have to say it again: I really and truly made a big mistake saving Amadeus Jaubert's life. It was bad enough his torturing little Junaynah with some absolutely jejune rhyme about a girl who lost her sheep, but when he started playing with her toes, calling them little piggies going to the market—it was enough to make a decent Muslim vomit—I had to get out of the room before I strangled him. Little piggies! At least the meat of the sheep could be eaten, if only the little girl in the stupid rhyme hadn't lost them! I kissed Zaynab on both cheeks and took my leave before I lost my temper and threw her squishy husband off the balcony.

"Tell Father I'll come to visit him before I leave."

I knew better than to argue with her.

17

FATHER WAS, AS USUAL at this time in the afternoon, in his study on the second floor. The door was locked. When I asked him to let me in, he said he was busy and told me to come back in an hour. Figuring it was either cognac or opium he was busy with, I left and returned an hour later. The door was still locked.

"Father, I have to talk to you. It's about Zaynab. Please open the door."

It took him five minutes to do it. He looked a bit bleary-eyed. "Didn't I tell you to bring her home?"

"But she—"

"No buts, boy! Just you bring her home! Now!"

"Father. She's made her plans. I can't—"

"Can't? Your *can't* is what I tell you you can't! Her plans are what I tell her she can! Bring her! I'll not have her dallying with the French like a collaborator. I'll not have her compromising the family name. Now go!"

"I already told her, Father."

"Tell her again! Pull her by the hair! I'll have no fingers of shame pointing at me! Now go bring her!"

Father redirected his shaking finger from my face to running it under the verses of the Quran he was reciting in a mumble. I turned, shaking my head, and looked around his prayer room. The door of the book cabinet where he had once kept his liquor and intelligence reports for Napoleon was closed and locked. Fingering my prayer beads, straining to speak with respect, I said, "You shouldn't have let her go with the French from the beginning."

"Don't mince words with me, young pup!" he shouted. "I told you to bring her!" His face had turned crimson. His fingers fumbled over the page, which wouldn't turn. He slammed the Quran shut and got to his feet with difficulty. His growling face, with its deeply etched lines of worry, was a palimpsest of fury written over fear. Three years of the French had aged him thirty.

"Bring her, I say!" He aimed his finger at me as though it were a weapon. "Bring her or you'll be no son of mine, and she no daughter!"

I left before I said something I would regret. Mother met me on the way out. She was distraught. She took me by the hand and had me sit with her beside the refreshing coolness of a small bathing pool in the women's section of the villa, our modest harem. "He's not been himself lately," she whispered, though there was no one around. "Poor man. What he's suffered." She sighed, played with her prayer beads. "Maybe with Zaynab home he'll feel better."

"Why should that make any difference?"

"He needs to feel he has a position, at least in his own family. He's lost everything else. Even his self-respect."

"He still has his religious titles he wanted so badly."

"He's afraid the Ottomans will take them after the French have gone."

"I'm sorry, Mother, but the old man brought it on himself."

"Don't be hard, Zaki. Who knew what was going to happen? One turn here or there and he could have been thought of as a great man."

My brow arched in surprise. The sardonic smile that curled the corner of my mouth vanished under Mother's reprimanding countenance.

"He did what he thought he had to do. He did what seemed right at the time." She shrugged in despair. "It's not his fault that the situation changed. Who knows what is the right way in times like these? Umar Makram fled like a coward in defeat to Syria with Ibrahim Bey, and returned with Ibrahim to be hailed as a conquering hero. Your father stayed to help his people and is called a collaborator. How do you know what to do in such stormy times that blow men like feathers in the wind?"

"Father was right to stay," I rejoined sweeping my hand across the surface of the water. "But don't make excuses for him, Mother. He's always calculating the wind and going with it. Now he wants Zaynab to marry old Musawi."

"He's desperate to regain his position."

"First he offers her to Napoleon," I said removing my sandals to hang my legs over the side of the pool and bathe my feet in the cool water, "then he offers her to Menou as a second wife, and now it's to old Shaykh Musawi as a third or fourth wife. He treats her like a pawn, and each time he moves it, he degrades her all the more."

"Like all other men treat their daughters, Son."

"A pawn doesn't move backward, Mother. Zaynab won't accept being treated like that. She never has before; she certainly won't now!" For emphasis I kicked my feet in the pool, unintentionally raising a tiny rainstorm around us.

Mother sighed. "That girl. The French have made her rebellious."

"No. They've made her the Zaynab she always wanted to be."

"More Zaynab than Zaynab. More Ayesha than Ayesha." Mother removed her sandals and swung her legs around to join me, bathing and kicking her feet in the cool water. "Your father blames me for her; I didn't bring her up right. Do you know that he threatened to divorce me and take another wife?"

"The old fool. He just threatened to disown me and Zaynab if she doesn't come back. She won't. She's leaving with the French."

"Dear God! She can't!" Mother's arms folded in deprecation over her breast, as though the Angel of Death had fluttered its dark wings over her. "It will destroy him, the family, all of us."

"It will destroy her if she doesn't go."

"He would never let it happen. He may have suffered a loss in position, but he is still shaykh of the Bakri clan and Zaynab is still his daughter. Have her come back, Zaki, please! I beg you. Otherwise ... it will be the end of everything. He'll blame me for it. He'll divorce me. He'll disown you. The family will be finished. I might just as well end it now and drown myself here." I told her to go ahead, but she'd have to lie perfectly flat on the bottom of the pool and not move because it was so shallow. She gave me a good splashing with her cupped hand. "Get Zaynab back here or I'll drown you! Ungrateful son."

"She won't come back. Why don't we drown Father?"

"I seek refuge in God!" Mother cried, bringing her beads up to her face to ward off the evil that my words had conjured. "How often have I dreamt of that," she whispered after a pause, looking around her as though

230

to make sure there were no evil jinn around to hear. Then: "Zaki, please, listen! Zaynab must return. I beg you, Son, on my soul—please go get her!"

"She's decided. It's too late. There's no going back on it. Her life is now with the French. Her life with the family is finished." Having to say this to Mother made me feel like I had picked up an ax and hacked the family into pieces—limbs, love, relationships, and responsibilities flying in every direction.

"No! She can't! She has a responsibility to the family."

I had to leave. This was tearing at my insides. Poor Mother—I didn't doubt the old man had it in him to divorce her or bring a young second wife into the house. The humiliation would kill her. She was only forty and still a fair-looking woman, but I could understand why, if our pool were deeper, she might tie a brick around her waist and jump in. Bracing myself, I told Mother that Zaynab's first responsibility was to herself (I almost added "and to her baby," but caught myself), and as I spoke the words, a little voice at the edge of my mind chided me about how much I was beginning to sound like a French savant.

"Zaynab's responsibility is to her family," repeated Mother.

"That's the only thing you and Father agree on: family tradition. That's not enough anymore, Mother." I withdrew my feet from the pool and strapped on my sandals. "I have to go."

"Zaki. Believe me, he will divorce me if she doesn't live up to her responsibility. Talk to Zaynab. Tell her she has to come back. Force her to come back if necessary!"

"She doesn't see her responsibility that way anymore, Mother. She has a responsibility to herself. She has her own life to lead."

"What blasphemy! How can she just think of herself? What is she without her family?" Mother broke into tears. She was in such despair, and I felt so wretched for having told her what I had, that I lied and promised to do what I could to bring Zaynab back. Then I left, relieved to be gone from the house.

The family had fallen apart. The French's departure was proving more devastating than their arrival.

The long-awaited evacuation began the following day. Article 12 of the treaty guaranteed the right of anyone in Egypt to leave with the French, regardless of religion or gender. It also guaranteed security of wealth, property, and any family that the evacuees left behind. Article 16 guaranteed the security of everyone remaining in Egypt who had associated with the French: no one would be accused, prosecuted, or harmed in any way for having cooperated with, served, or aided the French, whatever form the association had taken.

The several thousand Egyptians who had registered to leave were instructed to assemble with their baggage along the river at either Giza or the Island of Rawdah, whichever was more convenient. The local people evacuating were mainly Copt and Syrian Christians who had prospered with the French and who would be leaving much of their ill-gained wealth behind for the Ottoman pasha and his officers to confiscate. It was a prudent sacrifice, since the written guarantees of security signed by Grand Vizier Yusuf Pasha were deemed no more valuable than the scraps of paper Europeans used in their disgusting way of cleansing themselves after defecating. Also leaving were dozens of Egyptian women who had married soldiers, and several hundred Muslim men and women who, for one reason or another, figured it would be wise not to be around for a while, at least not until the dust settled and time had worked its power of forgiving, if not forgetting. They all swore they would return, for their roots went deep in the Nile mud of Mother Egypt, or *Umm al-Dunya*, as we lovingly called our country: Mother of the World.

The departing Muslims were mostly young women who were alone or had babies with them, or who had compromised themselves with the French and had been repudiated and abandoned now that the soldiers were returning home. Rather than remain in Egypt and face possible punishment, they had chosen loneliness, poverty, and insecurity in an unknown world that promised them little else than contempt. The young women with babies were huddled together in an isolated group in a corner of the stationing post by the river, looking frightened and vulnerable, a breed unto themselves, costumed as they were in their grotesque mismatch of French and local dress, as though lost in the twilight of these two worlds that had briefly come together only to be torn apart. Those who had dared step across the divide were now left hanging over the widening abyss. The lucky ones were those whose husbands had been killed, for they would receive pensions and live well enough in France, though they would be lonely, longing and heartsick for their Egyptian homes and their warm, nosy, comforting friends.

As I watched the young women gather by themselves along the river across from the Island of Rawdah, their children clinging to their skirts and their meager possessions all in bundles, I wondered how many of their kind were not there, how many had chanced the forgiveness of their people to remain, and I thought of Hawa, the Eve of Niqula Qapitan and his French masters. Niqula had taken the lesson of his unfortunate Eve and was leaving. With him was the Turkish janissary who had served the French as chief of police; Yusuf, the leader of the Coptic brigade; Thanks-To-God Shukrallah of the Coptic tax-collecting and house-wrecking crew; Bartholemew, a longtime Greek resident of Cairo, who when the French came went from bottle seller to chief executioner; and the Syrian Christian translators, whose French was as bad as their Arabic. Sailing with them would be the rest of the dregs and sleaze who had traded themselves to the French with obscene ease. But it wasn't just the unprincipled and unwise who were leaving. The grand patriarch of the Coptic church and community, a distinguished old man who had kept his distance from the French and advised his community to do likewise, was also leaving, for he knew the Ottomans would execute him as an example to the Copts that Ottoman justice was stern: what the body does, the head must pay for. The established price was separation of one from the other. Rumor had it that even Shaykhs Sharqawi and Sadat, who had been arrested in the Citadel as collateral against any trouble by the citizens, were thinking that the journey to France with their captors might be advisable if they wished to keep their heads in place. But that was only a rumor spread by people who wanted to express their disgust of the shaykhs, who looked like collaborators; it was in general the older, highly placed shaykhs, the elite, who were marked down as such.

The boats coming from Damietta were delayed. At first it was a blessing, for each day's delay was a day more that Zaynab and Junaynah could grow stronger for the long journey. But as Father well knew and Mother had said, man is but a feather in the wind of destiny. Who can, in the brevity of life, tell blessing from curse?

When I'd returned home without Zaynab, Mother went crying and fainting to her room and Father flew into a rage and cursed and disowned both of us. I believe fear was behind his destructive emotions. An aberration of history was being corrected in a way that left him out, and he was afraid. To show that he wasn't, he cursed the world and everyone, ranting on behind his veil of rage. He had sacrificed himself for Islam, Egypt, and History and had been rejected and scorned. In turn, he rejected the world, all of it, including the high ulema, of which he was an important member, and even al-Azhar, of which he was a leading member. And so too he rejected that part of the world closest to him, his family. Or so I was convinced.

His terrible boil of fear and wrath gathered first to be leveled on Zaynab for having, like History, disobeyed him. He cursed and disowned her. The more he cursed and disowned her, the more it tore his heart, as though his curses were thrown back on himself, for he loved her in his way—it was the love of a lord and father who demands obedience but when disobeyed continues secretly loving even as he blusters his pent-up rage at the world gone wrong. He cursed Zaynab for disobedience, and me for having failed to bring her back, and Mother for having failed to bring up decent children. She had reared a brood of scorpions, and he would divorce her. It seemed that fear and disappointment had so robbed the proud man of his senses that he could express it only in rage and threats of denouncement. I tried one last time to reason with him, this time as forcefully as I could, explaining that we must all accept responsibility for our acts and face the consequences. When he sent Zaynab to Napoleon, I asked him, did he really think the general would marry her, or was he just out to fulfill some personal ambition? He spit in rage and ordered me to hold my tongue.

"No, Father, not this time. I will speak. If Zaynab has caused you pain, then it is only because of your ambitions. You gave Zaynab to the French, and when you did, you gave yourself to them as well. She is not for you to give and take back as it suits you. You can disown the French and your collaboration with them, but Zaynab will not."

His face went a deeper red. His eyes sharpened on me in surprise. "What are you talking about?"

"You know what I'm talking about. The boxes that came here every week. Your twenty-five Mamluks. Your reports to Napoleon. You spied for the French. You were Napoleon's chief agent. How many Egyptians were executed because of your reports, Father? How many? Fifty, eighty, two hundred?"

He stepped back, wincing with each salvo of numbers, his face turning from crimson to ash, as though my words had punched the life from him. For a while he couldn't speak. When he did, his fateful words came as judgment on us all—deep, hoarse, wounded, trembling:

"Out! Out! Out of my house! I curse you! You are no son of mine, and Zaynab is no daughter! Out! Let me not set eyes on either of you again! Out!"

I returned to Mother, kissed her good-bye, and left, pierced by her heavy sobbing and cries for God's help as she doubled over and collapsed by the side of the pool, clutching her beads.

Father, if I can call him that now, had long ago lost my respect. His ruthless ambition and heartless treatment of Zaynab had obliterated the goodness I had once seen in him.

I passed a sleepless night in the shell of what had been the institute. The next day I learned that Father had married a fourteen-year-old peasant girl. Further humiliating Mother—nay, almost murdering her by virtually cutting her heart out—he brought his child bride home to live in the same house. Mother moved back to her old house on the other side of the city, where she cried her eyes out, calling for God to end her misery and her life. I moved in with her to keep her from harming herself.

"Bring Zaynab to me," she cried in anguish. "Where's my daughter now that I need her? Why have they abandoned me? Bring Zaynab! Bring Noha! I need my children!" I didn't believe my ragged heart could bear any more tearing than it had suffered already, but Mother's mournful tears made it clear there was no end to what the heart can endure.

I kept all that had happened from Zaynab, who was safe with Jaubert up at the Citadel, and prayed for the ship to come and take her away from This madness which was closing in on us like another plague, like God gone vicious in vengeance.

I was riding my donkey across town from my mother's house in the Jawdariyyah Quarter to see Zaynab for what I thought would be the last time. The ship was expected early the next morning and she and Jaubert wanted to transport their crates of luggage to Rawdah Island beforehand so they wouldn't be rushed. I had volunteered to help them. While passing through Khan al-Khalili and the al-Azhar Quarter on my way to Azbakiyyah and the institute, I met my friend and fellow student Faysal, son of Shaykh Sharqawi, the young man who had at one time wanted to marry Zaynab. (It seemed a century ago.) We dismounted, shook hands, and sat in rickety wicker chairs outside the front of a little teahouse to chat over tea. I told him I was sorry that his father had been arrested and taken hostage at the Citadel. Faysal shrugged, saying he was sorry that mine had not been arrested.

"From now on," he said, "those who are the most harmed by the French will be the safest."

"Who would have thought a few months ago the French would be leaving?"

"It will never be what it was before." Faysal cautiously looked around to see if anyone might be listening—Ottoman agents were everywhere. "Some things will need rethinking once the French are out."

"Many things," I agreed.

"We'll be the ones who have to do it, Zaki."

"It won't be easy."

Faysal chuckled. "What in this world that's meaningful is ever easy?" When I agreed and told him he sounded like a French savant, he nervously looked around again. "For God's sake, Zaki, guard what you say. You're my dear friend, like a brother, but please, allow me to put a noose around my neck by myself."

I apologized and we touched our tea glasses together, as we had seen the French do when they were imbibing, and smiled at each other. I didn't feel so alone anymore. Warm interaction with a friend was worth ten thousand prayers. In fact, I said this exact thing to Faysal, adding that it was a hadith (something the Prophet was reported to have said or done)—one that I had read in Bukhari's authoritative collection, I added for authenticity. Faysal took it with a nod of acceptance until he realized, helped by the teasing smile that broke loose on my face, that I had made it up, and he laughed and took my hand in his. "Zaki, you are exactly what your name means: a very clever guy!"

He then asked me if what I had learned at the institute was useful. Could it benefit Egypt?

I told him I thought certain things could be very useful: French science and mechanics, medicine, the system of organization and administration. "France's judicial system transposed into Shari'ah principles would be very beneficial. We have to learn to make steam and electricity. And to fly air balloons and drop bombs from them. Did you ever hear of people electing leaders?" He shook his head. "Well, we might have to think about that too, Faysal."

He put his hand on mine and said in a low voice, "You know, Zaki, I secretly envied you studying at that institute. But I couldn't do it myself. My father, he's not as open and free as yours."

"I don't know if those are the right words for my father, Faysal. You know how he felt cheated out of the religious titles before the French came? Well, he ended up getting them. And I'm afraid the time is coming when he will have to pay."

"Whatever the words, it took a lot of courage to do what he did. You too, going to the institute." Faysal drained his glass of tea.

"That was Zaynab's courage. She literally dragged me there. You know how insistent she can be."

"Zaynab." He looked down. "How is she?"

"The same as ever. Crazy."

"God made a mistake making her a female." He no sooner said the words than he took my arm. "Excuse me for saying so, Zaki."

"I've said worse about her."

He smiled. "You know what she once told me? That when she died, she wanted to be buried with the sultans and imams in Qurrafat al-Sughra. The royal burial grounds where no woman is buried. Can you imagine?"

"Easily."

"What man could satisfy her?"

"My father hoped it would be none other than our long-lost Napoleon."

"That wasn't right. He shouldn't have offered her."

"There were dozens of others who did the same."

We ordered hubbly-bubblies and sat quietly smoking, soothed by the sound of the gurgling water and the pleasant fragrance of the perfumed tobacco. In the narrow street in front of us, porters carrying heavy loads on their bent backs, supported by strong ropes around their sweating foreheads, were passing by one way and the other, joined by overburdened donkeys being coaxed along by peasants with switches, and colorfully dressed water and juice sellers who had polished containers slung over their shoulders and were clinking their little glasses together in case their hoarse shouts had not sufficiently alerted everyone around to their presence and what they were selling. The French had used horse-drawn carriages and wheeled carts for transportation and portage; we used donkeys and strong men with bent backs.

"Did Napoleon—"

I knew what Faysal was going to ask. "No, he sent her to the institute without as much as looking at her. She married the institute and lost her virginity to books and French grammar."

Faysal smiled sadly. "Zaynab wouldn't marry a mere man."

"Do you know what they called her?"

"Everyone knows: Napoleon's Egyptian girl." Turning somber, he puffed on the stem of his coiled pipe and stared down at his empty glass. "She's leaving with the French, no?"

"Yes."

"Be sure she does, Zaki."

Something in his voice alarmed me. I asked why he said that—was something up?

"No reason. It's just better that she does," he replied.

"I know she should leave, Faysal, but tell me what made you say it. I can tell by your voice. Why? Why is it better that she leaves?" He shrugged, smiled wanly, shook his head. "There's something going on, Faysal. Tell me. What is it?"

"Nothing important."

"Everything's important. What is it?"

He sighed, shrugged. "It's only gossip. Nothing important."

"This is no time for secrets. Tell me."

"I don't know if it's true. Just something I overheard in the mosque."

"So?"

"Some people were talking about bringing a case against Zaynab. It's so disgusting I didn't want to say anything about it, and it's only empty talk anyway. There are so many ugly rumors and gossip you hear these days, you can't take any of it seriously."

"Zaynab is innocent."

"It's not so much Zaynab they were talking about. It was your father."

"Him?"

"They want vengeance for his dealings with the French."

"What's he done that others haven't?"

"I'm just telling you what I heard. They were talking about bringing a case against Zaynab and forcing your father to testify on her behalf. They want to humiliate him by forcing him to testify for a daughter who's been charged with immoral conduct. I don't know how true it is. The city's crawling with rumors."

"There are no witnesses, no proof, no testimony ... how could they charge her with immorality?"

"Listen, Zaki. It hurts me to say this. It involves my own father. But you know how jealous those shaykhs are of each other. Your father was a big man under the French. They'd do anything to ruin him. Especially Shaykh Sadat. He secretly hated Umar Makram's guts when he was top dog before the French. Then it was your father's guts he hated when Napoleon gave him all his titles and offices."

"Sadat?"

"All smiles and sweetness on the surface, but underneath he's a cesspool of snake poison and envy. People say he's already scheming to take over your father's place once the pasha is back in power."

I regarded Faysal in silence and sipped the last of my tea. As we were sitting there, a gang of Turkish-speaking Christians from Anatolia and the European provinces of the empire—Bosnians, Albanians, Bulgarians, whatever—came swaggering down the street. Only a week ago they had been dandies in French uniforms lording it over us as soldiers. Now they were in Ottoman uniforms, and acting even worse. They pushed a fruit vendor out of their way, overturning his carefully arranged pyramids of peaches and oranges and calling him an "Egyptian animal," laughing loudly and looking around at everyone in the street as though casting the insult to all of us who could hear it. Faysal and I exchanged glances and pretended not to notice them.

"The Ottoman agents know everything, Zaki."

"Everything?"

"That your father disowned Zaynab. If they get her to court, your father would be forced to testify in defense of a girl he's disowned. He'd be made to look like a fool. Worse, why he disavowed her, what she did with the French—it would all come out. He'd be humiliated."

"That's the least he deserves."

"It's the humiliation to Zaynab that I'm worried about. If she's brought to court ..." He waved his hand before him as if to chase away the thought. "We've been humiliated enough, Zaki. None of us deserves any more. I'm afraid of what the new pasha is going to do."

"Zaynab won't be disgraced. She's leaving for Paris."

He patted me on the shoulder. "I'm sorry, Zaki. But life in Paris can't be worse than living here in dishonor."

We shook hands, mounted our donkeys, and went our separate ways—Faysal up the road to al-Azhar Mosque, I down to the French Quarter in Azbakiyyah and the defunct Egyptian Institute.

18

SOLDIERS WERE HURRIEDLY LOADING up their wagons, carts, donkeys, and camels for the long desert trek to the sea, where English ships awaited to transport them back to France. Most of the civilian evacuees were at the encampments at Giza and Rawdah Island, waiting for barges that would take them down the Nile to Alexandria. The Egyptians among them, fearing that the people might attack them for planning to leave with the defeated enemy, had retreated up to the Citadel with their possessions. They were followed by the sick and infirm who had been removed from the French hospitals, which were thereafter left to rot.

Azbakiyyah was fast becoming a ghost town. The evacuation treaty allowed the French to take whatever they could transport. The four hundred camels the grand vizier loaned the French to help transport their loot had been taken over by the officers. The common soldiers, left to buy or steal their own means of transporting their loot, had for several days been commandeering anything with wheels or legs.

When I reached military headquarters, a party of soldiers asked me how much I wanted for my donkey. Upon my informing them that it wasn't for sale, they pulled me roughly to the ground. Overtaken by a momentary blood-surge of angry manliness, I resisted, upon which they kicked my sides in and left me lying in the dust, holding my ribs with one hand and shaking my fist at them with the other while gasping for breath in voiceless protest as they led my donkey away. I painfully got to my feet, dusted myself off, straightened my turban, and continued on to the institute, for the moment oh so glad to see the French leaving us in the abject humiliation deservedly imposed upon them by the English.

At the institute, the crates to be transported had been loaded onto carts. Zaynab was up and dressed in the high military leather boots Pauline had given her and her white caftan and crimson sash, with her raven hair falling beneath her blue turban and down the sides of her face and over her shoulders—colorful as the revolutionary flag the French loved to wave around. Motherhood had added a glow to her beauty. Jaubert had Junaynah cradled in his one arm and was singing her some sadistic rhyme about a wind that sends a baby in a cradle crashing to its death from a treetop. Thank god the poor child couldn't understand. Whenever I heard him coo and baby talk and sing those grotesque nursery rhymes, I wanted to punch him in the mouth to shut him up, freshly regretting my unwise act of having saved his life.

"What happened to you?" he asked, seeing my dusty and crumpled condition.

"Nothing. Some French soldiers took a fancy to my donkey, so I let them have it. When's the boat coming?"

"Tomorrow sometime."

"In the morning?"

"Who knows? Are you in such a hurry to see us leave?"

"Yes. So we can live in freedom and independence. Isn't that what you taught us?"

"Hah! Under your Ottoman Turks? Mark my words, dear brother-in-law. Once the pashas are back in power, you're going to wish we never left!"

Zaynab served us tea and some sugary French buns. "You won't be bored with us gone?" she asked me.

I replied that I had hidden away some French books from the institute that would keep me occupied for a while.

"You stole books from our library?" Jaubert's brow was arched in stern disapproval.

I laughed in sarcasm. "The Egyptians steal; the French liberate! You bloody people are carting away half our cultural heritage!"

"But those books belong to the French state!"

"And those thousands of crates of manuscripts and art being taken from Egypt, who do they belong to?"

"But to us! You no longer have a state for anything to belong to."

I turned to Zaynab. "You know, you're going to have to learn a whole new logic in France." She wasn't listening. Her lips were pursed in troubled thought.

"Now that I'm strong enough," she said distractedly, as though to herself, "I should visit Father and Mother and Noha." She looked at Jaubert, whose scowl at my crime was now directed down at the poor baby locked in the crook of his arm. "There's plenty of time for a visit," she added, now looking at me.

"No!" I ordered peremptorily. "It won't do any good."

"But I may never see them again."

"That might be all for the better. Father's not exactly delighted that you're leaving."

She smiled sadly. "How's Mother?"

"She's unhappy you're leaving, of course, but she understands. Otherwise she's perfectly fine crying all the time."

It was no mystery to me that Zaynab had no idea what was going on at home, which though just down the road from the French Quarter in Azbakiyyah was completely impervious to the rumors and gossip that in Egyptian society spread with the speed of Berthollet's electricity. Faysal, who lived some distance away on the opposite side of the city, knew in detail what was happening in Shaykh Khalil's home, while Shaykh Khalil's own daughter, who lived practically next door in the French Quarter, hadn't a clue. Europeans and Egyptians inhabited the same city but were totally ignorant of each other, as though they lived in separate worlds, one sealed off from the other by invisible walls, except for that tiny minority of Egyptians who were now about to leave.

"I'd like to see Noha and her husband. Imagine her marrying a Mamluk!" Zaynab turned back to Jaubert, who had shamelessly resumed his cooing and coddling baby Junaynah, who looked bored to tears. "Couldn't you arrange for a carriage?" Zaynab asked him. "Mother could meet us at Noha's house. I might even try making it up to Father."

Jaubert was wrinkling his nose and squinting and grinning like an imbecile at the poor baby, who turned her tiny head, obviously trying to ignore him. "I suppose. If you really want to?" he replied, looking like a monkey with his baby faces. "Zaki could take you."

Before it went any further, I offered to bring Mother and Noha to her, and maybe even Father if I could soften him up. Zaynab's eyes widened in hope: "Will you?" I promised I would.

I shook Jaubert's armless shoulder good-bye and embraced Zaynab, sure I would never see any of them again. Jaubert offered me his donkey, which I declined, saying I'd only end up giving it to some poor soldier out of pity. Then, taking what I thought would be my last look at them, I started off.

In the Jamiliyyah Quarter, a great crowd had gathered in a swirl of dust, just at the corner near Mother's house. A chorus of frenzied cries rent the air: Whore! Prostitute! Slut! Shoe for every French foot! Approaching the corner, I caught sight of the young woman at the center of all the commotion. Her clothes had been torn from her; filth from the street had been smeared over her naked body. She was being pelted and pulled by the hair. "Take her to the judge!" an old woman cried. "Strike off her head first!" another woman cried back. Clutching my aching ribs, I squeezed through the hysterical crowd and continued on to my mother's house.

Mother was in bed weeping, wretchedly wailing to God, begging to know why He had humiliated and rejected her. Noha was at her side, trying to console her. I hadn't seen Noha in a long time. She had grown and matured into a young woman since her marriage to the Mamluk—and had become a lot more forceful: "Why isn't Zaynab here?" she demanded the moment she saw me.

The mention of Zaynab brought a heart-wrenching wail from Mother. "Oh! Zaynab! My daughter! Where is she when I need her? Why has she abandoned me? Why doesn't she see her poor mother in her hour of misery?"

Yes! Why doesn't she? demanded Noha. Zaynab was leaving, I told her. She was going with the French. Mother and sister looked at me in stunned silence. I repeated it: she had decided; she was going. Mother clutched her breast.

"Why should she leave?" Noha asked. "What has she done to run away?"

"Nothing. Everything. She's studied with the French."

"So? Half the women of Cairo have done a hell of a lot more than that with the French! You should tell her what Father has done to Mother. Or should I tell her?"

"It's too late," I replied. "She's already on the boat by now."

"Damn her! I can't believe she's doing this to us. Mother's threatened with divorce, Father's taken a wife younger than me, and Zaynab's left with the French without even a good-bye."

"Father won't divorce her," I said. "It would kill him to have to return the dowry written into their marriage contract."

"I hope so. My husband told me that the boat has been delayed. There's no reason for Zaynab not to say good-bye to us."

"How did he know about the boat? Did he take over Rustam's old spying job for Father?"

Noha's color deepened. "Never mind that," she snapped.

"Who's he spying for? The English? Murad Bey? The grand vizier, Yusuf Pasha?"

"He works his own intelligence operation. Do you want me to tell him to bring her? He can do it. She can't leave without saying good-bye to her own mother."

I hesitated a long moment before speaking, and when I did, I affected as grief-stricken a tone and visage as I could. "I didn't want to tell you, but now I see I have to." I sighed deeply before continuing. "Zaynab is sick. It may be the plague."

Mothers arms went from her breast to her face in appeal to God to save her daughter from the plague. Noha scrutinized me from the corner of her narrowed eyes and said the French would take no Egyptian to France who had the plague.

"It's not yet absolutely certain she has it," I countered.

But Noha had grown up and matured during the three years of occupation; she wasn't fooled. "Zaki. What's really wrong? You're hiding something."

"You're right, I am. My cowardice. This morning some soldiers beat me and stole my donkey right in the middle of the street in broad daylight, with people all around. Only a few houses away from here, a girl is being stoned to death for doing no more than what you and your girlfriends did, going to Tivoli. Thieves are looting stores and homes everywhere. Law and order are breaking down; people are being murdered."

"I'm not afraid. I'll go."

"And get raped and worse. The French have become as bad as the Mamluks. I'll go. Give me an hour to bathe my battered ribs and put on clean clothes."

Tears were streaming down Mother's drawn cheeks. "When Zaynab sees what's happened, she won't leave for Frangistan, and Shaykh Khalil will come to his senses and divorce that chit of a peasant."

"Of course he will," Noha consoled her. "Everything will be all right once she comes back. How could she possibly leave? Father will forgive her."

Mother's wet eyes shone with hope: "Son. Go to your father. Tell him Zaynab is coming back. Tell him she begs his forgiveness."

I soaked for an hour in a tub of hot water, then I had one of Mother's servant women rub down my aching sides with mint oil compounded with a garlic and herbal distillate that the French doctors had thought quaint but devoid of all curative power. Restored, I donned fresh garments—robe, caftan, turban—and mounted my second donkey of the day for the return trek to the villa, this time to see Father, for Mother's sake.

Father was having a hard time with his new life. His chief servant, an old Circassian manumitted slave who had been with the family since before I was born and had been more of a loving father to me than Shaykh Khalil, told me that Father had been locked up in his prayer room for days.

"With his child bride? Or is she too busy playing with her dolls?"

"More likely playing with your father's young Mamluks." The Circassian's ancient face wrinkled into a painful smile.

"Just what the old shaykh deserves." I went up and knocked on his prayer room door. "Father. It's me. I have to speak to you. It's urgent."

"Go away, no son of mine. Nothing is urgent to me that concerns you. Or Zaynab."

"Father! Please! Be merciful!"

"Mercy is for God. Go away!" I tried the door; it was locked. "Be gone with you!" he shouted.

"Father!"

"It's too late for you to call me that!" The hardness in his voice cracked in self-pity.

"It's about Zaynab. She wants to see you. She begs forgiveness."

"Hell and damnation to her! She is no daughter of mine to forgive."

"Father! Open the door! Let me at least speak to you face-to-face."

He didn't reply. His silence reached through the door like a cold hand gripping my throat, freezing my tongue. I remained awhile, waiting for a word from him, even of rebuke, but the silence on the other side of the door was his final statement that we no longer existed for him, as though the family had never been. I embraced my old Circassian teacher and left.

I avoided the streets filled with looting soldiers and young gangs and took the narrow back alleys. A plague-stricken beggar in rags dragged himself toward me on legs that had withered and twisted up behind him like dead branches. I threw him a coin and spurred my donkey on, not knowing where to go or what to do. Coming out onto Azbakiyya and the gutted ruins of Tivoli, I dismounted and sat in the roofless skeleton of what had once been the Grand Hall. Little remained of Tivoli but the razed integuments, most of the structure having been stripped away to build barricades. As I sat there gazing around me at the ruins in bittersweet reverie, I could hear the merriment of music and laughter echoing from the solitary stones of the structure's hollow innards, could see through my closed eyes the ghosts of young girls and officers whirling about the ballroom in their endless dances; the phantoms of jugglers and card players; the hucksters, hustlers, and tricksters; the magicians, fire eaters, sword swallowers and snake charmers; the laughing girls kicking up their legs on carousels; the French boy-soldiers racing donkeys and camels and falling off, laughing hilariously. The ghosts in the stones still sang with the coquettish giggles and flirting glances of the café girls; the whispers and turning heads; the unveiled, blushing smile; the soldier's wink. Even the ghosts would soon be gone.

As I was rising to leave, a horseman spurring a scraggly nag along the canal bank passed across my field of vision like one of the phantoms in my mind. The man rode with what was certainly a single-minded intent that bespoke of pressing urgency, his shoulders bent over the saddle, his head close to the mane, the tail of his black cloak streaming behind him like a satanic comet. So hard was he driving the scrawny mount that it seemed the beast would expire underneath him and topple with him into the canal. It must have been a matter of great dispatch—death, plague, murder, surprise attack, English invasion—for no Egyptian would have otherwise spurred an animal so strenuously as to risk killing it, let alone exposing it to confiscation by the departing soldiers. Startled, I watched the dark figure beat the emaciated beast until horse and rider disappeared into the complex of palaces that once housed French military headquarters, the institute, and the residences of generals, commanders in chief, and Pauline, the sweetest ghost haunting my emptied world.

Unnerved by the horseman, I returned to Mother's house rather than wander aimlessly around the dangerous streets. Mother and Noha were drinking tea and picking at a tray full of frosted French cakes. "Zaynab said she would come tomorrow," I lied. "She wanted to come but the French wouldn't let her leave. The situation is too dangerous."

Mother and Noha exchanged glances. A sixth sense told me something was up. When I left them an hour or two earlier, they were in deep distress; now here they were, sitting comfortably on cushions, gorging themselves on sugary French cakes like pampered housecats. I took a small, honey-soaked cake from the plate and between bites told them Father had locked himself up in his prayer room. "He plays with his beads while his child bride plays with his Mamluks." This returned Mother to her tears.

The servant woman poured me a glass of mint tea as I was examining the quality of the gooey cake between my fingers. "Where did you get the cakes?"

"Daud Kashif brought them," Mother replied, wiping at her eyes. "He is able to get anything we want."

Daud Kashif was Noha's Mamluk husband, kashif being the title given to a Mamluk emir's chief lietenant. "He was here?" I asked.

Noha said he had left a short time ago and would be back soon—hopefully with Zaynab, she added. Her Mamluk had influence with the French.

I threw down my cake and jumped up. "I have to stop her!"

Noha looked startled. "What for?"

"They want to shame and humiliate her."

"Who does?"

"Father's enemies." I turned to leave just as the outer door swung open and the excited voice of Mother's old servant woman came from the courtyard. A second later, the front door opened and Noha's Georgian Mamluk entered. His black cloak that almost touched the ground identified him as the horseman I had seen less than an hour earlier, racing his worn-out nag toward the French compound. Behind him was a woman covered from head to foot in a black robe and veil. She removed the veil. Seeing Zaynab, Mother and Noha leapt to their feet with shrieks of joy and embraced her.

19

ZAYNAB'S EYES LOOKED BLOODSHOT from crying. Daud Kashif had obviously spared her no detail of Father's new wife and Mother's suffering. When the hugging and kissing had finished, Zaynab angrily rounded on me for not having kept her informed of what was happening at home. Noha's eyes shot daggers at me, while Mother's grief-stricken look made me feel like I had plunged a dagger into her heart. Turning from the three women's accusing eyes with a French-like shrug of innocence, I told them that Father's enemies were planning to arrest Zaynab on charges of immorality in order to force him to testify in public that she was innocent.

"Nonsense," Daud scoffed. "You shouldn't believe the empty talk going around. Who told you such lies?" Something in the man's voice and expression didn't ring true. It was too strained, too eager to convince. I could still see him riding hell-bent on that sickly nag he would have spurred to death to reach his destination. Overeager people make my skin prick up with distrust and suspicion. When I asked him how he knew they were lies, he replied with another question: "How could Zaynab be arrested? There would have to be witnesses." The stupidity of the question increased my distrust. Witnesses could be bought for the price of an egg. Daud Kashif was too eager to have Zaynab stay.

"Innocent people have been taken to court before," I answered him testily, "and found guilty, witnesses or no witnesses."

Zaynab's cheeks had deepened in color. "Please," she begged, "there's no sense talking about it. I'm leaving for France. I have no choice!"

"Daughter! No!" cried Mother.

"Of course you have a choice!" exclaimed Noha. "You're the only one who can make Father feel he's regained his honor. With all of us together as a family, we can—"

I stopped Noha short, saying we could do nothing—it was settled. Zaynab was leaving and that was that. There would be no more discussion of it!

Noha persisted: "Why? Why is it so important for her to leave?"

"Because she must," I replied, taking a step toward the door to bring an end to the discussion.

"Why must she?" Noha asked belligerently, arguing that Zaynab's reconciliation with Father would bring the family back together.

"I'll go to him and beg his forgiveness," Zaynab said.

"Zaynab! No! It's no use," I exclaimed. "He wouldn't see you. I already tried to talk to him. He's cursed us both."

She put her hand to her mouth. "Why?"

"He's sick. He feels everyone's betrayed him—the French, the shaykhs, the people of Cairo, me, you, Mother, his family. Ever since General Bellier struck him on the face he's been out for revenge against the world."

Zaynab looked at Mother in despair—and Noha, she didn't know what to do. Mother begged Zaynab not to leave them. Noha assured Mother that Zaynab wouldn't abandon them. Zaynab turned to me in appeal.

"She's leaving on that boat tomorrow, and that's that! Discussion over!" I exclaimed, fists clenched.

"What does Zaynab say? France or family?" Daud Kashif asked.

Trembling in anger, I thrust my clenched fists up to his white, mustachioed Georgian face. "What the hell business is it of yours? This isn't your family. You have no say in this matter! You're just a slave Mamluk from nowhere, Georgia!"

"Zaki! You're talking to my husband!"

"That's your mistake, Sister! Zaynab is leaving!"

Noha dismissed me with a look of contempt and took Zaynab by the arm. "I can't believe you would do this to us. Is going to France more important than Mother? Than the family? More important than me, Zaki, all of us?"

Zaynab opened her mouth but then just shook her head and bit her lip. Unable to speak, she embraced Noha and Mother and went and sat on a cushion in the corner of the room, quietly weeping with her head in her hands. Mother and Noha stood looking at her, wondering what it was that was so distressing her. As they sat down by her side, consoling her and asking her what was wrong, Daud stepped forward and said he would go and bring Shaykh Khalil.

"If he wouldn't see me," I retorted, "why the hell would he see you?"

"He will see me," Daud said forcefully, returning my steely glare. "And he will listen to me."

We stood facing each other with clenched fists. Noha came and stood between us, telling her husband to go to Father and bring him here, or at least have him agree to see Zaynab. "Maybe if he hears her ask his forgiveness, he'll relent. We have to make him feel his honor is restored. We have a duty to him and the family."

"I'll go with you," said Zaynab. "It will save time."

No, Daud replied, he could travel faster by himself, and it would be easier for him to talk to Shaykh Khalil if he went alone. I agreed, as it would have been dangerous for Zaynab to travel outside the French security zone, even veiled.

When Daud had left, I apologized to Mother and Noha for my behavior and then took Zaynab to another room to ask her if Daud had seen Junaynah. No he hadn't, she replied.

"Good," I said. "Does Jaubert know you're here?"

"Yes."

"Why did he let you leave?"

"He had no choice. I couldn't go without coming here after Daud told me what had happened. You should have told me, Zaki."

"No, I shouldn't have. Your life is done here. I'm taking you back to Jaubert as soon as Daud returns."

"You don't think Father will come?"

"No. He won't come. The man's to be pitied—slapped by the French after all he did for them. But no one forced him to serve them."

Zaynab sat down on the cushions lining the wall of the room. She looked washed out from nerves. "He did a lot for Egyptians too, Zaki. He made the right choice sending me to Napoleon."

I didn't tell her what she already knew, that he'd had his own selfish reasons for doing that. On the other hand, I couldn't judge the old man too harshly. Shaykh Umar al-Makram had run like a dog with its tail between its legs when the French came, and then returned with the Turks like a shining hero. The people were now chanting his name in the streets as though he'd conquered the French singlehandedly. They'd forgotten that he ran away with the Mamluks while the other shaykhs stayed, shouldering their responsibility to guide the people under occupation, and ended up covered in shit for their efforts. If Napoleon had stayed, if Egypt had become the cornerstone of his commercial empire, Father would have been the shining hero and Shaykh Umar would have been picking apricots in Palestine. Tell me: who was right and who was wrong?

We sat silently for a minute. Zaynab asked what was going to happen to Mother. I told her I didn't know. Whatever happened, I'd take care of her. I asked her if she would be all right in Paris. Zaynab shrugged: "Why shouldn't I be? Amadeus will be there."

We joined Mother and Noha. Mother was brushing Noha's long hair. Our little sister was now a comely young woman of eighteen. Pity she ended up marrying a Mamluk, even if he was a kashif, had money and prestige, and was good-looking.

We waited for two nerve-racking hours. It was getting late. I was sick with worry. "He's not coming," I said. "I'm taking Zaynab back."

"You can't," Noha said. "The longer Daud's away, the more likely it is that he'll come back with Father." When I told her that I didn't trust her Daud, she asked, "What's there not to trust?"

"He's a Mamluk, like the rest of those greedy louts. Rootless slaves ready to sell themselves to the highest bidder."

Noha replied that he wasn't like that—he was a good Mamluk. No such thing, I said, and I asked her whom he was spying for. The English, she replied matter-of-factly. When I asked how she knew, she shrugged as though it were of little importance and said that her husband had told her that a party of Mamluks had made a secret agreement with the English against the Ottomans in case they tried to kick the Mamluks out after the French departed.

"The Mamluks knew there was going to be big trouble once the French were out," she said.

"And now it's the English," I said. "There's no end to it. Get rid of one Frangi and another comes. Like cockroaches. We should throw the whole fucking lot of them out—French, English, Mamluks, Ottomans, the whole fucking lot."

"With what?" Noha asked, surprising me with how aware she had become. "Our prayers? Our beads? Our pyramids? The English have a secret alliance with Alfi Bey, the French with another Mamluk leader, the Ottomans with another. They're getting ready for the fight over Egypt when the French have gone."

"All this talk of fighting. Haven't we had enough?" Zaynab put a hand to her breast. I could tell she was thinking of feeding Junaynah. I went to the window and peered out of the small, diamond-shaped openings of the wooden latticework. The street had emptied and was now silent. With a chill running up my spine, I wondered what fate had befallen the young woman the people of the quarter had been tormenting.

"It's time Zaynab got back," I repeated. "In a few hours it will be dark."

Another hour passed. I signaled to Zaynab that we could wait no longer. She nodded and looked at Mother, who was resting against her on the floor cushions. She was about to say something when the courtyard gate squeaked open. A chorus of loud voices made us jump nervously.

"Daud!" exclaimed Noha.

I looked out the latticed window. Several men in black robes were coming up to the house; I had never seen them before. They banged hard on the door. We froze in our places. Zaynab's face had gone white. Mother's old servant woman entered, looking frightened. "Men from the court," she whispered. I heard Zaynab's breath catch in her throat.

"Stay where you are," I told her, and I went out to meet them.

There were six of them: grim-faced, bearded men. I stepped outside and, closing the door behind me, asked them what they wanted. One of them stepped forward and handed me a document. It bore the seal of the religious court. I read it. It was a court order for the presence of Zaynab, daughter of Shaykh Khalil al-Bakri, to defend herself against charges of immoral conduct. The document also bore the Ottoman seal and the signature of the chief military judge in Egypt. The hairs stood up on my arms; a wave of burning nausea rose from the depths of my stomach.

"What fool has made these baseless charges against my sister?"

"That will be made clear in court," the leader of the six answered peremptorily.

"Where are your witnesses? You can't arrest her without testimony from four witnesses."

"She's not under arrest. She's only requested to appear in court to defend herself."

"That she will! Thank you. I'll inform her tomorrow."

"You don't understand. She is to come now."

"That's impossible. She's already left."

The men stared at me with cold eyes, neither speaking nor budging, their black cloaks and tunics, their cruel visage casting the specter of death around them as a cloud about to burst.

"She went to her father's house in Azbakiyyah," I added.

"We know otherwise. Our orders are to bring her with us. Now."

"I will bring her tomorrow."

"Our orders are to bring her now." The man's rising voice rang with impatient authority.

"You have no right to demand that. I'll bring her tomorrow."

"Right? What is that? Something you learned from the French? Those days are over! The French no longer have authority. The sultan's military judge now has authority. Bring us Zaynab, daughter of Shaykh Khalil al-Bakri!"

"But she's sick. She can't come. Tomorrow. Tell the judge we'll be there tomorrow morning."

The men exchanged glances. They drew themselves up as if to force their way in. I took a step back and braced myself squarely before the entrance with my back against the door and my arms folded in front of me. "You're not dishonoring this house!" We stood facing each other a long second, each waiting for the other to make a move. Then I heard the door open behind me and a woman's voice saying she would go with them. I turned. The woman was completely draped in a black robe and veil. "What are you doing?" I demanded.

"It's all right. There's no proof against me." Her voice was strained and unrecognizable, from fear, I imagined.

"Zaynab! No!" I blocked the door so she couldn't pass. Two of the men pulled me aside and held me. "Zaynab! Don't go!" I cried out, trying to free my arms.

"It's no use resisting. I'll be back." She stepped outside and the men surrounded her.

"Zaynab! No!" I flung myself at them. They pushed me away so forcefully that I stumbled backward to the ground. Then Mother appeared unveiled at the door, screaming for Zaynab not to go. She ran out to pull her away from the men. "Go back, woman!" one of the men ordered, pushing her away. I got to my feet. Mother was standing at the gate, looking down the street and screaming Zaynab's name as the men carried her off. I stood next to her, watching. When they were out of sight, we returned to the house. Mother called up the stairs that they were gone. Zaynab came down from where she had been hiding.

"Noha's idea," she explained, trembling.

20

It certainly looked like Noha's Mamluk didnt waste any time betraying her and her family for his pieces of gold. I told Zaynab I would deal with the slave son of a whore once she was out of the country. Zaynab asked what would happen to Noha when they discovered the deception.

"She'll be fine. Either they'll be too embarrassed to do anything, bringing in the wife of their chief spy, or Noha can say she thought she was the daughter they wanted. I hope she divorces her Mamluk before I cut his throat."

Zaynab slipped her long, black robe over her shoulders and adjusted the veil around her head. "What would they have done to me?" Her eyes stared out at me from behind the leather-bordered eyeholes of her black mask. I told her I didn't know. "I keep thinking of what they did to Hawa," she said, shuddering.

"It wasn't a court executioner who cut off her head; it was her Mamluk husband. Let's go."

Promising to return one day, Zaynab lifted her veil to kiss Mother, who held her tightly and called up to God to protect her daughter from the Franks of Frankistan. She would have been wiser to ask God to protect her from her own people. We waited in the courtyard while the servant woman made sure the street was clear. When she gave us the signal, we entered the street and headed for Azbakiyyah. We had gone a short way when we heard a woman's muffled cry coming from an alley just ahead of us. We stopped. Noha came running out, unveiled. The top of her torn robe was hanging down from her shoulders. "Run!" she screamed. That same instant, the six men who had taken her away charged out of the alley, caught up with her and threw her against a wall, and rushed us. We didn't have a chance. I was pounded to the ground; Zaynab was seized and her veil pulled off. A seventh man appeared from near the alley. He was covered in a woman's black face mask and hooded robe. From where I lay sprawled on my back, I could see the heels of his boots beneath the hem of the robe. Zaynab was pulled before him and her head forced up. The masked figure nodded.

I sprang up from my knees. Before I could reach him to tear the veil from his face, one of the men struck me on the chest with a club; another kicked me in the groin. As I hit the ground, I saw a club come swinging down on me and instinctively raised my arm over my head. Zaynab's scream ringing in my ears was the last thing I heard before a paralyzing pain shot through my neck and a burst of blinding light exploded at the center of my brain. The light gave way to a plummeting vortex of dark silence that devoured both scream and pain, and then my consciousness.

When I came to, my eyes opened to the worried face of Noha, who was kneeling by my side. Above her stood Mother and her servant, clutching each other and thanking God I was still alive. They helped me to my feet and back to the house, where I soaked my head in cold water. As soon as I felt able to walk on my own, I told Mother and Noha to wait there for me and headed for the Ottoman military court, which had already been reestablished in accordance with the evacuation agreement. It was in the Palace of Justice, about a mile away in the southeast quarter of the city, below the Citadel. With every step, my head, groin, and ribs throbbed with pain. But the worst affliction of all was the thought of Zaynab's public humiliation.

The military court had already assembled. The two guards grudgingly let me enter after I convinced them I was the brother of the accused girl and gave them each a coin. The small courtroom was filled with about thirty men. Half of them were standing at the rear, the other half at the front next to the dais upon which the broad-turbaned judge sat cross-legged. Disheveled and unveiled, Zaynab stood before him, several paces from the foot of the dais. Two guards stood behind her. The accusers and witnesses against her, a motley lot of sad-looking men of various ages who had obviously been rounded up off a not-too-respectable street, faced her at the side of the dais. The seedy collection of louts wore soiled robes, their ragged turbans having been so awkwardly wound around their scruffy heads that the shredded ends dangled loosely out from the folds. The turbans, obviously someone's attempt to make the witnesses look like upstanding members of the community, as legal witnesses should be, only succeeded in adding a comical touch to the travesty. One barefoot bumpkin, scraggly and unwashed, was idly picking his nose while staring vapidly at Zaynab with a dumb grin on his toothless face. He appeared to be so doped with hashish that he didn't know where he was or what was happening.

I forced my way to the front and stood beside Zaynab, who looked terrified. Seeing me, she smiled. I squeezed her hand. The guard tried to move me away, but I resisted. "She's my sister!" I cried out to the judge. "I have the right to defend her!"

Right! The meaningless word flew out of my mouth like a wild bird, banged up against the walls of justice, and fell dead in front of the judge, whose hand was raised for me to be silent.

"Oblige me a moment, oh learned scholar of the holy law," I continued brashly, jerking myself free of the guards trying to restrain me. "Are these the best that the conspirators against my family could find, these paragons of purity and prosperity?" I shouted, pointing at the sorry beggars who were supposed to be witnesses. "Are these the defenders of moral rectitude who bear witness against my sister, the daughter of Shaykh Khalil al-Bakri, shaykh of al-Azhar, former Naqib al-Ashraf? I ask you, from what sewer were these fine *sayyids* fished out?"

A chorus of laughter rose up from the men in the rear. In a voice surprisingly more civil than my own, the judge ordered me to be quiet. But then Zaynab, heartened by my temerity, cried out that it was an insult to her dignity to be brought here and confronted with these degrading accusations by such disreputable witnesses. "I've done nothing! I've never seen any of these people in my life. What could they have to testify against me?"

"You haven't heard the charges," the judge replied. "How can you know what they have to testify?"

"It's a sham!" I shouted out. "The witnesses have been put up to this and paid to discredit my father, to discredit the shaykhs and religious

258

scholars! They want to defile the good names of Egypt's most respected families!"

The judge motioned for the guards to take their hands from me. "In respect for your father, Shaykh al-Bakri, I will permit you to remain by your sister. But let me remind you, young man, as a religious student yourself, you should well know the procedures of the court. Charges against your sister have been made and registered with the court. The accusers and witnesses are here to testify, and the accused has presented herself to the court to defend herself. The burden of proof rests with the accusers. If they fail to prove their case, they will be fined an amount fitting the harm done, according to our Shari'ah law. Wrongful accusations can be as harmful as the crime itself. The court has no choice but to hear the case brought before it. Is that clear?"

I remained silent. Zaynab followed my lead. The sense of fairness struck by the judge's firm but calm statement, delivered in eloquent classical Arabic, evoked a rising murmur of approval from the audience of men behind me. One of the spectators enthusiastically declared, "He's right—the judge is right! All must be heard in turn!" A ripple of laughter followed. Someone else shouted, "Now that Ahmad the water carrier has pronounced the honorable judge to be right, the court can proceed." More laughter. Even some of the brain-dead, doped-up witnesses laughed. I was encouraged. The atmosphere seemed not to be all that hostile. Perhaps justice might play a larger part here than the plotters had planned.

The judge's mild demeanor made me think that the man realized he had been put in a false position. As an Ottoman military appointee he would have Istanbul's imperial interests foremost in mind, but he was at the same time an educated man, a religious scholar imbued with the sense and ideal of Islamic justice. He could have studied religious law with my father. In any case, he certainly knew of and respected him, and therefore couldn't have sympathized with those who were out to humiliate and discredit him or his daughter—unless he had been bribed to or ordered to by the grand vizier or the new Ottoman pasha of Egypt. My hopes were tempered by all the possibilities of bribery and intrigue.

The judge reread the charge: "Zaynab, daughter of Shaykh Khalil al-Bakri, stands accused of having associated with the French in a morally corrupt and dishonorable fashion. Will the witnesses please step forward and give testimony." Four men then stepped forth and identified Zaynab, giving almost identical statements. Speaking haltingly and mechanically, as though they'd poorly memorized the words, each testified in turn that he had seen Zaynab at various times wearing French clothes and dallying with French soldiers in a manner morally repugnant for a Muslim girl from a venerated family. Several men in the audience grumbled in agreement at the end of each statement. The four testimonies given, the judge then asked Zaynab what she had to say in her defense.

"I repent of anything I did that appeared immoral." Her voice quavered. Surprised by it, considering how confident she'd sounded before the witnesses testified, I turned to look more closely at her and saw fear in her eyes as she stole quick glances at her surroundings. Surveying the room myself, I could understand what was frightening her to the point of trembling: the intimidating presence of the judge, and the Muslim court filled with men of her own religion and culture, but unfamiliar men, less educated men moved by emotion, prejudice, and fear. I could feel her suffering, that sense of female shame her culture and parents had driven deeply into her since early childhood, particularly now that she was so far from the French who had taught, protected and befriended her, and with whom she had come to feel comfortable. I could see how stripped she felt, how naked, vulnerable and defenseless. The strength, dignity and confidence that had blossomed in her during the three years the French had been in Egypt seemed to have been stripped away from her in an instant. She was visibly trembling. I could feel in myself the fear and terror she had to be suffering in that claustrophobic courtroom.

The judge asked, "What did you do that was immoral?"

"I dressed in the French way."

"And?"

"I spoke to Frenchmen."

"And?"

"And that's all."

"How far did your social intercourse go with these Franks?"

"Speaking. Dressing. That's all."

"And?"

"Nothing more."

"The witnesses against you said you were dallying. Flirting. Displaying your ornaments."

"If that's what their eyes told them they saw, I repent of it. But I did not."

I interrupted. "Your Honor. I was with my sister all the time. She spoke with French scholars—that's true. I too spoke with them. We spoke with them together. The shaykhs of al-Azhar spoke with them. Many served on Bonaparte's various diwans, if you remember. Some of the highest of them received honors and titles from him. But Zaynab did nothing to display her ornaments. There was no flirting. She did nothing immoral. I was with my sister. I protected her."

One of the witnesses declared, "We saw her!"

"And so you must have seen me as well!"

"Flirting with Frenchmen?" the judge asked in surprise.

"Talking to them!" I shouted above the laughter.

The judge asked Zaynab if she denied the accusations against her. She answered, "I deny the intent of immoral conduct. If the witnesses saw me dressed in the French way and speaking to Frenchmen and they thought it immoral, then I repent of offending them and acting as I did. What more do they want? I did nothing immoral."

"So you don't deny the charges?"

"Not of dressing and speaking, as I said. That is not against religion or immoral."

Several voices in the rear of the courtroom exploded in a torrent of hate: "Shame! Shame!"

"Shoe for every French foot!"

"Slut!"

"Whore of foreigners!"

"Strike the sinner's neck!"

The judge raised a silencing hand. When the outbursts had subsided, he looked sternly down at Zaynab. "I repeat. Do you accept the charges of moral corruption?" Shaken by the vicious hate of the men behind her, she looked up at him in confusion without speaking.

"Your Honor," I interjected again. "I stand accused with my sister. What she did, I did. If she's guilty, then I am guilty with her. But guilty of what? Of speaking with Frenchmen? Of dressing like them on occasion when in their society? Of learning their language? Of learning about them and their machines and skills so that by understanding the strengths of our conquerors, we could better defend ourselves and our religion? If that is a crime, then we stand guilty, but I remind you of what the Prophet said: 'Seek knowledge though it be in China.' Well, China came to us, speaking French."

The court was stunned to silence by the mention of what Muhammad had said. The judge gazed down at me in a kind of stupefied wonder. "But ... but what concern was it of your sister to learn from them? What concern could it be of any girl to learn anything from anyone?"

"I don't understand. Why wouldn't it be her concern? Everyone's concern?"

"I agree, you obviously don't understand. Women have not the capacity. Your sister's vain attempt to learn led her to the evil she is in."

"What evil? Was Ayesha evil? Was the wife of the Prophet and daughter of abu Bakr, my ancestor, evil because of her intelligence? Ayesha boasted about how intelligent she was in making herself so loved by Muhammad. If it's true, as you say, that women have no capacity to learn, then what did Zaynab learn to lead her to evil? Isn't it ignorance that leads to error, and error to evil? Learning deepens faith. In any case, Your Honor, my sister has repented of trying to learn from the foreigners. But I am not repentant. Our intent was to learn for the sake of our own community. The language we spoke and the way we dressed are irrelevant."

"You mean the way you undressed!" someone shouted from the rear.

I turned to face my attacker and was met by worse abuse from him and his two or three companions, who I am certain had been planted there. "Your sister's a whore!" one of them shouted. Then the others: "Bonaparte's whore!" "Strike her neck!" "You are your sister's pimp!" "And her father! Cut his neck too!"

Zaynab put her hands to her ears. Each outburst was a sword cutting into her. Fists clenched, eyes glaring, I shouted back, "Who's paying you? You filth who disgrace your religion and sell yourselves! You pimps and whores stuffed like cabbage in one rotten skin! You take money to testify in court! May your miserable, dried-up, rotten hearts roast in hell!"

"Strike her brother the pimp's neck too! Their heads that have swilled the devil's wine of false knowledge are ripe for the cutting!"

The commotion continued in spite of the judge's threats to clear the courtroom. Above the clamor, I cried out to the judge, "Your Honor! Yes we associated with the French to learn! They conquered us with their tools and the weapons of their industry. They draw power like magic from steam that comes from the pumps that drive their machines. In that lies their strength over us. Next the English will be upon us. They are already! We have to learn, and learn fast, before the Franks take over the lands of Islam and make of our religion a defeated, vicious mockery of ourselves!"

This agitated the crowd in the back all the more. The uproar was deafening. "Traitor! Defeatist! What is there to learn from people of the devil who value hot mists of water, this thing you call 'steam'? May the fire of hell roast you in steam!"

The judge clapped his hands for order. When he had finally brought control, he addressed Zaynab. "Do you have anything else to say in defense of your behavior?"

She remained silent. The outbursts from the men in the rear had paralyzed her with fear.

"Nothing?" the judge repeated. His voice was sympathetic, as though he wanted her to speak up for herself. I nudged her.

At last she replied: she repented of all she had done. What she had done, she had done dutifully, and now repented of it. She had broken the traditions of the community and repented the offense.

The judge reflected on her statement and asked what she meant by saying that she did what she did dutifully: what was dutiful about it? She didn't answer.

"What was dutiful about your behavior?" he prodded.

I answered for her. "She means she dutifully obeyed our father, Shaykh Khalil." This brought a murmur of surprise rippling through the audience.

The judge asked her if what I had said was true. She nodded without speaking. The judged waited patiently a full minute before resuming his questioning: "How is it that obedience to your father leads you now to repent?" Zaynab maintained her silence. The judge persisted. "What did he have you do?" She shook her head.

Again I answered for her, saying that Father introduced her to Napoleon and that began our association with the French—our occasional association. "We visited the institute, as did some of the shaykhs. Jabarti, Mahdi, Attar, many shaykhs visited it. It was a place of learning."

"Your father initiated this ... this association, as you call it?"

"Yes," I replied.

"I'm asking the accused."

"I stand accused with my sister."

"You may stand, but you haven't been accused or charged. I'm asking your sister. Zaynab, speak up, girl! Your father initiated your contact with the French that led to … to your speaking their language and behaving in their ways?" The judge waited for her reply. "Will you not speak for yourself?"

"How can she?" I replied. "She's charged with immoral conduct, and you're asking her to implicate our father."

"I'm asking her to explain herself," the judge replied.

"She's bound by her sense of honor and tradition not to."

"Let the father speak for her!" one of the witnesses shouted.

"And for himself!" another added. "Let's see if he's truly a shaykh and a man of God, or a hypocrite!"

"Let him testify so we know if he's the one who made his daughter a whore to the French!"

The judge waved them into silence and looked at Zaynab. "Do you want your father to testify for you?"

She replied no, she didn't: "I'm the one charged, not my father."

The judge said that while her father was not charged, he could testify on her behalf. The judge sounded sympathetic. He seemed to want to help Zaynab. He asked again if she wanted her father to testify. She continued looking down at the floor without replying. From the back came a cry: "The whore's afraid! She's afraid her father will testify against her!"

"A whore has no father!"

The judge aimed an angry finger at the men in the rear, warning them that one more outburst and they would be expelled from the court. He then straightened his turban, took a deep breath to calm himself, and again asked Zaynab if she didn't want her father to testify on her behalf. Again she didn't reply. The judge looked up at the ceiling in exasperation. "I'm asking you one last time. Do you want your father as a witness?"

He waited for her to speak. When she didn't, and the same men in the audience began acting up again, he looked at me as if he was not sure what to do next. Eyes focused on Zaynab, he declared in a voice loud enough for everyone in the crowded courtroom to hear, "There is no shame or dishonor, no implication of immorality or wrongdoing, if a man be called upon to bear testimony for the good name of his daughter." Rising from his cushion, he ordered an officer to bring Shaykh Khalil al-Bakri to the court. Then he disappeared into an adjoining room.

Zaynab turned to me in fright. "They're going to bring him!"

"It's all right. The old man has to share in the humiliation."

An hour passed. We were sitting on the floor. Zaynab was fidgeting nervously with the side locks of her long hair. "What's taking so long? I have to feed Junaynah."

The officers who had been sent to bring Shaykh Khalil returned without him. Minutes later, a court messenger called for me to follow him into the judge's private room. I gave Zaynab an encouraging smile and followed the messenger.

"Your father refuses to testify," the judge told me when we were alone. "He claims to be too sick to appear."

"Can he submit a written testimony?"

"No. He has to appear. Orders from the new pasha."

"I swear to you, my sister is innocent."

"Innocence has nothing to do with it! The peace of Egypt has to do with it!" He pulled off his turban, ran his hand through his gray hair, and sighed in distress. "This isn't going right."

He had me sit. Turkish coffee and glasses of water were brought, and after sipping his coffee, the judge spoke again: "The pasha wants an example made of those who were close to the French. Not just the pasha— it goes to Istanbul. To Sultan Selim."

"Can't you just dismiss the case?"

The judge shook his head. "It's not up to me. The shaykhs have tasted some authority under the French. They formed diwans; they made decisions; some of them played a leading part in ruling Egypt with the French. The Ottomans see it as a threat to their authority. The shaykhs have to be shorn of their pretensions. They have to be shown who is in power. Examples have to be made of them. Your father is at the top of the Ottoman list." We remained silently staring in different directions. Our eyes met. "Your father's presence is necessary. But I can't force it. If he is forcibly dragged to court by Ottoman officers, the public sympathy he will gain from it will outweigh the loss of prestige he would suffer testifying for a daughter charged with questionable behavior. It can't appear that he's being forced or persecuted. You are his son—can you not convince him to appear? Once he testifies, I can clear your sister's name."

I explained that Father and I were not on speaking terms. And then, as I was drinking my coffee, I had an idea: "Your Honor, why not simply order Shaykh Khalil to come and take custody of Zaynab? It could look like the charges against her have been dropped, and all he has to do is come and fetch his daughter. Once he's here—"

The judge's gray eyes met mine. "I could then have him testify."

The judge wrote out a court order giving Father custody of Zaynab and sent two officials to deliver it. I rejoined Zaynab, who was sitting huddled in fright on the floor. I told her that the judge was ordering Father to come and take her home.

"What about the charges against me?"

"They've been dropped. All the judge wants is for Father to make an appearance in court."

"When will I get to feed my baby?" She was gnawing on her lips nervously.

"Jaubert's feeding her. You'll go home with Father. I'll tell Jaubert what happened, and when it's dark we'll come get you."

"There's really no danger?"

"No. Everything's settled."

She didn't accept that it was; she looked terrified. Fear had taken control of her. A tiny drop of blood appeared on her lower lip where she had bitten into it. "What if he refuses to testify?" she asked.

"He can't refuse. It would destroy him."

"But what if he does?"

"I don't know. There would be a fine, a public lashing maybe. But it can't happen. The old man's not that ... that self-destructive."

The witnesses who had testified against Zaynab were watching us as they sat with their backs against the judge's dais. Zaynab glanced at them and turned away, closing her eyes with a shudder. "I'd rather take the lashing than have Father come."

It was another hour before the court officials returned. Father was walking proudly between them.

21

A LL EYES WENT TO Shaykh Khalil. Dressed in a white robe overlaid by a richly embroidered caftan with an ermine collar, and with a high, elaborate turban surmounting his regal head and a long, carefully manicured, reddish beard covering the lower half of his face, he stood with exaggerated dignity at the side of the dais—a tall, erect, impressive figure among the ordinary folk filling the court. He kept his chin lifted slightly with his eyes raised above everyone's heads, with the air of a man who has found himself in a place far beneath him but who stoically accepts it by lifting himself beyond it, as though the place didn't exist or perhaps he wasn't there, as though what was happening was of no consequence; he was leagues above it all. He kept his gaze elevated and away from us, not once glancing in our direction. Zaynab grasped my arm in fear.

The judge at last entered and settled himself on his cushions. Everyone stood. The judge thanked Shaykh Khalil for his presence and recited the charge that had been brought against his daughter: "She has been accused of associating with the French and affecting their ways to a degree that goes beyond the limits of moral decency for a Muslim girl. What do you have to say for your daughter, Shaykh Khalil?"

The moment the judge started speaking, Shaykh Khalil's passive expression froze in surprise. His eyes widened and his face went as red as his henna-dyed beard. He stared at the judge, shaking his turbaned head in protest, and drew the court order from inside his caftan. "I was summoned here only to—"

The judge cut him short. Raising his hand, he said, "You were summoned, and you are here. Again, the court thanks you for your presence. Now, what do you have to say concerning your daughter's conduct, Shaykh Khalil?"

Father's lips trembled wordlessly as he unfolded the court order for Zaynab's release and approached the dais. The judge again raised his hand. "First things first. What do you say to the charges against your daughter?"

The old man looked stricken. Perspiration had broken out over his forehead. His mouth opened and closed as though he were gasping for air, like a fish out of water. With his head turning from side to side, as if in search of a way out, he reminded me of an animal caught in a trap. The pressure of Zaynab's hand increased on my arm.

"Your Honor," I called out. "Please list the precise charges again in case Shaykh Khalil didn't fully understand."

The judge obliged: "Flirtation and coquetry."

"Not fornication or adultery," I clarified. "Simply affecting French ways. Is that correct?"

The judge nodded, adding, "And associating with the French in a way unbefitting a Muslim girl—that is, going beyond the established limits of behavior. What do you say on behalf of your daughter, Shaykh Khalil?"

He wiped his forehead with his hand and stared at the judge. A terrible silence filled the courtroom. Everyone waited for the shaykh to speak. Even those who had been planted to provoke the court were stilled to silence in the gripping tension.

"I ..." He broke off.

The judge waited: "Yes?"

There was another long silence. Zaynab couldn't stand it any longer. "Father!" she cried out. "For god's sake, say something for me!"

The old man closed his eyes and turned his head away. The judge broke the ensuing silence. "Shaykh Khalil, you're a religious scholar. You know the legal formality when sufficient evidence is lacking to sustain a charge. The accused must have supporting testimony for moral character. What do you say in your daughter's defense?"

At last the old man spoke. "I ... I know nothing of this girl." He mumbled it so weakly that hardly anyone heard him. His feeble response destroyed the princely stature his demeanor and attire had created. There was a murmur throughout the room as people discussed what father had said. The judge asked him to repeat himself so everyone could hear.

"I know nothing of this girl. I am innocent of her."

A stunned silence seized the room. The angry buzz of flies circling in the hot, stagnant air filled my ears. I couldn't believe what I'd heard. Father had uttered the legalistic formula that affirms a female's guilt by not defending her innocence: *Ana bari'a minha.* I am innocent of her. I have nothing to do with her. She is no concern of mine. Do with her what you want. Ana bari'a minha: three little words that confirm guilt by denying responsibility—the most horrifying words a girl could hear from her father.

"Father! What are you saying?"

The old man refused to look at Zaynab. "I know nothing of the girl," he repeated in a low, mumbling voice, his head turned away from her, gaze fixed over the judge's head.

The judge appeared nonplussed. He leaned forward, squinting. "Shaykh Khalil. Do I understand you to say that you will not testify on behalf of your daughter's good character before this court?"

The old man stood like a column of white stone: mute, rigid, cold, his face drained of the hot blood of embarrassment that had risen to it minutes ago. His silence was unbearable.

"Testify for your daughter!" I screamed at him. He winced as if stung. "Testify! Testify!"

"Yes! Testify for your whore of a daughter!" some paid lout shouted, and at a signal from the judge two guards forcibly removed him.

"One more outburst," the judge warned, "and out you all go!" He looked down at the old man. "Now. Shaykh Khalil. Before I can release your daughter to you, you must testify to her innocence of the charges. I need your assurance of her innocence. I ask you: is she innocent? Yes or no."

Father's former air of superiority had melted away, leaving him a crushed, frightened semblance of a man, squirming like a wild animal trying to escape its cage. The judge leaned farther forward on his cushioned dais.

"Will you then not speak, Shaykh Khalil?"

"I know nothing of this affair."

"Father! What are you saying?" The judge motioned Zaynab to be silent.

"I know nothing of her," the old man repeated. The words came out like wind from a broken reed, a hoarse, hissing whisper.

"What do you mean you know nothing?" cried Zaynab. "What is there to know? What is there you don't know?"

The old man didn't blink an eye. He kept looking straight ahead of him with his head straining upward as though struggling to lift off from his body and escape the world below.

"Look at me!" she screamed. "What are you so ashamed of that you can't look at me?"

The judge gestured her to silence with a sympathetic frown, nodding his head and raising his hand. "Please. I will ask the questions. Shaykh Khalil. Understand me. I need a declaration of testimony assuring the court of your daughter's innocence before she can be released to your custody. A simple word of affirmation. Tell me: is she innocent?"

Like a dead man struggling to speak, the old man opened his mouth but no words came out. He opened it again, and this time we heard the three dreaded words, hushed and dry, crackling in the air like desiccated leaves: "Ana bari'a minha."

"Father!" Zaynab's arms went out toward him. "What are you saying? You are innocent of me? I am as innocent as you. Speak for me, Father!"

The courtroom fell silent. Everyone waited for the shaykh to speak. He said nothing. Then the gallery in the rear burst into abuse: "He rejects his daughter!"

"Strike the whore's head!"

"And her father's! He led her into whoredom!"

"One as corrupt as the other!"

There was no controlling them. The outbursts shook the old man to life. "I am innocent of the girl!" he cried out above the clamor, his face a tortured grimace of muscle and nerves.

"Coward!" I shouted at him. "Coward! Scheming hypocrite!"

"Father! Why do you deny me?"

The crowd exploded in fury:

"The whole family's corrupt!"

"The shaykh has corrupted them all!"

"Himself as much as son and daughter!"

"Strike their heads! The whole family of them!"

The judge ordered the gallery cleared.

While the guards were expelling the spectators in the rear, Zaynab ran up and knelt before the old man. Clutching his robe, she turned her

270

face up to him in appeal. "Whatever I have done, Father, I beg you, don't deny me! In my heart I am innocent. I don't know why I'm here, but if I have offended you, I repent. Take me from here! Please! Father! Take me home!" The old man folded his arms in front of him. His head remained tilted up and away from her.

When the guards had finished clearing the gallery, the judge allowed Zaynab to remain on her knees next to Father, and asked Shaykh Khalil if he persisted in disavowing himself of his daughter's conduct.

"She is no daughter of mine," he replied.

Zaynab flung her arms around his knees. "For the mercy of God, what have I done to deserve this cruelty? I obeyed you in everything. I repent if I have done anything to disappoint you. Tell me what you want me to do, and I will do it." Still hanging on to his robe, she broke down.

"Her repentance belongs to God. I have nothing to do with it."

"Father!"

A huge crowd had gathered around the courthouse and was pressing against the doors and windows, shouting that the shaykh had denied his daughter. Then a chant went up among the crowd that God had granted victory to Islam. "Death to traitors and whores of the French!" they howled, along with other frenzied cries in celebration of religion's triumph over evil. The feverish shouting whipped the people into hysterical fury. Their cries for blood and the shaykh's head put the final cracks in Shaykh Khalil's crumbling composure. His face was contorted by a spasmic quiver of nerve-jerking muscles. "The girl is out of my hands." His voice was thin, tremulous.

The judge rose from his cushions. "I will need a legal consensus from the chief mufti to decide what to do. I can't decide on my own. I haven't the authority."

"No, you don't! But I have!" The stern words, spoken in a thick Turkish accent, boomed like a cannon through the room. We all turned. Filling the entrance stood the newly appointed Ottoman governor, Mehmet Khosru Pasha. Next to him was a Turkish soldier, hardly older than a boy, holding an Ottoman field standard, to which were attached two horsetails designating the pasha's rank in the Turko-Mongol imperial hierarchy, which went back to Ghengis Khan and the great Mongol Empire. Behind the pasha and his standard-bearer stood his Albanian guard in a French-styled uniform. Mehmet Khosru Pasha himself looked strikingly like a French general. These were the sultan's French-trained New Order troops we had heard about. With their diaper-like trousers that hugged the crotch, cutaway field jackets, epaulets, visored caps, and high boots, and their swords sheathed at their sides and hanging from their belts, it was as though the French had returned as Turkish-speaking pashas. We gaped at the un-Islamic attire of our new pasha and his Albanian guard, and had it not been for the seriousness of the situation, I would have burst out laughing. The sultan thought that if you dressed like Napoleon, you fought like Napoleon.

Our new pasha strode imperially to the front of the courtroom and mounted the dais without removing his boots. Motioning for the judge to sit back down, he stood facing Zaynab and Father with his hands on his hips and his legs parted, his long, curled mustache adding to his cruel visage.

"You want a quick judgment?" he asked severely, staring down at Zaynab, who was still on her knees by Father's side. She remained silent with her head bowed in terror. "Good!" he snapped harshly. "You shall have it! What defense do you have for dallying with the French military dressed like one of their women?" She looked up, saw the ferocity in his eyes, and lowered her head. "Come! You wanted a quick judgment. Let's be finished with this!"

"I repent of my conduct, your excellency," she mumbled.

"Speak up, girl! Let's hear you!"

"I repent of my conduct."

"Well you should!" The pasha then looked at Father. "You! Shaykh! What do you say for your daughter?" The old man's lips quivered in terror. "Let's hear it!" the pasha shouted at him, showing no respect for his scholar's turban.

"I am innocent of her," he mumbled inaudibly.

"Louder!" the pasha ordered harshly, in Turkish. Shaykh Khalil repeated the words. "That's clear enough!" The pasha signaled to the captain of his Albanian guard. "Take her!"

"Where are you going to take her?" I demanded.

The pasha turned his fierce glare on me. "Who are you?"

"Her brother."

"Then say good-bye to your sister."

"Why? What do you mean?"

272

Zaynab clutched at Father's robe. He moved away from her. "Father! Don't forsake me!" she cried.

"I have nothing to do with this," he whimpered.

The pasha jumped down from the dais and stared fiercely into the old man's terror-stricken eyes. "Nothing?" He looked down at Zaynab, who was still clutching Father's robe with both hands. "You! Girl! You should have known better."

"I repented!"

"Too late." The pasha motioned for the guards to take her out.

"No!" she cried.

"Where are you taking her?" I demanded.

"She's been judged. Case over."

"You can't," the judge exclaimed. "Your Excellency doesn't have the legal authority!"

"I have the power invested in me by Sultan Selim III."

"The sultan has no concern in this," I said. "This is a case of religious law."

The pasha turned to me with a scowl. "Religious law?" He drew his sword from its sheath and held it high. "This is your religious law! Take the girl to the courtyard!"

Two guards took Zaynab by the arms; she screamed and kept hold of Father's robe. "Father! Don't let them take me!"

I fell to my knees and held her around the waist to keep the Albanians from dragging her off. "Stop them!" I appealed to the old man. "For God's sake, stop them! Have some mercy in your heart! Say she's your responsibility!"

My appeal had no effect. He was trying to leave. Zaynab kept hold of his robe even as the guards were pulling her away.

"He has given his testimony! Now go!" The pasha shoved me back with his boot. "Take the shaykh as well. The father throws the first stone."

The old man's eyes rolled upward in horror. "No!"

"Yes!" The pasha patted him on the shoulder. "As a good Muslim and shaykh of the Holy Law, you will do your duty. You condemn, you throw the first stone."

The judge rose to his feet. "This has nothing to do with the Holy Law. It's against—" His protest fell silent before the pasha's threatening eyes and words:

"Enemies of the sultan and his Islamic empire are enemies of religion and the Holy Law. Be careful you don't fall among the enemies. Now draw up the order of execution."

"Execution?" The judge took a step back as though he had been kicked. "No! I can't do that!"

"I am sure you can—and will!" The pasha circled his saber over the judge's head and brought the flat of the long blade slamming down on the lectern with a terrorizing crack that made everybody jump.

Even after the guards had wrenched Zaynab's hands from Shaykh Khalil's robe, she and I hung on to each other, only to be brutally yanked apart, and Zaynab hauled to her feet. When I lunged forward to hold her, several other guards pulled me back. Kicking and screaming for Father to save her, Zaynab was picked up and carried out by the Albanian soldiers. The old man was pushed along after her. The pasha and the rest of his men followed.

"It's not legal," the judge said feebly, standing alone on the dais. "It's not legal what you're doing." No one paid him any attention.

Outside, a huge crowd had gathered around Zaynab, Father, and the Albanian guards. Some people jeered at Father, pummeling him and grabbing at his robe, calling him "shaykh of drunkards," accusing him of condemning his daughter to save his rotten skin, and spitting on him. They would have done worse had the guards not held them off. A young scamp in rags squeezed through the guards, snatched the shaykh's turban from his head, and ran off into the crowd, trailing the long, white band behind him. Other children grabbed it and ran, sailing it through the air like a kite.

"Look," someone shouted, "the old shaykh lost his turban!"

"And soon the head it was on!"

Zaynab struggled against the guards who were dragging her toward the center of the square. She kept trying to turn and look behind her, pleading with Father to save her life. "I can't die now!" she cried out to him. "Save me, I beg you! I'm innocent! Tell the pasha I'm innocent!"

Pushed roughly along by the Albanians, the old man had his arms up over his bare head, protecting himself against the blows raining on him from the pressing crowd.

Zaynab was forced to stand at the center of the square. The old man— even now, so many years after that day, I find it difficult to call him Father—was pushed a short distance away and forced to face her. He kept turning his head one way or the other so as not to see her, but the pasha's Albanians kept forcing his head in her direction and making sure his eyes were open. People from every side were shouting insults and hurling filth from the street at him, while Zaynab's voice rose above the clamor, begging him to have mercy and tell the pasha she was innocent.

The pasha forced a fist-sized stone into the old man's hand and ordered him to throw it at her. The old man dropped the stone and backed away in a daze. A guard pushed him forward and forced the stone back into his hand, threatening him with his rifle butt if he dropped it. A grimace of confused agony contorted the old man's face. He shook his head and dropped the stone again. The guard glanced at the pasha, who gestured for the stone to be given back to him.

Zaynab ran up and flung herself at the pasha's knees. "I'm innocent, I swear to God! Let me live!"

"I didn't condemn you. He who will throw the first stone did."

The guards dragged her back and kept her in place with their bayonets. She fell to her knees and with her arms crossed over her breast cried for mercy, turning first to Father, then to the pasha, who ordered the old man to get on with it. The miserable old shaykh couldn't raise his arm.

"You know the tradition, Shaykh. You're a man of the Holy Law. You found her guilty. You condemned her. Throw!"

The old man raised his head up to heaven. Closing his eyes, he drew his arm back, let out a howl of anguish, and let the stone fly.

"Father! No!" The stone fell short. "Forgive me!" she screamed. "Tell the judge you forgive me. Tell the pasha! I can't die—not yet! Oh god, please, I beg you!"

The old man turned and staggered back with one arm over his eyes. I broke through the guards, seized the stone, and hurled it at him with all my might. It struck him on the shoulder. He shrieked and flung his arms in the air as though he'd been shot. When he tried to flee, the mob blocked his way and roughly pushed him back. In the confusion, I grabbed Zaynab and started running with her. I knew we didn't have a chance, but it was better to be shot trying to escape than to be slaughtered like docile sheep.

The Albanians were on us before we'd gone three steps. Zaynab was torn from me; I was beaten to the ground with their rifle butts. The Albanians would have crushed my skull had the pasha not ordered them to stop.

I was held by two guards about ten paces from where Zaynab was being held. Shaykh Khalil al-Bakri was dragged back and held directly in front of her at about the same distance. At a signal from the pasha, Zaynab was forced down on her knees. A wooden block was placed at her side. One of the pasha's Albanians stood by with an ax cradled in his brawny arms.

"Zaynab!"

Her eyes found mine. Staring at me, she shook her head slightly from side to side. "See after her!" she called to me.

I didn't believe it was going to happen. The pasha was staging it to terrorize us. He wouldn't have a young girl executed on such flimsy grounds. Zaynab closed her eyes and tilted her head down, as though accepting the inevitable.

The pasha was growing impatient. He ordered a guard to go see what was taking the judge so long in issuing the fatwa. A desperate hope leapt into my heart: if the judge refused to sign the fatwa legalizing her execution, the pasha would not be able to proceed. Her life would be spared! Legal formalities hadn't prevented Ottoman pashas from spilling blood in the past, but perhaps French legal influence had come with the sultan's New Order uniforms and westernized reforms.

Minutes later, the guard returned with two documents. "At last!" The pasha scribbled his signature across each of them and kneeled to pin one to the front of Zaynab's robe. She raised her head to him. Her eyes opened. Her lips parted as if to speak but then closed. The pasha patted her on the head as though she were a child. "Don't worry, girl. You won't feel a thing."

She gazed at him a moment, then at her father, whose eyes were turned up to heaven, lips busy in prayer. She looked around at the mob that was excitedly awaiting her execution, then up at the sky, and finally at me. "Zaki!" Her voice was hardly more than a whisper. "See after Junay—"

Before she could finish, one of the Albanian guards, acting on a signal from the pasha, pushed her down with his boot against the small of her back. With his foot planted there, he took hold of the rope binding her hands behind her and pulled it up to keep her from moving while another guard placed the block under her neck with her chin over the edge. The second guard then took the end of her long hair and pulled it forward over the back of her head to expose the bare white nape of her neck. She was wearing the pharaonic gold and bead earrings Marcel had found when digging around the burial tombs at Saqqarah. The guard tore them from her ears and threw them in the dust, and then yanked her hair forward to keep her neck stretched taut over the block. I cried out her name. Someone in the crowd behind me shouted, "Talk to her while you can! In a second she'll be roasting in the fires of hell!"

The executioner planted his feet firmly on the ground by the block. Then he positioned his huge hands along the haft of the ax and slowly raised it. He held it high a long moment, so long I thought he hadn't the heart to do it. When he brought it down slowly, with the sharp edge barely grazing her neck, hope welled up in my heart that the pasha would bring the mock execution to an end. But the executioner was only taking aim, measuring his length of stroke in order to make a clean job of it. The next instant he brought the ax swiftly up again and in one continuous, circular motion swung it viciously around his bulging shoulders. I shut my eyes and screamed her name to block the thud of the ax from my ears. But I heard it. The crowd was quiet for a few seconds. The silence gave way to a hushed murmur at the awe of death, and finally to loud, jubilant cries of emotional release: "God is great! God grants victory! Islam is saved!"

Let loose by the guards, I doubled over on my knees with my hands over my face and my forehead pressed to the dust, as though in prayer. I remained in that position and wanted to die in it. I didn't want to open my eyes to see what I would see if I opened them. But then I felt a tap on my shoulder and heard the pasha say that the body was mine to bury as I wished.

"All is according to God's will," he said. "From Him everything comes; to Him everything returns."

I lifted my head. A burial shroud had been draped over the body. I looked away. A gang of ruffians was harassing the old man, who was stumbling blindly about the courtyard, trying to escape. They were pushing him from side to side, spinning him around, pulling at his clothes, taunting him as the murderer of his daughter. They pushed him toward his daughter's corpse. He resisted, thrashing his arms and stumbling, reeling as he struggled to get away from them and out of the courtyard, holding his arm over his eyes and crying for them to leave him alone. The guards made them scatter, but they regrouped to carry on tormenting him, pulling and tearing at his clothes. They dragged him from the courtyard onto the dusty street, where they ripped away his shaykh's cloak, tore it to pieces, and stomped it into the ground. They threw dirt on him and groped at his robe, trying to strip him naked, but other less violent people intervened to keep the mob from going too far. So they left off tearing away his remaining clothes and satisfied themselves by covering him with filth from the street, dancing around him, and taunting him with shouts of what a fine religious shaykh he was, condemning his daughter to save himself, as the old man staggered backward with one arm still across his eyes and with the other flailing away in self-defense from the mob, like a drunk about to fall.

I remained with my head bowed, kneeling in the dust, a long time. The lowering sun cast long shadows across the emptying square. When it was dusk, I crawled to the dark form that was partly covered in the shroud. Her hands were already cold. I untied them and set about slipping her body into the sack-like shroud, beginning at the feet. Then I picked up her head. Her eyes were closed. As though afraid to bruise her cheeks with my rough hands, I gently wrapped her head in its long, soft hair and placed it in the shroud.

After tying the mouth of the shroud with the shaykh's turban that I found trampled into the ground, I hoisted her body over my shoulder and started for Qarrafat al-Sughra, where the old burial ground called the Abode of the Dead lay at the foot of Muqattam Plateau, beneath the Citadel. It was the cemetery of kings and emirs, of great imams and scholars who had been laid to rest over the centuries in domed mausoleums and mosques. It was where the Bakri family, since ancient times, had been traditionally interred in vaulted crypts. It wasn't far. As I carried Zaynab there, blood drained from her body and seeped through the shroud, running onto me.

In the dark shadows of the clan's crypts, I laid her down and stripped off my bloody clothes. Above me, the Citadel shone in the brilliance of an almost-full moon. I found the crypt that the shaykh had thoughtfully provided for himself and his family long before Napoleon's arrival, and forced open the heavy door, stone groaning on stone. The forbidding blackness within gaped back at me. I entered. Groping blindly in the eerie chill of the musty vault, I found the sarcophagus that the old man had reserved for himself thinking he would be the first laid to rest in the crypt. I struggled with the heavy stone slab that covered it, and finally I was able to slide it around so that it was perpendicular lengthwise to the basin of the sarcophagus.

Returning to where Zaynab lay in her blood-soaked shroud, I sat with my back against a tombstone, and gazing up at the moon, I spoke to her. I promised her I would finish the work we had started together. I promised her I would take care of Junaynah as I would my own daughter. I would live every day for the child. I would do everything in my power to have her become all that her mother had wanted to be. I would love Junaynah as I loved Zaynab, and I would gently guide her. I vowed myself to mother and child.

I know the dead don't hear, but I had to speak to her. Speaking to her gave me the strength to go on and do what I had to do. So I went on speaking to the moon and Zaynab, feeling her alive in me and me alive in her, our spirits united, and I vowed with all my heart and soul to do what she would have wanted me to do and would have done herself. Speaking my thoughts aloud to her gave her life, and gave me the will to go on.

I have never stopped speaking to Zaynab, aloud sometimes. Even now, twenty years after that bloody day, I often catch myself talking aloud to her, particularly when people stop and turn to see if I'm addressing them and then look at me as if I'm just an old nut babbling to himself, which I am.

Having told Zaynab all that needed saying, I rose to my feet and stood over her for several minutes. Then, with a shudder of crushing sorrow, I carried her into the black crypt and eased her into the sarcophagus. I shoved the cover back over the basin, pulled shut the crypt's heavy stone door, and departed.

Before rounding the escarpment of Muqattam, I stopped for a last look. The Abode of the Dead lay in peaceful silence under the full moon.

22

THE STREETS WERE DESERTED, more for fear of the arriving Ottoman military than for fear of the departing French. Even before the Ottomans fully regained the city and established order, the pasha's government had managed to outdo the French in crushing the people by taxation, sequestration, and outright confiscation—facets of rule the Ottomans practiced far more expertly than maintaining order.

Approaching Shaykh Khalil's estate, I caught a whiff of smoke. It hung in the empty fields bordering the canal in Azbakiyyah and grew heavier as I continued on. What had appeared to be flickering lanterns in the distance were glowing embers from the gutted innards of the partially burnt house. I prayed to God that the old man had been incinerated in it.

The wails and moans of a woman were coming from inside the walls. Stepping over a fuming ceiling beam, I entered the grand hall and made my way toward the noise. A young girl was in an adjoining room, curled up on a heap of cushions. Seeing me in the orange glow of the smoldering planks, she raised a hand in defense with a moan for mercy and tried to cover her nakedness with a cushion. I found a rug among what overturned and broken furniture remained and spread it over her, convinced by her youth and attractiveness that she was the old man's new wife. When I told her who I was, the terror left her eyes and she began telling me between wails and sobs how a mob of young street people had smashed up and looted the house, and then torched it and raped her over and over, even as fire was blazing all around them. She said she had been brutalized by the whole mob and fallen unconscious before they had finished with her. When she came to, she was alone in the dying fire.

I asked her what had happened to Shaykh Khalil. She didn't know: "The pasha's men took him to court. The mob came later." She turned her face away and moaned. "I was warned not to marry Shaykh Khalil. I didn't want to; my father forced me. Shaykh Khalil will divorce me, and who will marry me now?" She buried her face in a pillow and sobbed. "It would have been better if they killed me!"

I left her crying and went to the courtyard, where I stripped off my clothes, which were soaked in Zaynab's blood. Having immersed and cleansed myself in the circular pool, I gathered several smoldering planks from inside, fanned them into flames, and burned the clothes. Watching the smoke rise, I whispered Zaynab's name. The ache in my soul seemed more than I could bear.

My room was in a part of the house spared by the fire. I donned clean clothes, packed some others the looters had overlooked, and then removed a purse full of gold coins I'd secreted under a tile in the floor. My silver-handled Bedouin dagger, in its curved sheath of semiprecious stones, was in its place in a box on top of a high cabinet. I fixed it on the belt under my caftan, tied a sash around my waist, and departed. The wails of the old man's bride followed me into the terror of the dark night, hurrying me to my intended deed of vengeance.

Mother and Noha knew of Zaynab's death, but when I told them where I had interred her, Mother seemed not to comprehend. The losses she had suffered one after another having numbed her mind, she kept looking down at the floor, shaking her head and mumbling incoherently while fingering her prayer beads.

I asked Noha where her husband was. She didn't know. I told her our house had been torched. She already knew. "Do you know where Father went?" I asked.

"We heard he's staying with Shaykh Sadat."

"I'd like to kill the old man. And your Mamluk along with him."

"That would be too kind for Father. Let him live and suffer for what he's done. He's already dead, from what I hear."

"And your husband?"

"Leave him to me."

I looked at her without speaking. She turned from my gaze and glanced at Mother, who was sitting on her cushions, staring vacantly at the floor and mumbling. At forty, she looked like an old, broken woman.

"Let me be the one to slit his throat."

"You won't get away with it," Noha said. "He has powerful friends—spies, Mamluks, Ottomans. The pasha."

The pasha wouldn't regret the loss of a Mamluk, I told her.

"No. Leave him to me," she insisted. "I want to be sure he's the one who betrayed Zaynab."

"Who else could have?"

"I don't know. One of the servants might have been bribed. But if Daud did it, I will find out. And I will avenge my sister. I swear to God!"

The servant woman brought us tea. We didn't speak further about the matter of vengeance.

Daud Kashif arrived at last. He gave a splendid performance, acting as if he had no idea what had happened. When he asked what was wrong with Mother and where Zaynab was, I wanted to plunge my bedouin dagger deep into his heart and turn it slowly.

"You don't know?" I replied, straining to control myself.

"Know what?"

"Didn't you leave here for Shaykh Khalil's house?"

"I never got there," he replied. "Some French soldiers stopped me on the way. They wanted my horse. When I resisted, they threatened me. I drew a sword to defend myself and wounded one of them in the arm. They were about to kill me, but luckily an officer came by and stopped them. I was arrested and locked up in Azbakiyyah until an investigation was made. I was released a little while ago. But not my horse."

Noha and I were looking at him with hard, cold eyes. "Then you don't know?" she asked.

His eyes darted from mine to Noha's and back to mine again, searching, expectant. "What is it?"

I told him: "Zaynab was taken and executed just after you left."

His expression of pained amazement was almost convincing. I didn't tell him he was the only person who could have told anyone where Zaynab was. Why bother? He had already been judged. His execution was close at hand.

He sat down heavily on a cushioned divan with his head in his hands. "How could they have known?"

"That's what we were thinking," said Noha.

He looked up, saw us staring down at him. His eyes widened. "No. You're wrong. I'm innocent. It wasn't me. I swear." Noha said there was no way of knowing who it was. "It's natural you suspect me, but I swear it wasn't me. I didn't tell anyone. I'll swear to it on the Quran." Daud put his hand over his heart. "I had no reason."

"It's over. Nothing can undo it. Life goes on." I pressed the inside of my arm reassuringly against the handle of the dagger under my caftan and, excusing myself, rose to go to bed. It had been a long, hard day, and I was still in shock over Zaynab's cruel and unjust death. I bade Noha and her husband goodnight and climbed the stairs to my bedroom on the second floor, thinking with every step that the pain in my heart would ease once my dagger had done its work on Mamluk Daud.

I lay awake all night, waiting to be done with it. When the first gray light of early dawn appeared between the parted shutters outside my window, I rose from bed and pulled the dagger from under my pillow. The steel blade slipped easily from its sheath. Holding it at my side, I stole barefoot down the hall and quietly opened the door to the next room, where Noha and her Mamluk lay in the protection of a suspended mosquito net.

I stood over them. In the shadowy half-light, I imagined them looking up at me from behind the gauzed blur of netting. Their breathing, one's followed by the other's, assured me they were asleep. I moved to his side of the bed and pressed the dagger against the netting until the tip was just over his heart. My arm stiffened for the plunge. A donkey brayed in the street; I hesitated. A short gasp came from beneath the netting. Noha's eyes were open. Sitting half up, she put her hand between my blade and her husband's breast. I pressed down. The point just penetrated the skin on the back of her hand, bringing a tiny dot of blood to the surface. I increased the pressure; she didn't move her hand. We remained frozen in that position a long moment: I pressing the tip of the dagger to the back of her hand, she appealing to me with her eyes and a shake of her head for me to hold off. It was a full minute, but finally I backed off, nodded good-bye to Noha, and returned the dagger to its sheath.

I went to mother's room and kissed her softly on the cheek as she lay mumbling in her sleep. A minute later I was on my way.

I had to go by foot. It was just after dawn, but the streets were filling. Azbakiyyah was in chaos. The French were in their final stages of evacuation, and as expected, looting had become a general mode of employment. Draft animals were especially coveted, as the French needed to haul their artillery and their loot. At military headquarters, infantry and cavalry were forming in columns in front of their drummer boys, ready to march out in a feeble pretense of glorious triumph to the full blare of bugles and trumpets. I learned much from the French, good and bad, but one lesson the previous three years had driven home to me was that of all things in God's universe, governments and militaries were the greatest liars and hypocrites. It was a lesson prepared by the Ottomans but underscored and universalized by the French. As individuals, there was much good in them, but as officers in uniform or agents of government, I would as soon believe or trust them as I would walk barefoot over nests of scorpions and cobras.

The savants had already gone. I searched the empty buildings of the institute, asking everyone I met where Amadeus Jaubert was, but received only hurried shrugs. The French had been so eager to come; now they couldn't get out fast enough.

In front of the commander in chief's residence, an officer was hitching an emaciated nag to a wheeled artillery piece. I asked him if the savants were leaving from Giza or Rawda. "Rawda," he growled, eyeing my Egyptian robe and caftan with hostility, or perhaps looking to see if I had anything worth taking. "The asses are gathered at Rawda."

When he'd finished harnessing the horse, he whacked its scrawny rump. It neighed and bucked against the weight of the load, too feeble to get it rolling. It was then that I recognized the animal. Examining it more closely, I asked where he'd found the sorry-looking thing. He narrowed his eyes and asked me why I wanted to know.

"It's not important, but I'd like to know." I unhitched the dagger and sheath from the belt under my caftan. The soldier went for his sword, but left off when he saw I was presenting the weapon to him as a gift. "It was given to me by Napoleon himself," I lied. "Just tell me when and where you got the horse."

"Napoleon," he said appreciatively, examining the bejeweled dagger and sheath, weighing the heavy, solid silver of the handle in his hand and rubbing his finger over the rubies and sapphires. "Yesterday. A couple soldiers forced it from this Turk," he said, packing the dagger in a saddlebag with the rest of his booty. "There was a scuffle. The Turk struck one of the soldiers and was arrested. He was later released. That's all."

"You say a Turk. Would he have been a Mamluk?"

"What's the difference? He said he was a Mamluk officer, but it's the same thing, no? Mamluks are Turks."

Mamluks are Turks! Three years here and they knew less about Egypt than we knew about France, without our ever having been there or even being sure such a place existed! "What time was it when you took the guy's horse?"

"About this time yesterday. Late afternoon."

"When was the man released?"

"Last night. We released him after an investigation had been made into the incident and a report was written. But his horse was sequestered by military order. Sorry. If he wants it, he can retrieve it in Alexandria."

"This animal will never make it to Alexandria. Look at it. It's half dead already."

He shrugged. "So we lose a horse and shove the cart into the Nile. What's that to what we've lost already in your rat hole of a country?"

"So who invited you?"

I ran for the river. In the quarters of the city outside Azbakiyyah, the incoming Ottomans and Mamluks were busy looting the shops of whatever the outgoing French had been unable to carry. Egyptian merchants were already regretting the departure of the French, and they hadn't left yet. The new taxes and levies announced by our pasha had softened people's feelings toward their old rulers from over the sea. How fickle people were. When the French announced their departure, the people had cheered, greeting each other with "Happy day to you, blessed year!" and had uncomplainingly paid the new tax the French had levied to cover the cost of their evacuation. Now they were longing for yesterday's oppressor. My poor, beloved Egypt, Umm al-Dunya, Mother of the World—Mother that every rich fucking Egyptian, Ottoman, Mamluk, and foreigner since Alexander the Great had raped and plundered.

The riverboats were anchored off the Island of Rawda, which rose up like a green thumb in the middle of the Nile. The savants, European merchants, and all others of European nationality were being transported to Rawda on sturdy boats that had been specially provided for them. The non-European passengers (or "orientals," as the French had labeled them) were being ferried across in makeshift rafts, rowboats, and dilapidated falukas—anything that floated or came close to floating. A large crowd of departing Egyptians, Syrians, and Greeks had gathered at the bank and were scrambling hysterically to board the flimsy craft—pushing and shoving, and some even falling over the riverbank into the water, their bundles and rolled-up rugs and crates of belongings following them in. In their roiling frenzy not to be left, the wharf beneath them threatened to break up and sink. The French soldiers had long ago given up trying to maintain order.

There seemed to be many thousands of them, but in fact fewer than two thousand of our locals had elected to evacuate, most of them Greeks, Syrians, Copts, Jews, or Mamluks. Anyone who had served as a translator was there, as was anyone who had transacted business with the French in a big and open way. They knew their names were on the pasha's list. The Egyptian evacuees were mostly young women. Shaykh Hasan al-Attar, who had been pretty close to the savants at the institute, had already hightailed it for Syria, having packed up his books, jumped on his donkey, and left like the wind the very moment he knew the French were leaving.

I pushed my way onto a raft, which threatened to capsize because people had loaded their pitiful bundles all on one side of it and were standing beside them lest someone make off with one. The raft miraculously made it across to Rawda. The moment I stepped onto the island, Jaubert was there to embrace me. Pale and haggard, his grief-stricken eyes red and drawn cavernously into his skull, he looked ready for the grave. He had heard the news and looked like he might not survive it. He had loved Zaynab so much that her death was sucking the life out of him.

I asked him how he knew about Zaynab. Sitt Nafisa had told Menou's wife, Zubaydah, who had told him. I asked after Junaynah, and through tears he said she was being nursed by a Coptic woman and was fine. I told him I had buried Zaynab with the kings, sultans, emirs, and scholars at Qarrafat al-Sughra.

"Only in death did she enter the world of men," he replied, and when he tried to smile, his face contorted further in anguish, and then, no longer able to hold it back, he broke down sobbing like a child. I held him to give him strength, but his tears brought out my own. When he gained control of himself, he noticed the bag slung over my shoulder. "I'm going with you," I explained.

He wiped his eyes and smiled. "Thank God! I was afraid you had come to take ... Come, come!"

I followed him up the gangplank onto a riverboat where a young woman was sitting on a rocking chair near the prow, nursing Junaynah. When the baby had finished suckling, the woman covered her breast and handed the child to Jaubert, who took her, kissed her cheek, and held her out to me in the crook of his one arm. "Hold her. I know you're not going to France for the ride."

I hesitated, for I realized how precious the child was to him and I had never held a baby before. When he extended his arm farther to me, I took the child and cradled her in my arm, cooing and rocking her as I had seen Jaubert do. It was amazing how easily I got over my embarrassment of this unmanly behavior. Junaynah regarded me in curiosity for a minute or two before her lids fluttered closed in sleep or boredom. The little thing couldn't wait to get on with life and emulate her mother. Jaubert patted me on the shoulder. "You'll have to find a wife in France."

"I have too much to do to have time for a wife."

"A good wife saves you time. When Zu Zu and I were translating ..." He couldn't finish. Saying her name was too painful. He broke down. Barely able to keep my own grief from bursting forth in tears, I embraced him, hoping to comfort him and myself, and on we went, crying in each other's arms.

A whistle blew. Sailors started hauling up lines, lifting anchor, hoisting sails. Soon the boat was on its way north down the great river, heading for Alexandria. The gray-brown buildings and minarets of Cairo gave way to palm groves, water buffalo, bronze-skinned peasants working up to their knees in the Nile mud. With Junaynah firmly in my arms, I leaned against the deck railing and watched my city slip away from me. The pink-and-dun mountain plateau of Muqattam, with the Citadel carved into its granite chest, loomed bright in the eastern sun. Jaubert stood beside me, his grieved visage raised to the morning breeze over the quiet river.

"I wonder how history will judge us," he mused in sad weariness, watching the Citadel grow smaller behind us. "I wonder if it will be said we did any good here." When I didn't reply, he sighed and looked down at Junaynah. "Whatever the historians say, out of all the death and cruelty, out of all the lust and greed of glory and good intentions gone wrong, something good came of it. Even if accidental." He touched the sleeping baby's cheek. "A little bit of her mother yet lives in the spirit and flesh. A living symbol of France in Egypt." Then, shrugging in the way of his countrymen, as though to disburden himself of such weighty reflections on history, philosophy, and legacy, the pondering of which the French race seem to have lovingly condemned themselves to for eternity, he put his arm around me, and together we watched Egypt sail by.

—〰—

I should say something about the old man. According to the infrequent communications I received in Paris from Noha and friends, he was stripped of all his titles and positions. Like an outcast snubbing his nose at society, he destroyed a second house he owned in the city, and using the stone and marble from it and his ravaged Azbakiyyah mansion, he built a villa on land that he owned on the other side of the river, outside of Cairo near the pyramids of Giza, far away from friends and relatives. In the six long years it took him to build it, no one crossed the river to visit him, nor did he visit anyone. All his wealth went into the new house. Year after year, he kept building and adding to it, so that people began saying he would die before he finished it. Others said he didn't want to finish it.

When the house was practically finished, he stopped work on it and started surrounding it with spacious gardens, fruit orchards, and palm and olive groves. With the landscaping finished, he resumed work on the main house, hanging doors and windows. When only the doors of the main entrance remained to be hung, he had a high wall built completely around the house, and so close to it that a man standing outside the house could stretch his arms and touch the surrounding wall with one hand and a wall of the house with the other.

People were astonished. They couldn't understand it. He had "blinded" the house, some said. And true enough, no sooner had the blinding wall been completed than he started bricking up all the windows—blinding upon blinding, they said. Not a single ray of light penetrated any level of the house except through the main entrance, which was still without doors. Some people said his habitual consumption of drugs and alcohol had taken hold of his mind. Others said there was more to it than that.

The house remained in that peculiar condition for several months, with no front door and him living in it, completely alone. Then one day he had his workers hang doors in the main entrance. When they had finished, he paid them and told them to go home, and then he went inside and closed the door. He never saw the light again. A week later, when he hadn't come out, one of the workers broke in and found his corpse.

He was interred in the sarcophagus he had provided for himself in his mausoleum in the Abode of the Dead, presumably in the same sarcophagus where lay his daughter, Zaynab. A few members of the immediate family attended the funeral. One of them is reported to have said he could smell the fumes of hell rising up through the earth to claim the foul soul of the corpse. Another defended Shaykh Khalil as an honorable man who served Egypt and its people well.

Who but God knows the hearts of men?

Here ends the testament of Zaki ibn Khalil al-Bakri.